GODDESS OF JUSTICE

DWAYNE CLAYDEN

BAD ALIBI PRESS

Copyright © 2021 Dwayne E. Clayden

All rights reserved. No part of this publication may be reproduced, distributed, or transmitted in any form or by any means, including photocopying, recording, or other electronic or mechanical methods, without the prior written permission of the publisher, except in the case of brief quotations embodied in critical reviews and certain other non-commercial uses permitted by copyright law. For permission requests, write to the publisher, addressed "Attention Permissions Coordinator," at:

dwayneclayden@gmail.com

DwayneClayden.com

Publisher's Note: This is a work of fiction. Names, characters, places, and incidents are a product of the author's imagination. Locales and public names are sometimes used for atmospheric purposes. Any resemblance to actual people, living or dead, or to businesses, companies, events, institutions, or locales is completely coincidental.

Published in Canada by Bad Alibi Press

Printed and Bound in Canada

Cover Graphic by Travis Miles, Pro Book Covers

Editing by Taija Morgan

Proofing by Jonas Saul

Formatting by Dwayne Clayden

Goddess of Justice / Dwayne Clayden—1st print ed.

ISBN: 978-1-989912-04-1 (pbk), 978-1-989912-05-8 (e-book)

 Created with Vellum

Valerie West
My continual support through the craziness
of living with an author.
Here we are, at six novels!

ALSO BY DWAYNE CLAYDEN

The Brad Coulter Thrillers

CRISIS POINT

OUTLAW MC

WOLFMAN IS BACK

13 DAYS OF TERROR

GODDESS OF JUSTICE

The Brad Coulter Thrillers Continue in 2022

BONDED LABOR

The Speargrass Thriller Series

SPEARGRASS OPIOID

SPEARGRASS VENGEANCE (FALL 2021)

Short Story

HELL HATH NO FURY—AB Negative. Anthology of Alberta Crime

CHAPTER ONE

November 22, 1980

A STREETLIGHT FLICKERED, ILLUMINATING THE ROAD FOR A moment, then plunging it into darkness. The drug dealer, in his early twenties, leaned against one of the broken streetlights. His cigarette glowed intermittently, giving away his location. Cigarette in his mouth, he rubbed his hands together, then wrapped his arms around his thin body. Dealing on a cold November Saturday night required dedication, or maybe, desperation. He had a product to sell and junkies willing to venture out to get their fix. He stomped his feet, shivered, and took a long drag. The smoke, mingled with his breath, formed a cloud in front of him on his exhale.

Dice watched from the shadows of the crack houses across the street. Once an affluent area of Calgary, Alberta, Victoria Park had become the armpit of the city. House after house, block upon block of crack dens. Dice had to admire the dealer's choice of location. He'd have steady business until well into the early hours of the morning. Unfortunately for him, tonight would be his last night in business.

Sirens, wailing from several directions, broke the silence. A police cruiser raced past, then another. Seconds later, an ambulance passed, followed by another cruiser. The emergency vehicles stopped outside a house a couple of blocks past the dealer. When he'd heard the sirens, he'd slipped back into the shadows. But not so far that Dice couldn't see him.

Unfazed by the police presence, the dealer moved from the shadows. As crackheads popped out of the houses to see who'd overdosed this time, the dealer made further sales. Such was the life cycle in Vic Park.

An hour from now, the scene would be repeated with another overdose, a fight over drugs, or a domestic assaults, and knifings were common.

Dice waited in the shadows until the ambulance sped away. A few minutes later, the cops came out of the house with three men in handcuffs. The cruisers left, and the addicts headed back to their homes.

This was the time to act. The streets would be quiet for at least half an hour.

Sliding a beanie low, jacket collar up, Dice staggered toward the dealer, who was working on another cigarette, making him easy to find—just follow the glow.

The dealer heard the footsteps and pushed away from the streetlamp.

"You got guts. The cops were just here."

Dice nodded, pretended to trip on the curb, and lurched toward the laughing dealer.

"Seems you've got a head start. Whatever you need, if I don't have it, I'll get it. Name your poison."

Dice whispered, "Crack."

"Jeez, you'll have to talk louder than that."

Dice staggered toward the dealer and stumbled again. Before Dice hit the street, the dealer reached out a stabilizing hand.

"Maybe you don't need nothin' right now."

Dice's hand came up holding a hunting knife. The long blade thrust upward, just under the sternum, pointed toward the dealer's left shoulder.

The blade pierced the dealer's heart. With one hand on the knife, Dice shoved the dealer back against the pole, twisted the knife, then let his body slide to the sidewalk.

The dealer grabbed his chest with his right hand, blood spewing between his fingers. Eyes wide, he mouthed, *Why?* His eyes stared past Dice as life spurted out of his body.

Dice wiped the knife on the dealer's hoodie, slid it back into a sheath, and headed north toward downtown.

CHAPTER TWO

Detective Brad Coulter sat at the back of a classroom in the hotel conference center. He stretched his lean six-foot-one body out, legs well under the table, leaned back, and stared at the ceiling. He wondered why these places put up fancy chandeliers, yet the sliding walls were a dull gray cloth. Sure, it was practical, they could make the rooms bigger or smaller, but who cared about the lighting. He was in the sixth row of tables. He always sat at the back. Each table had a crisp white tablecloth, a jug of water and, best of all, a bowl of Jolly Ranchers. Twenty-three other detectives were in the class.

Today was the second day of the Crime Scene Management Course. It was further punishment from Brad's boss, Deputy Chief Archer. In October, Brad returned to work after a two-and-a-half-month leave following the murder of his fiancée and their unborn child. He was immediately immersed in a series of sniper shootings that shocked the city of Calgary. Deputy Chief Archer discovered Brad had returned to work under false pretenses, and he was suspended. When the snipers said they would only communicate with Brad, he was brought back in, and later that day, they tracked the snipers. One was now dead, the other awaiting trial.

Before Deputy Chief Archer could terminate Brad for falsifying a return-to-work letter, Mayor Roger Kearse recognized Brad and his team as heroes. Mayor Kearse had been adamant Brad remain a cop and keep his position in Homicide. First, Archer and Coulter agreed on a one-month unpaid leave where Brad would assist Crown Prosecutor Jenni Blighe with the case against the surviving killer, Logan Hirsch. It kept Brad out of the public eye, away from cops who felt Coulter had crossed a line, and it allowed him to use his law degree after passing the bar exams earlier this year. Brad also used the time to take his dog, Lobo, for daily runs, keeping in great shape.

The second part of Archer's plan was to keep Brad busy taking courses and, therefore, unavailable to respond to homicides and not on the roster. Last week, he'd attended classes on Multi-Culturalism and Media Relations.

This week it was Crime Scene Management, the new course name the identification bureau geeks adopted to make themselves feel important. At least after today, he'd get a three-day break. The instructor was his good friend and academy classmate, Sergeant Bill Sturgeon. He'd heard Sturgeon's rant many times over beer. He even looked the part of a professor. Stocky build, thick salt-and-pepper—more salt—hair combed back, a bushy mustache and a herringbone blazer. Gray eyes roamed the classroom. The only things missing were leather patches on his elbows and a pipe. Although, having his friend as an instructor wasn't enough to keep Brad awake.

"Crime Scene Management is changing. We cannot have the first officers on scene and detectives wandering around contaminating the area. The Crime Scene Unit needs to be the first at the scene to video, take photos and identify evidence before your size-twelve boots grind everything into the carpet or ground. Before your donut-sticky fingers touch everything."

"That's hurtful," a detective said.

"Truth hurts," another replied.

Sturgeon waited for the laughter to subside.

Brad's head bobbled, then his chin returned to his chest.

He woke out of his snooze when he heard his name.

"Those are the essential points of Crime Scene Management. Coulter?"

Brad's head popped up, his brown eyes frantically trying to focus. He sat upright and rubbed a hand through his shaggy brown hair.

"Yes, sir."

"Can you remind the class what any three of the essential points we just discussed were?"

Brad shook his head, hoping to clear his brain and dig up three points. He couldn't. "You've covered them so well, it would be pointless for me to take up your valuable time repeating them."

Sturgeon headed toward the back row, narrowed eyes on Brad. He repeated the steps as he counted them off on his hand. "First, preserve the crime scene. Second, keep pertinent evidence uncontaminated. And third, scene and evidence protection at a crime scene begins with the first arriving officer." Sturgeon surveyed the class. "It's apparent we need to take a break."

Chairs scuffed the floor as cops headed out of the classroom to smoke, grab a coffee, or both.

Sturgeon strode over to Brad. "Thanks a lot, buddy. I appreciate the support."

Brad poured two coffees and handed one to Sturgeon. "I've heard this before."

"I know, but backing me up wouldn't hurt, would it?" Sturgeon took the coffee. "This would be better with Scotch."

They wandered back to Brad's table and sat. "I'll buy you a beer when we're done today."

Sturgeon snorted. "How about I just take the cash?"

"Beer, or nothing." Brad popped a Jolly Rancher into his mouth.

"Beer it is." Sturgeon eyed Brad down and back up. "I miss a memo about appropriate detective clothing?"

Brad glanced down. "What?"

"Black button-down shirt, jeans, and what are those? Cowboy boots?"

"I'll have you know the shirt and jeans are Harry Rosen."

"Does he know you have them?"

Brad ignored the comment. "They're Italian and the boots are Roper lace-ups. Cowboy boots are stupid to wear if you get in a foot chase."

"Yeah, I don't worry about foot chases." Sturgeon sipped his coffee. "I'm a bit worried about your masculinity, though."

"Asshat," Brad mumbled.

Sturgeon leaned close, his voice a whisper. "I had an interesting call Saturday night."

"Do tell." Brad's eyebrows arched.

"A drug dealer stabbed in Vic Park."

Brad's hand stopped halfway to his mouth. "That doesn't sound exciting. In Homicide, we call that a regular Saturday night."

"Sometimes a Sunday, occasionally a Wednesday, and often a Thursday," Sturgeon added.

"What's special about a dealer getting stabbed for his drugs?" The Jolly Rancher clicked on Brad's teeth.

"That's the interesting part—he wasn't robbed. He still had his cash and drugs."

Brad shrugged. "The killer got spooked. Any cruisers in the area?"

"A few minutes before, the downtown guys responded with EMS for an overdose. They hauled three crackheads away."

"You're losing me." Brad grabbed another Jolly Rancher and popped it in his mouth.

"The dealer was stabbed once."

"Lucky for the killer, unlucky for the dealer." Brad worked the Jolly Rancher free from his straight, white teeth with a finger and leaned back in his chair.

"Not lucky." Sturgeon pointed to his lower chest, then left shoulder. "The knife entered under the sternum up toward the left shoulder."

Brad's chair rocked back to the floor. "Right through the heart."

Sturgeon rolled his gray eyes. "Finally, I got your attention."

"That's not a common street method of murder. Too clean, too precise."

"Exactly. Special training."

Brad swallowed the Jolly Rancher. "Armed forces?"

Sturgeon sat back and sipped his coffee. "That'd be my first guess."

"But why?"

"Not my job." Sturgeon smirked. "I collect evidence. You do the detecting."

"There was a similar murder earlier this year." When Brad returned to work in October, Griffin had given him two homicide cases where the investigation stalled. One was of a drug dealer in Victoria Park who was stabbed under the ribcage and up into his heart. Brad didn't get to investigate it before the snipers struck. Now it appeared the murders of the two drug dealers may be linked.

"Yup. Not as clean as this one. Some hesitation stabs, then the fatal blow."

Brad nodded. "Send me the case file."

CHAPTER THREE

THE NEXT MORNING BRAD PARKED HIS BLACK FIREBIRD IN THE association parking lot, grabbed his coffee, let Lobo out, then crossed the street and headed down the alley to police headquarters. He nodded to the desk sergeant on their way to the stairs. On the second floor, they passed the tribute to fallen members. Brad stopped, as he did every time he passed here, and remembered two close friends who had died in the line of duty—his partner Curtis Young, and his friend, Tina Davidson. Young, killed by bank robbers on a highway outside the city. Davidson, kidnapped, tortured and murdered by Jeter Wolfe, the same monster who had taken his fiancée from him. Lobo barked from the door to the detective bullpen. Brad nodded to the memorials for his friends, then headed to his German shepherd's side.

They wandered through the maze of metal WWII-surplus office furniture to his back-corner desk.

Brad tossed his black gloves on his desk, removed his parka and hung it in a coat tree. He dropped into his chair, put his feet on his desk, leaned back and sipped his coffee. Lobo crawled under the desk and was soon snoring.

He picked up the file of reports from Saturday's stabbing homicide. It wasn't his case, but his interest was piqued by Sturgeon's comments. Besides, he didn't have a case that required his attention, and it was unlikely Archer would assign one to him. Detective Don Griffin, Brad's current partner in Homicide, would be in court for the week. Maybe when Griffin was back and could take the lead on a homicide, Archer would let Brad work murders. Brad was on his own unless the shit hit the fan which, given his history, was likely.

The report from the first cops on the scene was brief and lacking detail. They arrived, they saw a body, they called EMS and their sergeant. No weapon was found, but there were no details of any search. The case was referred to detectives. Typical of a street cop's report, and even more typical of an event that happened in Vic Park.

The Patient Care Report from the paramedics had been detailed, but most of it concerned their treatment. The victim was found pulseless and breathless, leaning against a streetlight. Blood covered his chest and pooled on the sidewalk.

Paramedics transported the patient to the Holy Cross Hospital minutes away. A trauma team had been waiting in the emergency department, but it was quickly determined the patient was dead with no hope of resuscitation.

The detectives who responded were from the General Investigative Services. They handled a variety of cases, but not homicides. Brad figured that night no Homicide detectives were available, and since Archer had put Brad on the sidelines, GIS got the call. Their report was thorough, but with no leads. As Brad expected, no one from the area reported anything. Certainly, nothing they were going to tell the police. The victim had one hundred and seventy dollars on his person, mostly in fives. He had a pass for the shelter and a package of gum. The case was listed as *open*.

The autopsy was brief and to the point. The victim had one stab wound, and, as Sturgeon said, the blade entered beneath the xiphoid process in an upward stroke to the left shoulder. The knife pierced the left ventricle through to the right atrium. The inside of the heart was a mess of lacerations. The medical examiner speculated that once the knife was inserted, the attacker twisted the blade, ensuring the destruction of the heart and a quick death. The toxicology report noted marijuana and heroin.

Brad flipped to the dispatch report. The call came in to 911 at 11:10 p.m. The first cruiser was there at 11:12, and EMS thirty seconds later. The response time was excellent. The question was how long the victim had leaned against the pole before anyone checked him. It was strange he still had drugs and cash in his pockets. If he'd been found by crackheads, both money and drugs would be gone, and it's unlikely they'd call 911.

Brad flipped a few pages further in the dispatch report. The 911 call was made from a payphone on Sixth Avenue SW. Nothing to follow up there beyond the question of why someone would walk over eight blocks to call 911. There were plenty of payphones between the murder scene and where the call came from.

The dealer had a long record—over twenty charges for drug possession, dealing, and a couple of related assaults. Nothing deemed serious enough to warrant actual prison time, according to the records. All before he was twenty-one years of age. No doubt his juvenile records would be as impressive. Still, no one deserved to die like this.

Brad opened the envelope containing the crime scene photos. After a glance, he realized they were useless—dark photos of a pole, blood on the sidewalk, and nothing else. Several footprints in the snow of different-sized footwear were identified, most with a Vibram sole, like the boots police and paramedics wore. Maybe Sturgeon and his classes were onto something. This crime scene had been contaminated.

He checked the evidence list. Most notable was the lack of a murder weapon at the scene. The killer either kept the knife or tossed it. There was nothing in the notes about finding the knife, but blood smears were noted on the dealer's parka. The investigating officer suspected the knife was wiped clean on the dealer's coat.

The evidence list contained dozens of needles and syringes, small plastic baggies, and food and drink containers that went on for pages.

It wasn't a robbery or a drug theft. The murder was up close and personal. *Who? Why?*

Brad swung his legs off his desk, stood, grabbed his winter parka, and headed out of the office. Lobo slipped out from under the desk, stretched, then jogged to catch up.

"I'm going to a crime scene."

The secretary didn't glance up from her typing.

Brad parked his black Firebird on Eleventh Avenue just east of Macleod Trail and headed to the light pole. As he hiked, he slipped on a black beanie and matching gloves. The police tape was gone, but it wasn't hard to identify the large brown stain on the sidewalk under the streetlight. He studied the dilapidated houses. Once the pride of Calgary, they were an eyesore and the hub of the drug culture.

He snorted at the thought of finding a witness. Uniformed officers had gone door to door. He'd been assigned that task hundreds of times. First, you seldom got any information worth using. And second, you got a ton of abuse. Worse in this neighborhood.

"I was minding my own business."

"No, Officer, I didn't see or hear anything."

Insult the cop. "Get the hell off my porch, pig."

And his personal favorite, because it was used the most: "You got a warrant?" Idiots. He didn't need a warrant to ask questions. They watched too many 70's TV cop shows like Columbo and Streets of San Francisco. Although, Starsky and Hutch didn't worry about needing a warrant.

Brad studied the scene. If he'd stabbed the dealer, which direction would he escape? West was back to busy Macleod Trail. A chance to fit in, but there had to be a lot of blood on the assailant's clothes. Even in this area, a bloody shirt would stand out. North was out for the same reason. South would take you to the Stampede Grounds. Also, if there were no events on the grounds, the probability of security spotting you was high. They wouldn't be asleep yet.

That left east. A few blocks east, you'd come to the Elbow River with many wooded pathways. Further east led into Inglewood, which wasn't a much better neighborhood than Vic Park. Decision time. Did the killer go east, because that was the smart direction to go? Or did the killer go north and was the one who made the 911 call? If so, why would the killer call 911? Despite the 911 call, Brad's gut said the killer went east.

He headed back to his car and let Lobo out. They checked the drainage gates and sewers where a knife could be tossed. After ninety minutes of Lobo sniffing ditches, drains and sewers, they'd struck out as far as a murder weapon was concerned. At the river, he followed the paths, not sure what he was searching for, but hoping he would know when he found it. No luck.

Brad shivered and flexed his gloved hands. Despite evidence having been collected from around the scene the night before, Lobo found at least twenty baggies that no longer contained drugs, dozens of syringes and needles, and various pieces of clothing including a disproportionate number of bras and panties. The farther they searched from the site of the murder, the more crap they found.

Well, they'd given it a shot. Brad dumped the garbage into a box in the trunk and poured a bottle of water into a bowl for Lobo. Next would be a bath for the dog to get the grunge off.

While Lobo drank, Brad leaned against the car and again envisioned the murder. Someone got close and personal. No defensive struggle by the dealer. Someone he knew. A user?

That narrowed it down to the entire neighborhood. He gritted his teeth and opened the back door.

"Lobo, *hup-hup.*"

Lobo took one last slurp of the water and jumped into the car.

CHAPTER FOUR

THE COURTROOMS WERE ALL THE SAME—PALE WOOD PANELING on the walls, uncomfortable cherry-wood spectator benches, then the bar, past which were tables for the prosecution and defense, a witness stand, jury box, and the judge's bench. In the left corner were the Canadian flag and Alberta's provincial flag. A portrait of the Queen was hung behind the judge's bench. It was the third day of the trial. Crown Prosecutor Jenni Blighe had completed the prosecution's case yesterday. As she waited for the judge to reach a verdict, she picked lint off her navy-blue skirt and brushed wrinkles on her jacket. With this case, she'd been too busy to get her clothes to the dry cleaners. At least she'd had time to wash and iron her white blouse. She crossed her toned legs, dangled a black shoe off her toes and glared at the judge.

The victim, Laura Turner, a petite, blond, sixteen-year-old, sat behind Blighe. She was sobbing and being comforted by her mother.

The judge was taking his sweet-ass time deciding the verdict. Blighe stared at her notes in the folder on the prosecution table, tapping one French-tip nail against the pages. The seventeen-year-old, accused of raping his high school classmate at a party, was going free. Blighe's blue eyes blazed in his direction.

The accused was Burke Bailey Baldwin, a handsome young man with a firm jaw, dimpled chin and wavy jet-black hair. All of that concealed the sick person he was inside. Smarmy little bastard.

During the trial, he had leaned back in his chair at the defense table, lips twisted into a smirk as his lawyer brought the girl to tears. His parents, seated behind him, showed no emotion. On the visitor benches in the courtroom were a dozen of his high school friends, who spent most of their time whispering and laughing as they stared at the victim. One teen rolled his tongue around the inside of his mouth, then blew a kiss to the girl. Another repeatedly stuck the index finger of his right hand into a circle created with the thumb and index finger of the second hand. This had the other boys snickering, but it had garnered only a stern glare from the judge.

The defense had made Laura the subject of the trial. Nothing Blighe tried could turn the focus back to the accused.

Her objections were overruled by the judge, whose obvious bias oozed from his pores. His 'boys will be boys' attitude twisted her stomach.

In her summation she'd stood and given it one last shot. "Your Honor. While my learned colleague"—a term that meant anything but *learned*—"has portrayed this as the victim's fault, this is a sixteen-year-old, naïve girl, who repeatedly tried to get away from the accused who screamed 'no' until the accused put his hand over her mouth, pinched her nose, and rendered her unconscious. A young girl who trusted a classmate and then was viciously raped. She did everything she could to tell this ... this *predator* she was not a willing participant. Yet the accused refused to listen to her pleas. Your Honor, the facts speak for themselves. The accused is guilty of not only assault, but rape. The evidence presented is clear."

The judge waved his hand at Blighe, frowning. "Ms. Blighe, please take your seat and save your arguments for your appeal. The facts, as you say, are not clear. This girl went willingly with the accused to a bedroom. She was at a party and had been drinking. Despite her protests and tears, there is reasonable doubt in this case, and I find the accused not guilty."

The judge rose and left the courtroom. Blighe put her head in her hands, strands of short blond hair slipping free and hanging in her face. She breathed deeply, but her muscles were tense and her head throbbed. This was not justice, far from it. Predators like the accused should not be allowed back on the street. She had missed something. Could she have presented the case differently? Not with this judge. His decision was made before court started. If the court system didn't protect young girls, then who would? This was her worst defeat in five years as a crown prosecutor.

As a victim of a stalker, she knew firsthand the terror a male could bring into the life of a female. She still had nightmares about Jeter Wolfe. Eventually, he'd left her alone and found other victims. But those events changed her life. Already divorced, her ex-husband had petitioned the court for sole custody of their two children, citing that Blighe's job as a crown prosecutor had put the children's lives at risk. Blighe hadn't had the heart to fight in court. She'd installed a security system in her house, purchased a gun, and practiced multiple times a week. Months of self-defense courses had her prepared for an assault. But it was no way to live, always on edge, not trusting anyone.

Two months ago, outside a courtroom, a man put his hand on her shoulder. With her new instincts from self-defense training, she'd grabbed his wrist, bent it back, and had him on his knees screaming. The man was searching for courtroom 202. She profusely apologized. She had mixed emotions. First, she'd responded to a threat with decisiveness and had protected herself. But the man's screams brought attention in the hallway. Court security had raced toward her until she waved them off.

If the courts couldn't protect young girls, who would? Being a skilled prosecutor wasn't enough.

She slid her tailored jacket off her chair, draped it over her arm, grabbed her files, and headed back to her office. Tonight's workout would be intense—there was a lot of stress to release.

CHAPTER FIVE

After Brad's fiancée was killed in his house by Jeter Wolfe in July, Brad demolished the house and sold the lot. Now he lived with Lobo on a farm west of the city. The house was seventy or eighty years old and under a thousand square feet.

Brad changed into an insulated gray Calgary Police Service sweatsuit, a fleece jacket, a watch cap, and his favorite white North Star sneakers with three red lines up the sides and a good grip for running in snow and on ice. He slid on his black leather gloves, then he and Lobo followed their familiar path down the lane from the farmhouse and into the forested hill toward Bearspaw Dam. Several times he hit a patch of ice and fought for balance. Fortunately, he didn't crash onto the ice or into a tree. Lobo raced ahead, sniffing for squirrels, checking out piles of crap, probably from coyotes, and tracking other scents only he could smell.

They took a break at the bottom of the hill. Lobo sprinted

to the river and tentatively placed a paw in the water. He withdrew it quickly, then bent over and drank. He tested the water again, then lay down under a tree.

Brad stretched beside Lobo and worked out the problems with the murder of the dealer. On the one hand, a dealer getting killed was not a newsworthy event, and it was a low priority for Homicide. But since there were no active cases to occupy his time, he'd keep busy with this one. The method of killing was unusual. Stabbings weren't uncommon, but few were fatal. This was different. A single stab through the heart. Precise, no hesitation, and life threatening. Not a fluke or a lucky cut, but planned and deliberate. Not a frenzy or spur of the moment. Planned, targeted, and executed. But nothing in the dealer's history suggested he'd be targeted like this.

He thought of the stabbing two months ago that had occurred in Vic Park as well. A dealer named Billy Tuck. Interestingly, he'd also had cash on him when he was recovered on the sidewalk. At twenty years old, Tuck also had a lengthy rap sheet with minimal time served. The unique method of the stabbing connected the two cases firmly in Brad's mind, though Tuck's death hadn't been as clean.

One thing stood out. Despite numerous charges and convictions, both dealers, Billy Tuck and Vito Sotelo, had spent less than two months in jail—total. Lucky? Excellent lawyer? Screwed-up court system?

Brad remembered a conversation he'd had with Maggie's father, Judge Ethan Gray, the night they'd met at Maggie's paramedic grad. Even then, Brad had concerns about the court system. It wasn't a justice system, it was a legal system that ensured two things: the law was followed, and the rights of the accused were protected, more than the victims.

Still, all those minor charges related to drugs didn't add up to a targeted murder. There must be something else.

He whistled. Lobo raced past and was back on the hunt. They jogged up the hill back to the farm, then headed to the barn he had converted to a gym. Despite its age, it was structurally sound. He'd power-washed the cow and horse stalls, replaced the insulation, and added a furnace.

He'd even been able to get a timeworn truck running. It was perfect for hauling stuff around the farm. He wasn't sure how it would hold up on the highway, though. No sense getting new license plates.

Lobo headed to his bed in one horse stable while Brad started his workout. Soon Lobo was snoring, and Brad was grunting and sweating.

CHAPTER SIX

JIMMY DUGGAN HAD BEEN A REGULAR CUSTOMER AT THE CECIL Hotel Tavern for over fifteen years. When his wife died at fifty-five and left him a decent inheritance, the tavern became his home away from home. Most of the legacy now belonged to the bar.

The Cecil Hotel was in the east end of downtown. Never a five-star hotel, it had been built in 1912 to accommodate travelers and blue-collar workers. After prohibition ended in Alberta in 1923, the entire main floor was converted to a tavern. Now, fifty-seven years later, it barely rated one star. Downtown had over a dozen low-end hotels, but the Cecil was at the bottom. The fake paneling on the walls had faded and peeled, the ceiling had water spots, and the threadbare carpet was a dull gray with darker circles—not a design, but decades of spilled drinks. The tables were scarred with names and graffiti carved into the wood. The lighting was minimal, which was beneficial—you wouldn't know how disgusting the tavern was. Police regularly responded to the bar. It was the number one location the police were called to.

The Cecil Hotel's recent claim to fame was a robbery in '79 last year where two employees were killed for one hundred dollars from the cash register.

Jimmy Duggan stood, slightly hunch-backed, and fumbled in his blue polyester pants pockets for his car keys. He stumbled and grabbed a chair for balance. No one noticed. Everyone here kept to themselves. Funny that they came here to get away in a tavern filled with guys trying to get away. With half the lights burned out, that didn't help in the search for the keys.

After several frustrating moments, he noticed them on the table, next to the half-dozen empty beer bottles. Keys in hand, he searched for his wallet. Not in his polyester pants, front or back pockets. He glanced hopefully at the table. Nope. He squinted as he searched around. Maybe he could sneak out tonight. But if he did, he'd be banned here, and as rundown as it was, he liked this bar.

He staggered and reached for the back of his chair again for support. His hands landed on his worn black parka. Of course. He slid the parka off the chair and rummaged in his pockets, finding his wallet. He pulled out several dollars, tried to do math in his head, gave up and slapped a ten on the table. That should cover it.

Duggan lumbered toward the door, bumping into several tables as he wound his way through the bar. He reached out an arm to push the door and slammed into the dense wood. He moved back, pulled the door open, and stepped into the dark November night. Gloveless hands in his pockets, hunched over, he kept the icy wind away from his face.

His legs knew the way and led him down the block to the intersection where he'd cross the avenue to the parking lot and his Buick. It was the same route every night.

Duggan's eyes tried to focus on the pedestrian light. He was sure it said, *Don't Walk*. Fairly sure. Then the light changed to walk—he was mostly sure. He stepped off the curb. Halfway across, he was illuminated in the lights of a car. An engine revved. Duggan gasped.

The car struck Duggan's right side. His lower body absorbed the impact, shattering his hip and femur. A blazing pain shot up to his brain. A scream started low in his throat. His momentum carried him over the hood where his head and face impacted the windshield, extinguishing the scream.

He rolled across the roof—clouds, snow, then more clouds flashed before his eyes. A shoulder caught a corner of the trunk, and he slammed into the pavement, rolling several times, and coming to rest face down.

No air passed through his broken nose.

Through shattered teeth and a broken jaw, his breathing came in gasps. The ice-covered road was soothing on his shattered face. People sprinted toward him as if in slow motion. Voices called to him.

His body shuddered with the cold, and his eyes closed.

CHAPTER SEVEN

The tones in Fire Station 1 blared, and the voice of the dispatcher came across the speakers. "Medic 1. Pedestrian hit, corner of Fourth Avenue and Macleod Trail SE. Unconscious. Injuries unknown."

Amir Sharma and his partner, Jill Cook, shoved their chairs back from the kitchen table where they'd just sat down to eat their dinner, five hours after it had been cooked.

Sharma took one last, long glance at the roast beef, mashed potatoes, and the rest of the gourmet meal. He licked his lips, his tongue brushing over his dark mustache. For a thin guy, he could really pack away the food. But not tonight.

They raced out of the kitchen, then across the garage floor to the ambulance. They donned matching standard-issue EMS parkas and black wool beanies and climbed into the ambulance.

"Medic 1 is responding," Cook said into the mic.

Cook and Sharma had been partners for three months. She'd completed the paramedic program two years ago in 1978. She slid a black knit beanie onto the frizzy, light-brown hair that hung to her shoulders.

Sharma hit the lights and siren as they exited the station. The ambulance slid across the icy driveway in front of the station and out onto the street.

"Slippery?" Cook asked.

"You think."

Sharma fought for control of the ambulance. He swung right out of the station the wrong way on a one-way street, then right again, also the wrong way onto a dim one-way street. A block ahead, they saw the stopped cars, and a crowd of people gathered near the far sidewalk. A couple of people —dressed in parkas, beanies, scarves, and heavy mitts— stepped away from the patient and waved the ambulance toward the crowd.

"Helpful." Sharma tapped the brakes, and the ambulance slid toward the crowd. The tires hit a clear spot, and Sharma stopped the momentum. "I never would have figured out this was an emergency scene."

Cook grinned. "They're trying to be helpful. You know, maybe we're the blind paramedics."

"Tell dispatch we're on the scene," Sharma said.

Cook glared at him. "Thanks for telling me that. I didn't know I had to call dispatch." She grabbed the mic. "Medic 1 on scene. Police not on location yet. We have a crowd."

"Roger, Medic 1. Police were notified and are responding."

As Cook exited the ambulance, she slid on her black gloves and opened the side compartment to grab her kits. Sirens sounded from several directions. She caught up with Sharma at the patient.

"Paramedics," Sharma said. "Move back and give us some room."

Cook knelt next to the patient's head and Sharma near his waist. Cook slid off a glove and pressed on the side of the patient's neck with two fingers. "Weak, rapid pulse, too fast to count. He's got facial bruising and lacerations. He's missing some teeth and I'm sure the bones around his eyes are fractured. He's unresponsive with gasping breathing. Mid to late sixties, maybe older. He's cold to touch." She glanced at his lower body. Both legs were splayed at unusual angles.

"Fractured pelvis, femur, probably both tibia and fibula," Sharma said. "We need to get going."

"He was on his face, so I rolled him onto his back," a bystander in a suit with a long Burberry overcoat said.

"Did you protect his neck?" Sharma asked.

"Uh, no," the good Samaritan said.

"I see," Cook said. "Well, come here and hold his head for me."

"I'm not sure—"

Cook glared. "You already touched him. Get over here."

Overcoat man knelt next to Cook, and she placed his hands on the patient's neck, fingers extended to open the airway. "Don't let go until I tell you to." Cook glanced at him. "What happened?"

"It was a hit and run," Overcoat said. "He was in the

crosswalk. A car pulled away from the curb and sped up. He kept going after he hit this guy."

"You saw a man driving the car?"

"Well, no. But I'm sure—"

"Thanks." Cook saw a half-dozen cops heading toward them. "You guys, can you get the stretcher and spineboard?"

One cop stepped forward. "I will."

Cook eyeballed the cop. Sandy-blond hair, wispy mustache with darting eyes that missed nothing. She'd seen him at a lot of calls—his nametag said Robson.

"Great, Robson." Cook swung back to her patient. "We need to get out of here quickly."

"Roger that." Robson waved to a couple of cops standing at their cruiser. "You heard the lady. Stretcher, post haste."

Cook took the patient's left hand and set it across his chest. A thin gold band glittered from the fourth finger. She glanced around. "Was there a woman with him?"

The guy holding the patient's neck shook his head. "He was the only one in the crosswalk."

Cook nodded. His wife might be getting bad news tonight.

"I've got his legs immobilized." Sharma tied the last knot and eyed his handiwork. "It's not great, but it will do. They can figure this out at the hospital. Once he's loaded, I'll get us there in minutes."

When the cops were back, they slid the patient onto the backboard, placed a cervical collar and secured him to the board. The police helped lift the patient onto the stretcher and then into the ambulance. Sharma raced around to the driver's door. Cook glanced at Robson. "Ride with us for continuity."

He jumped into the ambulance and shut the back door as the ambulance began moving.

Robson stared at the unresponsive patient. "He's going to die, isn't he?"

"I expect so." Cook started an intravenous.

"Before we get to the hospital?"

"Nope. There's a rule. No one ever dies in the ambulance."

"A rule?"

"More a guideline. Although, I have had some patients die the second the stretcher wheels hit the floor at the hospital."

"Paramedic superstition." Robson nodded. "I get it." The odor of booze displaced the air.

"Sometimes being drunk works in their favor," Cook said. "When they get hit, they're flexible, and they just bounce."

"But not this time."

"Not this time."

A steady beep—Sharma was backing into the ambulance bay at the General Hospital. When he stopped, the back doors opened, and a half-dozen paramedics helped them slide the stretcher out of the ambulance into the emergency department and race down the hall to a trauma room.

The trauma team was waiting. The patient was transferred from the EMS stretcher onto the trauma room gurney and surrounded by gowned trauma specialists.

Sharma, Cook, and Robson stepped out of the way.

A nurse handed Robson the patient's wallet.

"I'll start cleaning and restocking the ambulance." Sharma gathered their equipment.

"I'll be right there," Cook said.

"Yeah, sure." Sharma rolled the EMS stretcher with their blood-stained equipment toward the ambulance bay.

"Are you going to help him?" Robson asked.

Cook grinned. "Sure. As soon as I get my report done and I'm sure you want a witness statement from me."

"That I do," Robson said. "I need to make a phone call and check out this guy. I'll meet you in the coffee room."

Cook sipped her coffee as she wrote her Patient Care Report. The door opened and Robson stepped in, a wallet in hand.

"Your patient is James Duggan. Sixty-eight years of age. He has a record for two *dozen* impaired driving charges. His license has been suspended many times, but he keeps drinking and driving. The most recent charge was from a month ago, and his license was suspended for six months. We found his car. It has tons of scrapes and dents. Appears he played bumper car a few times after nights of drinking."

"Ironic that he gets hit while drunk."

"Even more ironic if the hit-and-run driver was drunk."

"True," Cook said. "Any word on that car and driver?"

Robson shook his head. "Not yet. Downtown cruisers are searching. It's likely the car was stolen. Frequently, the drivers dump the car in an underground parking garage, then take a cab home, or get a friend to drive them. We might need to wait until morning and see who reports a stolen car. The Crime Scene Unit might get some paint samples from the scene or Duggan and tell us what model of car we're searching for."

The overhead speakers came to life, and a calm voice said, "Code 99, trauma one. Code 99, trauma one."

Cook glanced at Robson. "You've got a traffic fatality now."

CHAPTER EIGHT

When Sergeant Caterina Toscana arrived, the scene was a hive of activity. She slid her five-foot-eight frame out of her van, black Sorel boots crunching in the snow, and walked toward Briscoe. Biting wind whipped her short, raven hair around her face. She pulled out a police-issue fake-fur hat and shoved it down on her head. She hated the hat and reminded herself to get a wool watch cap. She leaned into the wind as she pulled on insulated gloves. At least she'd remembered to bring these tonight.

Sergeant Jerry Briscoe had everything under control. Fifth Avenue was barricaded to traffic, and police tape encircled the entire block. His police issue parka wrapped his thick body and was zipped tight to his jaw. Unlike Toscana, Briscoe seemed to love the fake-fur hat—maybe it kept his bald head warm. He had the flaps down over his ears and tied under his chin.

"Where the hell were you?" Sergeant Briscoe peered eye to eye with Toscana.

She could tell by his scowl this would not go well. "It's barely after eleven. I just got on duty."

Briscoe shook his head, chewed his bottom lip, and snarled, "You're a district sergeant now. You're at a higher standard. If you're on time, I consider you late."

Toscana rubbed her gloved hands against her arms, frowning. "But, Sarge—"

His thick finger was in her face so fast, she stepped back. "And don't ever backtalk me. Now get up to date on what is going on here and manage this scene."

"Yes, sir." Toscana headed over to the Crime Scene Unit huddled in the middle of the road.

Sergeant Sturgeon pushed off the road, stood, and buttoned his brown knee-length overcoat. "Got in shit, did you, missy?"

"He's an ass."

"That he is." Sturgeon shrugged. "But he's also right."

"He's not my boss," Toscana said. "I'm a district sergeant just like him."

"Nope, not like him," Sturgeon said. "You're new to the job."

"I'm thirty-one." Toscana's brown eyes blazed. "Young has nothing to do with it. He does this shit because he can."

"He's got ten years more experience, and in this case, he's right."

"I know." Toscana gazed away.

Sturgeon blew on his gloved hands. "Do you want to know what we've got?"

She nodded, eyes narrowing. "Yeah, that'd be great." Toscana's enthusiasm was back.

Sturgeon grinned and rubbed his gloved hands together. "Not much."

Her shoulders slumped. "Oh."

"Luckily, we don't need much." Sturgeon smiled. "There are no skid marks. The driver didn't hit the brakes. Some witnesses say the car was accelerating."

"Trying to make a yellow light?"

"Nope. Witnesses all say the light was red for traffic, and the walk light for the victim was activated."

"Another drunk?"

"Possibly, but that's your job," Sturgeon said. "We've found shattered glass from a headlight, likely the right one, and a few flecks of paint. Once we analyze it, we'll know the car and model. But for now, you are searching for a dark-brown car. That should help for your cruisers circulating through downtown."

"That's all?" Toscana's shoulders sagged.

"All for now. We'll keep the road closed until mid-morning so we can investigate in daylight."

Toscana nodded, then she heard her radio call sign. "501," dispatch said. "522 found the suspect vehicle. It's on the third level of The Bay's parking garage."

"I'm on my way." Toscana glanced at Sturgeon.

"I'll send a team over."

She jogged to her van, keying her mic. "501 responding. Tell 522 not to approach the car and to seal off that parking garage."

CHAPTER NINE

Dice exercised, eyes gleaming and with a wide grin, rock songs blaring from the stereo. It was the ultimate high—the thrill of ending a life. Sleep had been impossible after the Saturday-night killing of the drug dealer.

Everything about that night was incredible. How easy it was to pick a target. The stupidity of the dealer. But most of all, the feel of the knife as it thrust upward. The first pop through the skin, then the second as the knife breached the diaphragm. For a moment, the heart pulsed through the blade to the handle. Then the dealer's wide-eyed terror. The warmth of the blood and watching the dealer's soul, if there was such a thing, leave his body and journey to Hell—the perfect destination for him.

Drugs wouldn't stop flowing because the dealer was dead. Someone else would sell the drugs under the broken streetlight. Let him go for it. Perhaps Dice would strike there, again.

Last night's hit and run hadn't been as up close and personal, even so, there was the thrill when the man's body collided with the bumper, windshield, and finally, as he bounced off the trunk.

Thanks to thorough research, Dice knew the man's habits—boring habits. Still, when it was time, there was anxiety. No amount of planning could cover every eventuality. What if cops were at that intersection? What if the stolen car stalled? What if the stolen car was damaged when it hit the drunk? What if someone reported the license plate to cops before the car was dumped? The car had been found too soon. That information was locked away until it was needed for another vehicular adventure.

Otherwise, everything worked perfectly—one fewer drunk driver on the road. Dice did a fist pump and then a few jabs and uppercuts while shuffling around the room like a heavyweight boxer. The euphoria of the kill ignited all senses. Midway through chin-ups, a plan formed for the next victim.

The intense daily workouts had Dice toned, strong, and agile. The shooting range was on the list for later today. Several hundred rounds a few times a week. Not yet an expert, but accurate and consistent at close range.

The early morning workout complete, Dice showered and prepared for work. The bathroom mirror reflected eyes that gleamed, a flushed face and a wide grin. The hot shower gently massaged Dice's head, neck, and shoulders. As a fog filled the bathroom, the euphoria lessened.

After the shower, Dice stood in front of the closet. The dark sweatpants, hoodie, gloves, and winter beanie from the night before, were stuffed into a garbage bag. That would go into the dumpster outside the court building.

There was one outfit suitable for tonight.

Clothes were important—a power suit, but not too powerful. And shoes, comfortable for standing and walking, but in fashion. Not like the sterile, comfortable, and obvious shoes detectives wore. Those were a dead giveaway. So was the cheap off-the-rack suit. For Dice, that would never do. Today was extremely important.

CHAPTER TEN

Thursday morning Brad wandered into the detective bullpen after eight carrying a garment bag. Most of the desks were occupied, and the steady peck of fingers on typewriters filled the room. Cigarettes burned to the filter in ashtrays and the odor of coffee mixed with the smoke—a great place to think.

Lobo sniffed at the desks as they worked their way to Brad's domain in the far corner. Lobo slid under the desk and curled up.

Brad shoved his black gloves into the pockets of his winter parka, then hung it on the coat tree behind his desk. He hung the garment bag next to the parka. He flopped into his chair and checked for anything interesting from the night before. Nothing caught his eye. He figured Sturgeon would be in his office, and it was time to bug him about any new results from the dealer's murder. Brad left Lobo asleep under his desk, grabbed a coffee, and headed down the hall to the renovated Crime Scene Unit offices. He breezed past the secretary. "Coulter, to see Sturgeon."

She glanced up. "He's busy—"

Brad continued down the hall and into Sturgeon's office. It was about the size of a broom closet. The desk was a step up from Brad's WWII-surplus, fake-wood veneer over pressboard. But, unlike Brad, who worked in a room with twenty other detectives, Sturgeon had his own office. There was something for that. Now if only there were a place to sit. A file box occupied one chair with piles of file folders on the other. His desk was covered with crime scene photos.

Sturgeon didn't glance up, but said, "Sure. Come on in. I'm not busy at all. You're dressed up today. Job interview?"

"I have court this afternoon. You appear tired. Did you miss your morning coffee?"

Sturgeon glanced up from comparing fingerprints. "Morning coffee? I've been at work since last night dealing with a death. I'm living on coffee."

Brad stared at Sturgeon, confused. "I saw nothing significant from last night."

"You wouldn't. It was a traffic fatality. Hit and run. Totally beneath the gods of Homicide."

Brad shrugged. "I had an excellent sleep. Heck, Lobo even let me sleep until about six-thirty."

"Arse." Sturgeon pointed to a chair. "You might as well sit and make yourself at home like you generally do."

"Don't mind if I do." Brad set his coffee on Sturgeon's desk, moved the box to the floor, plopped into a chair, leaned back, and locked his hands behind his head. "What's so important about a hit and run?"

"Hit-and-run *fatality*. Old guy crossing the street a block from the Cecil Tavern when he was hit. He died in hospital." Sturgeon rubbed the stubble on his chin. "We found the car last night in The Bay's parking garage. I had it towed here. It's the right car. The windshield is cracked with blood and hair. There are dents in the hood, roof and trunk. The right headlight is broken."

"You've got the driver?"

"No, I don't think so."

Brad's eyebrows furrowed. "Why not?"

"Sergeant Toscana sent a cruiser over to the registered owner's house in Altadore about three this morning and woke him up. He was sober. His wife said he'd been with her since he came home from work at five-thirty."

"Of course, the guy has an alibi from his wife." Brad reached for his coffee.

"His kids, as well. They were awake until about nine. He didn't have a drink all night. We'll take his photo to the Cecil and other nearby bars today and see if anyone can identify him."

"Dead end there." Brad sipped his coffee. "Where was the car stolen from?"

"Down the block from his house. The houses are close together, and no one has a garage. Street parking is at a premium."

Brad reached for the crime scene photos. "Was the car locked?"

Sturgeon snatched the photos away before Brad could grab them. "He says so."

"What did you find in the car? Fingerprints? Tissue?

Coffee cup? Chip bag? Convenience store receipt? Bodies in the trunk?"

"Well, damn, why didn't I check for those." Sturgeon glared. "The answer to all is no. We were at the crime scene all night. We'll process the car this morning. Now get the heck out of here. Unlike you, I have work to do."

"About that." Brad leaned forward. "Anything from the drug dealer murder?"

Sturgeon shook his head. "No. Why? Do you expect something?"

Brad stood. "I guess not. Have a great day."

"Arse," Brad heard as he headed down the hall.

CHAPTER ELEVEN

At one-fifteen, Brad grabbed his gray pinstripe suit jacket and light blue shirt out of the garment bag and slid it on. He adjusted his navy tie, then headed out of the detective bullpen, down the second-floor hallway past the memorial to fallen officers and toward the court building. Coming the other way was a lady in a black pant suit with a white blouse. Her short raven hair was combed behind her ears.

"Toscana?"

She stopped. "Detective."

He did a double-take. "I didn't recognize you. What's with the serious business suit?"

"I just had my promotion interview. If I pass, then I'll be a full-time sergeant, not just in an acting role."

Brad stepped back as a group of uniformed officers raced past on their way to court. "How did it go?"

Toscana shrugged. "How do you ever know how an interview goes? I've had some I was sure I nailed and was passed over. Some sucked, and I got the job. I'll just have to wait."

"I'm sure you did fine." Brad glanced toward the executive offices, then back. "I hear you are doing a superb job."

She laughed. "If you heard that from Briscoe, I'd be surprised. He's riding my ass all the time."

"I know the feeling. You know he will never stop."

"That's a frightening thought." She lifted a thin eyebrow. "Where are you going all dressed up? That's a fine gray suit. You attending as a lawyer?"

Brad laughed. "Nope. I'm testifying from a case earlier this fall. If you can't dazzle them with brilliance, then bluff with a nice suit."

"I'll have to remember that." Toscana smiled and adjusted his jacket collar for him. "Have fun."

Brad shivered as he took the outdoor walkway from police headquarters over to the court building. It was only twenty feet, but it chilled him to the core. He was testifying in courtroom 201. Court started at one-thirty, but he'd be lucky if they called him to testify at all today. As he strolled, he reviewed the domestic assault from over two months ago. He'd responded to a call with Detective Don Griffin, where an asshat named Vinnie Bevan was beating up his girlfriend, Sylvia. A fight ensued during the arrest and Brad had, some said, *aggressively* subdued the suspect.

Brad headed to the front of the courtroom to check in with Prosecutor Jenni Blighe. She leaned over her table scanning the files she'd laid out. The view was impressive to say the least. She was all business. It made sense in court, even though they'd worked together for a month preparing documents, evidence and strategy for the trial of Logan Hirsch, the surviving sniper.

She wore a dark blue skirt and jacket, and a white blouse with a large blue bow tied at the neck. Her blond hair hung straight, barely touching her shoulders. She glanced to the side as Brad approached.

"Good afternoon, Detective."

"Prosecutor Blighe. Nice power suit. The bow is a lovely touch."

Blighe snorted. "Flattery won't help you today. You know the defense attorney Harry Townsend is going to come after you for excessive force."

"He's tried before. He can give it a go again."

"Just keep your answers brief and stay calm." She rotated to face him and glared. "I'm serious. Don't get in a pissing match with him."

"Me?" Brad stared at Blighe in mock terror.

Blighe glared back. "You are a cop testifying, not a lawyer. Remember that."

"Yes, ma'am." Brad nodded.

"Go wait in the witness room. I'm calling paramedic Jill Cook first so she can describe the injuries. Then Detective Griffin and Sergeant Briscoe. You're the last witness. Have a snooze.

Brad sat in the corner of the witness room with his head back against the wall, eyes closed. The aged pine paneling hid the soundproofing. The chairs were comfortable, better than the rigid courtroom benches. Better still, the air conditioning kept the room at a perfect temperature for sleeping. They'd just called in Briscoe. Once he completed his testimony, they'd call Brad. He was the last person in the room, which suited him fine. He appreciated quiet moments like this—he sought them out.

However, his brain was not cooperating. Rest and relaxation were not an option. He opened his eyes and stared at the white ceiling tiles. How could something that happened less than two months ago seem like forever ago? Worse, though, was that he didn't have a great recollection of that night. It had been his first night back on duty. He was champing at the bit to work. The night had been slow until the assault came in. Since they were the closest unit, they'd responded.

The door to the interview room opened and a voice called, "Detective Coulter."

Brad glanced up and followed the uniformed bailiff to the witness box in the courtroom where he nodded to the judge and was sworn in. He shrugged his shoulders to relieve the tension. Not that he was a stranger to court, but more was at stake today. He glanced around the courtroom. To his right, at the table opposite Blighe, sat the accused, Vinnie Bevan and his lawyer, Harry Townsend. He had been a defense lawyer for over twenty years and seemed to be in court every day. Tall, with salt-and-pepper hair slicked back, a hawkish nose, and beady eyes, the man came alive in court. He was impeccably dressed in a dark blue pinstripe suit, white shirt, and blue tie with shoes that gleamed from the florescent lights.

Crown Prosecutor Jenni Blighe approached. "Good afternoon, Detective Coulter."

"Good afternoon, ma'am." He stood straight, his hands clasped behind his back.

"Please state your name and spelling for the court."

"Detective Bradley Coulter. C-O-U-L-T-E-R."

"Detective, you are a sworn officer of the Calgary Police Service."

"Yes."

Blighe consulted her notes. "Were you on duty the night of October 4, at approximately 2200 hours?"

Brad nodded. "Yes, I was."

"Can you please, in your own words, describe the incident you attended."

"I was working with Detective Don Griffin. A call came on the radio for a domestic assault. We were the closest unit."

Blighe stepped away from her table and took a few steps toward Brad. "Isn't it unusual for detectives to respond to the initial call?"

Brad shrugged. "We are cops, and we were closest. Domestics can be tricky to handle. Additional cops are better than too few."

"I see. Continue."

"We double-parked out front and raced up the stairs to the second-level apartment. As we ascended the stairs, we could hear an assault in progress."

"Objection." Defense Attorney Harry Townsend stood buttoning his blue pinstripe jacket. His gray eyes sparkled as his performance began. "Speculation by the detective. He had no way of knowing what was happening."

"Sustained."

Townsend was technically correct, but Brad's statement was still heard in court. The judge couldn't unhear something.

"On the way up the stairs, we heard shouts and crashing. In the shouting, we heard the victim—" Brad glanced at the defense lawyer. "Sorry, *a female voice* screaming for help. When we entered the apartment, we saw a skinny guy, the accused"—Brad pointed at the man seated next to Townsend—"Vinnie Bevan, standing over the victim. Bevan held the victim's hair in his left hand and was poised for a punch with his right fist."

"Objection." Townsend leaned forward, ready to stand. "Again, the detective seems to know things that didn't happen."

The judge pursed his lips. "I'll allow that."

This time Townsend stood. "Your Honor—"

The judge held up his hand. "Detective, have you ever witnessed a fight?"

"Yes, sir."

"And in any of those fights, did someone draw back their arm and throw a punch?"

"Certainly."

"I stand by my decision to overrule the objection. I am confident the detective can identify risk." The judge stared at Townsend until he sat.

Blighe nodded to Brad. "Please continue."

"We had drawn our pistols because we were unsure what the threat was. I shouted to Bevan twice to put his hands where I could see them. The accused refused my requests and punched the victim, his girlfriend, Sylvia, in the jaw. Blood and spit spattered the bedroom wall. I raced to the bed and dove at the accused before he could hit her again."

"Objection."

The judge waved Townsend back into his chair.

"I dove at the accused. We crashed into the wall and then slid onto the floor. The accused continued resisting arrest, and with the help of my partner, Detective Griffin, we subdued and handcuffed Bevan."

"Anything else you want to add?" Blighe asked.

"Yes. The paramedics treated Sylvia in the apartment, and then moved her on a stretcher out to the ambulance. As the accused was being escorted from the apartment by uniformed officers, he said, 'I'll finish this later, bitch.' Then he broke free from the officers. Fearing he would hit the victim again, I subdued him. The uniformed officers took him away."

Blighe nodded. "I'm sure Mr. Townsend is going to question the force you used. Can you explain that for the court?"

"Absolutely. You've already seen the photos of Sylvia taken at the hospital. Bevan exhibited extreme violence toward her. I had no way to know what he would do next—my goal was to subdue him as fast as I could."

"Did you punch him?"

"I did, to stun him. He was obviously out of control. Sorry … to me, it appeared he was out of control."

Blighe asked her next question. "And the second time you had to subdue him?"

"Again, he appeared furious. As he pulled away from the uniformed officers, I was afraid he'd knock over the stretcher and continue his attack on Sylvia. I was also worried about the safety of the paramedics."

Blighe nodded. "Thank you, Detective. I'm sure my learned colleague has some questions."

Townsend stood and smoothed his jacket, taking his time as every defense lawyer did.

"Detective, do you recall the words you used when you told my client to put his hands on his head."

"I believe I said, 'Police, hands where I can see them.'"

Townsend nodded. "That sounds right for your first order. You said my client did not comply. Is it possible he couldn't hear you?"

"Sure, that's possible."

Townsend's eyebrows raised, and he cocked his head.

Brad suppressed a grin. "Because he was so focused on beating his girlfriend."

Townsend held his hands out to the judge.

The judge chuckled. "I believe you stepped into that yourself, counselor."

Townsend made an act out of studying his notes. "What did you say to my client the second time?"

"When the accused did not comply, I repeated my order."

Townsend consulted his notes again. "Would it be accurate to say your order was along the lines of, 'Let her go, or I'll spray your brains onto the walls?'"

Brad nodded. "That sounds like something I'd say."

"You threatened my client with death?" Townsend asked.

"It was an assault in progress right before me. I had already given the accused a chance to stop. Sylvia's life was under direct threat."

"Yet, you didn't shoot, you tackled and assaulted my client."

Brad hated this part of the court game. "I'm confused. Are you upset I didn't shoot your client?"

Townsend puffed out his chest and grabbed his jacket lapels. "Detective, I get to ask the questions."

"Sorry, I'm just confused."

"Let's move to later that night, when my client, was *handcuffed* ..."—Townsend paused for effect—"and was being escorted to a police cruiser. You said you were afraid for the victim, which is honorable. But I understand other officers had to restrain you from further assaulting my client. That, in fact, your attack left my client gasping for air and near death."

"The accused continued his attempts to attack Sylvia on the stretcher. During the scuffle, he may have been struck in the throat."

"May have, Detective?" Townsend cocked his head and frowned. "Or you punched him in the throat?"

"I can't say for sure how it happened."

Townsend stood directly in front of Brad. His way to intimidate Brad. *Good luck with that.*

"Detective, you are under oath." Townsend folded his arms across his chest and paused. "Do you want to revise that statement?"

Brad scrunched his eyebrows. "I'm not sure what your question is?"

"The question, and I'll state it clearly for you, is that, isn't it true you deliberately struck my client in the throat with intent to inflict a potentially life-threatening injury?"

Brad glared at Townsend. "I believe earlier you counseled me on not guessing what someone was thinking or their intentions. It seems to me you are taking some vast leaps into my mind and my intentions. Let me assure you, my intention was to ensure Sylvia and the paramedics were safe and the accused would harm no one else that night."

Townsend approached the judge, arms outstretched. "Your Honor, I am not on trial."

"Could have fooled me," Blighe said.

Townsend shot Blighe an icy glare. "Your Honor, please advise the witness to answer my questions."

"Counselor. Be sure you are asking a question."

Townsend consulted his notes. "Detective, this was your first night back at work, correct?"

"Yes."

"After two-and-a-half months on leave."

Blighe jumped to her feet. "Objection, Your Honor."

"To what, Ms. Blighe?" the judge asked.

"To the direction of this questioning. Detective Coulter's leave and the reasons for that leave are not relevant in this case."

"Your Honor," Townsend said. "I believe the detective's state of mind is relevant."

The judge sat back, fingers steepled under his chin. "You may continue, Counselor, but tread carefully."

"Thank you, Your Honor." Townsend nodded to the judge and stepped in front of Brad. "Detective Coulter. Can you please explain, for the benefit of the court, the circumstances around your leave?"

The judge leaned forward on his bench. "Counselor."

Brad glanced at the judge. "Your Honor, I will answer that question."

"Very well, Detective."

"On July 15, my fiancée, Maggie Gray, a paramedic, was murdered by Jeter Wolfe in our home. Our unborn child also died that night. In the confrontation, I was shot by Wolfe, and I returned fire."

"Killing Mr. Wolfe."

"Yes. After counseling, I returned to work. October 4 was my first night shift back at work."

"About the counseling—"

"Stop right there, Mr. Townsend," the judge said. "I warned you."

Townsend held up a hand. "Just trying to establish a state of mind."

"Find another way."

"Were you angry the night of my client's alleged assault?"

Brad shrugged. "No."

"I understand the alleged victim was blond."

"You know that," Brad said. "The photos reveal a blond lady, Sylvia, severely beaten by your client."

Townsend rolled his eyes. "Your Honor."

"He answered your question. Move on." The judge sat back.

"Your fiancée was—"

Blighe was on her feet. "Objection. Mr. Townsend has been counseled."

"Sustained. Mr. Townsend, if you have questions regarding the assault, please ask them. Questions will be considered a breach of my directions, and you will be penalized. Am I clear?"

"Yes, Your Honor." Townsend continued his questioning for another thirty minutes, asking the same questions in different ways, but Brad's answers remained the same.

The judge set a date for sentencing in two weeks, and the accused was released on bail.

After court, Brad and Jenni Blighe headed to a corner pub, the Jolly Judge, that was perfect for lunches and dinners as they worked late into the night on the sniper case. Despite the name, it was not in the courthouse but in an old sandstone building that was converted into apartments. On tap were several Scottish beers, but Brad had developed a taste for fine Scotch.

Brad ordered two Scotch and headed to a booth in the back corner. The waitress delivered the drinks as Blighe slid into the booth.

Brad hung his suit jacket on a hook at the top of the booth, loosened his tie, then sat.

Blighe grabbed her drink and held it out. "That went well." They clinked glasses.

Brad sipped the Scotch. "We had the judge on our side."

"That's not happening so often nowadays." She told Brad about the rape case.

Brad shook his head and sipped the Scotch. "How does that happen? Where is the accountability?"

"If you think it's awful today, wait a few years. The scales of justice are already tipping toward the accused. If you think you were on trial today, just wait. Cops will have to defend every action, and any perceived mistake will cause an acquittal."

"That's a real cheery thought after you won a case. I'd hate to drink with you when you lose."

"We haven't won yet." Blighe twirled her drink. "I'm not naïve anymore. We've talked about this. Jeter Wolfe changed our lives four months ago. Yours more than mine."

"It's not a competition," Brad said. "Jeter Wolfe affected a lot of lives and none in a moral way. He's gone. Good riddance."

"I live in fear every day." Blighe took a drink, then stared at the table. "I always carry mace, even when I jog. I'm taking self-defense courses and bought a gun. My house has more alarms and cameras than a jewelry store. If I'm lucky, I sleep for two hours at a time. My husband has custody of the kids because I'm terrified to have them in the house with me. They know I'm scared, but they don't understand. They want their mommy."

Brad leaned across the table. "Jenni, that's no way to live. Wolfe is dead. He can't hurt you."

"But to stop his revenge plan, you had to shoot him. It shouldn't get to that." She took a sip of the Scotch. "The courts should protect people. Prison isn't the answer for everyone, but when you have a record like Wolfe, or rape a teenage girl, or get your twentieth impaired charge, you should be in jail. Not out so you can strike again."

"The system isn't perfect, but it's better than the public hangings of the last century."

"Are you sure?" Blighe snorted. "I'll bet that was a deterrent."

"Was it?" Brad drank some Scotch. "What if you stole food so your children didn't starve? Does that mean you deserve to hang as a punishment? Or get your hands cut off?"

"I'm talking about violent offenders." She leaned forward and tapped the table with a finger. "The ones with a trail of destroyed lives. That shithead Burke Baldwin and Tony Bevan. I don't see the Goddess of Justice agreeing that severe punishment in those instances is too harsh. I like the code of the old west—wanted, dead or alive. Dead is easier."

"Easier, but right?" Brad sighed. "Don't get me wrong. I'd love to be a lawman and work under those conditions. But until someone comes up with a better legal system, we're stuck with this one. If I must stand and defend my actions in court, I'm pleased to. If the defense lawyers want to put on a show for their client, go for it. But I will continue to do what needs to be done, within the law, to bring the accused to you with high-quality evidence. You present the case as best as you can, then it's up to the judge or jury. Our best is all we can do."

"Are you sure about that?" Blighe finished her drink and ordered another round.

CHAPTER TWELVE

DICE CARRIED A MUG AROUND THE KITCHEN ISLAND, INTO THE living room, and stood in front of a wall covered with maps, photos of houses, photos of potential victims, and details of their daily routines. To make room, the couch was shoved to the side so the entire wall could be used for planning.

Dice sipped the hot drink—so many choices. They were all low-life scum-sucking pigs, all on the street, released by a corrupt court system.

Three targets were crossed out by a thick, red Sharpie pen. Three was a worthy start. It had been a mistake killing the second dealer the same way as the first. Lesson learned. In the future, the murders would be so dissimilar, they'd never be connected. Three victims, if they could be called that, who had never met, and whose paths had never crossed. Three crimes with no evidence pointing to Dice.

Knowing how the cops thought was an advantage. Understanding how the Crime Scene Unit did their job and what they searched for was essential.

Dice considered several options—someone as despicable as the drug dealer and the drunk driver, but dissimilar. Today, a new name made the list. He'd have to wait his turn until the surveillance was done. Dice knew about this piece of shit, and justice needed to be swift. The red Sharpie circled his name. But not tonight—other plans had been made. Tonight, Dice would take it to another level.

CHAPTER THIRTEEN

Early Friday morning Brad sat in the back booth at a truck stop restaurant, sipping coffee and reading the paper. With no court appearances scheduled for weeks, he was back to wearing jeans, a button-down navy shirt and hiking boots. His parka and gloves lay beside him on the bench.

What this place lacked in décor, it made up for with the best breakfast in Calgary. His workday-morning routine comprised a stop at Gerry's Convenience for a coffee or two, then later breakfast or lunch at one of two locations. If he was hungry in the morning, breakfast. If he got hungry later, then lunch. If not, he'd survive on coffee for the day.

Nothing of significance in the morning paper—Mayor Kearse was still basking in his role in the apprehension of the snipers. Brad shook his head. He still couldn't believe Kearse had gone from crime reporter to mayor in a few months. He flipped through the paper to the sports section.

Sugar Ray Leonard regained the WBC welterweight

boxing crown in New Orleans when Roberto Duran quit in the eighth round, saying 'no más.'

Brad was on the second page of the business section when his senses went on alert—not a threat, but something had changed in the diner.

He folded the top section of the paper over and peered toward the front. He recognized the man at the door.

It was Sergeant Kent Jackson.

Four years ago, when Brad was a constable on the street, Jackson had been his district sergeant. They had a love-hate relationship. Brad loved to push things to the line—right to the edge. Jackson dragged him back. Jackson had encouraged Brad to try out for the tactical support unit. Brad passed the testing, and Jackson was the first sergeant of the TSU.

Brad hadn't talked to the man for close to two years. Yet here he was, at the truck stop diner Brad came to in order to be away from cops.

There was no doubt this was Jackson, but he had aged. Hair and mustache more salt than pepper, weathered face showing deep lines, and dark circles around his eyes. He still had the swagger Brad remembered. His shoulders were broad, long arms reaching past his waist, hands spread wide, like a marshal in the old west heading for the showdown on Main Street. His customary toothpick was protruding from the corner of his mouth. Although, today Jackson was wearing a black suit that hung loosely on his tall frame.

Jackson's eyes roamed the diner, then came to rest on Brad. His long strides had him at Brad's table in seconds.

"Coulter."

"Sergeant," Brad said.

"Mind if I join you." Jackson hadn't waited for an answer. He took a seat across from Brad.

The waitress rushed over, topped up Brad's coffee, and filled a mug for Jackson.

"You look great, Sarge."

"Cut the bullshit, Coulter. I look like hell. I know it, you know it, so let's not BS each other."

"What brings you to the restaurant?"

Jackson's eyes held Brad's, then glanced down. He reached for the coffee and took a sip, then glanced over the brim of the mug. "Searching for you."

Brad wasn't sure what to make of that and didn't have a clue why Jackson would search for him. Heck, he wasn't even sure what unit Jackson was working in. He wasn't in uniform.

"You heading to an important meeting with the chief?" Chief Hamilton wore suits instead of a uniform.

"Interviews for district sergeants this week. Lucky me. I get to interview twenty-one candidates."

"You were a great district sergeant. You'll pick the right people."

The two men stared at each other for a few moments. Staring contests were something Brad typically won. But not with Jackson. Brad was the one to break eye contact. He stared at his coffee, grabbed it and took a sip.

"Besides the delicious food, great coffee and wonderful conversation, what's up?"

Jackson took another sip, eyes still on Coulter. "I told you I was looking for you."

Brad held his hands wide. "Well, you found me."

Jackson nodded. "Yup, I did."

Brad shifted uncomfortably in his seat. He didn't understand why Jackson was making him so nervous. He would like to think he had matured and was confident. Something about Jackson finding him here, the fact he was here, had Brad's Spidey senses tingling.

They sat in silence for a few moments. Jackson sat back, pulling his long arms across his chest. "This is a shitty year for you, Coulter." Before Brad could answer, Jackson continued, "A lot happened. Not a lot of it pleasant. The thing is, as much as I hated to admit it four years ago, you are a moral man and a great cop. It's a shame sometimes that life deals us shit sandwiches too hard to choke down." Jackson leaned forward, put his meaty hands on the table, and shifted. "No polite way to say this, so I'm just gonna tell it like it is. You are fucking lucky you're still a cop. You know you crossed the line last month. The reason you're still carrying a badge and a gun is because of Mayor Kearse. Deputy Chief Archer is tired of babysitting you—tired of covering up your messes. That's my job now. I did it before, and I can do it again."

"What the heck does that mean?" Brad asked.

Jackson leaned over his coffee and whispered, "What it means is there will be no bullshit from you. If you were a cat, you've used all nine of your lives. If you were on a sinking ship, your life preserver is missing. If your toenails touch the line, you are done. Do I make myself clear?"

"Sure. I guess so." Brad chewed a lip, then shook his head. "Actually, I'm not sure what that means."

"What that means, Coulter, is that you report to me."

"I'm still confused. Are you my partner, or my boss?"

"Right now, I'm your worst enemy. I have been assigned as the staff sergeant for Homicide."

"Sarge, we have a staff sergeant in Homicide."

"Yup, you're right. There's a need for another. I got the job."

"How does this work?" Brad asked.

"Everything you do, plan to do, or haven't thought about doing, goes through me. You will always keep me informed on where you are, what you are doing, who you are talking to, and what your next steps are. No freelancing and no running operations off-the-cuff. No fudging the system or playing fancy with the rules—none of that. Think about it as being on double-secret probation. I want to know when you wake up. I want to know what you have for breakfast. I want to know when you leave for work, and when you arrive. I want to know when you pick up a file or set the file down. You take a shit, I get to know. Questions?"

Brad licked his lips, surprised how dry they were. "Ah, yeah. You are the sergeant. No problem."

Jackson leaned back, but his large hands gripped the edge of the table. "What are you working on?"

Brad grinned because the answer was easy. "Well, Archer doesn't want me working on the street, so he had me going to training classes for the last seven days."

"Did you learn anything?"

"I learned a ton."

"You pay attention to any of it?"

"Sure, you know I did."

Jackson's face soured like he had bitten into a lemon the

size of a watermelon. The sourness quickly changed to disbelief. "Right at the start, I said no bullshit. I meant it."

Brad cringed. "All right, there was one first-rate course. Sturgeon's Crime Scene Management was excellent. I heard most of it before, but it made sense."

"Out of the seven days of classes, you learned one thing?"

Brad cocked his head to the side, pressing a finger to his lips as if he were concentrating. "That about sums it up, Sarge."

"And you have no cases?"

"Not officially."

Jackson rolled his eyes. "Oh god, give it to me straight."

Brad nodded, took a long drink of coffee and set the cup down. But no sooner had the cup hit the table than the waitress was over with a refill for them.

"No official cases. Sergeant Sturgeon told me about a drug dealer who was killed earlier this week in Victoria Park. Other than the training classes, I had nothing going on. He suggested I investigate. I did."

"So?" Jackson's hands spread wide.

"Nothing to say. There aren't any leads."

"Really?"

"There is one suspicious thing," Brad said. "About two months ago, there was a similar homicide. A drug dealer in Victoria Park was killed in the same way—the knife under the ribcage to the heart. Couple things. One, it's a specific way of killing somebody. Two, neither the drugs nor the money were taken. Three, in the first case a few months ago, there were several cuts on the abdomen, a lot like the hesitation marks we see in suicide. I think this was the killer's first murder. The killer knew what to do, knew how to do it, but that's a long way from doing it. It's a long way from understanding the upward force required. The first murder was practice, or the first one in a series."

Johnson leaned back. "That's interesting. What are your next steps?"

Brad leaned back and shrugged. "I don't know. I went to the crime scene and looked around. This crappy November weather messed with anything that might be at the crime scene. By the time Sturgeon and his Crime Scene Unit arrived at both scenes, the cops and paramedics and god knows who else, trampled over the scene. Any evidence that relates to the killing was lost in the tons of forensic evidence left by thousands of drug deals."

"No shit."

"I don't think that investigation is going anywhere."

Jackson slowly nodded, eyes boring into Brad. "Any of that story changes—and I mean any part of it—you let me know."

"Got it, Sarge."

Jackson slid his police business card over to Brad. He picked it up and checked the back where there were two phone numbers.

"Day or night, 24/7, you let me know."

"Got it."

Jackson slid out of the booth, stood, slipped on a parka, and picked up his gloves. His lips pursed. "Sorry about what happened to Maggie. I liked her a lot. I don't care what you do in your personal time, but when you're at work, you're dialed in." Jackson took a last sip of coffee, put the cup back on the table, and glanced at Brad. "Thanks for the coffee." Jackson spun on his heel and strode to the entrance.

Brad watched Jackson leave, then ordered breakfast. If Archer decided that Brad needed a handler, Jackson was a sound choice. He was a straight shooter. Like he'd said to Brad, no bullshit. He could live with that. Jackson was at the top of the list of men Brad admired, and as hard as it was to admit, he could use some mentorship.

He flipped the paper open and reached for his coffee.

The server asked, "Refill?"

Brad replied, eyes never wavering from the paper. "Thank you." He heard the coffee pouring into the cup and smelled the tantalizing aroma. For the second time his Spidey sense kicked in. So much for a peaceful breakfast. "And for the lady."

Brad folded the paper over. Across the table sat Sadie Andrus, newly hired chief investigative reporter for CFCN TV—one of the youngest in the channel's history at a fresh-faced twenty-eight. She slid a bright-red wool jacket off her shoulders, letting it pool on the booth at her waist. Her wavy auburn hair hung past her shoulders.

During the sniper crisis a month ago, Sadie had hounded Brad for inside info on the shooters. Mostly, it didn't work. But then the sniper started communication through her to Brad. They made an agreement where they respected each other's careers, but there were times they could work together. Sadie was given the complete story and access to all components of the investigation. That brought her to national attention and her new job.

"Thank you. I'd love a coffee." She watched the waitress pour, her brown eyes mischievous as she slipped off black leather gloves one by one, laying them on the tabletop. She adjusted the low collar of her tight black blouse.

Brad set the paper on the table. "How did you find me?"

"I'm an investigative reporter." She added two cream and two sugar to the coffee.

"You're stalking me."

Sadie tilted her head back and flashed a toothy smile. "You wish." She took a sip. "Must be wonderful being a Homicide detective when there are no homicides. Dress in jeans and casual button-down shirt. Hiking boots. Start work late. Have breakfast, read the paper. What's next? Manicure and massage."

Brad rolled his shoulders. "Oh, a massage. Great idea. I'm feeling tense."

She smirked over her white mug, smudging the porcelain with a blood-red lipstick print. "From your afternoon in court yesterday?"

"You take your job seriously."

"Nah. I heard about it from our court reporter. The way he tells it, you were doing the questioning and Harry Townsend was on the defensive." She tossed her hair over her right shoulder. "Were you just messing with Townsend or were you trying to deflect from his questions?"

"Wow. Right to the jugular."

"Hey, I'm not judging. I'm all for street justice."

"Are you baiting me, waiting for me to confirm street justice?"

"This isn't about a story." She smiled demurely. "As a member of the fairer sex, I'd be glad if you tuned up some asshat beating a defenseless woman."

Brad chuckled. "Asshat? Look at you, all grown up and using cop lingo. Besides, that's not how it happened."

"I heard she was blond." Sadie's fingertips played with a strand of her hair.

Brad shook his head and leaned back. "Wow. This is not the reporter of a month ago. Again, right to the point."

Sadie reached across the table toward his hand, then quickly withdrew it. She winced and swallowed hard. "Sorry, too personal."

"We have an agreement. Digging into my personal life is something I'd expect your predecessor *Anus* Ferguson to do. Not you." He picked up the paper and flipped it open.

On cue, the waitress set Brad's breakfast on the table. Pen poised on her notepad, the older woman smiled at Sadie. "Have you decided what you'll have?"

"I'm not staying."

"She's staying," Brad said from behind the paper. "Take her order."

Sadie beamed at the waitress. "Brown toast and strawberry jam. He's grumpy until he gets his breakfast."

The server glanced at Brad, shrugged, then headed to the kitchen.

"I didn't mean to pry," Sadie said. "Sometimes, I don't think before I talk."

Brad placed the newspaper on the table, took a few bites

of the eggs, then tossed his fork onto the plate more vigorously than he'd planned. He leaned toward Sadie. "We agreed. My private life is off limits, always."

The waitress set the toast in front of Sadie.

"Sorry, I guess I was leaving." Sadie grabbed her black crossbody purse and wool jacket.

The waitress rolled her eyes.

Brad, eyes on his plate, said, "She's staying." He placed several strips of bacon on his toast.

Sadie set her purse and jacket back on the bench. She grabbed a knife and spread strawberry jam on her toast, then peered across the table. "A bacon sandwich?"

"That could be the lead on the evening news." Brad continued eating, dipping the sandwich into the egg yolks. He glanced at the paper and began reading.

They ate in silence for several minutes.

"How's the new job?" Brad asked.

"It's great." Sadie's face brightened, highlighting freckles across her aquiline nose. She leaned forward on the table. "Most of the time I pick my assignments. When there's a breaking story, I'm offered it first. Since shit follows you, you'll see me frequently."

"Lucky me."

"You can play gruff, aloof cop all you want. You don't fool me. You like the attention. I know you like action. If appalling stuff didn't find you, you'd go hunting for it. That's just how you're wired."

Brad licked his lips and wiped his mouth with a napkin. "You think you've got me all figured out."

Sadie grinned. "Yup."

"I'm not that complicated. Just a cop doing his job."

"You would have made a great marshal in the old west."

Brad smirked. "Funny, just the other day I thought that about someone else."

Sadie set her napkin on her plate and pushed it farther onto the table. She finished her coffee and slid to the edge of the booth.

"I should get going."

"What? No further interrogation?"

"Nope." She beamed. "I just wanted to see how you're doing."

Brad glanced around. "Listen. A drug dealer was killed Saturday night in Vic Park. It didn't get any press. It might be a story worth pursuing. Then check back about two months ago. You might find something similar."

Sadie slipped on her red jacket, black fur pom beanie and gloves, then grabbed her purse and slung it over her shoulder. "That's not much of a tip."

"The best I have. Thanks for buying breakfast."

"Wait, I bought it last time."

"True, but I gave you a story to follow." He sipped his coffee and went back to reading the paper.

CHAPTER FOURTEEN

SATURDAY NIGHT, DICE PARKED ACROSS FROM THE FEDERAL building and headed to Third Avenue, known as the hooker stroll, the worst-kept secret in Calgary. While Dice had done surveillance over the past two weeks, dozens of police cruisers had slowly driven down the avenue, stopping to talk to the hookers, exchanging jokes, and on a warm night, some hookers lifted their shirts and flashed their tits. It wasn't unusual to see an ambulance cruise by occasionally.

The bus bench had been the perfect place to sit and watch. That bus stop was used by at least a half-dozen different bus routes, so it was normal for someone to sit there for a while waiting for the bus they needed. Dice wore dark oversized pants, a dark T-shirt, a dark hoodie and a dark baseball cap with the bill pulled down low. Sitting in the open, Dice was invisible.

The hookers gathered in groups across the street. Maybe for safety. Some hookers were young, so perhaps the older hookers were looking after the young ones. Motherly, in a disturbing way. Old or young, they were the victims as far as Dice was concerned. Victims of the men who brought them into prostitution slavery. Victims of the men who preyed on them.

They were victims, but Dice had no interest in them. The plan wasn't to save every hooker, but to eliminate men who abused them. It was close to eleven—shift change for the cops. Police presence in the area would be limited for the next twenty to thirty minutes.

Dice picked up a garbage bag of bottles and cans and lumbered to the intersection. When the light said walk, Dice ambled across the avenue toward a trio of hookers. The oldest, likely early twenties though she looked late thirties, stepped toward Dice.

"You want a lady or three for the night? We'll give you a special deal." She glanced at the other girls who laughed.

Dice had watched them on other nights when it was slow, teasing the homeless men who wobbled past digging in the garbage for cans for recycling and their next drink.

"No thanks," Dice said. "I'm looking for a guy."

"A guy." The hooker put both hands over her mouth. "Well, break our hearts, right, girls?"

The girls laughed again. The youngest one said, "Give us a chance. You won't regret it."

"Thanks."

"You change your mind, you know where to find us."

The black Lincoln Town Car was easy to find; there weren't that many of them downtown at this time of night and just one on the hooker stroll. Dice waited in the shadows for a couple of minutes. The driver's window was open a few inches, and smoke floated out into the night. The driver was having his every-half-hour cigarette.

Dice pushed away from the wall, staggered toward the car and placed a hand on the hood. Dice choked with a sound like vomiting.

"What the—" The driver opened the door. Before he could exit, Dice pushed off the hood and fired two shots into the driver's head. The blast propelled him back into the car, leaving a red stain on the passenger seat and window. Dice leaned into the car and fired two shots into the back-seat passenger. One shot entered under his chin and exited through the back of his head, shattering the rear window and creating an explosion of maroon with bits of bone and hair on the remaining glass. Dice tossed the driver's legs back into the car and closed the door.

CHAPTER FIFTEEN

Briscoe had just left headquarters after the evening briefing for the Saturday night crews when the call came in.

"All units downtown. Third Avenue and First Street SW. Not sure what to call this, but caller from payphones says, to quote, 'something hinky goin' on in a Lincoln Continental.'"

A couple of units booked on the radio, and Briscoe figured he would head that way. Sergeant Caterina Toscana was going to be late, and Briscoe was covering her area and his own. It wasn't unusual for 'something hinky' to be going on near the stroll on the weekend. Hell, every night. That was part of the charm.

Briscoe was the second unit there. He slipped out of his van and jammed the fake fur hat onto his bald head. He slid on gloves as he ambled over to the Lincoln. Constable Robson arrived at the Lincoln first, had a baton out, and was about to tap on the driver's window when he stopped, groaned, and stepped back. Briscoe shoved past him. "You never seen a hooker and her john—"

"Ah, shit." Briscoe was not prepared for the two frozen red spatter patterns on the car glass. The two dead men were a lot different from a hooker servicing her client. Way different. Briscoe was a veteran cop, and he made the adjustment instantaneously.

He keyed his mic. "Dispatch, 401. We've got a double homicide at this location. We're gonna need additional manpower to shut this area down, and the Crime Scene Unit."

"Roger, 401. Calls being made. I'll contact Homicide."

"Negative, dispatch." Briscoe glanced around the scene. "I'll notify Homicide."

Briscoe swung and bumped into Robson.

"Get your partner and push these people back."

The buzzing was becoming annoying. Brad brushed at his ears, hoping to chase away the mosquito. He pulled the quilt up around his neck. Lobo jumped on the bed and lay close to Brad. What the farmhouse lacked in character, it also lacked in heat. Winter was going to be brutal living here.

The buzzing started again. Brad sat up, pissed off, and shrugged off the covers. He started shivering. Lobo groaned and rolled over, eyes closed. What the heck was that? Beside his head, his pager buzzed and bounced. Brad snatched the pager off the nightstand and glanced at the display. *From dispatch—Briscoe wants you to attend a homicide.*

He swung his feet off the bed onto the icy floor and sat on the edge.

"Get up, sleepy mutt. We're going to work."

Lobo stood, yawned, and stretched his front paws. He followed Brad around the house while he changed, got his gun, badge, and a black ball cap to keep his longer-than-regulation hair in check.

"All right, boy. Game on."

The drive downtown took twenty-five minutes over snow-covered roads and black ice. He could have been to the scene sooner, but he needed a coffee to wake up and warm up. It would be a long night. Brad swung onto Fifth Avenue and quickly came to a police roadblock. Ahead, a bank of lights around a dark car. From the curb across the street, other bright lights pointed toward the car. *Ah, lovely. The media is here.* He parked behind the accumulated police vehicles and rolled down a couple of windows so Lobo would have fresh air. "I'll be back, buddy."

Lobo snored in response.

Brad slid out of the car. It was colder than when he left the farm. Storm coming in. He grabbed his blue parka from the trunk, slipped it on, and replaced his ball cap with a black beanie and gloves. He sipped his coffee as he wandered to the squat form of Briscoe.

"Hello, Sergeant."

Briscoe stared out from under the fake fur hat at the coffee. "Kind of you to finally grace us with your presence."

Brad sipped the coffee again. "Ah, that tastes so delicious. Did the victims get deader?"

"What?"

"Are they deader now than when you first called for me?" Brad sipped his coffee.

"No."

Brad pointed to the Lincoln. "Did you solve the murder?"

"No."

Brad shrugged. "Then I guess it doesn't matter whether I got here earlier. You still need me."

"Fuckin' rookie." Briscoe smirked. "My coffee?"

Brad nodded to his black Trans Am. "Over there. Be careful. Lobo is in the back sleeping. You might lose an arm if you disturb him. He hasn't had a decent bite in months. You know I'm not technically on the roster for homicides."

"Yup. That's why I paged you. You need to be doing actual work, not going to classes."

"Archer will have your ass," Brad said.

"He's welcome to it." Briscoe headed toward Brad's car, then stopped. "Oh, you might want to get to work quickly. Staff Sergeant Jackson is on his way."

Brad shouted after Briscoe. "What about an update?"

"You should have thought about that when you left my coffee in your car. Walk around, do your detecting thing. Then we'll talk."

Brad wandered toward the Lincoln. After each step, he re-analyzed the scene. Six- or eight-year-old black Lincoln Continental. The outside was clean, which, in November, was difficult to do. Someone cleaned the car every day. The winter tires had deep tread. Snow and slush had drifted around the tires, so the car hadn't moved in a few hours. A light skiff of snow had gathered on the roof. Finally, he was at the open driver's door. Its window was down a few inches. He'd have to ask Briscoe, but Brad had heard that all doors were closed when the cops arrived. So, maybe not as when they found it.

The driver's upper body was tilted to the right, partly on the passenger seat, his jacket open and showing a shoulder holster and gun. His feet were both to the far left, not a place you would have your feet. That made little sense. If he were the driver and saw the shooter, he'd do one of a few things: reach for his gun, put his hands up hoping to stop the bullet or the shooter, or try to get out.

Brad stepped back. Something else was wrong. His brown eyes swept the inside of the car again. Someone had closed the driver's eyes. That meant there was contact with the body. He would have to let Sturgeon and his Crime Scene Unit know. Probably the paramedics.

He dialed the clock back an hour. The pimp is in the back-passenger seat of his fancy car. The driver is both chauffeur and bodyguard. If someone approached the vehicle, the driver might roll down his window. If he wasn't expecting the person, he'd tell them to fuck off. Maybe show off the gun, so they got the message.

Why was the window down a few inches? Brad peered at the pavement beside the car. Cigarette butts. So, the driver was blowing the smoke out the window. Still made little sense. Then why didn't the killer shoot through the glass?

Because the shooter didn't have to. The driver opened the door but wasn't threatened. Who could that be? Hooker? Drug dealer?

Brad surveyed the crowd gathered behind the police tape. A nighttime mix for downtown. A few twentyish adults dressed for a night at a bar, the homeless watching the excitement, and in the shadows, hookers wondering if they'd be able to work again tonight. A couple news vans were pulling in behind the crowd. Briscoe wandered over, sipping his coffee.

"Okay, you've had your coffee. Give me an update."

"Sure." Briscoe sipped the coffee a few times.

"Today?" Brad crossed his arms.

"Oh, right. 911 calls started coming in after eleven. The 911 calls were vague, and the call taker thought it sounded like a hooker and john were going at it in the car."

"How did they come to that conclusion?"

"Most of the calls came from the payphone by the liquor store. No one gave their name. The callers knew what had happened but didn't want any part of it. They didn't want a dozen police cruisers racing up here."

Brad glanced around. "Yeah, I get that."

"When we got here, the car door was closed. We were about to tap on the driver's window when I saw the bodies."

Brad held out a hand. "When I arrived, the door was open, and the driver's eyes were closed. Who screwed with my crime scene?"

"That, your highness, god of detectives, was the paramedics. There is this thing we do when someone is hurt or maybe dead. We call the paramedics, because I don't know anything about paramedic shit."

"Okay. That makes sense, sorry."

"I got the area cordoned off, and we waited and waited

for you. We waited so long the media is already set up across the street. They were waiting for you, as well."

Brad took a deep breath, exhaled, and took a three-hundred-and-sixty-degree turn. "You've got guys interviewing everyone here?"

"Yup. The street people say they saw nothing. The others, gawkers, came after we showed up."

"Get your guys to canvass the crowd again and see if anyone saw a homeless person around the Lincoln. Make sure they check drainage grills and garbage cans for a weapon or clothing."

"Already got them on that." Briscoe tracked cops on either side of the street.

"Do you have a video recorder?"

"No." Briscoe's head swung toward Brad. "Why? Are you making a movie?"

"No. I want to record every person who is standing outside the police tape."

"You think the gunman is watching?"

Brad shrugged. "You never know. I can't think of a reason for the giant chauffeur-bodyguard to open the door unless he wasn't threatened."

Briscoe nodded. "Hooker or dealer … or homeless person."

"Brilliant," Brad said. "Homeless person."

A police van pulled up and Sergeant Toscana stepped out and surveyed the scene. Briscoe rolled his eyes.

"She's not that bad," Brad said. "Give her a chance."

Briscoe ignored Brad and peered across the street. "I see someone who can do the recording for you."

"Great, who?"

Briscoe grinned and pointed.

Brad headed to the crowd around the crime scene. Several cops made sure the onlookers stayed behind the police tape. As he approached, a brilliant light blinded him.

"Detective Coulter, can you tell us what's going on here?"

Brad shielded his eyes with his arm. "Ms. Andrus, tell your cameraman to shut the fuc—the *camera* off, please. We need to talk."

Sadie straightened the lapels of her knee-length white parka. Black leather boots covered her legs up to the lower edge of her parka. She wore a white knit beanie with a pompom on top. "On the record or off the record?"

"The light?"

She nodded to the cameraman, and he extinguished the camera light.

"How was your day?" She smiled. Her white teeth accentuated by deep red lipstick. "I haven't seen you since breakfast this morning."

A couple of cops at the tape line grinned. Brad blinked a few times and glared at them. They looked away.

"I need a favor."

"I already had dinner," Sadie said. "Drinks later would be great."

The cops grinned again.

"Will you shut up and listen?"

"Sure, since you asked so politely." She flicked her auburn hair over her shoulder.

Brad stepped close enough to smell her citrusy perfume and whispered, "I need your cameraman to pan the crowd. Get a closeup video of everyone."

Sadie put her hand on his arm. "Now, Detective?" Sadie's voice was louder than it needed to be. "That sounds like fun. I'd love to."

The cops had their full attention on Sadie and Brad.

Brad quickly stepped back. "It's important."

Sadie grinned. "Why do you need that, and why would we do that?"

"Off the record, it's possible the killer is here."

Sadie glanced around. "Why do you think that?"

Brad shrugged as he watched the gathering crowd. "A hunch."

"And what do I get?"

"The scoop when I break this case."

Large flakes of snow started falling. Sadie shivered and held her arms tight over her chest. "It needs to be better than your stupid lead this morning. That went nowhere. Who cares if a dealer killed another dealer? That's community service in my mind."

"Wow." Brad shook his head and frowned. "So young, yet so cynical."

Sadie glared. "Film for the scoop."

"Yes."

"I'll have to call my boss."

"Do it quick before the crowd gets bored or the snow chases them home."

CHAPTER SIXTEEN

COFFEE IN HAND, BRAD ENTERED THE OFFICE OF THE MEDICAL examiner Sunday morning and headed past the vacant reception desk. He continued down the dull white hall to the autopsy suites. He peeked in the windows and doors until he saw a body on the table, then stepped inside.

Three people stood around the body—the medical examiner, his assistant, and Sturgeon. He wore green surgical scrubs, a green cloth hat and booties. He snapped photos of the deceased before the autopsy, then throughout the postmortem.

"About time," Sturgeon said. "Did we ruin your Sunday morning sleep in?"

Brad didn't know how Sturgeon could handle this. It was like imprinting the image in your mind forever. Brad did not need new images stored in that special file in his brain.

It had thrilled Brad to work in Homicide, but autopsies were something he had never adjusted to. He knew autopsies would be an essential part of the job, but he still felt queasy every time. It didn't affect Sturgeon. Trying to convince your mind the person was dead and couldn't feel anything didn't work. Sturgeon suggested Brad should view it as evidence gathering and no different from any other part of a homicide. That didn't work either.

Brad changed into the surgical greens. He'd become an expert at watching the autopsy, but not seeing. He forced his mind to happier thoughts. But sometimes they went to Maggie, and that was worse than the autopsy.

The bonus today was he got to view two autopsies. *Shit.* Recovering the bullets or fragments was a key part of the case. Well, it would be once they found a gun.

This body was that of Owen Judd. Only twenty-seven, Judd's body had been abused like he was fifty. Scars dotted both arms, but no new injection sites. Maybe he was one of the rare ones who kicked the heroin habit. Or, more likely, he had found something better. Maybe cocaine.

The Y-cut was completed, and the ME was removing organs. Perhaps Brad would have a salad tonight.

The ME said, "I have one bullet. Made a mess of the heart." He pulled the bullet out and set it in a tray filled with saline. The lead was in decent shape—a 9mm. With the blood and tissues washed off, Sturgeon put the bullet into an evidence bag. Further organs were removed, and the assistant weighed each one. The ME kept up a steady description of everything they were doing for the recording. Sturgeon continued to take photos.

Brad wondered if he should paint the farmhouse.

A second bullet was lodged by the spine. This bullet was

in worse shape—it had mushroomed, probably from multiple impacts on bones. Rather than a complete round, it appeared like someone had used a potato peeler on it. It went into the saline, then into an evidence bag. An hour later, this autopsy was complete. *Just in time.* Brad needed a coffee.

The autopsy on the driver, Anthony Moss, went the same as the first. Brad was running out of cheerful places to take his mind. At one point, he drifted off and nearly fell from the stool. That would have been a disaster. He would never convince them he'd drifted off. They'd assume he'd passed out from the autopsy, and he'd never live that down. Sturgeon would take pictures before checking to see if Brad had a pulse.

Both bullets taken from Moss had disintegrated into fragments. From the four bullets, they had one that would give a proper analysis. But that was all they needed.

What Brad needed was fresh air. He left the autopsy suite and headed straight to the parking lot where Sturgeon joined him.

"I thought you were going to drop in there," Sturgeon said.

"Just tired," Brad replied.

Sturgeon grinned. "Sure. I had my camera ready."

"I knew you would. Any thoughts?"

Sturgeon nodded and held up the evidence bags. "One bullet for analysis. They shot the chauffer from close, within a foot to eighteen inches. Owen Judd, from further away, but not much. The driver was shot first, then the shooter leaned into the car and shot Judd."

"Both up close and personal. Besides the bullets, anything else to help us?"

"The bullet is our best evidence, but only if the gun has already been used in a crime. If not, we keep it on file and check guns when we get them."

CHAPTER SEVENTEEN

AFTER THE AUTOPSY, BRAD HEADED TO THE TV STUDIO. HE SAT at a monitor in a tiny viewing room off the newsroom of CFCN TV. The room was under six by six with a short table and a video recorder with a monitor. The soundproofing added to the claustrophobic feeling. Sadie arranged for the video, but Brad had to watch it at their station.

He sat with a technician in a viewing room. Brad had him run the tape in slow motion. Occasionally he'd have the tech stop, zoom in on a person, and then print the image. After three hours, everyone appeared suspicious. A half-dozen paper coffee cups littered the table and floor. He increased the volume as the news came on a TV.

The primary story was about the shooting downtown last night. It identified the dead as Owen Judd and Anthony Moss. Another part of the deal. CFCN got to break the news before the other stations.

The video showed Sadie at the scene with her back to the police tape and the Lincoln. Sergeant Sturgeon and his crime scene techs were labeling evidence and preparing the car for transport to the police garage. Staff Sergeant Jackson and Briscoe stood off to the side in conversation. They must have filmed this segment after he talked to Sadie. He didn't understand how she could be relaxed and refreshed at that hour. He rubbed the stubble on his unshaven face.

The monitor switched to the weather report—freezing rain followed by heavy, wet snow. *Perfect.* Brad went back to the video of the crowd.

What type of people hung around a murder scene? Besides cops and reporters? Maybe crime writers. If that was it, there were a lot of crime writers in Calgary.

He set the photos across a table—at least three-dozen pictures. His selection had been less than scientific—people who appeared suspicious. He shook his head. He could see himself saying that in court. What a waste of time. He had these photos, but nothing to compare them to. Useless.

He stepped out of the viewing room, headed down the hall and knocked on an open door. Sadie glanced up. "Any luck?"

"No."

"Remember, if you find a witness, you promised I get the scoop."

Lobo had slept most of the day while Brad attended the autopsy and watched the video. Now that Brad was home, Lobo was ready for action.

Lobo sat at Brad's feet, staring up expectantly.

"All right. I'll get ready."

Brad changed into his cold-weather running gear while Lobo raced around the house. When Brad opened the door, Lobo bolted down the path and out of sight. Brad shivered as a blast of icy air hit him. He glanced at the sky—overcast, and darkness was fast approaching. He and Lobo knew the path in daylight or darkness. He shivered again, then set a steady pace. The first mile passed with Brad running on automatic. One foot in front of the other, breathe in, breathe out. His body was in a rhythm, his mind resting. His brain started to function as he jogged down the hill to the dam.

Birds swooped low across the path; others chirped in the trees. Squirrels scrambled up trees and nattered at Lobo from branches overhead. The sun was over the horizon. At the water's edge, he felt the icy chill.

Bits and pieces of the past few days floated around until the shooting last night clicked into place. A pimp and his bodyguard killed. Sadie was right. Who cares? Some rival was making a play for the prostitution business on the stroll. Out with the old, in with the new. By tonight, those girls would have a new boss. Maybe better, maybe not, but the trade on the street would continue and not miss a beat.

However, two men were dead. Brad was a cop—not any cop, but a Homicide cop. His job was to solve murders. Not just ones he thought were worthy of his attention, but all homicides. Still, it was difficult to get energy to address these two murders. Without having checked yet, Brad knew they would both have extensive police records that included assaults on women. It was a possibility that one of his ladies had had enough—bang. That could fit. The driver wouldn't worry about a hooker approaching the car. He would be relaxed, even indifferent.

That fit to a point. But so far, they knew of four shots. All nicely placed in the two men in tight groups. Fatal shots. Not shots someone with a grudge could do. You don't buy or steal a gun off the street and place your first four shots exactly where you want them to go. Hell, trained soldiers miss half of the targets they shoot at in combat. And shooting at a silhouette in a gun range is a lot different from pulling the trigger on a human. If he stuck with the hooker theory, then the hooker had some significant gun experience. That was worth following up. An arrest for possession of a gun—not uncommon with the hookers. Past military experience? Doubtful.

Lobo, full of energy, blasted past Brad as they ascended the hill. The squirrels chattered at Lobo, but today he didn't care. He had the scent of something and hunted with his nose to the ground.

As they crested the hill, Lobo spotted two deer. They glanced at him, then raced off. They quickly put distance between them and Lobo, but he didn't give up. Brad slowed to a fast walk and watched the race. *Keep going.* If the deer let Lobo think he had a chance of catching them, then Lobo would keep running and be exhausted by the time they got home. Lobo disappeared out of sight. Brad continued to the house.

Brad was outside the house when Lobo came panting around the corner. Lobo lay, all four legs splayed out. Brad grabbed Lobo's water bowl from the back porch and set it in front of him. He didn't stand as he gulped the water his human served him.

Brad headed over to a bench and sat, legs stretched out in front of him, arched his back, and closed his eyes.

CHAPTER EIGHTEEN

AGAINST HIS BETTER JUDGMENT AFTER THE AUTOPSIES, AND IN the freezing rain, Brad was cooking steaks on the BBQ. It was refreshing to take a break from the cases and relax with friends on Sunday night. It had become a tradition. Sunday dinner with whoever could attend.

When Sam and Emma Steele arrived, Lobo followed them around the house. Charlie Zerr was in the kitchen, helping Annie with the salads and baked beans. Like she needed help. Brad sighed. It appeared those two were getting serious.

Sam Steele came out to the BBQ and handed Brad a beer. Steele and Brad were two of the original Tactical Support Unit members. Initially they'd been fierce competitors but had become best friends. They were built the same, six-one, a hundred and eighty-five pounds of pure muscle. Steele, at twenty-eight, was four years younger than Brad. When Brad had moved on from TSU, Steele had remained and was partnered with Charlie Zerr.

Steele tapped the neck of Brad's beer bottle. "I heard you picked up an interesting call this week. I thought Archer had you sidelined."

"Briscoe called me directly." Brad drank thirstily. "Ah. I get to keep the case—double homicide. Pimp and his driver."

"That's called community service, isn't it?" Steele leaned against the deck railing.

"You can say that to me but be careful saying that anywhere other than here," Brad said.

Steele shrugged. "Still, maybe once we could win the game of attrition."

"There'd have to be more than two deaths of asshats each week." Brad flipped the steaks. "It would help if the courts locked these guys up when the crown presented a solid case. It seems defense lawyers and the shitrats are winning."

Steele gulped his beer. "True. Hey, do you know what you call one hundred lawyers on a sinking a ship?"

Brad rolled his eyes. "No."

"An excellent start."

"If I were gone, who'd save your ass and cook your steaks?"

"Excellent point. I don't mean you. Maybe a shipload of defense lawyers."

"Now you're making sense." Brad gulped his beer. "We're not the only ones frustrated. I talked with Jenni Blighe after court the other day."

"Like, you talked in the hallway?" Steele grinned over his beer.

"We went for drinks."

"I see."

"Jesus, Sam. We worked together for a month on the sniper case. Nothing there."

"A month?" Steele's eyebrows rose. "Continue."

"Jenni works her butt off to present a well-thought-out case to the court, but the judges search for any fault in the case, and side with the defense. I haven't seen her that mad since Jeter Wolfe was stalking her. I worry one day Jenni will have enough, and she'll lose it in court, or worse."

"She's just venting," Steele said. "Jenni knows she can talk to you."

Brad stared off the deck to the snow-covered barn. "No, it was deeper than that. Jenni has changed a lot in the last six months. More cynical. I see it in her eyes."

"Do you blame her?"

"Of course not." Brad flipped the baked potatoes. "We're all fighting a battle with the courts. It's getting worse."

"I heard that drunk who was killed had over twenty-five charges for drunk driving."

"Perfect example. He was a danger to everyone—he should have been locked away."

"Thank goodness for karma. It killed him before he killed someone." Steele held out his bottle, and they clinked bottlenecks. "Hey, uh, I heard a rumor this morning."

"Uh-huh. If you don't hear a rumor by ten, start one? What did you hear?"

"A few cops from downtown were talking about this reporter who was, uh, especially friendly with a detective."

Brad's hand stopped mid-flip of a steak. "What did they say?"

Steele sipped his beer. "I'll slow it down for you. Apparently ... this reporter ... mentioned ... she hadn't seen the detective ... since that morning."

Brad tossed the steak back on the grill. "Ah, crap."

Steele's eyes widened. "It's true?"

Brad's shoulders slumped. Damn Sadie. He did not need this shit floating around. He'd have a talk with her. Then he realized that was what she was hoping for. Or maybe she was just messing with him. Who knew what that woman thought?

"No, it's not true."

"There were rumors about you and Sadie during the sniper case. This appeared to fit."

"Stinking rumors." Brad drained his beer. "None of their goddamned business. Nothing is happening, and nothing happened before. She's a reporter hunting a story, and I'm always in the middle of a shit show. That's all."

Steele sipped his beer and smirked. "Wow, I touched a nerve."

"Just get me another beer."

When Steele went inside, a pregnant Emma Steele slipped out onto the chilly deck. In the last month of pregnancy, her face was pale with dark circles around her eyes. She appeared exhausted. She'd pulled her dark brown hair back in a ponytail and wore a police-issue black beanie.

"Get back in the house," Brad said. "I don't want to deliver your baby on my deck."

"I don't either." She rubbed her belly. "I'll wait another month."

Brad glanced at her bulging blue down parka. "How are you feeling?"

"Enormous as a house and waddling like a duck."

"You're gorgeous." Brad winked.

"You're such a smooth-talking liar." Emma leaned against the house. "Have you talked to Charlie lately?"

Brad shook his head. "Some, why?"

"Annie has said nothing?"

Brad set the BBQ fork down. "What's up?"

Emma stepped closer to the heat of the BBQ. "Charlie tells everyone he's fine, and he's healed from the helicopter crash, but Sam says that's not so. Sam frequently sees Charlie rubbing his leg and limping. Especially after a long run. Charlie's complained about the cold affecting the leg."

"Ah, shit." Brad sighed. Six weeks ago, when they were hunting the snipers, Charlie Zerr's helicopter was shot down. It crashed into the Bow River and Charlie had serious injuries including a damaged spine, fractured femur and broken hand. "I should have known he came back too soon."

"You'd know." Emma smiled.

"Touché. I'll keep my eye on him."

Emma gave Brad a quick peck on the cheek. "Thanks." She glanced at the BBQ. "I don't know how you do this. I'm going back inside."

CHAPTER NINETEEN

After an early jog with Lobo in the dark, chilly December morning, Brad was warming up with coffee from Gerry's. He slid between desks in the detective office, heading to his cubbyhole in the back corner. He stopped five feet from his desk, coffee halfway to his mouth. Staff Sergeant Jackson sat in Brad's chair, dark boots on his desk, giving a toothpick a thorough workover. His black suit jacket was open and a striped, red tie, too wide for fashion, lay on his white shirt.

"Hey, Sarge. You're up early."

Brad slumped into a chair across from his desk.

Jackson swung his long legs to the floor and leaned over the desk. "I tried to make it simple for you. Let me remind you. Tell me everything you do, including when you take a shit."

"I thought you were just being colorful. But since you want to know, I had a great shit this morning, right after my jog. I rarely take a crap until after I've had coffee, but today for some reason—"

Jackson pounded a fist on the desk, then pointed a shaking hand at Brad's chest. "Not today, Coulter. No backtalk, no comedy act, no innocence. On Saturday night—that would be about thirty-four hours ago—you attended a double homicide. Not a burglary. Not someone passing counterfeit money. A fucking double homicide. Do you call me? Let me know what's happening? No. I arrive on scene and you have already left. I had to get my information from Briscoe and Sturgeon. But I think, no problem. Coulter will call me Sunday. This morning, I'm walking down the alley and the chief's driver drops him at the back door. The chief talks to me like I know what happened thirty-four fuckin' hours ago. I play along like I know all about the murders. I tell him I'll see you this morning and get an update. I can't find you."

"Ah, Sarge. I didn't want to wake you up in the wee hours of Sunday morning. The guys were dead, so there wasn't anything you could do."

Jackson's jaw was clenched, and his eyes ready to pop. His finger was shaking uncontrollably. "I see. Tell me about Sunday mid-morning, and no, I don't go to church. Afternoon, Evening? What about first thing this morning? Heck, I would have visited your new farm Sunday, but apparently you were entertaining."

Brad looked away. "I'm sorry. You are invited the next time I have friends over."

Jackson's large hands slammed onto the desk, eyes ablaze. "Coulter, that was not the point. We are not friends and I don't need to hang out with you in my off-duty hours. I'm not even thrilled about sitting here with you now. But those were the orders to me from Deputy Chief Archer. I plan to follow his direction. My orders to you are that you keep me informed every second of every day. Is that clear enough?"

Brad nodded. "Yes, sir."

"Tell me about this double homicide."

Brad slid his chair close and told Jackson everything from the initial call to the autopsy.

"Any leads?" Jackson asked.

"Nope," Brad said. "The murder weapon is a 9mm, more common than the cold. I watched hours of television video trying to find witnesses, a familiar face or someone showing too much interest. But I struck out."

"Excellent analogy." Jackson stood. "Because if you screw up again, you're benched. Is that clear?"

CHAPTER TWENTY

Dice stood before the living room wall and used the red Sharpie to place a large X on two pictures—victims three and four. Dead. These killings had upped the game. The Homicide Unit was investigating. Not that they cared about the pimp and his driver, but the killings were out in the open and innocent people were around. A shooting scared the public. When the public was scared, Mayor Kearse felt he needed to protect and make promises the police would have to keep. Dice still couldn't believe that a drunk TV reporter could become mayor. If the citizens knew half of what Dice knew, they'd run him out of Calgary. Heck, out of the province. Kearse thought his secrets disappeared when he became mayor. But Dice knew where the skeletons were.

Today, Dice had other problems. Despite not being on the roster for Homicide, Coulter showed up at the double murder. Everyone knew about Coulter. The local hero. The tragic death of his fiancée.

The problem was, he was an excellent cop. If he sunk his teeth into this, he wouldn't let go. Not that there was anything for him to work with. Dice was meticulous in planning. The killings had gone exactly to plan. The gun was stolen from a drug dealer, who stole it from another dealer, who bought it from a pawnshop. The guy who pawned it stole it from a house he broke into so he could pawn stuff and have money for drugs.

Even if Coulter found the gun, it would trace back to the home robbery years ago. Coulter might waste time with the original owner, but that would be a dead end. Maybe he'd find the pawnshop, but the trail would end there. Coulter finding the gun wasn't part of the blueprint, but the gun was part of the bigger scheme.

As for Coulter linking the murders—the three events had nothing in common. He probably didn't even know about the two drug dealers. He would focus on the pimp and whoever he'd pissed off, which would be every girl turning tricks for him—likely a few other pimps he had put in the hospital and out of business. Maybe he'd had his driver teach a lesson to an aggressive customer about how to treat a lady.

The crimes broke most of the rules. Cops were anal on motive and method. Killers who murdered more than one person generally had a modus operandi, an MO. The killings may vary somewhat as the killer improved his technique but would have similarities. The weapon was the same—a knife, a gun. The victim was similar—a teen, with long brown hair, and green eyes or some such physical description.

Dice made sure the cops could not apply their tried-and-true methods of a homicide investigation.

No, even with Coulter investigating, all was well. Still, he was an unplanned factor, and his participation in the murders had to be addressed. He was now part of the problem. Dice placed his picture on the wall.

Dice slid a finger over the pictures. Who was next?

CHAPTER TWENTY-ONE

Dice headed down the dark alley toward the tattoo parlor. They normally closed by nine, but Dice had begged for an appointment at nine-thirty, saying that because of work, the appointment couldn't be earlier. Agreeing to pay extra for the time didn't hurt.

The alley had been excellent cover, but now Dice, dressed head to toe in black, would be exposed to the traffic on Edmonton Trail for about fifteen seconds. Head down, Dice jogged to the door and knocked.

A guy with long hair, a beard, and full arm tattoos peered out the door window, then opened the door.

"You Aaron?" Dice asked.

"That's me."

Dice stepped forward, grabbed his shoulder, and thrust a knife under his ribs to his heart. His body shook as his hands tried to grab Dice's neck. Blood spewed from his mouth, and he made gurgling sounds. Dice eased him to the ground, then stepped around him and behind the reception counter.

Dice opened the cash drawer and took the money—not a lot. Under the counter was a strong box. Dice tried to open it, found it locked, and used the knife to pop the lid. The box was full of cash. Dice stuffed the money into a plastic bag and shoved it in a pocket.

Dice headed down a hall. There were three closed doors, two to the left and one to the right. Dice listened at the one on the left—no sounds, then stepped to the right and listened at the first door. Muted voices. Perfect.

Dice drew a gun, slowly rotated the doorknob, and eased the door open. The room was lit by powerful lights aimed at a bed in the corner. No one heard the door open.

A camera situated to the right filmed the action on the bed. Beside the camera, a man gave directions. On the bed, a man, mid-thirties, was screwing a teen. To the left, two other women dressed in petite bathrobes watched, their eyes filled with terror.

One teen glanced at the doorway, saw Dice, and gasped.

Dice had already chosen targets. The first bullet struck the man on the bed in the back of his head. He collapsed on the screaming girl.

Dice swung to the right as the director glanced left. The bullet struck his jaw and exited behind his ear. As he collapsed, he knocked over the camera, exposing the cameraman to the third and fourth bullets, mid-chest.

Now the girls were screaming. The girl on the bed frantically twisted to get out from under the body. As she slid off the bed, she clawed at her face, trying to remove the blood, brains, and bone.

"Get cleaned, get changed, and get out of here." Dice handed a plastic bag of money from the cash box to the closest girl. "Say nothing to anyone. But if the police stop you, say …"

The three girls grabbed their screaming friend and raced out of the room.

Dice lifted the camera back into position, then hit the pause button.

CHAPTER TWENTY-TWO

SAM STEELE AND CHARLIE ZERR MET SERGEANT BRISCOE AT A coffee shop on Memorial Drive and Edmonton Trail at 10:30 p.m. The waitress had barely finished pouring their coffee when dispatch radioed Briscoe to call in pronto. Briscoe finished the phone call, waved to them and headed out the back door. When they caught up to him, he told them an anonymous call had come in that three teens were acting strangely and wandering around Sixteenth Avenue without winter parkas. When the street cops talked to them, the girls eventually said they were held captive and forced to do sex tapes. But someone had come in, killed all the men and told them to get out.

Steele and Zerr followed Briscoe's van to the scene. No time to be discreet, Zerr pulled up to the front of the parlor. He and Steele jumped out, grabbed their rifles, and headed to the house. Zerr limped through the snow as they ascended the front steps. Steele shouldered open the door. A man lay in a sizable puddle of blood. Zerr stepped past Steele, his gun sweeping the reception area.

Steele knelt next to the victim, slid off a black glove, and reached for a pulse. He shook his head. With a hand signal, Steele directed Briscoe to remain by the door.

Zerr stepped to a hall and again aimed his rifle. Steele brushed past and into the parlor toward six chairs.

The room was empty. Steele headed back to Zerr and gently gripped his shoulder. Then Zerr stepped forward. The first door on the left was open and empty.

Zerr stopped in the room's doorway on the right and held up his fist. Steele stopped behind Zerr, who pointed to a door on the left.

Steele opened the door and peered in—empty. He stepped past Zerr and checked the second room on the left. An unoccupied bedroom. He nodded and mouthed, *Clear.*

Zerr nodded and stepped into the room to the right. "Sweet baby Jesus."

Steele moved to his left. "Ah, shit." He keyed his radio. "Dispatch, TSU has cleared the scene. No hostiles. But we have four DOA. I need the Crime Scene Unit. I'll get Sergeant Briscoe to contact Homicide."

Brad had been at Maggie's gravesite when he received the page from Briscoe. Brad wasn't sure how Staff Sergeant Jackson would react to Briscoe circumventing the system and again paging Brad directly, rather than having dispatch call the next Homicide team. The drive took less than five minutes.

Brad parked his Firebird behind the TSU truck. He stepped out of the car. Lobo stuck his head out of the back window. He loved hanging his head out the window and letting the wind blow over him, no matter how cold the weather. "Lobo, stay." Brad scratched Lobo's head.

Brad headed up the sidewalk. Déjà vu washed over him. A few years ago, when they were fighting the Gypsy Jokers and Satan's Soldiers biker gangs, his TSU team had raided this tattoo parlor. A senior member of the Jokers, Eldredge Hammond, had managed the place. Brad had chased him down in an alley and was about to make the arrest when a police dog raced past and took Hammond to the ground. Roger Kearse, then a CFCN reporter, and his cameraman, caught it all on tape. Brad glanced around. No media here yet.

He jogged past a constable running crime scene tape around the scene and up the front stairs where Steele and Zerr waited.

"This was the Jokers' place," Steele said.

"Yeah, I was just thinking about that. I heard someone else runs this now."

Steele led Brad inside. "This guy must have answered the door."

Brad surveyed the scene. "Someone he expected or trusted?"

"That someone had skill," Charlie Zerr said, limping up behind them. Zerr was in the second intake to the Tactical Support Unit and had quickly become friends with Brad and

Steele. He was not imposing—five-ten and one hundred and seventy-five pounds. But as a former US Army Ranger, he was the best trained and qualified member of TSU. Now that Brad was a detective, Steele and Zerr were seldom apart.

Zerr pointed to the victim at the doorway. "Up to the heart with one stroke. Precise and deep. His heart probably stopped before he hit the floor."

"I've seen this before," Brad said. They stepped around the body to the hall.

"It appears they'd expanded beyond tattoos." Steele pointed to the bedroom. Brad stepped to the doorway.

He whistled. "That tells a story, doesn't it?"

A male was propped up on the bed against the wall. Dried blood smeared the wall behind his head. Blood soaked the bed sheets between his legs. His eyes were wide, staring ahead. His penis was shoved into his mouth.

The second victim, closest to the door, sat on the floor against the wall. The right side of his jaw and face was missing. His penis hung out from the gaping hole.

The third victim, near the camera, was positioned the same as the others. He was naked from the waist down and blood pooled around his groin. His penis was also stuffed in his mouth.

"This is personal," Brad said. "Very personal."

"The camera was still running," Steele said.

"That might be a clue," Zerr blurted.

"You think?" Brad replied.

Zerr glanced at the camera. "I mean, well, maybe the killer didn't know it was running."

"Everything is too precise," Brad said. "I doubt the killer made that mistake."

"We were meant to see the video," Steele said.

"Possibly," Brad said. "Maybe it's the porn, maybe the killing, or even a message to us."

"What type of message?" Steele asked.

Brad shrugged. "I'm not sure. Message to pimps and pornographers. This is the second homicide scene that involved the sex trade."

"You think they're connected?"

"No sense getting ahead of ourselves. We let the facts talk to us." Brad scrutinized the room. "What does the evidence tell us? Not, does it verify our hypothesis?"

"That's brilliant," Steele said. "Did you just make that up?"

"Coulter?" a familiar voice bellowed from the hall.

Brad, Steele, and Zerr swung to the voice.

"What the heck are you doing?" Sturgeon strode toward them slipping off his tan sheepskin gloves and unzipping his brown knee-length overcoat. His winter overshoes were covered with white booties.

"What I always do," Brad said. "Examining the scene and searching for evidence."

"Did you not learn anything from my class? You remembered *my* quote about evidence, but not the part about contaminating the crime scene." He glared at Brad and then Steele and Zerr. "I understand you two clowns coming in here to secure the scene. But Mother of God, Coulter, why are you in here?"

Steele and Zerr retreated behind Brad. "Uh, I guess that's my fault. I asked them to bring me in."

Sturgeon glanced at the floor. "Well, look at that. A few bloody boot prints. Oh my. Is that a Vibram tread? Does anyone here wear boots with a Vibram tread?"

Steele and Zerr glanced at their feet.

Sturgeon's eyes narrowed. "I need your boots."

"Sure," Steele said. "We'll go to the station and bag them."

"No, I need them now."

"But I don't have a spare pair with me," Zerr said.

"I don't bloody well care." Sturgeon took two evidence bags out of his kit. "In here, boys."

They glanced at Brad for support. He held his hands high and stepped back.

"Where do you think you're going, mister?" Sturgeon asked.

"I'm done in here. I'll get your reports in the morning."

"Not so fast. I need your boots, as well."

Brad looked down at his feet. "But I didn't step in the blood."

"But you wandered around *my* crime scene." He pulled out another evidence bag. "Now."

"You can't be serious?" Brad asked.

Sturgeon chuckled. "Not this time, boys. Next time, you'll be walking in socks."

Brad stood by the open car window and scratched Lobo's head. A light snow was falling. The streetlights had a hazy glow from the frosty air and snow. The street was blocked off to traffic.

"Your dog is a pig," Steele said.

"Well, he is a police dog." Brad zipped his parka, slid on gloves and a black beanie.

Zerr rolled his eyes.

Steele pointed to a line of frozen drool down the side of the car. "Your pretty Trans Am is an icy mess."

"Are you done here?" Zerr stomped his feet and blew into his gloved hands.

Brad laughed. "Not likely. Why?"

"Let's get a beer," Zerr said. "We'll change and meet you somewhere."

Brad glanced at the tattoo parlor, the ring of police cruisers and the crowd gathering behind the yellow police line tape. "I should probably hang around here."

"And do what?" Steele asked. "Stand out here and get covered in snow until you freeze? Sturgeon isn't letting you near that crime scene until morning, at the earliest. You've got uniformed guys to keep gawkers away."

Then they were blinded by a bright light.

"Detective Coulter, do you have a comment on this situation?"

"Ah, shit," Brad said.

Steele and Zerr exchanged grins. "We'll save you a seat." They slipped away as the light focused on Brad.

"We understand there are multiple dead in the tattoo parlor. Can you confirm this?"

Brad held a hand over his eyes as he crossed the street.

"Jeez. Shut that light off. What's with the cameramen and the bright lights?"

Sadie nodded to the cameraman. "It's okay." She was wearing her knee-length white parka, white knit beanie with a pompom and leather boots. The light went out.

"How was your day?" Her bright smile was highlighted by dark pink lipstick.

Lobo was barking frantically and trying to get out the window.

Brad blinked, trying to focus, and turned to Lobo, then back to Sadie. "Lobo, quiet. Ms. Andrus, why do you do that at every scene?"

"Not every scene, just the last couple." She leaned over the police tape and grinned. "It gets your attention."

Brad held out his hands. "Next time, Ms. Andrus, try, *hey, Detective Coulter.*"

Her white-gloved hand touched her chest. "Oh, we're being formal, are we, Detective Coulter?"

Brad clenched his jaw and sighed. "In this a professional setting, yes."

"But if it's not professional, then it's Brad and Sadie." Her eyes sparkled.

Brad dropped his head and his shoulders sagged. He stomped his feet as his toes tingled from the cold. "Ask your questions, Ms. Andrus."

She nodded to her cameraman, and the lights were on again. Brad raised a hand to the light, then lowered it. He stared unseeing at the camera.

Sadie shoved a microphone at his mouth. "Detective

Coulter, with you on the scene, I gather it is a murder investigation."

"It is an investigation of multiple suspicious deaths."

"For my viewers, a few years ago, the Gypsy Jokers Motorcycle Club owned this tattoo parlor—"

"Gang."

"What?"

"They're not a club." Brad glared at the camera. "They are organized crime."

"Right, a gang. But the bikers don't own this place anymore. Do you think the Hells Angels want it back? Is this the start of another biker … gang war?"

"It's too early to assume anything." Brad brushed snow off his shoulders. "Until the Crime Scene Unit has done their work, the victims are autopsied, witnesses interviewed, and evidence analyzed, it's impossible to make any predictions or assess blame."

"Detective. Are you assuring Calgarians this is not another gang war?"

"That's not what I said. It's too early to come to any conclusions."

"Is this an attack on the sex trade? With the murder of a pimp—"

Brad smiled. "Thank you, Ms. Andrus." He spun, headed to his car, opened the door, and started the engine.

The camera light went out. As his eyes adjusted again, and before he could pull away, Sadie was tapping at his window. Lobo barked as Brad lowered the window.

Sadie leaned on the car door. "That went well, don't you think? You're getting comfortable with TV interviews."

"Of the many things I would like to perfect, that's not one of them. Have a safe night." He put the car in gear.

Sadie leaned farther into the car. Lobo jumped over Brad and licked her face. She jumped back, wiping her arm across her cheek.

"I guess he likes you."

Sadie regained her composure. "I interview you because you know what you're talking about. You don't give me the complete story, but you don't blow sunshine up my ass either. Besides, the public loves a hero."

"And you get excellent ratings."

"That I do." Sadie's grin grew wide. "Breakfast tomorrow?"

Brad pulled into the strip mall and parked in front of the pizza restaurant in Bowness. The restaurant's name was, The Place. Brad discovered the restaurant when it opened while he was in police training. It was close to where he lived, had great food, and was small enough you could hear yourself talk. Eight vinyl booths lined the walls with a half-dozen tables in the middle. On a late Monday night, there were only two other customers.

He stacked his parka on top of Steele's and Zerr's and slid into the vinyl booth across from Sam Steele and Charlie Zerr. Steele slid a beer over. Brad snatched it off the table and drained half the bottle.

"Tough interview?" Zerr asked. "Ms. Andrus has found the new poster boy for the service."

"We want you." Steele saluted. "For the Calgary Police Service."

Zerr clinked bottles with Steele.

"Abbott and Costello not available tonight? I get you two clowns?" Brad picked up a menu. "Did you order yet?"

"He's deflecting again," Zerr said.

"I noticed," Steele replied.

"I'm hungry."

"We ordered a pizza."

Brad glanced over the menu. "Charlie. How's your leg?"

Zerr punched Steele. "What the heck was that for?"

"For your big mouth," Zerr said.

"Nope. Sorry, buddy. I didn't say a word."

Brad nodded. "True story. Sam didn't say a thing to me."

Zerr rolled his eyes. "Right. What did Emma say?"

Brad gulped his beer. "Your leg is giving you some issues."

Zerr crossed his arms. "Nothing to worry about. It takes time to heal. But this shitty weather doesn't help."

"Helps me," Steele said. "I always know when it's going to get cold because you bitch about your leg."

Brad laughed and set the menu down. "Did you get spaghetti and meatballs for Lobo?"

"Are you serious?" Zerr asked.

"Oh, yeah," Steele said. "He's serious. Lobo loves spaghetti and meatballs. Spaghetti and steak are the only things Brad knows how to cook, so that's all Lobo eats."

"Not true," Brad said. "I do a mean eggs benedict."

Steele choked on his beer. "He and Lobo survived on steak and spaghetti for weeks until Annie caught on and started making meals for him and putting them in the fridge."

Brad tossed the menu on the table. "Carbs and protein. Perfect for an active lifestyle."

"And beer," Steele said.

"And beer. Electrolyte replacement." Brad waved to the waitress, ordered another round of beer, and spaghetti with extra meatballs for Lobo.

"That crime scene was a frickin' mess," Zerr said.

"More than one assailant?" Steele asked.

Brad shrugged and chewed his lip. "Or one extremely talented person."

"Are you thinking military?" Zerr asked.

"Aren't you?" Brad stared at Zerr. "If you hadn't been on the scene, you'd be my first suspect."

"Ah, but we were on scene," Steele said. "You weren't."

Brad stopped his beer halfway to his mouth. "Are you kidding me?"

Steele laughed. "All three of us could have done that."

"So could any TSU member," Brad said.

Zerr pointed his beer at Brad. "You got there awfully quick. You couldn't have been at home."

"Come to think of it, Ms. Andrus arrived at about the same time," Steele said.

"Are you starting this shit again?"

"They had breakfast the other morning," Steele said.

Zerr flashed his eyes at Steele. "Would you like to meet for breakfast, or can I just roll out of bed and make it."

"Christ." Brad's head dropped to his chest. "Are we in grade nine?"

The waitress set three beers on the table.

"Pleasant lady," Steele said.

"Great legs," Zerr said.

Brad glanced out the window toward his car and gulped his beer. His friends were messing with him. But, maybe, still too soon after Maggie. He swung back to them, twirled the beer bottle in his hand, then absently peeled the label.

"Jeez. Sorry, boss," Zerr said. "That got away from us."

"Yeah, sorry," Steele said. "This is like old times. For us, anyway. We didn't think about you."

"You guys are so wrong about Sadie." Brad leaned over the table and grinned. "Because her ass is her best feature."

Zerr spewed a mouthful of beer on his shirt.

CHAPTER TWENTY-THREE

BRAD SWUNG OFF MEMORIAL DRIVE, PARKED IN FRONT OF Gerry's, and grabbed two coffees. As he exited the store, Jackson was leaning against the driver's door. Was this guy going to hang out at Brad's favorite stores and restaurants, hoping to see him every morning?

Brad sighed. "Morning, Sarge."

"Coulter."

Brad extended a hand.

Jackson shook his hand and slid a toothpick to the other side of his mouth.

Brad glanced at cuts on the back of Jackson's hand. "Get in a fight with a cat?"

Jackson withdrew his hand. "Barbed wire at the farm. It doesn't cooperate at the best of times but worse in the winter."

Brad nodded. "Coffee?"

"What the hell happened last night?"

Brad set one coffee on the roof of the car and sipped the other. "There was a quadruple homicide."

"For Christ's sake. I know that. Why were you there?"

"Simple. I was paged."

Jackson slowly nodded his head. "By Briscoe, not dispatch."

"I was close, so I took the call. No sense getting anyone out of bed. I'm heading to the autopsies now."

"At what point were you going to call me?"

Brad scratched his head. "I figured I'd tell you this morning after the autopsies when I had additional information."

Jackson frowned, and the toothpick slid across his teeth. "But enough information to do a mini press conference last night."

"The press ambushed me."

Jackson rubbed his temples. "Sadie Andrus from CFCN News ambushed you."

"Correct." Brad sipped the coffee.

"Coulter, I'm not stupid. Archer told me about your relationship with Andrus."

Brad held up a hand. "Stop right there, Sarge. There is no relationship—never has been. Sadie likes to play games she thinks are funny."

Jackson waved his hand. "I don't care about your off-duty time."

"Am I off the case?"

"Archer thinks you should be off the street. I convinced him to let you handle these murders. That it was better to keep you busy. He agreed, for now. You need to keep me informed. I don't care how late or how early you call, but make the call. I need every detail. Leads, suspects, forensic evidence." Jackson's gray eyes bored into Brad. "Am I clear?"

"Yes."

"What?" Jackson bellowed.

"Yes, sir."

"That's better." Jackson slapped Brad's back and grabbed the coffee off the car roof. "Glad we understand each other."

Brad drove to the drab building of the Medical Examiner's Office. He parked in visitors' parking close to the front door.

He smiled at the receptionist and headed down the white hall to the autopsy suites. With four new bodies, he didn't need to know who was where. There would be a backup of postmortems all morning.

Sturgeon, dressed in green surgical scrubs, was sitting outside an autopsy suite reading the paper. Brad handed him a coffee. "The city paying you to read the paper?"

"No. The city is paying me overtime. I'm at nine hours so far. Likely be sixteen or eighteen before I head home." Sturgeon sipped his coffee. "Where the heck did you go last night?"

Brad yawned. "I figured you were mad at me, and there was no way you'd let me back into the crime scene until today, so I went home."

"And slept?"

"Like a baby." Brad rolled his shoulders and cracked his

neck. "Pleasant, long, hot shower this morning. I'm refreshed and ready to go."

"Asshole."

"Tell me a story about last night."

"While you were getting your beauty sleep, and I don't mind saying you need more, we were doing your work for you."

"How so?"

"We videoed the scene and took about thirty rolls of film." Sturgeon sipped his coffee. "The techs will process them this morning. We pulled a couple hundred different fingerprints off the walls and the objects in the room." He held up his hands. "Don't even ask about the objects. The room lit up like blue sky under the black light."

Brad clenched his jaw. "Disgusting."

"The autopsy is completed for victim number one at the front door. Zinovy Frolov. Perhaps you should have been here for that?"

"It's barely eight-fifteen."

"The ME came in early because of the lengthy list of customers, to get an early start."

"I guess you'll have to testify on the first. What did the ME find?"

"Knife inserted under the xiphoid, then up and into the heart. The blade was rotated, destroying the inside of the heart."

Brad nodded. "Extremely sharp knife."

"Sharp and skillfully used," Sturgeon said. "Just like the two drug dealers in Victoria Park."

"What about the knife?" Brad asked.

"At least an eight-inch blade," Sturgeon said. "Either a hunting knife or a tactical blade."

"Steele, Zerr and I were talking last night. Either military or tactical experience."

Sturgeon tapped his finger to his cheek. "Who do I know who fits that?"

"We decided all three of us. And Sergeant Jackson."

"Bingo. There's more." Sturgeon sipped his coffee and stared across the hall. "He killed two others with single shots to the head, and the last guy had a double-tap to the chest. Tight grouping."

"Did you find any slugs?"

"Yeah. One in the wall behind the bed and another in the wall beside the camera. We're examining them this morning. I'd say 9mm."

"Same as the pimp and his bodyguard shooting." Brad sipped his coffee and stared at the wall. "Maybe same gun?"

"I'll know later today." Sturgeon twisted as the door to the autopsy room opened.

"Sergeant Sturgeon," the ME assistant said. "We're starting the second autopsy. Nico Yudin."

Sturgeon stood and grinned at Brad. "Just in time."

"One Russian and I couldn't care," Brad said. "Two Russians, now I'm interested." Brad headed to the change room. He hung his leather jacket, gray button-down shirt, and black dress pants in a locker and left his hiking boots on the floor. He changed into green surgical scrubs and entered the autopsy room.

It was the smell that got to him. He could handle the cutting and ripping out of organs. It had taken time, but that was okay. The mix of blood, stomach contents, and bowels fighting with disinfectant made a concoction not meant for a human to endure.

He grabbed a stool and slid it close, but not too close, to the autopsy table. The asshat on the table was the rapist. Brad thought of volunteering to do the cutting. He would start with the suspect's dick, except the killer had already done that.

The attendant grabbed a scalpel and started the Y-cut—shoulders to high on the chest, then down past the belly button. The ME peeled the skin back, revealing the sternum and ribs. The attendant used bolt cutters to snip the ribs. When he was done, they lifted the ribs and sternum off as one piece. Brad glanced away. After he attended his first autopsy, it was years before he could eat ribs.

Brad took a few deep breaths of the foul air. *Well, that didn't help.*

The medical examiner came in, removed and weighed organs, and visually inspected the stomach contents.

This asshat was shot in the head, so there would be nothing of interest in the chest and stomach as far as the homicide was concerned. Maybe what he had for a last meal. Forty minutes later, they were ready to examine the head.

The medical examiner was recording his findings. Again, nothing Brad didn't know. The bullet had entered the left side of the head and exited the right, the explosion blasting the back of the skull across the wall. The bullet was through and through and into the wall—the first bullet Sturgeon found.

Brad remained seated while the next two autopsies were conducted. The bullet that struck suspect two entered at the left corner of his mouth and exited behind his ear—the second bullet found. That side of his face was missing.

The suspect, likely the cameraman, took two bullets to the chest. Both bullets entered the heart and then lodged by the spine. They were in relatively decent shape. Sturgeon slid them into evidence bags.

It was well after noon when Brad and Sturgeon exited the autopsy room.

"How about I buy you lunch?" Sturgeon asked.

Brad glared. "You ask because you know I'll pass. And don't tell me you're going to eat. This bugs you as much as me."

Sturgeon grinned. "Don't say I didn't offer."

CHAPTER TWENTY-FOUR

BRAD EXITED THE MEDICAL EXAMINER'S OFFICE AND STEPPED out into the sunlight—no snow in the forecast for today. He pulled his sunglasses out of his parka pocket. Before he put on the glasses, he noticed Sadie leaning against a CFCN News van parked behind his car.

She wore a long dark-blue snow parka that came to her knees, boots that covered her feet to her knees, dark gloves, and sunglasses. Her auburn hair glimmered in the sunlight and hung loose on her shoulders.

They'd positioned the van so it blocked Brad's escape. He headed to his car.

"I didn't see you at breakfast this morning," Sadie said.

Brad unlocked his car. "I tend not to eat before autopsies."

"That's probably best." Sadie leaned against his car and crossed her arms. "Wouldn't want to vomit on your leather jacket."

"Or my hiking boots." Brad glanced at the driver-cameraman still in the van. "What, no bright lights today?"

Sadie slid her sunglasses down her nose. "Seems bright enough out here. Should we do the interview?"

Brad crossed his arms. "There will not be an interview."

Sadie pouted her lips. "We don't have to do it here."

"No."

"No, not here? Yes to lunch?"

Brad reached out, slid her sunglasses off, and leaned close. "Read my lips. No interview."

"You could use some lip gloss." She reached into her pocket. "Want some?"

Brad opened the car door. "You are exasperating."

"No interview? No lip gloss? We're back to lunch, then."

"Sadie, please move your van." Brad slid into his car. "I have work to do."

"Dinner? About eight?"

Brad closed the door and started the car.

Brad sat in another claustrophobic room, this time in the Crime Scene Unit area. There must be some rule that video viewing rooms had to be tiny. A generic metal desk, office chair of undetermined age with minimal padding, and a video monitor and player on the desk. He had the lights off as he watched the video for the second time—this time watching the tattoo parlor, rape and murders. The first twenty minutes were hard to watch. He winced and looked away a few times as the girl was repeatedly raped.

They'd package it as porn, but it was vicious. Yet again, he was reminded what Annie had endured when she was held captive by Jeter Wolfe. He wanted to barf. Even his coffee didn't interest him. Between the autopsies and this, he might not eat for a month.

The rape was interrupted when the attacker's head exploded in a mist of blood, brain, and bone. Right after the gunshot, the girl's screams burst from the speakers. The victim frantically scratched and clawed at her dead attacker. Finally, she pushed him to the floor, rolled off the bed, and dashed past the camera.

A second shot rang out, then the camera wobbled and fell on its side. Two additional shots sounded. There were screams from several girls.

A muffled voice said, "Get cleaned, get changed and get out of here." A pause. "Say nothing to anyone. But if the police stop you …" He couldn't hear the rest.

It was hard to make out the voice. Maybe it could be enhanced. He'd ask Sturgeon. No identifying factors. It could be male or female—deep, but unnatural, and an attempt to disguise the voice.

The shots were seconds apart. It would take a skilled marksman to hit the head on the first shot, turn right, hit the head a second time, and then two shots to the chest of the third suspect.

Shooting like that was something the tactical support unit or special forces practiced. It was not something you typically learned at a gun range.

He scrolled through the tape in slow motion. The four shots took three and a half seconds. He wasn't sure he could do that.

After the fourth shot, the girls were told to leave, and then the video ended. Seconds later, the video started and panned the room. The rapist on the bed and the other two men shot and positioned on the other side of the room. He fast-forwarded until Zerr entered onscreen. Steele moved to his side. "Sweet baby Jesus."

CHAPTER TWENTY-FIVE

Dice watched the six o'clock evening news while working out. It was a recorded segment, shot late last night well after the murders. The tattoo parlor was in the background and cops wandered around the scene. The segment switched to an interview at the scene—a closeup of Detective Coulter. Dice stopped barbell curls and increased the volume.

"Detective Coulter, with you on the scene, I gather it is a murder investigation."

"It is an investigation of multiple suspicious deaths."

"For my viewers, a few years ago, the Gypsy Jokers Motorcycle Club owned this tattoo parlor—"

"Gang."

"What?"

"They're not a club. They are organized crime."

"Right. But the bikers don't own this place anymore. Do you think the Hells Angels want it back? Is this the start of another biker ... gang war?"

Dice increased the weights and listened as the interview continued—what a waste of time.

"Is this an attack on the sex trade? With the murder of a pimp—"

"Thank you, Ms. Andrus."

"As you heard, we are not getting a lot of information from the police. As we learn about this incident, we will update you. Sadie Andrus, CFCN News."

Dice set the weights aside and mopped the sweat with a towel. Generally, murder would get assigned to different detectives, unless they were connected. So far, there wasn't anything to connect them, but with Coulter on both cases, he might find the one thing that linked the deaths. He was getting too close.

This confirmed Dice's previous suspicion. There were two options. First, make Coulter the next victim. Second, get him off the case. The first option wasn't great. The death of any cop, but especially Coulter, would bring the wrath of the police service on Dice. Coulter had friends in high places. A distressed cop, mourning the loss of his fiancée and child, and eating his gun was a possibility.

Then it clicked in. There was one way that ensured Coulter would be removed from the homicides.

Dice grinned and started working out again. Tonight, another victim would make headlines.

Dice had parked in the back corner of the high school parking lot. A crowd was exiting the school into the cold, snowy night after having watched the junior and senior boys' basketball games. It was the last match before the city-wide Christmas Tournament this coming weekend. They scraped windows of frost, and snow was cleared from the hoods, roofs and trunks. The cars formed a mini rush hour as they exited. After ten minutes, the last of the spectators pulled out and the parking lot was quiet. Dice waited. The players would take time to shower, then head home. Dice was parked next to a 1979 Toyota Celica two-door hatchback. The Toyota was one of many new and sporty cars in the lot. Sixteenth birthday presents from parents with money to burn on kids with a powerful sense of privilege—which described half of this high school.

The back doors opened, and players trickled out. There were, give or take, ten players and three or four coaches left in the school. The coaches came out first and rushed to their cars, giving a quick sweep of the snow from their vehicles, and then raced out of the lot. A few players came out, started their cars, and burned donuts in the parking lot to the cheers of other players. Then the group broke up and headed to their own cars. A teen, being cool, wearing a school hoodie against the icy wind and snow, trudged toward his car—the car next to Dice.

Dice slid out of the car and popped the hood. As the teen approached, Dice said, "Can you give me a boost?"

The kid stopped and glanced over. "Uh, I don't have cables."

"No problem," Dice said. "I have some in the trunk."

There were several toots of horns as the other players headed home. Dice and the player were the last ones in the lot. Dice opened the trunk and pointed at the vinyl bag that held the jumper cables. "Grab those, please."

As the teen leaned into the trunk, Dice wrapped an arm around his neck and used the other arm to apply pressure. In wrestling, they called it the sleeper hold. In policing, it was a neck restraint. No matter the name, the result was the same, unconsciousness. Dice bound the player's wrists, then stuffed a rag in his mouth and secured it in place with a long strip of cloth. Dice slammed the trunk shut, slid back into the car, then drove out of the school parking lot. What needed to happen next couldn't be done here.

CHAPTER TWENTY-SIX

JAY ROBSON AND HIS PARTNER MAURA ROSSI PULLED OUT OF THE strip mall, each with a coffee. They'd been partners for close to a year. Robson's sandy-colored hair was a sharp contrast to Rossi's black hair, pulled back in a tight bun low enough that she could still wear her black beanie. Where Robson was fair skinned, Rossi's Mexican heritage showed in her complexion. Opposites in appearance and temperament, Robson was calm, methodical, and Rossi was quick-tempered and impulsive. They'd formed a tight bond.

When they'd come on shift at seven this morning, they'd been assigned a missing person file. A seventeen-year-old teen named Burke Bailey Baldwin II had not returned home after his basketball game the previous night. He was last seen by other players after ten walking to the Lord Beaverbrook High School parking lot.

"How many times did you sneak into and out of your house when you were a teen?" Rossi asked.

"More times than my parents knew about," Robson replied. "You?"

"A couple of times. My older sister moved back in with us when I was in grade eleven and she brought her yappy dog with her. The dog busted me a few times."

They had stopped to talk to the basketball coach, but he wasn't in yet. The first rays of sunshine were just peeking over the horizon as they drove around to the dark parking lot at the back of the school. Barely seven-thirty, there weren't many cars.

One car was parked in the back corner. It was parked with the nose into the hedge that surrounded the parking lot, covered with snow. They figured it hadn't been moved since the day before.

Rossi checked the license plate and got a match to the missing student. They slid out of the cruiser and zipped their parkas. Rossi wandered to the passenger's side, and Robson checked the driver's side.

Robson was first to the front of the car. "Oh, shit. We've got a problem."

By the time Brad arrived, police tape surrounded the entire Lord Beaverbrook High School parking lot, and officers were keeping the students well back. Briscoe wandered over to Brad, and they headed to the back corner of the parking lot.

"They reported the kid missing early this morning," Briscoe said. "He didn't come home from a basketball game last night. Parents didn't realize until they woke up this morning. Robson and Rossi got the call and came to the school." Briscoe led Brad to the front of the car.

Brad's eyes widened. "What the heck?"

A naked, frozen body was draped across the windshield and hood. The arms were tied to the side mirrors, his legs attached by rope to the bumper. Despite the snow overnight, the word 'Rapist' could be clearly seen carved into his forehead.

"Who is this kid?" Brad asked.

Briscoe blew on his hands and then rubbed them rapidly. "He's Burke Bailey Baldwin II."

"That's quite the handle," Brad said. "It sounds familiar." Brad snapped his fingers. "Jenni Blighe was telling me about him. He raped—"

"Allegedly," Briscoe said.

Brad frowned, and his eyebrows rose. "He raped a sixteen-year-old at a school party last fall—repeatedly. But the defense counsel Harry Townsend twisted it into a trial of the young teen, Laura Turner. Blighe said Townsend destroyed her on the stand, and then the judge acquitted Baldwin II."

"The family paid a lot to hire Townsend," Briscoe said.

Brad clenched his jaw. "Acquittal bought and paid for."

"Now he's the one who bought it," Briscoe said.

Brad glanced at Briscoe. "Callous, even for you."

Briscoe shrugged. "I believe in karma."

Brad stepped closer to the car.

"I wouldn't, if I were you," Briscoe said. "You already got in trouble for screwing up a crime scene."

"Whatever." Brad peered at the rope around the wrist. "See the chaffing. Even frozen, there are rope burns on his wrists. He was alive—long enough to fight against the ropes. There's one additional thing."

"What's that?" Briscoe asked.

"There's no way this kid was captured, stripped and tied to the car here. Not if he was alive. Heck, even if he were dead. Have you ever tried to take clothes off an unconscious or dead person?"

"Can't say I have." Briscoe lifted an eyebrow. "But I'd love to know how you know that detail."

"Oh, shit, Briscoe. Just ask any medical examiner or mortician. EMS doesn't even bother trying to take off clothes. That's why when we get the clothes as evidence, they're cut to pieces. Trust me. This kid was stripped somewhere else."

Brad sat in an empty classroom and stared at the posters on the walls—periodic table, rocket launches, world map, and mobile of the solar system. The door swung open, and Griffin marched in, followed by Jackson dressed in uniform. Jackson tossed his issue dark blue parka on a chair.

"Good morning," Brad said.

"Miserable frickin' day." Griffin slid off his parka and shook snow onto the floor.

Jackson flopped into a chair next to Brad. "Thought you two might need some help."

"You bet. All the students are jammed in the gymnasium. Briscoe has his street cops talking to every kid who was here last night. The rest are being sent home. The principal is rounding up the basketball players, their coaches, and the cheerleaders for us to interview."

"I'll take the coaches." Jackson left the room.

"I've got the players," Brad said.

Griffin frowned. "Come on guys, not the cheerleaders."

"Have fun with that." Brad smirked.

There was a knock. The door opened. The principal stuck his head in.

"I've got the coaches and cheerleaders in the next two rooms. Do you want the players here?"

"Sounds good." Brad stood. "One at a time. I want to talk to the guys who were closest to Burke."

"Sure," the principal said. "I'll bring the players in."

Brad grabbed two chairs and set them facing each other. He directed the first player to have a seat—tall and gangly with red hair and pimples.

"I'm Detective Coulter. What's your name?"

"Ben." He stared at his hands.

"Ben, do you understand why we are here?"

"Yeah, Burke is dead." Ben stared at his hands as he cracked his knuckles.

Brad leaned forward, his elbows on his knees. "Were you two friends?"

"Yeah."

"For how long?"

"We've been friends since grade seven."

"Tell me about the rape."

Ben's head popped up. "There wasn't any rape. Laura Turner made it up."

Brad stretched his upper body to within inches of Ben's face. "Were you there that night?"

"Sure, we all were." Ben shrugged. "We'd won the city championship the night before, and it was a celebration party."

Brad sat back in the chair. "Tell me what happened."

"There's nothing to tell. We were having a party."

"There was alcohol?" Brad cocked his head.

"Shit, are you a prude?" Bens slid his chair back. "Of course, there was alcohol. Our parents bought it for us. That was the deal. We all stayed at the party, and then they'd pick us up, so no one was driving."

Brad pursed his lips and nodded. "Tell me about Burke and Laura Turner."

"She'd been hot for him all fall. Laura went to all our football games and waited for him outside the locker room."

"Were they dating?"

Ben scowled. "No way. Burke wouldn't pick one girl. He could have any girls he wanted, and plenty wanted him. He was our best player, football and basketball."

Brad crossed his arms and stared. "That night at the party?"

"We were all drinking and having fun. Laura practically threw herself at him. Everywhere he went, she was right there, clinging to him. It was clear what she wanted. Next thing I know, I can't find them."

"Where did they go?"

Ben's eyes darted around the room. "Uh, I've said all I'm going to say. Maybe my dad should be here."

Brad held up a hand. "That's fine. What I need to know is

do you know of anyone who would want to hurt Burke?"

"Burke was a school hero. Everyone liked him."

"No one comes to mind who would want to kill Burke?"

Ben's brow furrowed. "Well, one person, maybe."

"Who is that?"

"Laura's father, Al Turner."

"Why?"

Ben chuckled. "Because he said he would."

Over the next two hours, Brad interviewed the remaining nine players. The further down the roster he went, the less information he could get. Burke had been friends with four other players. They all told the same story. Too much the same. They'd all pointed the finger at Laura's father, Al Turner.

Jackson and Griffin wandered back into the classroom and took seats across from Brad.

"That was ten pounds of nothing," Griffin said. "According to the cheerleaders, Burke was a perfect gentleman."

"The coaches aren't that generous," Jackson said. "While they all agreed he was an exceptionally talented athlete, there was also agreement that Burke didn't think his shit stunk. One coach said Burke was a pain in the butt and did as he wanted on the basketball court. 'A nightmare to coach,' were his exact words."

"What did the coaches have to say about the 'alleged' rape?" Brad asked.

"Baldwin the first is an immensely powerful man," Jackson said. "The coaches were careful with what they said."

"We're no further ahead," Griffin said.

"Is this murder somehow linked to the others?" Jackson asked.

"We certainly have a murder crime wave going on. Maybe it's the cold weather pissing people off," Brad said. "There's definitely a trend toward sexual offenders. It's like someone is saying, if the courts don't take care of this, I will. But there's no common ground, no modus operandi. Al Turner is the best suspect in this one."

Brad decided he'd show up unannounced and hope to catch Al Turner off guard. He parked in front of the house and hiked up the recently shoveled sidewalk. The sun was fighting through the clouds, but there was still an icy chill in the air. He knocked on the door and glanced around the snow-covered yard. The fence was recently painted and the house, a bungalow, was well maintained.

The door opened. A lady, mid-forties with a tea towel in her hand, stood in the doorway.

"I'm Detective Coulter." Brad held out his badge. "Is Al Turner home?"

She stared at his badge and wiped her hands on the towel. "My husband is asleep. He worked last night."

"What time did he come home?" Brad asked.

Her lip trembled. "About seven-thirty."

"Where does he work?"

"Invite him in, dear." A man dressed in sweatshirt and sweatpants stepped behind the lady. "Come in, Detective."

He showed Brad to the living room and extended his hand. "I'm Al Turner. Have a seat."

Brad shook his hand and sat on the couch. The room was neat and cozy. Afghans sat on the couch and chairs. Family photos lined the mantel above the electric fireplace.

"How can I help you?" Turner asked.

Brad leaned forward. "This morning, Burke Baldwin was killed."

"I see." Turner paled, his jaw clenched, and his hands shook. He licked his lips.

"I need to know where you were last night."

Turner nodded. "I was at work. I'm a mechanic at the Ogden Yards. I work night shift, eleven to seven."

"You were there all night?"

He sighed and stared past Brad. "Yes, I was there all night."

Brad leaned back and crossed his legs. "Someone can vouch for that?"

"Sure, at least ten guys. We were replacing an engine on a locomotive. We were together the entire night."

"I understand you made threats against Baldwin."

Turner nodded. Tears formed in the corners of his eyes. "Do you have children, Detective?"

Brad glanced away, thoughts straying to Maggie and what might have been.

"No, I don't."

"When you do, you will understand. My daughter was violated. Her attacker was found not guilty. His lawyer made my daughter the aggressor, describing her as a tramp. They destroyed her. Yes, I made threats. Wouldn't you? Wouldn't you do anything to protect your child? I was angry. I don't wish ill on any person. I won't shed any tears for him. But he destroyed my precious baby girl."

"I'll need the names of those men you work with." Brad handed his notebook and pen to Turner.

Brad's stomach rolled. He pushed down the waves of nausea. Turner's words echoed in his brain: *Wouldn't you do anything to protect your child?*

"Thank you for your time."

He took the notebook from Turner and rushed to his car.

It was close to three by the time Brad was back downtown at headquarters. He bundled up against the freezing north wind and trudged down the alley. The blast of warm air as he entered the back door revived him. He stomped the slush off his boots and brushed snow from his parka, then pushed through the second set of doors.

The desk sergeant glanced up. "Detective Coulter. You have a visitor." He pointed toward an interview room.

"Sarge, any chance you can grab me a couple of coffees?"

"Only because you asked so respectfully."

Brad shrugged off his parka, headed down the hall, and peered into the room.

Sadie faced the door. Her red winter jacket was over the back of the chair, black gloves and purse on the table. She wore a white blouse with at least three buttons unfastened, and a black knee-length skirt. Her legs were crossed with one black-booted foot swinging freely. She flashed her bright smile. "Detective, I worried you'd gone home for the day."

Brad sat, stretched out his legs, crossed at the ankles, and folded his arms. "Ms. Andrus." He glanced around the gray walls. "What? No camera lights?"

Sadie pouted. "Your sergeant wouldn't let my cameraman in. I could call him, though, if you want to do an interview." She stared at the framed glass on one wall. "Or you could just have someone watch us." She winked. "That would be fun."

Brad shook his head. "No one is watching. How can I help you?"

"Maybe by decorating this room. The gray walls are depressing, and your cleaners missed a few spots of blood. Better furnishings. A metal table and three aluminum chairs are hardly in fashion these days."

Brad rolled his eyes and sighed. "Sadie, what do you want?"

"You're not much of a detective if you're asking that question."

The sergeant set two coffees on the table.

Sadie glanced at hers. "Any chance I can get cream and sugar?"

The sergeant's shoulders slumped. "Oh, naturally. I'm sure there's no pressing police business." He spun on his heel and left the room.

"A teen was killed." Brad leaned forward. "We don't know who did it. We're following leads. Anyone who was at the basketball game last night at Lord Beaverbrook High School and has information should contact the police."

"You're getting particularly skilled at that."

Brad frowned. "Talking to the press?"

"No." Sadie laughed, then pushed loose auburn hair behind her ear. "Stating the obvious and offering nothing new."

"Then why are you here?" Brad slid a hand through his long hair.

"To see if you'd say something other than the obvious."

"Did you think I'd do that?"

The sergeant dropped two creamers and two sugar on the table and left.

Sadie leaned toward the door. "Spoon? Stir stick?"

"I wouldn't press my luck if I were you."

"With the sergeant or you?"

"Sadie, I'm exhausted and swamped."

Sadie poured the cream and sugar into the cup, then swirled it in her hands. "The murders are connected, aren't they?"

Brad stared blankly as he sipped his coffee. Who would blink first?

Brad stood. "I need to go."

"At least some of them must be linked. Someone hates sex perverts." Sadie stood and stepped toward Brad. "Blink once if I'm right."

"Always a pleasure to see you." Brad grabbed his coffee. "I'll have the sergeant show you out."

"There's a fine out-of-the-way restaurant in Chinatown. The Royal Garden. Say six?"

"Not tonight, Sadie."

"Headache?"

CHAPTER TWENTY-SEVEN

Brad read and re-read the murder files. They were connected, but nothing to point to a killer. After over three hours, his brain was mush, and his shoulders and neck were tense. He needed to relieve some stress.

He hadn't been to the shooting range since he qualified two months ago. He tried to get Briscoe to come with him, but Briscoe had 'a thing' with his kids.

The range was on the fifth floor in the middle of the police headquarters. It was well insulated, with concrete walls and thick soundproofing. Brad sniffed the air, heavy with the smell of gunpowder and lead.

He grabbed a handful of 9mm ammunition from a box on a shelf in the observation area and donned earmuffs and protective glasses. He stepped through the first door into no-man's-land. When the door closed, he opened the second door and stepped in. There were two other cops at the six-bay range. He didn't recognize the guy at the far end, but he recognized the cop third from the door, Sergeant Toscana. She wore a black, scoop-necked T-shirt and jeans.

She nodded. Brad nodded back.

He placed a target on the frame and moved it out five feet. He dropped the magazine from the pistol, ejected the bullet from the chamber, and placed them on the counter behind him. He filled three spare magazines with bullets, slammed in a magazine and chambered a round.

He rolled his shoulders and neck, arms loose at his sides, and wiggled his fingers like some western cowboy ready for a gunfight. Well, in some ways that was what this was about. Not the gunfight tonight, but the one that might be around the corner.

With his pistol holstered, he eyed the target. Then his left hand darted to his holster, the gun swung up to his chest then out toward the target. Shots rapidly exploded. He dropped the empty magazine into his hand and replaced it with a full mag. He slid the pistol back in his holster and recalled the target. It was his usual pattern. Five to the head, four to the groin and four to the chest. All tightly grouped.

With a new target at ten feet, he balanced his stance, and drew the pistol. On the fifth shot, the gun jammed. He slapped the bottom of the magazine, racked the action and fired.

For the next forty minutes, he shot at various distances, round after round, replacing the targets frequently and clearing the gun several times. As he recalled the last target, he felt a presence behind him. Toscana stood just off to the side and gave him two thumbs-up.

With a new target at five feet, he fired another magazine.

He repeated the process at ten, fifteen, and twenty feet. That was enough for the day. He swept the cases into a pile, collected the remaining bullets, and headed out of the range through the double doors to the observation area.

Brad tossed the remaining bullets in the ammo box on the shelf and set his pistol on the cleaning table. He pulled a small plastic container of cleaning supplies from his gym bag, disassembled the gun and cleaned the individual pieces.

"That was outstanding shooting." Toscana set her gun and cleaning supplies on the table next to Brad.

"Practice," Brad replied.

"That was brilliant."

"In TSU, we did a lot of shooting."

"That accounts for some of it, but you must be a natural shooter."

Brad glanced at her pistol. "You're shooting a Browning Hi-Power as well."

"I want to be proficient with it."

"It's a dependable gun when it's not jamming. Why not the .38 revolver?"

"Rules say I have to use the .38 at work. But TSU uses the Hi-Power and I need to be proficient. I'm going to be the first female member."

Brad stared at her targets. There was nothing wrong with her groupings. Not as tight as his, but they were all killing shots, and that's what counted.

"You've got excellent groupings on your targets. You'll be fine with your shooting."

"I practice a lot."

"You must be a natural."

Toscana was cleaning the barrel of her pistol. She glanced around.

"Something wrong?" Brad asked.

"I think I left a magazine on the counter on the gun range. I was so distracted by your shooting, I missed it."

"I'll get it," he said.

"I'll get it after I complete my cleaning."

"I'm nearly done," he said. "You keep going."

Brad tossed his cleaning cloth on the table. He stepped through the two doors and to the bay where Toscana had been shooting. Less than a minute later he came back into the room holding the lost magazine. "I had to search around. It must have fallen onto the floor and then you kicked it."

She took the magazine from him and smiled. "Thank you. There are still gentlemen in the world."

"Don't let that get out." Brad rubbed the back of his neck. "It would ruin my reputation."

"Oh, your reputation will survive."

Brad picked up the gleaming pieces of his pistol and expertly assembled the gun. Toscana did the same.

"Hey, I have some questions about TSU. Can I pick your brain some time?"

He glanced at his watch. "Do you work tonight?"

"Nope, my night off. I was done at seven this morning."

"How about now?" Brad asked. "I can't be late, or my dog will be pissed at me. But I need to eat. How about Olympia Pizza in Mount Royal?"

Brad was sitting in the back booth facing the front door, the back door behind his shoulder. For four years he'd worked this area as a street cop and had spent many hours here, sometimes just coffee or to get out of the cold, other times for one of the best pizzas in the city. He inhaled the fragrant aroma of garlic and tomatoes.

"You drive like a maniac." Toscana stomped the snow off her black Sorels and tossed her multi-colored ski jacket onto the seat before sliding in. She wore an unbuttoned red and black lumberjack shirt over her black T-shirt. "There was no way I was keeping up. Not on those icy roads."

"Another thing I learned at TSU. We seldom stopped when responding, not for red lights, traffic, traffic accidents we caused, not anything. If traffic was jammed, we drove on the wrong side of the road. Which works great. When people see a huge Suburban heading straight for them, they react fast."

A waitress with a red perm and large hoop earrings stopped by the table. "Can I get you anything to drink?"

Brad held his hand out to Toscana.

"A beer, Labatt's Blue, please," she said.

"Old Vienna for me," Brad said.

The woman's red hair bobbed, and she headed off to get their drinks.

The waitress came back with two beers. Brad ordered the pizza special.

"You may be right." Brad held out his beer, and they clinked the necks. "Acting sergeant, that's an accomplishment."

Toscana shrugged. "I worked hard for it."

Brad held up a hand. "I meant no offense. Truly, it's impressive."

"Sorry. I'm used to guys figuring I got the opportunity based on lying on my back." She pulled at the cuffs of her red and black lumberjack shirt.

"Well, you must have impressed the right people. What areas have you worked?"

"Right out of the academy, I was assigned temporarily to Vice. At first, I was thrilled they chose me. I worked hard in classes and figured I'd earned the opportunity."

"But—"

Toscana tilted her head to the side, raven hair swinging with the tips barely touching her shoulders. Her lips twisted. "They needed female a cop to play hooker so they could arrest the vermin that prey on the prostitutes. It had nothing to do with excellent marks or hard work, just that I was female."

Brad nodded, staring at his beer. "It doesn't hurt that you're great looking, also."

Her dark-brown eyes rolled. "Sure. The guys stared at me first. I was assisting in loads of arrests, but my name never appeared on any arrest reports."

Brad frowned. There were some sides to policing he didn't like. The archaic boys' club still had a firm hand on the police service. They'd be kicking and screaming and holding fast to the *timeworn* ways. He knew how hard it had been with Maggie as a student paramedic in the fire station.

"You must have done something right."

"My partner, Tony DeMarco, was outstanding. He was my sole backup most of the time. Too often, a guy would get rough, and I needed Tony. I can hold my own in a fight, but when you are in a tight skirt and six-inch heels, you lose any advantage. By the time Tony was through with the guy, I doubt he'd ever try to pick up a hooker again." Her eyes crinkled at the edges as she smiled.

"Those types of guys will find another outlet for their rage."

Toscana stared at her beer. "He was my mentor. I owe him a lot."

"The Italian connection couldn't hurt." Brad cocked his head. "Sounds like there's more to that story."

Toscana nodded and pursed her lips. "Yeah. It's not good spending most of your time with one person. There were other guys on the team, but Tony was my partner. We always worked night shifts on the weekend. The city shuts down after 3:00 a.m. Then it was the two of us alone in a car, and me dressed to the nines."

"Was he married?"

Toscana chewed her lip and nodded. "Nothing happened, but it was going to. He asked for a transfer. They made him a district sergeant in the northeast. I wanted to transfer there, also, but I didn't. For the next four years, I got some magnificent opportunities to work on some serious crimes. I did research, paperwork, and all the stuff the detectives didn't want to do, but it got my foot in the door. I'm sure Tony had a say in this opportunity."

"Do you still talk to him?"

"For the first couple of years we'd get together for beers or run into each other at The Cuff and Billy. Then the beers became infrequent and we haven't talked in two years. I heard he and his wife had a baby three months ago." Toscana took a long drink of beer. Her brown eyes glistened.

Brad realized it was time to change the topic. "What do you want to know about TSU?"

Toscana set her beer down and slid off her lumberjack shirt, leaned back and crossed her arms under her breasts. He thought they'd pop out of her T-shirt.

"I want to know everything. I want to know how I can get on TSU."

Toscana's arms weren't just toned, they were defined and bulging. She was a solidly built lady. "That might take more than a beer, something to eat, and fancy shooting."

Her eyebrows arched and she smiled. "I'm fine with meeting again."

Oh, oh. Was this only about TSU? Rather than feeling safe in the back corner of the restaurant, he felt cornered. Then he gave his head a shake. *Feeling a bit high on yourself, are you?* "Where do you want me to start?"

"How was the team originally formed?"

"That's a loaded question." He sipped his beer. "Some ex-military Airborne were robbing banks and Brinks trucks. They were an elite Canadian unit, not as skilled as the US Navy SEALS, but they were proficient. They stole all the guns and ammunition they needed. As well, they were trained in tactics and worked well together as a team. The police were hopelessly outgunned, and our revolvers and shotguns were no match. They'd already killed my partner." Brad's grip tightened on his bottle.

"Sorry," Toscana said, meeting his eyes.

Brad peered out the window. "Sergeant Jackson went to

Los Angeles and met with their SWAT team. He then convinced two members of LA SWAT to come back and train us. The SWAT guys told stories about stuff we have never encountered here. Riots, gang wars, and multiple homicides. They had some great tips. Like if you see one weapon, expect at least one more. Always carry a backup gun and a knife."

Toscana leaned forward. "Do you?"

"I thought they were crazy." Brad grinned. "But yeah, I always have a backup in an ankle holster. A CZ75 and a tactical knife in my belt." He stared at his beer. "They've both been handy to have."

"But you were selected for the team."

"We went through rigorous testing, and finally, six were chosen."

"Did any women apply then?"

Brad shook his head. "Remember, this was four years ago. There weren't that many women on the streets in 1976, let alone ready for the jump to that."

"How was training?"

"We spent two weeks with the LA SWAT guys and then hit the streets. That's when we realized we didn't know squat. We were highly trained, and nothing was happening. Then we had a couple of holy-shit calls. An estranged husband killed his wife in front of their kids, then barricaded himself in the basement."

Her eyes widened. "Oh my god. What happened?"

"I tried to talk him out. But in the end, it was suicide by cop. Then a young guy, high on glue, barricaded himself in a garage. One cop was killed, and five others injured."

"That was Detective O'Shea."

"Yup."

"Didn't the military end up coming?"

Brad frowned and took a drink of beer. "The ending was not Calgary Police's best moment. Later, the robbers got aggressive—a full-on assault on a bank near Chinook Mall. The bank was shot up, and the two ex-Airborne were stranded in the bank. They chose to shoot it out. By then, we were a cohesive team. The Airborne guys had added real-life experience than we did, but we had trained for something like this. Three Airborne were killed."

"Jeez, that was some start to the team."

"It was." It felt like so long ago. A lot had happened since. And not a lot of it cheerful. Or what was going well went to shit. If you believed in luck, which he didn't, then he was born under a bad sign. They say you make your own luck. He wasn't sure what he had to do differently. Brad drank his beer. This had started out as fun. Now he wanted to get out of here.

The waitress set the pizza on the table and glanced at Brad's drink. He held up two fingers.

"I need to get back to my dog soon. Do you have specific questions? Ask away while we eat."

"Sure. Sorry to take your time."

"That's fine." Brad grabbed a slice of pizza.

Toscana ignored the pizza and leaned forward, her brown eyes fixed on Brad's "How can I get on TSU?"

"That's going to be a huge uphill battle. I don't know of any Tactical or SWAT team with a female member." Brad bit off a huge section of pizza.

A grin formed and her eyes sparkled. "The Israelis?"

"They're in a league of their own." Brad wiped his mouth. "Not the group to compare to."

"But it can be done."

Brad twirled his bottle in his hands. "All the emergency services are stuck in a male 1950s paradigm. You know women have only been on the street for seven years. EMS has a few female paramedics, but only in the last few years. The Fire Department has no female firefighters or people of color."

"I applied for TSU earlier this year."

"So I heard." He grabbed another slice of pizza.

"I didn't make it. You know some guys there. Did they say anything?" She didn't meet his eyes.

"Nothing other than you had done well."

Toscana's shoulders slumped. Her confident, playful mood was gone. It was like her energy was exhausted. "But not good enough."

"I wasn't there, but I know it's extremely competitive. It's a major accomplishment that you are an acting sergeant. Heck, you probably aced your interview and you'll be a full-fledged card-carrying sergeant. That's not a small achievement."

"I'll believe it when it happens."

Brad grabbed another slice of pizza and chewed. It was like a switch was flicked and he was talking to a different Toscana. "To make TSU, you'd have to be the best in every test—best shooter, best physical shape, smartest, psychologically sound, and strongest. You might accomplish the first ones, but it's unlikely you'll be the strongest." He grinned. "I heard you bench pressed more than a current member, so you'll be okay. As long as you can carry a two-hundred-and-twenty-pound cop who is shot out of a building, you'll have a chance. That's the bottom line."

Toscana's lips pursed. "Yeah, I can do that."

Brad held up a pizza-greased hand. "It's a worthy goal. Keep doing what you're doing."

CHAPTER TWENTY-EIGHT

SHARMA MANEUVERED THE AMBULANCE THROUGH THE SNOW AND ice. There was no sense rushing tonight—they didn't need to get into a traffic collision. For a Thursday at midnight, the traffic was light. No one wanted to be out in freezing weather, not even to go to the bar. The back end of the ambulance slid through the turn onto Seventeenth Avenue as Sharma fought to straighten the vehicle.

"Damn, that was fun." Cook held tight to the handhold above her door as her right foot jammed into the floor.

Sharma glanced over at her foot. "Did your side stop?"

"Just a reflex."

Sharma got the ambulance under control, and they plowed through the snow toward the apartment building.

"Isn't this the same address we were at a few months ago?" Cook asked. "The boyfriend beat up his girlfriend. We transported her to the hospital, and the cops took him away."

"You mean the guy Coulter tuned up?"

"Twice. Yeah, that's the one."

"Shit. He was a nutcase. Make sure the cops are close," Sharma said.

"Dispatch, Medic 2. We're a minute from the address. Are the cops on the way?"

"Medic 2, CPS should be right behind you."

Cook glanced in the rearview mirror in time to see a police cruiser slide through the intersection over the curb and onto the sidewalk. "They're taking the long way."

Sharma maneuvered the ambulance to the curb, and they jumped out. Cook slid a black wool beanie over her frizzy light brown hair and grabbed the kits while Sharma keyed his radio. "Dispatch, Medic 2 on scene with police."

"Roger, Medic 2."

Sharma and Cook started up the sidewalk to the main door of the apartment building as Robson and Rossi caught up.

Cook glanced over at them. "Who was driving?"

Rossi stared at her boots. "That would be me."

"Don't worry," Cook said. "Sharma almost did the same thing."

"*Almost* is the key word," Sharma replied.

A squat man with bulging biceps held the building door open. "I'm the manager. I'm tired of the noise. I want them out."

"Have you served an eviction notice?" Robson asked.

"Sure. It don't matter. They no leave. You come before. Take him away. Next day, he's back. It's worse than before."

"What happened tonight?" Robson asked.

"Half hour ago, they start again. Yelling. Then sounds like

place is being wrecked. Screaming, shouting. I take no more. I call." He marched to the stairs. "Tonight, you make go."

Robson pushed in front of the paramedics and took the stairs two at a time. Rossi brought up the rear. When they stepped into the corridor, there were no sounds. Robson waved the paramedics behind him and, hand resting on the butt of his gun, he stepped down the hall. The apartment door was ajar.

He waved Rossi to the other side of the door, then said, "You two wait here."

Robson nodded to Rossi, nudging the door open with his foot. "Police. We're coming in." Silence. "Police, coming in." No answer. Robson stepped into the apartment, Rossi on his heels.

Cook and Sharma followed cautiously behind.

Robson continued left into the tiny bedroom, Rossi headed to the combined living room and kitchen. "Clear."

"You'd better come here," Robson said.

Cook entered the room and stopped short in the doorway. A barely recognizable male lay on the floor, legs splayed at weird angles poking out of the bathroom. His upper body lay in a pool of blood, his face smashed beyond recognition. Cook stepped over his legs and knelt at his head. Blood bubbled from his mouth and nose. "We've gotta move quick."

"Dispatch, 424. We will need detectives and Crime Scene Unit here."

"Roger, 424. We will notify," dispatch said.

Cook glanced up at Robson. "Can you and your partner grab our stretcher?"

"Better than that." Robson spoke into his mic again. "Two

cruisers just pulled up. They'll bring the stretcher in. We need to stay until the detectives arrive."

"Hey, where's his girlfriend?" Cook opened her paramedic kit and pulled out the airway pack.

"Her name is Sylvia," Robson said. "Another cruiser found her running down the street. She wasn't wearing a coat, was freezing and talking about a guy that beat Vinnie with a bat. The cops took her to a women's shelter."

Cook swept the blood away from the patient's face with gauze, then slipped in an airway. Blood bubbled out of the airway. She grabbed the suction, slid a tube into the airway and suctioned. The canister filled with blood.

Sharma had secured the patient's neck with a cervical collar and tied his legs together.

A loud noise came from the hallway—swearing, clanking of metal and something hitting the walls. Then four cops pushed the stretcher, at full height, into the room.

"You know that collapses, right?" Robson asked.

An exhausted cop leaned against the wall. "Thanks for the heads up on that."

Sharma lowered the stretcher. "We'll need a hand lifting him."

Robson glanced at the cop by the wall, who mouthed, "Screw you."

Robson nodded to his partner. They knelt with Sharma and Cook, then lifted the patient.

Sharma wrapped the patient in a blanket, then connected the straps. He pulled the stretcher out of the apartment to the stairwell. Robson and Rossi stayed in the apartment. With the help of the cops, they carried the stretcher down to the main level and rolled it out to the ambulance.

Robson and Rossi were sitting on the carpet outside the apartment, issue parkas across their laps, when Griffin and Sturgeon arrived. As they stood, Robson arched his back and groaned.

"Sorry for the wait," Griffin said. "It's not the night you get anywhere fast."

"He drives like my grandmother." Sturgeon pretended to hold a steering wheel close to his chest, then strained his neck forward and squinted.

"It could be worse," Robson said. "You could have been driving on the sidewalk." He glanced at his partner, who reddened.

"Bring us up to date." Griffin brushed snow off his blue parka and stomped his feet, snow falling off his black boots.

Robson filled them in. "There are a few things you need to see. Follow me." He led them to the bathroom door and pointed. "There's a baseball bat in the tub. The weapon of choice, if you go by the blood and hair. Might belong to the victim and used in the struggle." He glanced at Sturgeon. "But then, that's above my paygrade."

Sturgeon unbuttoned his brown overcoat and slid off his gloves. He peeked his head into the bathroom, then glanced over his shoulder.

"No, we didn't touch them," Robson said.

"We've been here before," Griffin said.

Robson nodded. "The paramedics, as well. But it was for the girlfriend."

Griffin stepped toward the living room. "But she's not here."

"Nope," Robson said. "A cruiser found her and took her to the Women's Shelter. They'll get a statement from her."

Most of the time, Sharma would have asked a cop to drive the ambulance. But with the snow- and ice-covered roads and after witnessing the cruiser careen onto the sidewalk, he decided it was best if he drove. That left Cook in the back alone with the patient, but there wasn't a lot she could do. This guy needed an emergency physician and a surgeon.

He pulled into the ambulance bay at the Foothills Medical Centre. A few paramedics hustled over and assisted lifting the stretcher out of the ambulance. Cook jumped out and they hauled the stretcher to the triage desk.

Cook stepped to the counter. "Approximately thirty- to thirty-five-year-old male, severely beaten, likely with a baseball bat. Unconscious, unresponsive. Pulse 130, weak. Blood pressure 140/86. Respirations shallow and eight a minute. I assisted ventilations en route. He has an airway in place and an intravenous to keep the vein open. Pupils unequal and reacting slowly to light."

"Trauma one," the triage nurse said.

They swung the stretcher next to the hospital gurney and with the help of the trauma team moved the patient. Sharma slid the ambulance stretcher out of the trauma room and into the hall.

Cook gave her patient report to the trauma team, then stepped back into the hall with Sharma.

"Someone gave that guy a shit kicking," Sharma said.

Cook nodded as she watched the trauma team work on the patient. "Part of me hopes it was his girlfriend. He had it coming."

"That's as vicious of a beating as I've seen. I don't think she could have done this unless he was unconscious."

"I noticed a baseball bat lying in the bathtub. That would do it."

Sharma cocked his head and chewed his lip. "Yeah, that would do it."

"Let's get X-rays and then a CT scan," the emergency physician said. "Make sure he has circulation in his legs and watch for compartment syndrome."

"I didn't think of that," Cook said. "When I splinted his legs, I didn't see a lot of swelling, but I had a faint pulse."

"The doctor just said to watch for it. If the swelling in the legs is severe enough, it decreases blood to the foot, and the pulse is not palpable, then the docs can deal with it. I should have mentioned that to you."

Cook's eyes cast downward. Her jaw clenched.

Sharma pushed their stretcher down the hall. "The trauma team is on top of this. Let's clean up."

CHAPTER TWENTY-NINE

Brad hauled a stack of files into the compact conference room and set them on the table. For the next hour, he posted victim and crime scene photos on the walls. Under each victim, he added notes from the crime scenes and autopsies. His gut told him the deaths were all linked, unlike the sniper case a few months ago, but the link wasn't obvious. He wasn't the first to notice and point out that their recent spate of homicides seemed to involve karma serving up a cold dish to victims that wouldn't be missed. Satisfied with his work, he stood back and reviewed each death.

The two drug dealers in Victoria Park were killed in the same manner, so in Brad's mind there was no doubt about the same killer. He further believed the murder of Billy Tuck, the first drug dealer, had been the first in the series. The killer had hesitated or struggled with the first kill, but made up for it in the second Vic Park murder of Vito Sotelo.

The hit and run of James Duggan, the drunk driver,

wasn't a perfect fit. He wasn't involved in the drug trade or prostitution. Too many DUIs, but just an elderly man who drank excessively. Now that Brad had posted the drunk driver, he didn't see the connection and contemplated taking Duggan off the wall. The only thing he had in common with the others was a lengthy rap sheet.

The killer appeared to be gaining confidence with the pimp and bodyguard murder. Killing two asshats at the same time took balls. Walking up and shooting the pimp Owen Judd and his driver-bodyguard Anthony Moss while they sat in their car was gutsy. The accuracy of the shots was significant. The shooter had serious skills. And that the killer had done this without a single witness was another testament to his skills.

The killings at the tattoo parlor were well planned and perfectly executed. To surprise the large doorman and shove the knife into his heart was impressive in a dark way. Where did the killer learn this? The knife to the heart was the same style as in both drug dealer murders.

The execution of the rapist, the pornographer, and the cameraman again showed proficiency with guns, the tight, expert groupings drawing a connection with the pimp and driver double homicide. The added touch of hacking off their dicks and shoving them in their mouths seemed over the top. Maybe personal? A sister, girlfriend or wife who'd been raped? That's a lot of anger.

Then another rapist is killed, Burke Baldwin II. This case he knew about from Jenni Blighe. She was as mad as he'd ever seen her when she lost that case. Brad couldn't imagine the trauma suffered by the victim not only with the rape, but then the humiliation in court. Burke's friends pointed the finger at the dad, Al Turner. Brad would follow up with a few phone calls to Turner's workmates to confirm his alibi for the night, but Brad's gut said the dad was innocent.

Brad's rage wouldn't be controlled if his daughter had suffered like that. Jeter Wolfe was already arrested when Brad had discovered what he'd done to Annie. Shooting Wolfe later was barely a consolation. Carving the word 'rapist' into the boy's forehead seemed intended to send a message in the same way as the pornography case, with the castration and intentionally posed bodies. Though the methods of murder differed for some, every victim on the wall had a criminal history.

Brad pulled a chair in front of the wall and flopped down. His head shook slowly, and he exhaled deeply. In the sniper case, it had helped to use the board to work out patterns. This time whenever he recognized a pattern, the next murder was different in some aspect.

Maybe he was trying too hard to find a pattern. The first two drug dealer deaths had to be related with drug dealers as the common variable. The method was the same. The hit and run was an anomaly.

The next seven murders were all related to sex crimes. The method varied, but in five of the seven, the killer used a gun with precision. They had to be connected.

Was he faced with two killers? One taking out drug dealers? The second killer with a huge hate for the sex trade? Except that the same method of stabbing had shown up in the pornography case as the drug dealers. Maybe two killers working together?

He flipped back through the files. Except for Burke Baldwin, the others all had long criminal records, and few had served any prison time. That brought his thoughts back to Jenni. If the court system was the link, who better to have inside information than a crown prosecutor. Still, as angry as she was, and even including the terror Jeter Wolfe had caused her, he didn't see her as a vigilante. Or did he? She was taking self-defense classes and had asked Brad to teach her to shoot. He shook his head. No. She had learned to shoot quickly, and was accurate, but he hadn't seen the precision the murders showed.

He leaned back in his chair and linked his fingers behind his head. He peered at the wall, reviewing each murder. Right to left, left to right. No one had stood out in the footage of the crime scenes that Sadie had let him watch, just a bunch of cops and gawkers. His mind connected common factors, and just like earlier, when he thought he had a pattern, he hit a dead end. He inhaled, slowly exhaled, then rubbed his eyes. It was there, somewhere—the answer, the link, the clue.

There was a knock and the door opened. Griffin and Sturgeon stepped in and grabbed chairs. Griffin glanced at the wall. "I see you're working on your homework collage. The teacher will love this. I see a gold star in your future."

Brad raised his middle finger.

"While you were dreaming of whatever you dream about, they called us to an assault last night."

Brad frowned. "They called you out for an assault?"

"It was a severe beating. Paramedics weren't sure if the guy would live. Robson was there. He made a smart decision and had us paged just in case the guy didn't make it."

"Is he alive?"

"Yeah," Griffin said. "He's in ICU. We just came from there. He's got multiple skull fractures. They rushed him to surgery early this morning to relieve pressure on his brain. His nose, jaw and cheeks are broken. One eye is severely damaged, and he may be blind in that eye. The list goes on. Rib fractures, both legs broken in multiple places. It's a miracle he's still alive."

"He may wish he hadn't made it," Brad said.

Griffin glanced at Sturgeon, who nodded.

Brad glanced from one man to the other. "Is there something you're not saying?"

"The assault victim is Vinnie Bevan," Griffin said.

Brad's eyebrows raised, his eyes widened. "Bevan? The asshat who beat his girlfriend. I was just in court on that. He hasn't been sentenced yet."

"Someone got ahead of the court," Sturgeon said. "Bevan's a frickin' mess."

"I love it when you use medical terms," Brad said.

"Add him to your wall of shame," Griffin said.

"I'm not sure he fits the pattern," Brad said. "Besides, he's not dead."

Griffin shrugged. "I'm not sure you have a pattern other than murders are coming fast and furious. It makes sense to think we have several killers."

Sturgeon headed to the door, then glanced back. "I need to get to the lab. A baseball bat was left on the scene, likely the weapon of choice. Might be the victim's, but I hope the attacker left it."

Brad slowed to a walk as they reached the lane to his house. Their run had been both invigorating and cold. Lobo was glad the pace eased and was glued to Brad's side. The yard light shone on a gray Honda Civic parked behind Brad's car. Annie. Two years ago, Annie's mother and her boyfriend were killed by Jeter Wolfe, the enforcer for the Gypsy Jokers Outlaw Motorcycle gang. Wolfe took Annie as his prize. Annie's tenacity and cunning provided the opportunity for her and another teen, Sissy, to escape. Annie's information on the gang was pivotal in Brad and TSU locating a meeting of rival bikers.

Brad and Maggie unofficially adopted Annie and helped her deal with the horrors she'd experienced. Brad paid for her apartment and her college education. After Maggie's death, Annie had returned the favor and cared for Brad.

As he passed Annie's car, he saw a glint of metal in the snow. He reached down and picked it up.

"Shit."

It was his tactical knife. It must have fallen off his belt, and then either he or Annie had driven over it. He loved that knife. It had been a gift from his partner, Curtis Young. It held a lot of sentimental value. Maybe it could be fixed.

Lobo sniffed the area, then bounded to the house. Annie opened the door and knelt. Lobo rewarded her with slobbery kisses.

"He was happy to be with me until he saw you. What brings you out on a wintery night in shitty road conditions?"

Annie tucked her blond hair behind her ear. "I was worried about you."

Having Annie in his life was a godsend. He wasn't sure if he'd have survived Maggie's murder without Annie. Annie had just turned eighteen and Brad was thirty-two, but they had a father-daughter relationship. Which pissed Annie off when Brad had opinions on her choice of boyfriends.

Brad shrugged. "I'm great."

"I left a bunch of messages."

"I've been busy at work. I didn't check the messages when I got home. We went for a jog right away."

Annie placed her hands on her slim hips. "Hm. Not checking messages again. Sounds familiar."

Brad held out his hands. "Whoa. I'm busy. The murders are stacking up."

"I heard." Annie headed to the kitchen. "On a great day, you don't eat well. I figured you were busy, so I bought groceries and made dinner. Fried chicken and fries."

"Not sure that counts as a healthy meal."

"It's homemade. Better than your fast-food, 'I'm busy' diet."

Brad showered and changed into shorts and a tattered University of Calgary T-shirt, and when he stepped into the kitchen, he was overwhelmed by the aroma of fried chicken.

"That smells great."

"It should," Annie said. "It's your recipe."

Brad hadn't realized how hungry he was, and he dove into the food. When his plate was close to empty, he paused and glanced up.

Annie was staring at him, blue eyes wide. "We need to

talk about your manners. Living alone has not improved dinner etiquette."

Brad shrugged. "Nasty habit. Eat and pee when you can."

"You've said that before." Annie leaned back and crossed her arms. "You aren't in a patrol car. You're not on the tactical support unit. It's okay to take your time with a meal."

Brad stabbed another piece of chicken. "How's college?"

Annie leaned back and shook her head. "You're deflecting."

Brad grinned, then stuffed a chunk of chicken in his mouth.

"College is fine. The first year was hard getting into a routine, and then there were the distractions in the spring. Second year is flying by. I won't be ready to stop learning in the spring. I don't know enough."

"Enough for what?" Brad asked.

"That's the problem." Annie took a long drink of milk. "I don't know what I want to do. But I know what I don't want to do—corrections. You'd have to be insane to do that." Annie stroked Lobo's head.

Brad set his fork down and sat back. He would let Annie work this out. This wasn't the time to interrupt or give advice.

"I guess I worry about what you'll think," she added.

Brad cocked his head.

"I see what you do, and all the different opportunities in the police service. That gets me excited. But I also see the toll it has taken on you. Then I lean toward law, but that didn't work out for you. I wonder why not? You've never talked about it. But some of it I can guess. You can't be a defense lawyer, that would make you crazy. However, the legal system isn't set up for success for a crown prosecutor. Jenni Blighe is an excellent example. You've talked about her frustrations. I enjoy being on the side of the good guys, but I don't know where I fit. That's why I don't want college to end." Annie stood, went to the fridge, and brought back two beers. "You going to sit there and say nothing?"

"Do you want advice, my thoughts?"

Annie frowned. "No, I just talked for ten minutes because I enjoy talking."

"Another time we can talk about me and the law. Tonight, you're missing a third option."

Annie's eyebrows scrunched.

"You need to talk to Sturgeon. There are some significant advances happening in crime scene analysis. The way we handle crime scenes is changing. The science behind analysis of evidence is at the edge of being revolutionary. I tune him out most of the time, but I know he'd love to talk about it. I can set that up if you'd like."

Annie sipped her beer. "I hadn't thought of that." She nodded. "Yeah. I could get into that."

Brad stood and collected the plates. "I'll talk to Sturgeon. I'll clean up and then I need a decent night's sleep."

When Brad had finished cleaning, Annie was still at the table sipping her beer. He left her with her thoughts as he headed to bed.

CHAPTER THIRTY

Most of the lights were out as Dice drove past the Town and Country Hotel and Bar. Built in the 50s, it had rapidly declined as owner after owner paid scarce attention to upkeep. The bar and restaurant occupied the main level, with three floors of rooms above. The enormous florescent streetlight was in darkness. A single motorcycle was parked by the side door. Dice continued a block farther, parked in an alley, popped the trunk, and pulled out a crowbar. Keeping to the shadows, the dark clothes and black balaclava blended into the night. Dice headed toward the side door.

A quick check confirmed the door was locked. That was expected. Dice wedged the end of the crowbar between the door and the frame and pushed. The frame cracked, and the door popped open.

On the far side of the bar a lone biker played pool, illuminated by the light over the table, with his back to Dice. Evidently, he had not heard the door crack.

Dice snuck across the bar, grabbing a pool cue on the way. The biker sank a shot and stepped to the other side of the table.

"What the fuck are you doing in here? Get out. We're closed."

Dice pulled the balaclava down and leaned the pool cue against the table.

The biker laughed. "Oh, woo. I'm terrified." He headed around the table toward Dice, who didn't move. He swung a meaty fist toward Dice's head, which was easily deflected. The biker grunted. This time the fist came from the left. Dice deflected that blow, then fired a series of punches at the biker's gut with a final fist to the biker's nose. Cartilage cracked, blood spurted, and he stepped back, grasping at his face.

Dice grabbed the pool cue and snapped it in two. Then Dice stepped toward the retreating biker and shoved the sharp, broken end deep into his gut and forced it up toward his heart.

The man gasped. Blood flowed from his mouth. His eyes widened, and his legs collapsed. His knees hit the floor first. He teetered there for a moment and then fell onto his face, which forced the broken pool cue deeper. Blood pooled around the biker's gut and seeped into the cracks in the floor.

I hate bikers. Dice slipped out the side door.

Brad parked near the street, far away from the dozen cruisers, and headed across the snow-covered parking lot to the front door of the Town and Country Bar. He ducked under the police line tape, identified himself to the cop shivering outside the door, and stepped inside.

He'd been in this bar a few times. The memories weren't all that pleasant. The odor of French fries, bacon, and beer mingled with a pine cleaning solution. Bar stools were in their place and chairs were positioned upside down on the wooden tables. All the lights were on, but the bar was vacant. Well, except for cops and the Crime Scene Unit techs.

Brad unzipped his parka, spotted Griffin by a pool table and headed over. "I see you've finally come back to police work."

Griffin glanced over his shoulder. "Screw you and the horse you road in on."

Brad slapped Griffin on the back. "A pleasure to see you, as well."

Griffin stepped away from Brad. "I was looking forward to a weekend off. What the heck was I thinking?"

Brad glanced past Griffin to the body on the floor. The handle of a pool cue stuck out of the dead man's chest. His T-shirt and Hells Angels leather vest were blood soaked, as was the wood flooring.

"Someone was a poor loser," Brad said.

"Seems so," Griffin mumbled.

Brad wandered around the perimeter of the body. "Who finds a dead body at four in the morning?"

"District cops were driving by about three. They routinely check on him when they're on patrol. This place closes at one and there's a guy who cleans up, then shuts off the lights and locks up. But some lights were on. The cops stop, peer in the front door and windows, and see nothing. When they walk around the side of the building, they see a door that's forced open. They call it in and when a couple of additional cruisers get here, they head in. That's when they found the dead biker."

"Do they know who he is?"

Griffin opened his notebook. "It's the guy who closes up—Arnie Fletcher. He's a Hells Angel and former member of the Satan's Soldiers.

Brad's brown eyes widened. "Ah, shit." Brad slid his hands through his hair. "I know this guy. Fletcher hung around with a biker named Lou LeBeau, who got himself blown up a few years ago. LeBeau and I had a confrontation here. Fletcher was one of his lackies."

"That when they beat the shit out of you?" Griffin asked.

"I don't remember it that way."

"Briscoe told me about it. You versus four bikers. Not betting odds."

Brad stared at Fletcher. "I got three of them."

"Close, but no cigar. You got other history with this guy?"

Brad glanced at Griffin. "Nah. I haven't seen him since that night."

"You're sure on that?" Griffin's icy stare was a shock.

"What the—?" Brad asked. "Yes, I'm sure."

Griffin held his hands out. "Okay. I've got this. Go home and go back to sleep. Nothing to do until the Crime Scene Unit finishes up. We'll catch up in the morning."

"You sure?"

Griffin nodded.

"I can stay and keep you company," Brad said.

"I'm sure you could. No sense both of us stuck here." Griffin spun away from Brad and strode toward the Crime Scene techs.

Brad nodded and headed for the door. He stopped before he stepped outside and glanced back at the pool table. Something wasn't right. Weird coincidence that of all the bikers, Arnie Fletcher gets killed. Brad didn't believe in coincidences. The answers would come to him. He headed to his car.

CHAPTER THIRTY-ONE

As Brad slid out of his car, the sun was fighting to break through the cloud cover. A good way to start the week. According to the weather report, it would be a brief reprieve and cold and snow would blow in later today. But a break in the awful weather had to be a good sign. With the sun shining, it would be a glorious day. He felt it in his gut. The break they needed would come today.

That was enough to put a spring in his step as he crossed Sixth Avenue with fresh Gerry's coffee. The sun was blocked by police headquarters as he headed down the alley. He was glad he had the coffees to keep his hands warm. An icy wind swept down the alley. Balancing the two coffees, he entered the back door and headed past the booking sergeant.

"Good morning, Sarge."

The sergeant glanced up, then swung his back to his newspaper, mumbling something unintelligible.

Holding the coffees in one hand, he fished out his wallet

and swiped it over the door scanner. The lock clicked, and he pulled the door open with one hand, then held it open with his foot as he juggled the hot drinks.

The detective bullpen was eerily quiet this morning. Boisterous conversations dropped to whispers. The click-clack of one-fingered typing was missing. Even the phones were silent.

Brad found Griffin at his desk. "Brought you a coffee from Gerry's."

Griffin grunted and pointed to his desk.

Brad set the coffee down and took his chair. "What's got you so engrossed so early? Did we get a lead last night?"

Griffin held a hand up as he concentrated on a file folder.

Brad sipped his coffee and peered at his partner. Whatever it was Griffin was reading, it had his full attention. Griffin might make fun of Brad for needing his morning coffee, but Griffin was no cheerleader before he had a cup or two. And ignoring a coffee from Gerry's was unusual.

Never a candidate for the cover of a fashion magazine, Griffin's suit was especially rumpled, like he'd slept in it. His eyes were bloodshot, and a frown creased his face. A half-dozen open folders were on his desk. Brad wondered if Griffin had been here all night.

Griffin gathered the files, stood and headed to the door. "Archer wants to see us ASAP."

"Did he say why?" Brad jumped out of his chair and followed Griffin out of the room and down the hall.

"Update on the murders."

"I had that figured out," Brad said.

When they stepped into the deputy's office, Archer's secretary said, "He's waiting. Go in."

They stepped into Archer's office.

"Sit, gentlemen," Archer said.

Griffin took a chair next to Sturgeon, leaving the chair opposite Archer for Brad. It reminded him of promotion interviews with senior police management. *Let the inquisition begin.*

Brad glanced around. Archer, Jackson, and Sturgeon were seated at the conference table. No one made eye contact with him, their jaws tight and faces like stone. There was a chill in the room, like someone had died, but the warm sunlight was streaming through a window. Apparently, he was the only one excited by the sunshine.

"I didn't know we were meeting until Griffin told me." Brad glanced around the table, cocking his head to the side. "Hey, guys. Lighten up. We're going to break this case today. I feel it in my gut." He rubbed his hands together.

All eyes were on Archer. "There are recent developments in the case. Sergeant?"

Sturgeon glanced down at his notes. "We analyzed a hair sample from the tattoo parlor crime scene. It didn't match any of the dead men or the girls. Not surprising, that scene was a disgusting swamp of body evidence."

"Did you identify the hairs?" Brad asked. "Were they the same person?"

"Well, no." Sturgeon avoided eye contact with Brad. "The sample from the parlor was canine."

"Are you sure?" Jackson asked.

"Yes," Sturgeon kept his gray eyes on his notes. "Human and dog hair are completely different. First, canine and human hair growth cycles are different. Multiple hair shafts emerge from each canine hair follicle as opposed to human follicles that only produce a solitary hair. Second, human hairs grow for two to six years where dogs have a much shorter growth cycle resulting in frequent shedding. Third, animal hair provides a protective function and is thicker than the human hair."

Brad nodded. "Well, that doesn't sound helpful."

"Agreed," Sturgeon said. "Then we did eliminations on known canine hair from our K9 unit." Sturgeon paused and stared at his report. "We, uh, got a match." He kept his head down. "Lobo."

"What?" Brad blurted. His eyes widened. He did a double-take in Sturgeon's direction. "Are you sure? No way." Brad shook his head, struggling to figure out where this was going. It made little sense. "Lobo was nowhere near that place."

Sturgeon's jaw clenched. "It's clearly a match."

Brad glanced at Sturgeon, rubbed his hands over his pants, then glanced at his palms. Dog hair. "That's my fault. I had Lobo in the car, and then I went into the crime scene." He picked a piece of dog hair off his palm. "There must have been a transfer of Lobo's hair when I was in the room. Shit. Stupid of me." Brad glanced at Sturgeon. "I guess I wasn't paying attention in your class."

Archer glared at Brad, then nodded to Griffin.

"When the girls from the tattoo parlor were interviewed, they all said the same thing," Griffin said. "That when they scurried out of the parlor, they saw a car parked beside the building. A black Firebird."

"That should be easy to track," Brad said. "There aren't that many black Firebirds in Calgary. I bought one of the few—"

"You see where this is going?" Archer asked. "It hasn't eluded our notice that you were recently in court regarding your scuffle with Vinnie Bevan, a man who is still in ICU after the severe baseball bat beating. Nor has your history with Arnie Fletcher, the Hells Angels biker recently stabbed to death with a pool cue through the heart."

"Chief—"

Archer held up a hand and continued, "It seems the unique and precise method of stabbing in that case correlates with the stabbings of two drug dealers and one victim at the tattoo parlor. And at that tattoo parlor, the remaining three victims were shot to death in a manner nearly identical to that of another recent crime scene—the murders of Owen Judd and Anthony Moss in their vehicle. Also, at the tattoo parlor crime scene, three of the victims were posed and mutilated as if to send a message. Not unlike the message 'rapist' carved into Burke Bailey Baldwin II's forehead. Griffin mentioned the wall of victims pinned next to your desk, some we hadn't even thought to include, such as the recent hit and run. They all share an underlying thread of connection though, don't they? You see why we're concerned."

They were staring at him. His eyes darted from one man to another. Did they believe he was involved? That was absurd. They had to know that. Screw the reports Sturgeon had given. "Come on, you don't think—you can't … this makes no sense."

"Brad, we're following the evidence," Jackson said. "We're telling you what we know. No one is judging."

"It sure as hell feels like I've been judged." Brad's Spidey senses tingled, and not in a good way. "You guys are freaking me out." He held out his hands like he was pushing them away.

Archer set a duty roster on the table. "You weren't on duty for any of the killings—"

Brad glanced at the roster, felt his face redden and his fists clenched in his lap. "That means nothing." Brad glared at Archer with his head held high, breath coming rapidly through his nose, lips pursed. His voice was louder and shakier than he intended. "I'm always scheduled for day shift. If there's a homicide at night, I get called in. That's the way Homicide works. Since all the killings were at night, yes," he growled, "I was off duty."

Archer ignored Brad and continued, "Yet for the tattoo parlor killings, you arrived quickly. Why were you in the area?"

"Oh, come on. I was … visiting Maggie's grave." His mouth was dry, but his palms were sweaty. He rubbed them on his pants again.

"I understand you visit frequently." Jackson's voice was calm with a country drawl. It was soothing. "That's reasonable. We're talking about a few months since—"

Brad's right leg bounced to a rapid beat. "I go sometimes, when I miss her—or need to talk to her."

"Late at night," Griffin snorted.

Jackson held up a hand. "I get it, I do."

"You guys are kidding, right?" Brad pushed his chair away from the table a couple of inches. He glanced around the table—they were all guys who knew him. Jackson clicked a pen in time with a clock. Sturgeon, head down, stared at his hands.

Archer nodded to Sturgeon. "He needs your pistol."

"You're serious?" Brad tensed, his back firmly against the chair. He felt cold, yet he was sweating.

"That we are," Archer said. "We're just going to test it, compare the ballistics to the bullets recovered from the pimp and bodyguard murders and the tattoo parlor scene."

Brad reached for his service pistol and saw everyone in the room tense. Griffin even slid his hand down to the butt of his gun. Jackson put a large hand on Griffin's chest. Brad carefully pushed the release on the holster, slid his pistol out with two fingers, and set it on the table.

Sturgeon, wearing latex gloves, reached for the pistol. He cleared the chamber and caught the expelled cartridge. He released the magazine and placed it in an evidence bag. "I'll need your spare mags, and your backup gun, as well."

Brad slid the spare mags out and set them on the table. He slid his backup pistol, the CZ75, out of his ankle holster. Sturgeon bagged the guns and magazines, pulled some hair samples, then left the room.

Brad set his hands on the table, then into his lap, then crossed his arms again. His leg muscles tensed with the surge of adrenaline, both legs bounced on his toes, and his hands dropped loosely to his sides—ready for fight or flight. He slid his chair back another couple of inches.

Brad was the only one who glanced up when the door closed. Now the heat from the sunshine was too intense. Sweat dampened his armpits and his forehead. He licked his lips again and grabbed his coffee. It was warm but wet. He swished it around his mouth, then swallowed.

"What happens now?" Brad stared at Archer. "Am I suspended—again?"

"Griffin will escort you to an interview room while CSU tests your weapons."

Brad's jaw clenched, his eyes ablaze. "Hold on." He pushed his chair back against the wall and stood.

Griffin jumped to his feet.

"Easy." Jackson placed a hand on Griffin's chest, then turned to Brad. His voice was calm and low." "There's considerable evidence that suggests you're a person of interest. Put your self in our position. What would you do? Give us a chance to work through that."

Brad's eyes narrowed. "Are you charging me with something?"

"Not at this time," Archer said.

"This is circumstantial bullshit," Brad said. "How is this possible? You all know me."

"We know you're under stress," Archer said. "What happened to Maggie would make any of us angry."

"Sure, I'm angry," Brad's eyes peered around the room. His look pleading. "I'm not a vigilante." Brad glanced at the door. "Am I under arrest?"

"I'd hoped we could clear this up this morning," Archer said. "Hang around at least until we have ballistics back."

"No thanks." Brad sighed.

Archer stood and locked eyes with Brad. "I'm asking you to wait for an hour. Two, tops."

Brad stared back. "If you're charging me, I want a lawyer. If you're not charging me, I'm out of here."

"I'm advising you to stay," Archer said.

Brad's shoulders slumped and his bright eyes dulled. "Is that an order?"

Archer shook his head. "Griffin will stay with you."

Brad closed his eyes. When he opened them the fire was back. "How about I keep working on finding the real killer while the rest of you wait for ballistics that isn't going to prove shit against me." Brad opened the door and jogged to the stairs with Griffin close behind.

Brad shoved the door open on the main floor and nodded at the desk sergeant. Griffin caught up with Brad at the back door and grabbed his arm. Brad jerked it away and glared at Griffin.

"Don't."

"Archer wants you to stay here." Griffin slipped between Brad and the door.

"That's not what Archer said. I don't have time for bullshit. I'm going to do my job, catch the murderer and clear my name. If you have a problem with that, take it up with the deputy chief."

"Running makes you appear guilty, you know."

"I'm not running." Brad rolled his eyes. "I solve homicides, and we have a lot of them to solve. Come with me."

Griffin held his spot blocking the door.

Brad glared at him. "Do you think I'm a vigilante?"

Griffin's jaw clenched and his eyes narrowed. "The evidence is pointing that way."

"Circumstantial evidence. You coming or not?" Brad deked past Griffin and out the door.

He stopped halfway down the alley and leaned against the wall, shoulders limp, fists clenched at his sides. His rapid breathing hit the cold air as puffs of mist. His heart pounded against his chest wall. It was like he'd used up all his energy defending himself. From what? He was innocent. In an hour they'd all feel stupid. So why was he worried? He got his breathing calmed and his heart slowed.

He sprinted out of the alley and across the street to his car. He slid into the driver's seat, a tight grip on the steering wheel, staring across the parking lot and grinding his teeth until his jaw ached. What had just happened? His heart raced again, and his palms grew sweaty. *I'm not guilty.* Yet they tried to tie him to the killings. They thought he was the killer. He had to clear his name. How long before they decided he was an outsider and blocked his access to case files or evidence. He banged the steering wheel. *Shit.*

He fired up the engine, headed west on Sixth Avenue, then up Centre Street. At Sixteenth Avenue he veered left, then right on Fourth Street. He swung into the Queen's Park Cemetery and parked across from Maggie's grave. He wandered over and stood facing the tombstone.

He wiped snow off the granite and collected his thoughts. *What the hell is going on?*

"Hey, Maggie. I miss you. I wish you were here. I'm in trouble. I did nothing wrong. Heck, I didn't even come close to any line."

He took a deep breath and stared at the sky. Wisps of clouds floated over, and giant flakes of snow fell.

"There's been a spate of murders. At first, they didn't seem related, but when I investigated further, I was sure the same killer was involved. Not like the sniper earlier this year. Like a vigilante is killing dangerous dudes—drug dealers, a pimp and his driver, pornographers, a rapist and a biker. That guy, Vinnie, who beat up his girlfriend is in the hospital. Not that clearing out the rabble isn't a splendid idea … I'm kidding."

He pulled his parka collar up and slid on a beanie.

"I'm being framed for the murders. They have Lobo's hair from one crime scene. But I take him to work all the time."

Brad stamped his heavy boots on the ground, knocking off the snow. "Witnesses reported my car at a crime scene before the murders. Today they took my gun for testing, and my backup. They're clean, but I'm worried. Since you … since Wolfe killed you, I've been screwed up. I've got a temper, and it's gotten away from me at work. Archer believes I'm a liability. He's still pissed off I forged my psych letter to come back to work. I need to prove I'm innocent, but I can't do that from jail. I don't know where to turn. I could sure use your advice."

Jackson knocked on the door and peered into Sturgeon's office. Jackson slid his lanky form into a chair and glanced around the cluttered room. "I like the decorating."

Sturgeon glanced up from a report. "You sound like Coulter. And trust me, that's not good."

Jackson leaned back in the chair and linked his fingers behind his head. "You have something?"

"We have to find Brad."

"I know," Jackson said. "By four, Archer will have every cop in the city hunting Brad. IA is on the case now."

"I'm not worried about IA. You and I have to find him first."

"Why?"

Sturgeon slid a file folder over to Jackson. "Ballistics is a match on his service pistol. The bullets that killed the guys in the tattoo parlor, the pimp and chauffeur, are all from Brad's gun."

"That's not possible," Jackson blurted. He leaned forward and stared wide eyed at the report. "Maybe someone switched guns?"

"First, Brad would know if his gun had been switched," Sturgeon said. "Second, we checked the serial number."

"Oh, shit." Jackson rubbed his hands rubbed his face. "Not possible. I know the kid. Despite his horrific luck, he didn't do this."

"At first I thought that." Sturgeon pulled the report back in front of him. He glanced down and shrugged. "There is a lot of room for error in some evidence. But you can't fake ballistics."

"Does Archer know?"

Sturgeon shook his head. "Not yet."

"I'll try to find Brad." Jackson stood. "You need to redo the ballistics."

"We did it right, we double checked—"

Jackson stopped at the door and held up a finger. "It is my opinion as the staff sergeant for Homicide that we need to reconfirm your results. Do the ballistics again … and take your time."

CHAPTER THIRTY-TWO

Brad slowed as he drove through the southwest neighborhood near Mount Royal College. It was well established, with older homes in decent repair, lawns cut, and large, mature trees providing shade. On the right side of the street, several apartment complexes stood out in contrast to the bungalows. Brad had chosen this four-floor building for Annie over a year ago. Twenty-four-hour security and the latest in locks. It was close to Mount Royal College, in Briscoe's district, and less than fifteen minutes from Brad's farmhouse.

He'd planned to talk things out with Annie. Minutes ago, on the radio news, they reported an unidentified police source had revealed Detective Brad Coulter was a person of interest by his own police department.

Brad turned right, then right again into the alley and parked behind the building. He headed to the back door and used his key, then took the back stairs to Annie's floor. He opened the stair's door and glanced at the four apartment doors.

He stepped to one and tapped lightly on the door. When he didn't hear anyone moving, he tapped again. He thought shadow passed over the eyepiece. The lock clicked, and the door opened.

Brad slipped past her into the apartment and closed the door behind.

"What are you doing here?" Annie asked.

Brad peered out the peephole.

"Are you okay?"

"Something isn't right." Brad followed the hall to the living room, his eyes roving from right to left over the leather chair against one wall, the leather couch against the other, and the coffee table in between. Criminal Justice textbooks were open on the coffee table, with notebooks and pens scattered over the surface.

He strode over to the window and drew the shades. He swung back, his eyes darting around the room. "Anyone else here?"

"No." Annie wrapped her arms across her blue sweatshirt. "You're acting strange."

"I've got an enormous problem."

Annie pointed to the dark leather couch. "Sit. Tell me."

Brad peeled off his beanie and slipped out of the parka. He glanced at his Roper boots. "Oops, sorry."

"Not important." Annie sat on the couch and slid her sweatpants covered legs under her.

Brad sat on the edge of the couch next to her. He told her about the meeting in Archer's office and the radio report.

"That's bullshit." Annie pulled her hair back and into a ponytail. "Maybe Archer has to play this legit. But not the other guys. What are they thinking?" Annie reached for the telephone. "I'll call Briscoe. He'll straighten this out."

"No." Brad put his hand over hers and stared, inches from her face. "No one ... no one can know I'm here—they'd have to turn me in. As it is, I'm putting you in danger. But someone needs to know this is bullshit. I need to clear my name."

"Just talk to Archer." Annie grabbed his hands and stared, pleading. "He'll understand."

"Listen." Brad shook his head and gripped her hands tight. "If I'm arrested, call Maggie's father, Judge Ethan Gray, and Jenni Blighe. But right now, I need you to do a few things."

As Annie drove up the lane to the farmhouse, the motion light came on. Lobo bounded around the corner of the garage and jumped at the window of her car. She got out and grabbed Lobo. They wrestled as he tried to lick her face. She shivered. The sun was setting, and the temperature was already dropping. It would be another minus twenty-five Fahrenheit night.

Lobo raced to the back of the car and sniffed the trunk. He crawled under the back of the vehicle, slid out and sniffed the trunk again.

His head swiveled to the right and stared down the lane. His hackles shot up and he barked. He jumped on his front paws, barking continuously, backing toward Annie. Then he circled her, barking in all directions.

Annie heard branches rustle. *Coyote? Wolf? Bear?*

Lobo was frantic, barking out into the night. Flashlights shone on her from all sides. "Police! On your knees. On your knees! Now."

Annie knelt.

"Hands on your head. Don't move."

Lobo stood in front of Annie, teeth bared.

"Call the dog off," a deep voice ordered.

"Screw you," she shouted. "Identify yourself."

A large man stepped toward her out of the bright lights and the deep voice spoke again. "Call the dog off."

"Who are you?" She stared into the glare of several flashlights.

"Royal Canadian Mounted Police. Last chance." The deep voice was confident. "Call the dog off or I shoot."

The fuckin' Mounties? Emergency Response Team. Their version of SWAT. Of course. Brad lived outside the city. "I don't know if he'll listen."

"Last chance."

"Lobo, off," Annie pleaded. She had to get Lobo to settle. She knew they'd shoot. "Please, Lobo, off."

Lobo stopped barking and sat in front of her. Several figures in dark blue tactical gear came out of the darkness. A loop on a pole was slipped over Lobo's head. He spun and barked and tried to bite the loop around his neck. The pole was twisted, and Lobo flopped onto his side. A black hood was placed over his head. Lobo fought vigorously, but the pole kept him at a distance from the Mounties.

"What the hell do you want?" Annie shouted as she stood.

"Stay on the ground," a deep voice said. "Where's Coulter?"

"I have no clue."

The cop, dressed in dark gray tactical gear with sergeant's stripes lowered his flashlight, rifle at his side, and stared down at Annie. "His car is at your apartment."

"He came by to visit." Annie shrugged. "He does that regularly."

"Where is he now?"

"He's not there?" Annie grinned at the Mountie.

"No. Only his car." He knelt in front of Annie. "Stop jerking me around."

"I'm answering your questions." She glanced behind her at the small farmhouse. "Did you check the house already?"

"Yeah. He'll need a new door."

The Mountie stood and waved to two tactical cops dressed in gray standing behind him. He nodded toward the car. "Check the trunk. Pry it open if you have to."

"Hey, don't wreck my car," Annie pleaded. "Take the keys. They're in my purse on the front seat."

She heard the driver's door open, then the trunk pop. "He's not here, boss."

"Shit," the Mountie sergeant said. "Cuff her."

A Mountie yanked Annie's arms behind her back and slapped on handcuffs. He lifted her by her arms and shoved her toward the house. She stepped over the damaged front door and destroyed frame.

"Brad will be pissed."

"Like I care." The Mountie shoved her into a chair. Two

men wearing black balaclavas stood before her—RCMP ERT patches on their shoulders.

"I don't know you," Annie said. "But you know who I am. And understand that Brad will be madder about what you did to Lobo than to me. I wouldn't want to be in your boots."

"I'm shitting bricks," the Mountie closest said.

"Enough trash talk," the sergeant growled. "Where's Coulter?"

"I don't know." Annie sighed. "I don't know any other way to say it. Why?"

"He's wanted for murder."

Brad watched from the door of the ancient barn. There was nothing he could do. ERT were doing their job, but he still wanted to kick their asses—although Annie was giving them a nasty time. He heard her call Lobo off. The German shepherd yelped, then barked again, but it was muffled.

Fuckers.

He peeked around the garage—they'd put a hood over Lobo's head and had him on a tether pole.

I'll kill them.

Brad had hoped he'd have more time.

Archer had called the RCMP and ERT had arrived in record time.

Brad's jaw clenched and his pulse pounded in his temples as they handcuffed Annie and led her into the house. There was nothing he could do.

ERT fanned out around the house. They hadn't started clearing the dilapidated out-buildings.

The RCMP had made two mistakes. First, they didn't bring K9. That meant they were hunting in the dark. Second, they had no clue what the lay of the land was. They didn't have time before they got here. That was all the advantage he'd need.

He rolled the old truck out of the barn. It wasn't registered, the plates were expired, but it was a vehicle they couldn't link to him. This was no time to play hide and seek until they left. He needed to leave. Annie could hold her own.

He picked his broken tactical knife and slid it into a parka pocket. With one hand on the steering wheel and his shoulder on the doorframe, he pushed the truck toward the hill. Once the truck had momentum, he jumped in and steered as best he could without power. The truck rolled down the hill in darkness to a road about a half-mile from his house. He started the engine but kept the lights off. As he drove away from his farm, he saw two black SUVs blocking the lane. No one was going in or out that way. Rookies. The farm had dozens of exits. Not that Brad could make a high-speed escape, but tonight the truck would do.

As clouds crossed the moon, the road was illuminated, but Brad was well out of sight. He glanced at the passenger seat and wished he had Lobo with him.

CHAPTER THIRTY-THREE

ARCHER STOOD OVER HIS DESK, PHONE TO HIS EAR. HE LISTENED for a minute, slammed the receiver down, and leaned on his desk. "Damn."

Jackson wasn't sure if he should ask what happened.

Archer took a deep breath and sat. "Coulter eluded us." He lowered his head and slid his fingers through his hair.

Jackson, the man, was glad Coulter had escaped. The cop, not so sure. "How'd that happen, Chief?"

Archer's head rose, and he glanced at Jackson and paused before answering. "I'm sure you're heartbroken. When your guys got to Annie's apartment building, Coulter's car was there, but he wasn't. Then Annie showed up at the farm. Lobo was curious about the trunk of her car. RCMP ERT popped the trunk, but he wasn't there either. I don't suppose you've got any ideas of where he'd go."

Jackson shrugged. "Those would be the first two places I'd check. Maybe the cemetery."

"I've got Griffin heading there with a few guys," Archer said. "But if Coulter's car is at Annie's, then how is he getting around?"

"Beats me."

Archer stood and paced the room. "This is a nightmare. How did the press get a hold of this so fast? We're in a pile of shit."

"For which part? That Coulter may be the killer or that we don't have a clue where he is?"

Archer groaned and sat. He opened his desk drawer and pulled out a bottle of Scotch. He poured two glasses and slid one over to Jackson.

"I'm confused," Jackson said. "Are we drinking, hoping we find Coulter or celebrating that he's out there solving the case?"

Archer glared at Jackson and downed his drink.

Griffin followed K9 through the darkening cemetery. He had police cruisers blocking all the exits. Behind him, six uniformed officers followed. They stopped, and he glanced at the map again, then pointed. K9 led the way.

They came to a fork in the road, and Griffin split the team in half. Each team worked their way opposite the row where Maggie's grave lay. On Griffin's command, they lit their flashlights and yelled, "Police."

The shouts echoed throughout the cemetery, but no one answered. Griffin glanced to the K9 dog straining at his leash.

Griffin stepped next to the handler. "So?"

"He has Coulter's scent from that disgusting T-shirt you brought, and he tracked it here. But there are no new footprints. The heavy snow of the last few hours covered any tracks. I'd say if Coulter was here, it was before the heavy snow. My dog will turn around and track right back to our cars. Coulter has been and gone."

"Shit." Griffin absently rubbed his neck. This was the second fucking time he'd been searching for Coulter. The guy was a pain in the ass. Coulter could frame it however he wants, he's running and that makes him guilty. He's made us all look stupid. Griffin grimaced and felt his stomach churn. He hated bad cops.

CHAPTER THIRTY-FOUR

THE CFCN NEWS VAN STOPPED CLOSE TO THE DITCH AT THE lane to Brad's farm. From here, the farmhouse couldn't be seen because of a thick stand of trees, darkness, low clouds, and the heavy falling snow. A dark SUV blocked the lane. A Mountie in gray tactical gear including balaclava strode over. "No one gets in."

"On whose orders?" Sadie asked.

"RCMP business. This farm is off limits."

Sadie lifted her mic higher. "What's happening?"

"Ma'am, please leave."

"I'm here to see Brad Coulter."

He leaned into the window, his rifle pressing against the van, and pushed the microphone down. "I don't care if you're here to confess to the Pope. You don't get in."

"He invited me."

"How pleasant. You two will have to have tea another

day." He stepped back and waved his hand down the road. "Move along."

Sadie nodded to her cameraman. They drove down the road about a half-mile and parked. The cameraman set up his tripod and attached the camera.

"Get some video of the RCMP at the entrance." Sadie slid out of the van and straightened her parka. She used the truck's side mirror to check her makeup, add red lipstick, and adjusted her black pom beanie. She did a mic check with the station, then faced the camera. The cameraman nodded, then the bright lights lit up the road.

"This is Sadie Andrus, CFCN News. I am reporting from Detective Brad Coulter's farmhouse just outside the city limits. Earlier, I received information from an unidentified police source that Coulter was wanted by his own police department for murder, and that a city-wide manhunt was underway."

The screen switched to black SUVs blocking the lane into Brad's house with the audio of Sadie's confrontation with the RCMP.

"We were confronted by members of the RCMP ERT in full tactical gear, including balaclavas. They denied us entry to the house and refused to tell us what was happening. They hustled us away from the scene."

The video switched to Sadie, with members of ERT a hundred yards behind her.

The door to Archer's office burst open. His secretary pointed to the TV.

"You need to turn on the evening news, sir. Channel 4."

Archer set his drink on the table, then switched on the TV.

"This is Sadie Andrus, CFCN News. I am reporting from Detective Brad Coulter's farmhouse just outside the city limits. Earlier, I received information from an unidentified police source that Coulter was wanted by his own police department for murder, and that a city-wide manhunt was underway."

The screen switched to black SUVs blocking the lane into Brad's house with the audio of Sadie's confrontation with the RCMP.

"We were confronted by members of the RCMP ERT in full tactical gear, including balaclavas. They denied us entry to the house and refused to tell us what was happening. They hustled us away from the scene."

The video switched to Sadie, with members of ERT a hundred yards behind her.

Jackson stood and stared at the TV. "This is not good."

Archer grabbed his phone and dialed. "Dispatch. Contact RCMP dispatch and order the ERT at Coulter's house to shut down that TV broadcast. Now!"

The camera focused on the outline of a house in the darkness. A single light illuminated the yard. Several interior lights were on.

The scene swung from the yard back to Sadie. "We have attempted to talk to the occupants of the house, especially Detective Coulter, but ERT has blocked our entry. When questioned, they would not give us a reason. Could it be that

Coulter is being held inside and interrogated by his own department?" Andrus glanced to her right. "I have little time. I have several ERT members running toward me."

The camera swung past Andrus and three ERT sprinted toward her.

"Shut that camera off or you'll be arrested," the lead Mountie yelled.

Sadie's voice broadcast over the image of the sprinting Mounties. "Since they could not arrest Coulter, they will be satisfied with arresting us." The cops were within ten feet.

The camera rolled along the ground.

Sadie shouted. "Get your hands off me. That hurts. You're breaking my arm."

Then both the video and audio went dead, and the face of the news anchor came on the screen.

"It seems we have lost the video and audio feed from Sadie Andrus," the anchor said. "We'll keep you posted on this developing story and the arrest of our news staff."

Archer stared at the screen, his eyes wide. "No. No. No. Idiots."

"You told them to shut it down," Jackson said.

"Not like that." Archer leaned on his desk and stared at the TV. "What were they thinking?"

"Maybe you should have sent out TSU."

"Don't you fucking start." Archer glared at Jackson. "Make sure the RCMP bring them here."

The door burst open again and Archer's secretary stepped in. "Sorry, again. Chief Hamilton is on the line for you."

CHAPTER THIRTY-FIVE

Brad swung the truck onto the highway and headed back to the lights of the city. The county roads crew had done an admirable job plowing the highway, but the huge flakes of snow were accumulating quickly. The truck plowed through the snow fine, but when the back tires hit the ice underneath, he fought to keep the truck under control as the back end slipped from side to side.

At the city limits, the roads were far worse. The road crews hadn't made it this far. After a few slides toward the ditch, Brad stopped and locked the four-wheel hubs. He slid back into the truck. In four-wheel drive the vehicle slipped less. He wished he'd tossed three or four hay bales in the back for added weight.

Instinct had sent him toward the city, but now he didn't know where to go. Heading to the home of anyone he knew was out. There were some recent advances in tracking credit card use, but he'd never paid attention when the fraud detectives discussed that. It just didn't interest him. Brad decided he needed to listen more and talk less. Best case was he had one night where he could use his card. In the morning, there was no doubt they would flag his bank account and credit cards.

He drove through downtown to the east end and stopped at the Army Surplus store. One stop shopping. He grabbed winter boots, several pairs of socks and gloves, a navy wool beanie, heavy lined gray and black camouflage pants and parka. He wandered around the store and selected a few additional items—one tactical knife, a four-D-cell metal Maglite, a penlight, and sunglasses.

The clerk eyed the purchases. "You heading to the arctic, buddy?"

Brad laughed. "Feels like it. Have you been outside tonight?"

"Can't say I have."

"Well, it's nasty. I'm a farmer, and I need to check the cattle in weather like this. I don't want to be discovered dead in the morning next to a frozen cow."

The clerk nodded. "Makes sense. This is the best stuff there is. You need anything else?"

Brad glanced around the shop. "Yeah." Brad set the knife blade on the counter. "I drove over my knife. Do you think it can be fixed?"

The clerk picked up the knife. "The blade is sharp. I don't think you can replace the plastic sheath or hinge, but I've got a do-it-yourself repair kit. You might be able to attach a handle or strap. I'll throw in a clip-on leather sheath."

Brad paid cash for the purchase.

Before he left the store, he changed into the winter gear. He had a few things to do before he searched for a room for the night. His stomach growled. Food first.

Brad headed down a dark back alley in Chinatown, through a heavy metal door, and up three flights of stairs. The Royal Garden Chinese Restaurant wasn't much bigger than the kitchen at Brad's farmhouse. It had tables for two dozen customers, but you'd be jammed in. Tonight, the blizzard kept most people at home. Besides himself, there was a Chinese couple across the room. The ceiling lights were dim, and a small lantern illuminated each table.

Brad sat in the back corner of the Royal Garden Chinese Restaurant in Chinatown. It was the perfect place to sit back and figure out what the heck had happened today, as well as his next steps.

Sadie was right, the food was outstanding. His chopsticks sped back and forth to Brad's mouth. He was starving. He figured he hadn't eaten in twenty-four hours. With about a dozen coffees in between.

In the corner to the left, on a shelf, sat a dated black-and-white TV. He glanced to the TV. Even Charlie's Angels couldn't keep his attention—at least not in black and white.

He cleaned his plate, leaned back, and took a large gulp of Coke. His eyes drifted to the TV. He thrust forward out of his chair and over to the TV. He increased the volume. Sadie was doing a broadcast outside his farm. He listened to her report, then saw the RCMP ERT racing toward her. The audio and video went dead.

Son of a bitch.

"That was a scene outside Detective Brad Coulter's home earlier tonight," the news anchor said. "Ms. Andrus and her cameraman were arrested. We could not speak to them, although our company lawyer is at police headquarters. We will interrupt programming as additional information becomes available."

An idea formed.

CHAPTER THIRTY-SIX

Steele slammed on the brakes and their SUV skidded sideways toward the three Mounties standing in the middle of the road. Steele threw the truck in park and they both jumped out.

"Get back in your truck," the ERT sergeant said.

"Move your fucking trucks," Steele said. "Or we'll push them out of the way."

"You're not getting past us." Two of the Mounties stepped forward, their rifles at the ready.

"You're fuckin' hilarious," Steele said. "Posturing with rifles won't intimidate us. You might bully a reporter and her cameraman. You're in shit for that."

"We don't want a fight with you," a Mountie said. "Go back to the city. You have no jurisdiction here."

A siren grew louder, and a black sedan raced toward them. The car slid to a stop. The driver's door opened.

Jackson stepped out. "What the hell is this? The shoot-out at the O.K. Corral?"

No one moved.

"You're a bunch of idiots." Jackson stepped between them and swatted the RCMP rifles down. He glared at the ERT team. "Put the fucking long guns away." He glared from Steele and Zerr to the ERT sergeant. "Make sure the cameraman and the reporter are not hidden away in your lockup. Order your men to drop the news crew at our arrest processing." He handed a radio to the ERT sergeant, who stepped away. They couldn't make out his side of the conversation. Finally, he returned.

"Pack up, boys. We're not needed."

The ERT trucks pulled away and Steele steered their SUV up the lane. Jackson followed. As they approached the house, Lobo raced around the corner, barking, fangs bared.

Steele slowly got out of the truck. "Whoa, Lobo." Steele cautiously held out a hand.

Lobo glared, hackles raised, growling. He blocked the way to the house. When any of them took a step, his barking continued. Then Annie strode around the corner, a shotgun at the ready.

"Oh, it's you three." She lowered the shotgun. "I thought Lobo and I were gonna bag us some ERT cops out of season."

"Those assholes will always be in season." Zerr headed over to Annie and kissed her. "You going to invite us inside?"

Annie glanced at Steele and Jackson. "Do I have to invite the other two?"

Zerr nodded. "I'm afraid so."

"Dang." She grabbed his hand, and they headed to the house. Everyone shed their winter gear in the entranceway. While Annie brewed coffee, the guys sat around the kitchen table.

Jackson stretched his long legs away from the table and clasped his hands behind his head. "This is a nightmare."

"How do you think Brad feels?" Annie glared from the coffee pot. "He's out there alone."

"He enjoys being alone," Steele said.

"No." Annie frowned, her eyes on the verge of tears. "He enjoys being alone *with* Lobo. There's a vast difference. Now he is completely alone." She sniffled, then grabbed the coffeepot.

Lobo wandered around the kitchen sniffing pants and socks.

"See," Annie said. "Even Lobo knows something isn't right."

"Sarge," Steele said. "Tell us what the hell is going on."

While Annie poured coffee, Jackson told them what he knew.

Annie sat, hands wrapped around the white coffee mug, and stared at the swirling steam. "That matches what Brad told me." Then she told them about helping Brad escape and the ERT team assault on the farmhouse.

"Why did Lobo think Brad was in the trunk?" Steele asked.

"Because he was." Annie grinned.

"I don't follow." Jackson sipped his coffee. "The Mounties didn't find him."

Annie smiled. "Brad's always thinking ahead. He knew either Calgary cops or the RCMP would be here. I stopped a mile from here. Brad left his T-shirt there, then headed off on foot. I drove here, into the gun sights of a half-dozen Mounties, sure Brad was in the trunk. They were pissed when he wasn't, so they took it out on Lobo and me."

"What the hell are you talking about?" Zerr asked.

Annie tried to cover her wrists, but Zerr grabbed her arm and saw the redness from the cuffs. "Son of a bitch. They're dead."

Annie pulled her hands away. "Not now, Charlie. After we help Brad." She stared at her coffee. The cup shook. "What do we do? We don't know where he is."

"He'll contact us," Steele said.

"He doesn't have a vehicle," Annie said. "I don't know how much cash he has. Every cop in the city and the RCMP are searching for him."

"Not every cop."

They hadn't heard the back door open. Briscoe strode in, shaking snow off his fake fur hat and stomping his overshoes. "I heard I could get a coffee here." He slid off his police issue parka and plopped into a chair.

Annie poured him a coffee, then got another pot brewing. "I guess none of us are sleeping tonight, so I'll keep the coffee going."

Briscoe sipped his coffee. "Ah. The lot of you look miserable, morose."

"Morose?" Steele said. "Where did you learn that word?"

"He used it properly, though," Jackson said.

Briscoe ignored them and drank coffee. "You know he's

not dead, right? You're acting like this is a wake. Get your shit together. We have to help him."

"We don't know where he is," Steele said.

Briscoe drank some coffee. His eyes sparkled. "But he knows where we are."

CHAPTER THIRTY-SEVEN

THE DESK SERGEANT HANDED SADIE A BAG OF HER BELONGINGS. "Sign here." He slid a form across the counter.

"It better all be here." Sadie glared at the sergeant as she put on her black knee-high boots, slid on her black parka and knit wool beanie, then wrapped her red silk scarf around her neck.

"Yes, ma'am."

"Don't fucking patronize me." She signed the form, grabbed her black purse, slung it over her shoulder, and stomped to the back door. She stepped out into the alley and slid on her leather gloves. Her cameraman had been released before her and went to get the van. She leaned against the outside wall in the back alley, waiting for her cameraman to pick her up. Cops came and went from headquarters. A few grinned as they passed.

Bastards.

An early sixties, rust-bucket truck drove slowly down the alley and stopped opposite her.

Now she wished there were cops in the alley. Her eyes darted up and down the alley, then to the back door. She had no problem screaming for help. But no cops were around. She thought about running. Then a head poked out the driver's window. "Sadie, get in. Now."

Coulter?

"Now."

She sprinted around the front of the truck to the passenger side. She was barely inside when the truck jerked away. The momentum forced the door shut. She grabbed the dash.

The vehicle continued down the alley, hit the ice on Sixth Avenue, and slid sideways. Brad regained control, then kept to a normal speed.

"Brad." Sadie swung in her seat to face him, but her back was jammed into the corner. "What the hell is going on?"

He glanced at her. "We need to talk."

She pushed farther away from him and crossed her arms over her chest. "Sure, now you want to talk." She gazed out the window and watched the night activity of the city. Midnight. The streets were nearly empty. She shivered at the icy air leaking through rust spots in the floorboards. She sighed. "Fine. What are we talking about? The fact I'm in a truck with a serial killer taking me who knows where to do who knows what to me."

"You wish."

Sadie rolled her eyes. "Whatever."

"Do you believe I'm the killer?"

Sadie scrutinized Brad. Her eyes narrowed and her chin quivered. Finally, she spoke. "Of course not."

"I'm being framed for the murders."

Sadie laughed, then covered her mouth with her hand. "Sorry. But that was funny coming from you. How many times have your suspects said that to you?"

Brad's cheek twitched. "Yeah. I knew you'd pick up on that."

"Why did you kidnap me?"

Brad's head swung to face her. "I offered you a ride. You accepted."

"Why are we talking? You haven't said it yet, but I'm sure you consider this conversation 'off the record.' What about your cop buddies, Steele and Zerr?"

"I can't get them involved and put their careers at risk." Brad veered south on Fifth Street. "You know they were at my farm. Archer will make sure everyone I'm close to is under surveillance. I'll bet they even checked Maggie's grave."

Sadie nodded. "But not me. I'm not one of your friends. Other than another 'scoop of the century' for me, what do you want?"

"I need a place to hide."

Sadie's eyes grew wide. "Are you out of your mind?"

"Someplace no one will search."

"Gee. Any place you have in mind?"

He glanced at her and grinned. "As a matter of fact—"

Brad parked in front of a forty-year-old sandstone apartment building on Royal Avenue. When it was first built, the rich and famous of the city lived there. They had a doorman and an elevator operator. Eventually, the doorman was replaced with a high-tech security system and the elevator operator, the only one they ever had, died five years ago, so the tenants operated the elevator themselves.

"I suppose I should be pissed you know where I live." Sadie opened the door and exited the truck.

"At one point, I worried the snipers would attack the media. So, yes, I know where you live."

"Are you sure you're not a stalker?"

"I accused you of that."

"Imagine that, two stalkers finding each other." Sadie punched in a code and a buzzer sounded. Brad opened the door and followed Sadie to the elevator. They exited on the fourth floor and headed to a corner apartment. Sadie unlocked the door and opened a sliding closet door where she hung up her parka, tossed her knit beanie onto the top shelf, and unlaced her boots. Brad eased out of his camouflage parka and boots.

Sadie prepared a pot of coffee. "I'm going to change. Make yourself at home. Not that you'd wait for my permission." She headed down a short hall. A door closed.

Brad stood at the kitchen island and surveyed the apartment. It still had its forties atmosphere. The walls were solid oak, as was the window trim. The floor was hardwood and polished to a glossy shine with several area rugs. Rather than decorate with modern furniture, Sadie had kept with the period. Two walls in the living room had enormous windows with incredible views of downtown. A third wall was covered with a full oak bookcase. The first section was filled with world history books. The second held textbooks on journalism, biographies of journalists, and a complete shelf on fashion. He grinned when he reached the third section. He recognized many of the authors' names—a shelf of Danielle Steele, *Are You There God? It's Me, Margaret* by Judy Blume, *Helter Skelter* by Vincent Bugliosi, and—Brad's eyes widened—*The Joy of Sex* by Alex Comfort.

Most notably, and certainly required reading by a journalist, *All The President's Men* by Bernstein and Woodward.

Brad sat at the kitchen table, leaned back and closed his eyes. It felt good to relax, even for a moment.

The door down the hall opened and a light patter of feet headed to the kitchen wearing extra-large Calgary Stampeders T-shirt and gray sweatpants. Sadie poured coffee into two white mugs with the CFCN logo and set them on the kitchen table. Sadie headed to the fridge and returned with cream and sugar. She scooped two spoons of sugar and two dollops of cream into her mug and stirred.

They drank in silence.

Sadie slid one leg under her and set the other foot onto the chair seat, cradling the coffee in both hands. "Lovely outfit. You getting your clothes tailored for you?"

Brad sipped the coffee and stared at Sadie. "It's a new fashion I thought I'd try."

"Don't get too used to army camouflage." She slid a loose strand of auburn hair behind her ear. "I hear prison orange is in."

Brad's eyebrows raised. "Thanks for your support."

Sadie set down her cup. "Most of the time you won't tell me diddly squat. That's fine, it's a game we play, and I accept the rules. Then today, I'm your best friend, maybe your only friend, and I'm supposed to say, 'Oh sure, Brad. Stay at my house. I trust you.'" She leaned over the table, eyes ablaze. "You have five minutes to tell me what is going on. Don't bullshit me, leave nothing out. Five minutes. If you don't convince me in five minutes, I call 911."

Brad puffed his cheeks and exhaled. "Okay. You get everything. You hold my freedom in your hands."

Sadie rolled her eyes. "Oh, for Christ's sake, drop the melodrama. Tell the story."

Brad started with the death of the dealer in September, then one a few weeks ago, and the recent murders. He thought some were related. She frowned as he talked about the evidence against him.

"That sounds like a circumstantial case."

He sat back, hands held out. "Sadie. Do you think I'm stupid?"

"What?" Sadie frowned and shook her head. "Where does that come from?"

"Am I stupid?"

"No, you're very smart, probably brilliant. What does that have to do with anything we're talking about?"

"Thank you." Brad sipped his coffee. "Do you think I'd be stupid enough to use my service pistol? That I'd drive my flashy vehicle to commit a crime?"

"You think *that* truck is fancy?" She smiled weakly. "When you put it that way. Who would do this?"

"The actual murderer."

Sadie rolled her eyes. "Of course, you'd say that."

"This murderer is devious. The murders were well planned. They were intended to appear different. We weren't supposed to connect them. But I did. This person thought far enough ahead to know they might need to set someone up for the murders. Who better to set up than the detective investigating? Some of those murders happened at previous crime scenes where I was involved."

"That implicates you further."

Brad took a deep breath, exhaled, and set the coffee mug on the table.

Sadie sat silent, staring at him.

He reached behind his back. Sadie stiffened. He set his handcuffs on the table, then placed his hands next to them. "Fine. Make your call. I won't resist."

Sadie stared at the handcuffs. The smart play was cuff him and let the cops deal with it. More than the smart play, she'd be the reporter who captured Brad Coulter. *CTV National Desk, here I come.* She headed to her living room window and stared down at Royal Avenue. She wrapped her arms around her chest. She loved the view of downtown. Royal Avenue below. Not the snobbery of Mount Royal, but not the crime land north of Seventeenth Avenue.

It was her move. The bright lights and Toronto—or the unemployment line. When she thought of it that way, how could there be any doubt.

She glanced back at the table. Brad hadn't moved. He

stared at his hands. The swagger, confidence, cockiness, and the damned sarcasm was gone. He wasn't Superman anymore. Whatever was going on, it was Kryptonite to him. Maybe the next in a lengthy line of Kryptonite. It was in his blood—he was poisoned. What the biker gangs had done. What Jeter Wolfe had put him through. What the snipers did to this city—all of it beat him up. But after getting knocked to the canvas, he got up again. This time, it wasn't the darkness and the evil of crime, it was his own department. And that, he couldn't fight.

Sadie headed back to the table. "You look awful."

Slowly, he glanced up. "Thanks."

She slid the handcuffs to him. "You might need these later. I have a spare room. You need some sleep. We'll figure this out in the morning."

CHAPTER THIRTY-EIGHT

Just before six in the morning, Sergeant Toscana wandered into the district sergeant's office and shrugged off her parka.

"Good morning, Briscoe. You're bright and early."

Briscoe was reclined in an old office chair with a steaming coffee on the metal desk. He glanced up from the newspaper.

"Toscana. How was your night?"

She grabbed the chair opposite Briscoe. "Cold, quiet, and a waste of time. We spent the night searching for Coulter. No luck. He's vanished."

Briscoe tossed the newspaper on the desk and reached for his coffee. "I heard everyone he's friends with is being watched along with their homes."

Toscana grinned. "You'll have a parade following you today."

"Probably." Briscoe sighed. "Coulter isn't stupid enough to approach me, and certainly not during daylight hours."

"So, I should keep my eye on you tonight?"

Briscoe grunted.

"This puts you in a terrible spot. Hunting your friend."

Briscoe drank his coffee, then licked his lips. "Personal feelings aside, Coulter needs to turn himself in. Let the process work. If he's innocent, justice will prevail."

Toscana shook her head and crossed her arms. "I'm not so sure I believe that."

Briscoe worked at something in his teeth with his tongue. "What do you mean?"

"You've been around a long time."

Briscoe grunted again. "Thanks. I'm not sure I can stand any more of this flattery."

Toscana leaned forward and held out her hands defensively. "I meant nothing by that, just that the court system is broken. How many times have you sat in court and watched one of your airtight cases fall apart on some technicality? Or worse still, the suspect is released from custody long before you finish the arrest paperwork?"

"I'm not sure which side you're on, Missy? That Coulter is innocent, and the courts will see that, or that even if he is guilty the courts will release him?"

"I'm just saying the courts are light on everyone." Toscana shrugged. "Guilty, not guilty, seems the same sometimes. We need a better system."

"Like France, guilty until proven innocent?"

Toscana's face brightened. "That might work."

CHAPTER THIRTY-NINE

TUESDAY MORNING, STURGEON SAT AT THE CONFERENCE TABLE next to Jackson and Griffin in Archer's office. They watched Archer pace behind his desk. Sturgeon stared at the picture of the Calgary tower at night behind Archer. While Sturgeon loved photography, he wasn't interested in technical aspects of the photo. He was doing everything he could to avoid Archer's eyes.

Chief Hamilton hadn't given Archer a choice. Hamilton wanted Internal Affairs to take over the Coulter investigation. Hamilton felt IA was best suited to deal with this.

Archer firmly disagreed and had said, "Yes. Sir." Then left the chief's office.

Sturgeon knew the conversation with Archer would not be pleasant. He'd met Griffin for coffee before they came to the meeting. Griffin was furious with Brad, which made sense. Brad had embarrassed Griffin. They were partners, but Brad had broken that bond. Griffin's hands shook as he drank his coffee. As far as he was concerned, Brad had proven his guilt by disappearing. No amount of talking could convince Griffin otherwise. He didn't accept Sturgeon's contention that Brad was under great stress. Griffin called it bullshit. If Coulter could get it together to track the snipers, then none of this was stress related.

Brad had gone over the line, gone to the dark side. They'd both seen it when he came back to work with an edge. For whatever reason, killing Wolfe hadn't been enough. Brad sometimes talked of the injustices of the court system. Brad had picked the path of a vigilante.

Archer was thinking about what Griffin had said. Sturgeon glanced toward Griffin, who leaned forward, jaw set.

Archer stopped pacing and leaned on his desk. "Let me get this straight, Griffin. You want to be the lead on the case because you believe Coulter is guilty."

"Yes, sir." Griffin's jaw was set. His eyes blazed with anger. "His actions proved it."

"He's your partner."

"No, sir, he was never a partner." Griffin inhaled and exhaled rapidly, his fists clenched. "We worked a case together, that's it. Less than a month. He's smart, but he does his own thing. He doesn't want a partner. Brad isn't the same guy he was six months ago. Not even close. The Brad we knew then would never consider being a vigilante. But the Brad who came back would."

"Maybe, but he was brilliant on the sniper case," Jackson said. "No one was close to making the connections."

Griffin leaned forward, anger in every fiber of his body. "I'm not saying he isn't smart and an excellent detective. He has slipped a cog or two in his brain. He's changed. And not in a healthy way."

Archer sighed and sat back, fingers steepled under his chin. "The chief has already assigned Internal Affairs this case."

Griffin chewed his lip and glared at Archer. "This isn't some piddly case about a cop getting free dinners at a restaurant or letting his best friend off with a traffic violation, it's multiple murders. And if you think those pissants from IA can solve this case, you're—"

Archer held up a hand and glared at Griffin. "Not another word."

"You know I'm right."

Archer clenched his jaw. "I can't argue with your logic. This is bigger than an IA investigation, but you work with Harker and Genereau and report to Jackson."

"Whoa." Jackson held up a hand. "I didn't ask to be involved. I don't want to be involved."

Archer swung on Jackson. "Oh, I'm sorry, Staff Sergeant." Archer's eyes blazed and his face flushed. "I didn't realize I had to ask permission before I assigned *my* staff sergeant to a case. And you, Sturgeon? Where do you stand?"

"The evidence is the evidence." Sturgeon shrugged. "I'm not deciding innocence or guilt. I will lead my team objectively and evaluate every piece of evidence, no matter who the suspect is."

Archer stood to his full six-foot-one height. "Imagine that. A cop taking his sworn oath seriously." He swung to Griffin. "Talk to Harker and Genereau."

Griffin stood and stomped out of the office.

Archer stared at the closed door. "Fucking incredible. One Homicide detective hunting another. This is a public confidence nightmare." Archer slumped into his chair. "Every department worldwide has gone through internal struggles, some—like the New York City Police Department—many times. It tears a department apart. This is new for us—we've been lucky. We're trusted by the public. That's going down the shitter."

"If Coulter is guilty of murder, then yes, you have a problem," Jackson said.

Archer glanced from Jackson to Sturgeon. When he spoke, his voice was low, his eyes boring into them. "I want him found and charged with the murders. The courts decide his guilt or innocence, not us."

Jackson leaned forward, his hands wide in front of him. "Chief, I'll find him, then we can talk to him."

Archer pounded a fist on his desk. "Jackson, I want Coulter arrested. Today. Sturgeon, I want you and your team to go over every piece of evidence again." Archer slumped in his chair. "Fuckin' Coulter. Pain in my ass."

Sturgeon pulled his most trusted evidence techs, Gayle and Angie, into his office and closed the door. Gayle was about five-six, with shoulder-length brown hair and sparkling eyes. Angie, a few inches shorter with blond hair and green eyes. With three of them in Sturgeon's office, there wasn't a lot of room, and only two chairs. Both Gayle and Angie stood.

"I have an important task." Sturgeon put his elbows on

his desk and rested his chin on his clutched hands. "Once I tell you what it is, if you don't want to be involved, I'll understand. I won't hold it against you."

They glanced at each other and shrugged.

"What I say next is confidential." He glanced from one lady to the other. "You talk to no one other than me. Clear?"

They nodded.

"Perfect." He sat back. "We're going over the Coulter evidence again. Right from the start, like we've never seen it before."

Angie hesitantly raised a hand. "Did we do something wrong?"

Sturgeon shook his head. "No. That's not it. When a cop is involved, we have to be sure of our conclusions."

"Coulter is your friend," Gayle said. "Do you think he's innocent?"

"He *is* my friend." Sturgeon sighed, glanced at the reports on his cluttered desk, then raised his head. "But that doesn't change what we do. The evidence will go where it goes. But I'd be lying if I said I thought he did it. That's why we will examine the evidence again. Is this a problem?"

Gayle said, "Not for me."

Angie shook her head. "Me neither."

"Great, let's get started."

CHAPTER FORTY

BRAD WOKE WITH A START. HE REACHED OVER THE SIDE OF THE bed, but Lobo wasn't there. He shook his head and cleared his eyes. Where the heck was he? He'd never seen this room before. Cream wallpaper with branches on trees with hanging birdhouses and a white comforter and pillowcases with white and pink roses. He blinked his eyes several times as if that would clear his head. He was in some kind of fashion hell. He grabbed a glass of water off the night table and drained it.

Shit.

It hit him. He was at Sadie's. Oh shit. What time was it? He didn't have his watch. He glanced at the alarm clock on the night table. It was nine in the morning. How had he slept this long? He glanced around for his newly acquired clothes. They weren't in the room. He glanced under the sheets. At least he still had his boxers. He wrapped a sheet around his shoulders and stumbled to the door. He peeked outside.

Sadie was sitting at the kitchen table, wearing the

Calgary Stampeders T-shirt and gray sweatpants, drinking coffee, reading the paper, listening to the radio news and watching the TV. How he'd slept through all that, he didn't know.

"Uh, good morning."

Sadie swung around. "Well, good morning, sunshine. We can have breakfast together and I don't have to stalk you."

"I seem to be missing my clothes."

"Oh, that. I washed them and ironed them, including the socks."

"Are you kidding?"

She sneered. "Yeah, I ironed nothing. I don't iron. That's what the dry cleaners are for. But I washed your stuff. They had a street odor to them. You'll find them in the bathroom." She pointed down the hall. "Consider a shower, as well." She went back to her coffee and paper.

Brad leaned onto the counter and stared at the mirror. He looked like shit. He must have slept at least six, maybe seven hours. He couldn't remember the last time that happened. After taking care of the toilet business, he started the shower. He let the warm water energize his neck, shoulders and down his back. He thought he heard a noise outside the shower. He peeked around the curtain. Nothing. It must have been his imagination. Then he thought about the shit he was in. No room in his brain for anything other than clearing his name.

Reluctantly, he shut off the water. He stepped out of the shower and toweled off. At first, he thought he could use a shave. Then he realized that it would add to his disguise. It would get better every day.

He dressed and headed down the hall. Sadie pointed to a mug. "Coffee for you."

Brad sat and grabbed the coffee.

Sadie increased the volume on the TV. "It's been on every hour since about 2:00 a.m." The screen said, *News Update*. The morning news anchor came on. "Good morning. We have a news update from last night. Sadie Andrus is reporting."

"Last night I received information that Detective Brad Coulter was wanted by his own police department for murder, and that a city-wide manhunt was underway."

The screen switched to the scene by the lane at Brad's house.

"Last night we were at Detective Coulter's house just outside the city limits. We were confronted by RCMP ERT members who denied us entry to the house and refused to tell us what was happening."

The video switched to the confrontation with TSU.

They watched the report in silence. Brad sipped his coffee "How long have you been awake?"

"Since about five-thirty."

"That's less than five hours sleep."

She nodded and stared at him. "It wasn't much of a sleep. Finally, I got up and stared at my phone. I reconsidered. Well, a career clarity moment. I needed to turn you in."

He nodded. "So, the cops will be here any minute?"

Sadie set her coffee mug on the table, then chewed her upper lip. "You never tried to stop me."

"Would it have helped?"

She shook her head. "No. If you'd tried, that would have settled it for me. You'd be dressed in orange."

"I don't think that's my color."

Sadie held her coffee with both hands. "No, I don't think so either." She stared at her coffee. "There's one more thing."

Brad sat back in his chair, feeling relaxed for the first time in twenty-four hours. "What's that?"

"When I called the station this morning, I heard something. I don't know how to tell you."

Brad shrugged. "Just spit it out."

Sadie licked her lips. "A reporter I know heard Sergeant Sturgeon say ballistics from at least two of the murders were matched to your gun."

Brad swung forward in his chair, spilled his coffee, and his jaw dropped. "That's not … I mean … no way."

Sadie squeezed her body as far back in the chair as she could, eyes wide.

Brad sat, frozen to the spot. Now what? "I need to get my gang together."

"Your gang? I'm sure you don't mean the Keystone Cops. Everyone you know except me is a cop. They can't help you. You told me they were all being watched. If they helped you, they'd be guilty of … well, I don't know exactly what. Assisting a fugitive or something. They'd lose their jobs."

Brad nodded. "They might, but that's their decision and I'll respect whatever they decide."

CHAPTER FORTY-ONE

ANNIE WOKE TO THE RINGING. SHE SWUNG HER LEGS OFF THE BED and into her slippers. She grabbed her housecoat and headed out of her room. The living room was littered with snoring cops. They'd talked until well after two in the morning. Couldn't one of them have answered the phone? She stepped over and around them and into the kitchen. She lifted the receiver off the wall.

"Hello." She hoped she'd hear Brad's voice.

"Good morning. Is this Annie?"

Annie glanced around the kitchen, like she'd see the person calling. She shook her head. "Yes, who is this?"

"We haven't met. I'm Sadie. I met a best friend of yours last night. Sissy."

Annie gasped. Her knees buckled. She slid into a chair. Sissy was the girl held captive with Annie in the biker's clubhouse. She was the girl who Jeter Wolfe had raped before he kidnapped Annie.

Annie and Sissy had escaped together, and what they knew helped take down the biker gangs. With the love and support of Brad and Maggie, Annie had overcome that nightmare. Sissy hadn't been as lucky. Sissy was dead. Annie wasn't shocked at the name, because it meant something. It meant Brad was okay. That was the code word they'd agreed on two years ago. Brad was with Sadie, or at least Sadie knew where he was.

Annie grabbed her chest and gasped. "Oh my gosh, I haven't heard from Sissy for quite a while. Is she doing okay?"

"Yes, she's okay. When I saw her last night, she didn't appear well. But she's a lot better this morning, and she wanted me to let you know she was okay. If you have time this morning, I'd love to meet you for coffee. Sissy gave me a few things for you."

"That would be fantastic." Annie processed the things she needed to do. "I need to shower and I'm out of the city. Where can we meet?"

"There's a new coffee shop on Seventeenth Avenue and Eighth Street. They make the most wonderful coffee."

"I'll see you there in an hour."

CHAPTER FORTY-TWO

SADIE SAT IN THE BACK CORNER OF THE COFFEE SHOP AND SIPPED her espresso. The shop still had the newly renovated smell with a heavy roasted-coffee tinge. What's old is new. The owners had gone for a fifties theme, with red-topped chrome tables and chairs and mismatched plates and mugs. Sadie couldn't care less about the décor—the coffee was amazing.

She watched the front door and the large plate-glass window. After she'd hung up, she realized she had no clue what Annie looked like, but Annie must have seen her on TV, so it was up to Annie to make contact.

As Sadie watched clients come and go, she realized Brad had taught her something. He always sat in the back corner facing the door. Sadie realized what she had missed by sitting with her back to the door. He'd even shifted his paranoia to her. She scrutinized everyone who came in and checked the streets for cops in cheap suits sitting in dark sedans.

A few times she perked up when an early twenties lady

came through the door. But none of them glanced at her. She checked the clock on the wall. 10:30. Was Annie late? Traffic heavy coming into the city? Took longer to get ready? She decided not to show?

Sadie glanced at her empty mug and headed to the counter for a refill.

When she returned to the corner table, a young lady sat where Sadie had been, with her back to the wall, sipping a drink. Her blond hair was pulled back into a ponytail. Her eyes darted around the room while keeping Sadie in her sight. Her hands were flat on the table, eyes sizing up Sadie.

"I'm Sadie."

"I know."

"Are you Annie?"

She nodded.

"You took my seat." Sadie cocked her head.

"I know." Annie grinned. "I've seen you on TV a few times. You're serious when you're on the air."

Sadie sat across from Annie. "I'm serious all the time."

Annie sipped her drink. "I doubt that."

"Why?" Sadie reached for her coffee.

"If you were serious all the time, Brad wouldn't be interested in you."

Sadie's hand stopped with her drink halfway to her mouth. "What?"

"Oh, come on. Girl to girl." Annie leaned over the table. "Surely that can't come as a surprise to you."

"He … he treats me like a necessary evil."

"He's never liked the press, that's true. For some reason, he's making an exception for you."

"Oh, I doubt that." Sadie sipped the coffee. "Brad is guarded about what he tells me."

Annie grinned. "But he tells you stuff."

"Sure." Sadie shrugged. "Not career-defining scoops, although god knows I've tried."

Annie laughed. "I always thought it was guys who were clueless." She shook her head. "He's in trouble, he could be charged with multiple murders, and who does he go to for help? Not me. Not his best friends. You."

"I don't think he had a lot of options."

"True. But he would never go to someone he didn't trust."

Sadie stared at the table. "I nearly reported him last night. Again this morning."

"But you didn't." Annie sipped her drink. "He knew you wouldn't."

"I'm not so sure. He was defeated last night. I got a feeling that if they arrested him, he'd be okay with it. That he didn't care anymore."

"And this morning?"

Sadie sipped her coffee. "The sleep did him good."

"Sleep?" Annie grinned.

"Yes, sleep." Sadie glared. "That's it."

"If you say so." Annie's grin widened.

"Enough with the chitchat." Sadie sat forward. "Brad told me about the code and what it means to you."

Annie nodded and stared at her mug. "It's crazy we didn't need to use it over the past eighteen months." Annie's eyes clouded over, then she stared out the window. "How much can a person take? How many times can their life go to shit and they're expected to jump back up?"

"Brad said you've been through some horrible stuff," Sadie said softly.

Annie's eyes scrunched. "I wasn't talking about me. Brad. Is he safe?"

"He's safe … for now. I don't think anyone will search for him at my place. But he's already going crazy. He wants to get out and clear his name."

Annie stared over Sadie's shoulder. "He can't go out until dark."

"He knows that. I get the feeling he doesn't enjoy being cooped up."

Annie snorted. "He doesn't."

Sadie sipped her coffee. "How's Lobo?"

"Wondering where his dad is."

"Brad is lost without him."

"Lobo is his support, his constant," Annie said. "That dog is fine tuned to his emotions. Now what? As much as it's a pleasure to meet you and have a chat, there's an enormous problem to solve."

Sadie set her mug on the table and leaned forward. Her voice dropped to a whisper. "There's a place where Brad takes Lobo for a swim when it's warmer. Tell Steele and Zerr to be there at midnight."

Annie nodded, set a wrapped present on the table. "Please give this to Sissy."

"A birthday present?"

"Better." Annie stood and headed out of the restaurant.

CHAPTER FORTY-THREE

BRAD STOOD BEHIND THE CURTAINS, STARING AT DOWNTOWN. HE knew cops out there were searching for him. They wouldn't find him. But staying in this apartment wasn't helping clear his name. He needed to find the killer. Something he'd been unable to do when he had free rein of the city and all the police resources at his fingertips. Staring out the window wasn't accomplishing anything.

He sat at the kitchen table and dumped out the contents of the knife repair kit. It was a mix of screws, miniature screwdrivers, glue, a slim container of a cleaning solvent and a tiny sharpening stone. He examined his blade. None of this stuff would help much. He used the stone to grind out a few nicks in the blade. He checked the kitchen and found a junk drawer with some white rope. He fashioned a loop out of the rope and glued it to the blunt end of the blade. That was the best he could do. He set the blade next to the leather sheath. Not that he needed that blade, he was carrying another tactical knife he'd bought at the store. Working on the knife was about exercising his brain. Now what? He clipped his new tactical knife behind his belt and, with nothing better to do with it, slid the leather sheath and broken knife into his boot.

Sadie had a desk that faced the window. He sat and searched for a pen and paper. He opened the drawer in the middle of the desk. Plenty of pens. He pulled out a couple. Pens that were given out for promotions—Calgary Herald, CFAC TV, CKQR radio and CFCN News, to name a few. The top side drawer was filled with, well, junk. Not even worth searching for paper.

He opened the second drawer—it was filled with notebooks. He picked one up and opened it to the front page, dated from June. It was a journal of the sniper case. More detailed than any notes Brad had written. The notes covered the crimes, locations, who she interviewed, questions she had about the case, names of people she wanted to interview. He found his name with red stars beside it. Well, she'd done her best to interview him. As interested as he was, he closed the notebook and put it back.

He opened the third drawer. It held a package of looseleaf paper and grabbed a handful of sheets. Then a file folder caught his eye. Good Brad said, "Close the drawer." Bad Brad said, "Ooo. Cool." He set the file on the corner of the desk.

For the next ninety minutes, he wrote everything he could remember about the cases. It wouldn't be as complete as his wall charts, but it kept him busy going over everything again. When he was done, he leaned back and rubbed his eyes. He rocked back in the chair and spun it, peering around the apartment.

When he'd swung back to the desk, the file folder caught his attention. He opened the folder and read. He flipped the pages faster and faster. When he finished reading, he closed the folder and slid it back in the drawer. He wasn't sure how he felt about what he'd read.

CHAPTER FORTY-FOUR

Steele shifted in the driver's seat of the Suburban. No matter which way he moved, something on his belt caught. They grabbed hamburgers at Peters' Drive-In and parked facing the tattoo parlor.

Steele stared at the converted house, willing a witness to walk out.

"You know they boarded the place, right?" Zerr sucked hard at the straw in his milkshake.

Steele dipped a few French fries into the ketchup up to his knuckles. He absently stuck the fries and his fingers in his mouth. "The girls in the porn den were the witnesses who said they saw a black Firebird outside when they escaped. But the cops didn't pick them up until an hour later, then brought them back to the scene. Do you think that's when they saw Brad's car?"

"Possibly." Zerr's cheeks pulled inward as he fought with the straw and shake.

Steele glanced over. "Wait until it melts. You'll give yourself an aneurism."

"I won't admit defeat."

Steele rolled his eyes and dipped fries in the ketchup. "They hadn't committed a crime, so they were released. Initially, they were picked up five blocks east and six blocks north. It can't be random. They were going somewhere specific."

Zerr stabbed the straw repeatedly into the shake.

"Would you put that down?"

Zerr stopped mid-stab, then set the shake down. "I was listening."

"How about offering some suggestions?"

"Sure. The address they gave was fake, but they were found a few blocks from that address. So, Watson, the address was fake, but not the area."

"That's brilliant, Sherlock. How does that help us?"

Zerr took an enormous bite of hamburger, then pointed the burger at Steele. "They're staying, living, squatting, whatever, in that area." Bits of hamburger and bun sprayed. "As horrible as it is, they're hookers. Not much prostitution happening on these streets. We have two options. First, we hang around that area tonight and see if we find them walking to catch a bus or cab. Or second, we cruise the stroll tonight. We can tell the downtown units to keep their eyes open for them. Shouldn't be hard to spot a pack of hookers."

Steele munched the fries. He pointed to Zerr with a fry. "We could do both. We let the downtown guys know we're searching for them, and we'll hang around up here. If they show up downtown, we're five minutes away. If they're up here, we find them."

Zerr grabbed the fry and popped it in his mouth. "Then what?"

"They lied," Steele said. "They didn't see a Firebird when they left, or they saw it when the cops brought them back. Or someone told them to say they saw the car."

"Who'd tell them that?"

Steele rolled his eyes. "The killer."

"Why?"

"Because, Sherlock, it's all part of framing Brad. The audio from the video that we couldn't make out said to tell something to the cops. I bet that was it."

Zerr chewed his hamburger and stared at the tattoo parlor. "That's elaborate."

Steele swiveled in his seat toward Zerr. "Not if the plan all along was to frame him."

"Okay, say I go along with that. Who's the killer?"

"That, my friend, is what we have to figure out."

Zerr nodded and sucked on the straw. "I'm in. Where do we start?"

Steele dipped the last of his fries. "I don't have a clue."

CHAPTER FORTY-FIVE

Brad heard steps in the hallway. He eased away from the desk, then stepped to the hinge side of the door and waited. A key entered the lock, then the deadbolt retracted. The knob rotated, the door opened, and a shadow stepped past. Brad shouldered the door shut.

Sadie screamed and dropped a box. Brad clamped his hand over her mouth. "It's me." He let go.

She swung around and punched him on the jaw. The blow caught him off guard and he stepped back into the wall.

"Don't ever fucking do that again." Her glare was icy cold. Her eyes flashed bolts of lightning.

He held his hands out. "Sorry, I need to be cautious."

Sadie stepped over to him and grabbed his shirt lapels. "Who the hell did you think had a light footstep and opened the door with a key? TSU? They don't fucking knock. You know that."

"Sadie, I'm sorry. You're right. My mistake."

She pushed him against the wall. "What?"

"I said I'm sorry."

She let him go. "That's better. I like it when a man apologizes and grovels."

She spun away from him, removing her red wool cap and jacket, untied her boots and kicked them into the closet. She strode past Brad and down the hall to her bedroom and slammed the door. His brain was still trying to figure out what just happened. Was she pissed at him or not?

He picked up the parcel wrapped in birthday paper. A tag had the name *Sissy* on it.

He took the box to the desk and opened it. Inside, packed in wax paper, was his first Browning Hi-Power 9mm and a holster that he'd used in TSU. Tucked underneath was a CZ75 9mm pistol in an ankle holster, and two boxes of 9mm ammunition. He grinned. *Thank you, Annie.*

When the Gypsy Jokers and Satan's Soldiers were at war two years ago, Brad had feared Maggie might be a target. So, for her birthday, he bought her a CZ75 and Briscoe had trained her to shoot. She'd killed two armed men holding her parents hostage. Now the gun he bought to protect Maggie might be the weapon that protected him. *Thank you, Maggie.*

He set the guns back in the box and closed the lid. Then rifled through the dozen pages of notes. He'd started with the stabbing earlier in the year, the hesitation stabbing. The next murder was the dealer. No hesitation this time. What changed? How did the killer gain confidence? Training? But how do you train for that? Military operation? Possibly. Where was the Airborne deployed? A reason to be away for a month. Some of Giles' and Torres' friends. Angry ex-military with attitudes. Or deployed Airborne, with bigger attitudes. The gap between the first two killings was because of deployment and the killer was back for an extended time.

That explained the dealer murder, and the killings at the tattoo parlor.

But none of this explained the knowledge of homicide investigation, how evidence is gathered and preserved, or the intricate planning of setting him up. That practically shouted cop. Yet combining the characteristics of the military with the police procedure knowledge brought up a handful of suspects—and if it wasn't him, then it was his friends, Steele and Zerr. Not a chance. Jackson? No way.

There were other cops who'd had the tactical training, but except for the newest team, Brad knew them all. Knew them well. What reason could they have for setting him up?

He sat back and flipped through his notes again. There was no bolt of clarity. He set the notes aside and slid a half-dozen clean sheets of paper in front of him. He tapped the pages with his pen, reviewing the evidence against him.

Dog Hair
He was always covered in dog hair.

Car at the Scene
Not possible.

At Maggie's grave. No proof. No alibi.

Death of Biker Arnie Fletcher &
Vinnie Bevan Attack on Girlfriend
Coincidences, but there's no such thing as coincidences.

Bullets Matched to Gun
Not a chance.

The ballistic match was the most damning evidence. He

didn't understand how this was possible. Aside from the fact that if he were the killer, which he wasn't, he'd never use his service pistol. Not that he'd say this out loud, but he had daily access to guns from shitheads on the street. None of them were traceable. So why use his own gun to commit a crime and risk having it tracked back to him? Why have that gun on him when Archer asked for it?

If anyone but Sturgeon had verified the ballistics, he'd have shouted that they tainted the evidence. But he couldn't deny Sturgeon's results.

He sat back in the chair and chewed the pen. His gun was the murder weapon. But it wasn't. He knew the feel of that gun. The grips fit into his hand like a handcrafted glove. He would know in a second if someone had switched guns.

The grips could be switched, but that was a lot of work and Brad's gun was never out of his sight, unless it was locked up, either at home, in his locker at work, or at arrest processing.

His work locker was the logical choice for tampering with his gun. But he couldn't remember the last time he used the locker. He hadn't worked out at headquarters in six months. There's no way this was planned that long ago. Unless it was?

He felt liquid in his mouth and then a horrible taste. He wiped his lips with the back of his hand and it came away blue. *Shit.* He'd chewed through the pen.

He raced to the kitchen sink and grabbed a handful of paper towels. He stuffed them into his mouth, then spit the rest into the towels. He ran the water, rolled his head under the tap and let the warm water run into his mouth, then out into the sink. He stuffed additional paper towel into his mouth, then rinsed again.

"Are you okay?"

He twisted his head toward the voice.

Sadie was standing beside the sink, a quizzical expression on her face.

"You are weird." She shook her head and headed to the front door. "I'm going for a jog. Keep doing whatever it is you're doing. I'll be back in an hour."

From under the tap, Brad watched her leave. At least it gave him an opportunity to clean up. He headed to the bathroom and stared at his image in the mirror. The left side of his lips and cheek were blue. He grabbed a bar of soap and scrubbed. Soap seeped into this mouth. He gagged and filled his mouth from the tap. After five minutes the blue was faint, and his cheeks were red and sore.

Shit. Shit. Shit.

He started the shower. He used soap and shampoo to get rid of the last of the ink. The bathroom was a cloud of steam. He wrapped a towel around his waist, opened the door and headed to the bedroom. He grabbed the bag on the bed, the shopping Sadie had done for him this morning. Underwear, socks, black T-shirts, black jeans, black sneakers, black coat and a black wool beanie?

She'd also picked up some toiletries. He debated if he should shave. Probably not. He grabbed the toothbrush, globbed some paste onto the bristles, and headed back to the bathroom. Although it was merely a few steps, he heard the deadbolt retract and the door open.

Sadie stepped in. They were face to face. Sadie in sweats and a hoodie. Brad in a towel.

Sadie tossed her keys into a glass bowl by the door. "By all means. Make yourself at home."

"Shit. I'm sorry. I'm just used to, well, other than Lobo, you see—"

"Forget it. But finish quick. I need to get ready to go to work." Her jaw clenched. "I'm not used to sharing either." She stomped to her bedroom and shut the door—not a slam, but damned close.

Brad spit out the toothpaste, rinsed the sink and went back to the room. He changed quickly and stuffed the clean clothes and toiletries into a gym bag. He grabbed, his notes, some fresh paper, and a handful of new pens. He started to leave but stopped. He grabbed the guns and ammunition out of the box, then loaded the guns and slipped spare magazines in the parka pockets. He slid the Hi-Power into his holster and slipped it into the small of his back. The CZ and holster were attached to his right leg. He grabbed his broken tactical knife, was about to toss it back on the table, then clipped it his left boot.

Brad stepped out of the apartment building into familiar territory. For four years he'd patrolled this area. He knew it like the back of his hand, day or night.

He followed Royal Avenue to Eighth Street, then headed north across Seventeenth Avenue. At Fifteenth Avenue he saw the perfect place to stop. He entered the Dairy Queen and ordered lunch. Seated in the back corner, he tore into his burger, hungrier than he'd realized. As he ate, he pulled out his notes, then tossed them aside. The bigger problem was who was doing the killing and why were they framing him.

Were they two separate problems that came together? The murders started before he was involved. A vigilante with a plan. Then, by luck of the draw, and out of boredom, he investigated.

As he drank his Coke, he worked on a plan and came up with two objectives—avoid the police and figure out who was framing him. To stay out of jail, he'd need to think like a criminal—which, technically, he was.

At what point did the killer target him? What was it he did that scared the killer and caused the killer to add Brad to the plan? It was brilliant. While the police hunted for Brad, the killer wasn't under suspicion. No one was hunting anyone other than Brad. Would the murders continue? Why not, if Brad was on the loose? In fact, if another homicide occurred, it would be even better for the actual perpetrator. He had no alibi. Not even a bad alibi.

CHAPTER FORTY-SIX

Jackson burst into Sturgeon's office and slumped into a chair.

Sturgeon glanced up. "You and Coulter, neither of you learned to knock. What the heck do you want?"

Jackson stretched out his long frame and placed his hands behind his head.

"Christ," Sturgeon said. "You two even sit the same way. You bored?"

"Staff Sergeant in Homicide isn't that busy of a job. Being the sergeant in charge of one cop—Coulter—shouldn't be that difficult."

Sturgeon raised an eyebrow. "But."

Jackson leaned forward. "How the hell does he do it? He's always in shit."

"The shit finds him, he doesn't go looking."

"Maybe," Jackson said. "But Christ, a vigilante?"

"You don't believe that?"

"No. You?"

Sturgeon hesitated.

Jackson's eyes widened. "Spill it. What have you found?"

Sturgeon shrugged. "Just the stuff you already know. The evidence points to Coulter. No matter how many times we analyze, it comes back the same."

"You've known him a long time. Is it possible?"

Sturgeon shook his head. "Even with Maggie dying, I don't see Brad doing the murders. He may tiptoe on the line, but he'd never cross over this far."

"I don't know." Jackson pursed his lips. "He was a long way over the line when he forged the psychologist's note to come back to work."

"Sure. But he came back to work, not to go rogue."

Jackson's eyes narrowed. "So you say."

They sat in silence for a few minutes.

"What do you think he's doing?" Jackson asked.

Sturgeon gazed around his office. "Clearing his name ... I hope."

Jackson fumbled around in a shirt pocket until he found a toothpick. He slid the toothpick from one side of his mouth to the other. "He doesn't have a lot of resources to do that. He can't use his friends."

"Are you sure?" Sturgeon wrinkled his brow.

"Shit." Jackson sprung forward and spit out a piece of toothpick, eyes wide. "Have you talked to him? Are you helping him?"

Sturgeon held up his hands. "I have no clue where he is, and I haven't spoken to him."

Jackson sat back, nodded and chewed on the toothpick. "He'd figure out a way to contact his friends, though."

Sturgeon shrugged. "I suppose so. But Griffin and his IA buddies have everyone under surveillance."

Jackson snorted. "Griffin is a great cop, but the other two?"

"They're wasting their time if they think Brad's friends will lead them to him. One of two things will happen. He solves the murders, or he turns himself in. But if he doesn't want to be found, they won't find him."

CHAPTER FORTY-SEVEN

BRAD SHIVERED AS HE SAT ON THE GROUND AGAINST THE boulder and listened to the Bow River flow past. The sun had set hours ago. He'd driven east and parked the truck. He'd hiked through a playground and into the east end of Bowness Park, better known as the 7 Bees.

This was where he and Lobo had come on daily runs for four years so Lobo could swim and fetch rocks. Later, it was the place he brought Maggie—then it was their spot. He felt the chill of the wind and shivered. Minus twenty-five degrees Fahrenheit with a wind chill close to minus thirty-five. Why didn't they just say minus thirty-five? He wrapped his arms around his chest. Military winter gear—bullshit.

There wasn't a day he didn't miss Maggie. After she died, he and Lobo had spent hours here every day. Sometimes late into the night. He didn't want to leave. But it became a place of sorrow—of depression. Then he was worried that one day he would come here and go to Maggie. He couldn't do that to Lobo, but ...

His friends were around, but he'd never felt so alone. He didn't believe in bad luck, but there was something, some aura around him that got people hurt. He should be able to protect them, but he couldn't, didn't. He'd been wrong to bring Sadie into this. He'd rectify that.

He leaned back closer to the rock and brought his knees to his chest, then circled his knees with his arms. He was in as tight of a ball as he could be. Small, a mere speck in the universe.

His head lifted. Someone was crashing down the path through the trees. *Shit. Shit.* Somehow, they'd found him. But damn, they were making a lot of noise. Brad rolled and faced the noise, drew his pistol and pointed around the left side. If they were coming from the west, then there had to be approaching coming from the east. What a stupid spot to be. He had no escape.

The crashing grew closer, then he heard the panting. The dark shape came over the top of the boulder and pounced on him.

Brad was knocked to the ground with Lobo planting slobbery kisses over his face.

"Lobo, enough. Out."

Lobo had no intentions of stopping. He kept his paws on Brad's shoulder, the slobbering getting worse. Two dark figures stood over them.

"Should we call Lobo off?" Steele asked.

"He's trying to lick off those wisps of a beard," Zerr said.

"Give them another minute," Steele said.

Finally, Brad rolled out from under Lobo and stood. "Lobo scared the shit out of me." Lobo raced around his legs.

"How is that possible?" Steele asked. "He was making more noise than an elephant."

Brad dusted the snow off his clothes. "I thought Griffin and IA had found me."

"You set up a meeting through that reporter and then you're surprised we're here?" Steele asked.

"He's tired." Zerr grinned.

Steele cocked his head. "From what?"

"Last night."

"Don't fuckin' go there," Brad hissed.

"Me thinks he doth protest too much," Zerr said.

Steele smirked at Zerr. "Annie said Sadie had a special glow about her."

"Are you two comedians finished?" Brad glared at his friends. "Nothing happened."

"Great idea. Plead the fifth," Zerr said.

"That's just in the US, numbnuts." Steele cocked his head. "Hey Charlie, you know what my question is?"

"What would that be, Sam?"

"If our dear friend Brad spent the night at Sadie's, then why the heck *didn't* something happen?"

"I believe he has lost his super power over women," Zerr said.

Brad smacked Zerr on his back. "If you two idiots are about done, whether my sex life is on or off is not the issue. I'm framed for murder. I have to clear my name. Are you two going to help me or audition for Saturday Night Live?"

"Hadn't thought of that," Steele said.

Brad glared. "Bring me up to date. What happened today?"

"Where to start," Zerr said. "Sturgeon matched ballistics to your gun."

"Yeah, I heard that. It's bullshit."

"The chief ordered Archer to bring Internal Affairs onto the case," Steele said.

"Ain't that fuckin' lovely," Brad said.

"It gets better," Steele said.

"Or worse," Zerr muttered.

Brad glanced from one to the other.

Steele frowned. "Griffin went to Archer's office and asked to be the lead on your case."

"Seriously?"

"Kid you not." Zerr stamped his feet and rubbed his arms. "He'll be working with Detectives Genereau and Harker from IA."

"Oh, shit. They hate me."

"They might have reason to," Zerr said.

"As I recall, you called them fucking idiots and stormed out of their interview," Steele said. "Archer had to intervene to save your ass."

Brad frowned. "I don't remember it that way."

"They already hauled us, Briscoe, and Annie in for the third-degree interviews."

"Sorry about that," Brad said.

"Are you kidding?" Zerr said. "Most fun I've had in a long time. They forgot that in the military I trained on evading and enduring interrogation. I spun them in so many circles they'll be dizzy for a week."

"Annie said she messed with them as well," Steele said. "Sturgeon has his two best techs going over the evidence to see if there's any way it's false or tampered with. Your picture is in every cruiser, shown at every briefing, in every newspaper, and on TV. You're a regular celebrity."

"Shit. I guess I should have expected that."

"Jeez, it's cold by the river." Zerr shivered and rubbed his right leg. "You couldn't think of a warm place to meet?"

"Muffin," Steele said. "Archer is doing the right things. He's getting immense pressure from the chief. They've got your farm, Annie's apartment, Briscoe's house, and Maggie's grave under surveillance."

"That's hardly original thinking," Brad said.

"They've got guys following us," Steele said. "It's fun leading them all over the city until we want to ditch them. That takes about fifteen seconds. They follow Briscoe home. Even at work he's got someone tailing him."

"He's not gonna like that," Brad said.

Steele grinned. "Oh, yeah. He enjoys messing with them by racing up Fourth Street and into the cemetery. They follow and then block all the exits. Briscoe sits there for about ten minutes, then leaves. They can't get the roadblocks out of the way fast enough, and he waves at the cops as he drives around them."

"Did you bring the stuff?" Brad asked.

"Yup." Steele swung a duffel bag in front of Brad.

"You got everything?"

Sam shrugged. "Annie gave us the list—older clothes for the homeless style, but not the 'jeez, you stink' kind. Binoculars, notebooks, cash, dimes for the payphone—everything."

"Where are you sleeping tonight?" Zerr asked.

Brad said, "I know a place."

"The accommodations of last night didn't work out?" Zerr asked.

"Too many people are getting caught in my wake. It was a mistake last night. I'm not putting Sadie or anyone else in danger."

"We'll find you someplace to hide," Zerr said.

Brad shook his head. "You guys are already too involved. Better if you don't know where I am. If I don't figure this out soon, I'll have to turn myself in."

"We're a long way from that happening," Zerr said.

"Maybe." Brad shrugged. "I need to find the hookers. Something's not right with what they said."

Steele nodded. "We thought that, as well. When we leave here, that's what we'll do. Leave it to us."

Zerr tossed over a plastic bag. "Subs, milk, water, juice, and toothbrush and paste."

"How do we get ahold of you?" Steele asked.

"You don't, too risky," Brad replied. "We meet here every night around nine. If either of us are followed, it's off. Otherwise, I'll get messages to you through Sadie and Annie."

"Reconsider your options," Zerr said. "You were safe at Sadie's place."

"That's a last resort." Brad clipped a leash onto Lobo's collar. He knelt and roughed up Lobo's head. "Be a good boy." Brad handed the leash to Steele, grabbed his stuff and headed out of the park to Lobo's frantic barking.

CHAPTER FORTY-EIGHT

BRAD PARKED BEHIND THE STONE-AND-BRICK BUILDING. A SINGLE light shone from a window facing the back parking lot. Brad sat in the truck staring at the window, wondering if this was a good idea. Maybe not the best, but he was out of options. After he'd left the park, he'd never felt so alone. Leaving Lobo behind was the hardest. Especially when Brad needed him.

A shadow passed over the window. Brad opened the truck door and headed to the church. He hesitated at the back door, then knocked. Not his usual, 'police' knock, but a friendly, hesitant knock. He heard noises from inside, then the door opened.

"Reverend Branton," Brad said. "I don't know if you remember me, but I was—"

"Of course, I remember you, Detective." Branton's smile was wide. His blue eyes sparkled. "I don't typically get visitors at this time of night. Is everything okay?"

"Would you mind if I came inside?"

"Not at all." Branton stepped aside. "Where are my manners? Please, come in." Branton, wearing a powder blue button-down shirt, navy pants and black wing tip oxfords led Brad down a short hall to an office with an antique desk littered with papers, books and magazines. "I'm working on a sermon for this Sunday. Doing research." Branton pointed to one of two recliners. "Please, have a seat." Branton hesitated at the other chair. "Can I offer you a coffee? Water?"

"I'd love a coffee. I know it's late."

"No problem. I have a pot on. I do my best work at night."

A few minutes later, Branton was back with two steaming mugs of coffee.

"Most cops I know take their coffee black. I made an assumption." Branton handed a coffee to Brad and sat.

"Good call." Brad sipped the drink and sighed. "That is what I needed."

Branton sat back and sipped his coffee. His soft eyes observed Brad.

They sat in silence for several minutes, neither willing to disturb the relaxed atmosphere.

"I don't watch a lot of TV," Branton said. "But from what I've watched, you are famous—or is it infamous?"

Brad slid forward to the edge of his chair. "I'm sorry. I'm putting you in a compromising situation."

Branton waved him back down. "Priest and parishioner confidentiality."

"You're not a priest and I'm not your parishioner."

Branton chuckled. "Minor details." He held his arms

wide. "This is a house of God. There's a reason we call it a sanctuary. You are safe here." He sipped his coffee and crossed his legs. "How can I help?"

For the first time in a long time, Brad felt comfortable, at peace. Mandatory sessions with the police psychologist Hans Keller had been adversarial. Talking with a psychologist he'd picked, Darlene Fricker, had gone better. He leaned back in the comfortable chair and closed his eyes. Then he started talking about Maggie.

Branton listened intently, never interrupting, eyes locked on Brad, fingers folded in his lap. Brad slumped in the chair when he'd finished his story.

Branton let a few quiet minutes pass. "Would you like me to offer my observations?"

Brad nodded.

"For someone so young, you have experienced more than 99.9 percent of people experience in a lifetime. Your chosen profession guarantees that. Your personal loss is extreme. One thing you haven't mentioned is your belief in God."

Brad leaned forward, but Branton waved him off with a smile.

"That doesn't matter," Branton said. "I'm not here to save or convert you. Suffice to say, you came here for sanctuary. If you believe in God, your faith is questioned. 'How could a loving God allow this to happen?' If you don't believe in God, then you believe you are the unluckiest person in the world. Either way, the pain is real and devastating. The road to recovery or acceptance is long, and each person travels that path at their own pace. Some believe in the Kübler-Ross Grief

Cycle. The theory is that we go through five stages of grief—denial, anger, bargaining, depression, acceptance. I'm not sure I believe it is as simple as that, but it's as good of a model as any. Are you with me so far?"

Brad nodded. What Branton said made sense. It surprised Brad he was so far down the path, if he was. When he first woke in the hospital and was told Maggie didn't make it, he'd been in denial. Forging documents so he could come back to work appeared to be bargaining. On his first full shift he lost it on the asshat who beat his girlfriend. He was angry. When he was suspended just when the sniper case had some leads, he hit depression. If he wasn't depressed, then what was left?

"I reached bargaining before anger," Brad said.

Branton shrugged. "It's a model. Each person will work their way through the stages in their own order, in their own time. From what you've told me, you are well down the path, past denial, anger, bargaining and depression. Where does that leave you? Acceptance."

Brad felt his gut clench. His mouth went dry, and he held his breath. Acceptance? Could he accept Maggie's death? It didn't feel right that acceptance was the last step.

Branton read his mind. "Have you realized that acceptance may not be the last step?"

Brad's head jerked up. "That's exactly what I was thinking."

"I have a theory on that." Branton shrugged, and his blue eyes sparkled. "Just a theory, or as some call it, my opinion. Some people will tell you that you must move on. I don't accept that. Moving on seems to mean leaving everything in the past, buried, never to be remembered. I believe you need to move forward. You don't forget the past, you honor the memories you want to, you don't let the awful memories weigh you down, and you forge a fresh path. Perhaps the road less traveled. I'm rambling and giving a sermon. I apologize."

"No need to apologize. It makes total sense. More sense than three months of counseling. I should have come to you first."

"You came here when the time was right."

Brad smiled. "Interesting, the circumstances that led me here."

"Can I be forgiven for saying, 'God works in mysterious ways'?"

"I don't believe in coincidences. I'll accept the mysterious ways theory."

Branton stood, grabbed Brad's mug and headed to the kitchen. Moments later he was back with two tumblers. "I hope you like whiskey."

"I'm acquiring a taste."

They sipped in silence. For the moment, the weight he'd been carrying was lifted off his shoulders.

Finally, Branton said, "I am a man of God, but I read the newspapers and watch the news. You're in a lot of trouble."

Brad talked about his current situation, being wanted for multiple murders by his own police service.

Branton let a quiet moment pass, then leaned forward in his chair. "Did you commit the murders?"

Brad gasped. "Of course not."

"Then you have nothing to fear." Branton's tone was light, welcoming, accepting.

Brad drank the last of the whiskey. "I need to go." He set the glass down and stood.

Branton waved him back to the chair. "Sit. I'll refill your whiskey. You shouldn't drive."

CHAPTER FORTY-NINE

A NNIE SAT IN BRAD'S OVERSTUFFED CHAIR WITH LOBO AT HER feet. She absently chewed on a sandwich and stared unseeing at the TV. When the eleven o'clock news came on, she jumped out of the chair and increased the volume. Lobo rolled onto his back and groaned.

"Good evening, and welcome to the CFCN News. We have a report from Sadie Andrus who, last night, reported that police had launched a manhunt for Detective Brad Coulter. Sadie, do you have an update for us?"

"Thanks, Todd. As you mentioned, last night we received word that Detective Coulter was a suspect in the recent murders. Police have been tight-lipped."

The last portion of the video where Sadie and the cameraman are knocked to the ground played with Sadie's voiceover.

"As you can see, the police did not want us anywhere near the scene. The local media have requested a press conference, but so far, the police have declined. However, I have information from an excellent source that Coulter may not be guilty of the murders. In fact, the source suggests Coulter has been framed. Knowing his department does not support him, he is working alone to clear his name."

"That is a bizarre twist to a bizarre story," the news anchor, Todd, said. "Sadie, did your informant give any reason Coulter would be framed for these murders?"

"Good question, Todd. I wasn't given that information."

"Incredible story. Thank you, Sadie."

Annie stared dumbfounded at the screen. Sadie had put her career on the line. Now all Brad had to do was clear his name, and his and Sadie's careers would be saved. If not, one would go to jail and the other to unemployment.

The apartment was in darkness when Sadie entered. She tossed her keys in the bowl, switched on the lights and checked the rooms. There was no sign of Brad. She knew he'd been upset or pissed off or some other irrational male emotion. She returned to the closet and hung up her red jacket and tossed her wool cap on the shelf. She leaned against the wall and untied her boots and tossed them toward the closet.

She'd had difficulty keeping her mind on the news today. All the coverage about Brad and the murders took center stage, and her bosses were smart enough to know she had inside information. Not that she'd shared it, but they'd made her do features all day on the murders and Brad's career as a cop. At least she could temper some information. The other stations were less sympathetic. Wolves circling the wounded animal.

Then her boss thought it would be a marvelous idea for Sadie to do the late-night news. It had taken all her energy to portray the perky news reporter they wanted. She'd left the station after taping the show.

Sadie thought about changing out of her tan skirt and black knit shirt, but poured a whiskey and sat on the couch, swirling the glass before taking a sip. Her eyes spotted a piece of paper with her name scrawled on the front. She swung her legs off the couch, grabbed the note, then sat down. Two sips of whiskey later, she flipped the note open.

Sadie,

Thanks for the hospitality.

That is a great tip about the Central Library. I'll check it out tomorrow afternoon.

Tell Annie I'm off on another adventure.

Will contact soon.

Sissy

Something had happened while she was on her jog. Did he think she told the cops he was here? Did he discover something new? No, it was something else. What was the library reference? She tossed back the whiskey, drew her black-stockinged legs under her and closed her eyes.

The ringing phone startled her. Sadie switched on the coffee table light and grabbed the phone. "Hello."

"Hi, Sadie. It's Annie. Sorry to call so late, but I'm worried about Sissy. Is she okay?"

"Hi, Annie." Sadie stretched and rubbed her eyes. "I

haven't seen Sissy since early this afternoon. She left a note. She's off on an adventure."

"I thought she was staying at your place for a few nights. You know until she got things worked out."

"Did her classmates meet her tonight? Did they give her the package?"

"I haven't heard from them. That's why I thought I'd check with you. I thought she was back there with you."

"She's in a difficult situation. Boy trouble and all." Sadie swung her legs to the rug and leaned forward. She grabbed her glass, then silently cursed that it was empty.

"In unrelated news, Internal Affairs interviewed me, Zerr, Steele, and Briscoe today."

"That must have been fun."

"It was. I got Detective Griffin."

"Isn't he Brad's partner?"

"You wouldn't think so, the way he acted. He's out for Brad's hide."

"You're kidding." Sadie stretched the telephone cord as far as she could and was just able to get her hand on the whiskey bottle.

"Nope."

"You've got me worried." Sadie filled the tumbler close to the brim.

"Sorry, I didn't mean to—"

Sadie heard the tension in Annie's voice. She was barely holding it together. She was emotionally strong, but when it came to Brad, Sadie was sure that was Annie's Achilles' heel.

"I'll tell you about it later."

Sadie gulped her whiskey. "How did the other interrogations go?"

"I'm not sure. We were told not to talk to each other. But that won't last. I'm sure they gave as much grief as I did." Annie sounded so tired. "We should meet tomorrow."

"Sure," Sadie said. "Same place at one?"

"Sadie, please call me if you hear from Sissy."

"I will. Goodnight, Annie."

Sadie replaced the receiver, then refilled her tumbler. She wandered to the window and gazed out at the snow-covered city. She shivered. *Where are you, Brad?*

CHAPTER FIFTY

Dice paced the living room, too keyed up to sleep. The workout over the last hour, the second of the day, didn't help.

Everything was planned so carefully, every step analyzed from all conceivable directions. Coulter's arrest was the culmination of all the planning.

Fists pounded against Dice's forehead. *Stupid. Stupid. Stupid.* All the planning and one minor detail derailed it all. Coulter hadn't been arrested. Coulter was free. Maybe the manhunt for him would solve the problem. It also allowed the killing to continue with the blame on Coulter. But Dice couldn't count on that. Coulter needed to be pulled out of hiding. Dice needed to feed information to Coulter, crumbs for him to follow. In jail or dead—it didn't matter. But Coulter could not be free to investigate. If he lived, the killing would have to stop, at least for a while. Future justice would have to be planned so there was no way anyone could ever link the killings.

Coulter dead was the best option, even if it meant a pause, and Dice had an idea forming. *Oh, yes. Perfect.* Believable and oh so sad. Dice practically cried. *Ha. Not a chance.* Coulter's death would bring days of celebration. But if Coulter was still out there ...

Dice stood in the shadow of a giant pine across the street from a tiny home in an older neighborhood overlooking downtown. One of the historic communities, it was home to many elderly homeowners. Urban renewal was starting with the outdated homes demolished for enormous mansions taking advantage of the view of the river below.

Light came from a table lamp and the TV. Now and then a man crossed in front of the window, changing the channel or fetching another beer. This man couldn't wait for his mother to die a natural death. He was helping her along. The courts believed his story that his mother was frail and had balance issues. That's why she fell a lot and it accounted for the bruises. Her mind was going and frequently she forgot to eat, which explained her thin, emaciated appearance. He cashed her support checks so he could care for her—and buy beer. Dice had watched in horror as against all probability, the judge bought his story, several times. Rather than stopping the abuse, he'd increased it. That ended tonight.

Dice, dressed in black, slipped across the street and around to the darkness of the back of the house. The door was weathered. A crowbar slipped easily between the door and doorframe. A quick turn of the wrist popped it soundlessly open with no damage to the door or frame. Dice stepped inside and followed the sound of the TV to the living room.

He was slouched on the couch with his stocking feet on the coffee table. A bowl of chips was lodged between his legs, several empty beer bottles sat on the table and a beer was in his hand. His eyes were glued to a late-night show. Don Rickles was doing a comedy routine. The man was laughing, the bowl of chips bouncing in his lap.

Dice pulled an eight-inch hardwood baton out of a back pocket and swung hard. The crack of his skull echoed throughout the room. Dice dragged the man off the couch and over a shoulder. The man didn't weigh more than a hundred and twenty pounds, but Dice was breathing hard by the time they reached the top of the stairs. Dice took a deep breath, then tossed the man down the stairs. A quick check determined the man had a pulse.

Dice hauled him back up the stairs and tossed him for a second time. This time there was a loud crack as his head bent at an unnatural angle.

A check produced no pulse. Dice used a gloved hand to pick up the man's beer bottle and then dropped it on the floor beside him. The bottle shattered.

A voice called from upstairs. "Edwin, are you okay? Edwin?"

Dice rolled the baton under the couch, called 911, said "Ambulance," set the receiver on the couch and slipped out of the house.

CHAPTER FIFTY-ONE

Brad woke to the smell of bacon. He loved bacon. He rolled onto his back and rubbed his eyes. For the second morning, he was in a strange room. He bolted upright, eyes scanning the room. Double bed and not much else. He peeked under the covers—he was wearing pajamas. He never wore pajamas. He swung his legs off the bed and headed to the door. With the door open, the odor of bacon was strong, and something sweet. Maple syrup? He followed the tantalizing scents to the kitchen.

Reverend Branton was at the stove. "Hope I didn't wake you. I'm an early riser."

Brad yawned and stretched. "We didn't stop talking until after two this morning."

"You know where the bathroom is. Take care of business, then come back."

When Brad returned to the kitchen, a plate of bacon and pancakes sat on the table, next to a large mug of coffee.

"This is delicious." Brad speared three pieces of pancake and sopped up the maple syrup.

"I have a class at seven," Branton said. "Make yourself at home."

"I'll head out soon. Thank you for giving me sanctuary."

"It's the off season, so that room is available anytime."

"You'll be sorry you said that."

Branton smiled. "Oh, I doubt that. It was wonderful to have company." He tossed the morning newspaper on the table. "You might find the lead story interesting." Branton headed out of the kitchen.

Brad grabbed the newspaper and flipped it open. In bold letters across the top:

Killer Cop at Large

Brad groaned and started reading. He didn't learn anything from the story but was surprised how much information the reporter had. It would piss Sadie off that she didn't have this type of inside information. Deputy Chief Archer stated that the search was on for Detective Coulter and they were following several promising leads. Homicide and Internal Affairs were working together on this manhunt. He reported there had been no further killings. Finally, a plea for Detective Coulter to turn himself in.

Brad headed down the hall to the bathroom. He did his best thinking in the shower.

CHAPTER FIFTY-TWO

STURGEON POURED THREE COFFEES AND CARRIED THEM INTO THE meeting room. He wasn't sure why it was called a meeting room. It had been an office, but the new staff sergeant decided they needed a meeting room. Rather than build one or renovate, he selected this office. Three of them barely fit around the table—four would overload the room. They'd covered the walls with photos, maps, and reports. It was impossible to walk in the room without kicking over a pile of folders. Heaven help you if you shut the door. The room temperature went up ten degrees with minimal air circulation. But leaving the door open, or even ajar, was an invitation to everyone in the section to stop by and ask questions or not so secretly ogle the walls.

Gayle and Angie were pouring over the tests they'd performed yesterday and the analysis from the RCMP crime lab.

He set three cups on the table. They grabbed the coffees and leaned back in their chairs.

"Why were you called out last night?" Sturgeon asked Gayle.

"911 call for a forty-five-year-old guy who fell down the stairs. He was drunk and broke his neck."

Sturgeon shrugged. "Not uncommon."

"True," Gayle said. "But the cops and paramedics who responded felt something wasn't right."

"How so?" Sturgeon asked.

"There was a 911 call, but other than a voice saying 'ambulance,' they said nothing else. The guy was obviously dead from the fall, but his mother says she didn't make the 911 call."

"Does she have dementia?"

Gayle shrugged. "I wouldn't say she's all there, but she could answer our questions."

"You said he'd been drinking?"

"Yeah. By the number of empty bottles, I'd say a half dozen. One was broken next to his head."

"Drunk falls. Dies. End of case," Sturgeon said.

Gayle nodded. "That would be true, except for the weapon we found."

"What?"

"A Billy club."

Sturgeon's eyes widened. "Police issue?"

"Yup," Angie said. "What street cops carry now. Not the sap you used to carry."

Sturgeon grinned and stared off. "Ah, there was nothing like a piece of lead on a spring wrapped in leather to get someone's attention." Sturgeon grinned, then jerked his head back to his team. "Great for bonking fish." He glanced toward the report. "Fingerprints?"

Gayle nodded. "Coulter's. Blood and hair consistent with the victim on the club. We'll know more today after the autopsy and blood and hair analysis."

"Coulter isn't that stupid," Sturgeon said.

Gayle shrugged. "You'd think that, but the evidence keeps piling up."

"Anything new from your re-tests?" Sturgeon asked.

"The tests are coming back the same," Angie said. "There's no reason to think someone tampered with the tests."

"I agree," Gayle said. "We've been focusing on the wrong thing."

Sturgeon stared over his coffee cup. "How so?"

Gayle pointed to the paper on the table. "Instead of trying to prove the tests are wrong, we should figure out how the right evidence got to where we found it. Same with the Billy club."

"I don't follow," Sturgeon said.

"If we agree Coulter is innocent, and we know the tests are correct, then we need to figure out how the evidence that implicates Coulter got there."

"Do you have a theory?"

"Dog hair?"

Angie nodded. "Yes. When we searched Coulter's car, there was dog hair everywhere. It's impossible for Brad to drive that car without getting dog hair on him. I don't think

Coulter had vacuumed that car for months—maybe over a year."

Sturgeon nodded. "I get it. We have a dog, and I'm forever cleaning fur off my clothes. It was worse when I was on the street. The dog hair clung to my dark wool pants."

Angie tapped the dog hair analysis report. "Exactly. Based on what we just talked about, finding dog hair, Lobo's hair at the tattoo parlor murders is a given. Coulter's clothes had to be covered with Lobo's hair. Every scene Coulter attended would likely have dog hair. So, we have two possibilities. One, the dog hair transferred from Coulter to the crime scene. Or, the second possibility, the killer planted it there. But that doesn't matter, because we already know that a transfer is likely to have happened. The dog hair evidence is inadmissible."

Sturgeon nodded. "Zerr and Steele are searching for the hookers who gave a statement that they saw Brad's car at the scene before the murders. They didn't find them last night. We'll have to leave that to them. The gun?"

Gayle glanced at Angie, who shrugged.

"That one is challenging," Gayle said. "You were there when Coulter took his gun out of his holster. You took the gun into evidence. Angie took it out of evidence and test fired it. Then she did the bullet analysis."

"So," Angie said, "the only person who could have replaced Coulter's gun with another is you."

Angie and Gayle stared at Sturgeon. He glared back. "And you two were doing so well up to that point." Sturgeon tapped the evidence bag holding the gun. "That's the gun

Coulter handed over to me. I'm sure you checked the serial number."

Angie nodded. "I did."

Sturgeon leaned back in his chair and linked his hands behind his head.

"How do we explain the ballistic evidence?"

Angie and Gayle stared blankly back at Sturgeon.

CHAPTER FIFTY-THREE

Morning rush hour was over, and the below-freezing temperatures and icy wind kept office workers inside. Brad headed down Fourteenth Street to Seventh Avenue, then turned east. With the gym bag slung over his shoulder, he practically skated on the icy sidewalk into downtown. He bought an extra-large coffee and continued toward the library. This was where he had to be careful. The downtown library was right next to police headquarters. He'd thought about going to another library, but the downtown library had the best archives. He needed to read the newspapers from the last week again.

He kept his head low as he approached the library door. He slid the coffee under the worn jean jacket and entered. He smuggled the coffee to the fourth floor and took a table in the back corner. He set the coffee by the table leg and headed to the newspaper section where he grabbed all the papers for the last week and returned to the table.

He pulled out a couple of pens and a notebook, then sorted the newspapers into a pile with the date of the stabbing on top, followed by dates up to the current day. He glanced around the room frequently, so the librarian didn't catch him with the coffee. It's not like he'd be arrested, but he didn't need the attention. But damn, he needed the coffee.

For the next ninety minutes, he read and re-read the news stories. The press had paid minimal attention to the first murders and didn't get excited until the pimp and his chauffeur were killed. Thinking he would find the answer somewhere in the columns was silly, but it helped his brain work through the chronology and filled in some blanks from the early cases that he'd forgotten.

One thing that caught his eye was a hit and run that occurred after the drug dealer and before the pimp. He'd follow up on that, as well.

He re-read his original notes and filled in some blanks. Then he listed the murders one by one.

MURDERS

Drug Dealer, Tuesday, September 9
Billy Tuck
Victoria Park

- The first in the string of killings?
- Hesitation—the killer had second thoughts, or this was his first kill?
- If his first kill, was it harder than the killer had imagined?

- Nothing from the press and about the same from the police.
- Lack of evidence or leads, so not worth pursuing.

It was easy now to see this as important, but at the time, he would have made the same decision.

Drug Dealer, Saturday, November 22
Vito Sotelo
Victoria Park

- There were two months between killings
- unless other killings not obviously linked.

He'd need someone to go back through the murders and suspicious deaths in the past six months. He tapped his pen on the pad, then wrote, *Sturgeon*.

Connection?

- The MO was consistent—a knife, not found.
- They were drug dealers who were not in jail.
- The murders required prior knowledge of the habits of the victims—surveillance.

Maybe someone saw the killer when the victim was being stalked?

But who in that area would tell the cops anything?

If these were the first two murders, there was nothing linking them to Brad. The closest connection was that he'd taken an interest in the first stabbing, then he caught the second case.

Pimp and Chauffeur, Friday, November 28
Owen Judd and Anthony Moss
Eau Claire

- Different weapon—a gun.
- Four murders, two different weapons:
- knife x 2
- gun x 2
- The shooting was extremely accurate.
- The killer blended into the neighborhood.
- Dressed as <u>a homeless person</u>?

If the killer had been dressed as a homeless person, he'd be practically invisible to anyone else in the area. In fact, most people went to great lengths to avoid the homeless. Not a suitable witness pool.

Tattoo Parlor, Monday, December 1
Zinovy Frolov, Nico Yudin, 2 more?? Names??
16th Avenue and Edmonton Trail

- Killer escalating
- four dead
- knife,
- gun
- Confidence?
- Thrill?

- Multiple weapons
- Scene staged
- Video evidence left
- Not just an escalation
- well planned and personal
- The penises in the mouth made a statement

Brad thought about a female killer.
That lead to two possibilities:

1. A victim
2. A close relative of a victim

Then again, if the victim was the sister or girlfriend, fiancée or wife, then a male might react this way and stage the scene. Now he'd talked himself into a circle.

Brad added his connection to the tattoo parlor. The Gypsy Jokers had owned that parlor two years ago. Brad had led a raid that shut the place down, for a while at least.

Teen Rapist, Wednesday, December 3

Burke Bailey Baldwin II
Lord Beaverbrook High School – Secondary killing location unknown

- Wealthy, pretentious family
- High school jock
- Shit-don't-stink attitude
- Raped teen Laura Turner

- Found not guilty
- Jenni Blighe the crown prosecutor
- Put on display at high school
- Laura's father, Al Turner, a suspect?

Biker at T&C, Sunday, December 7
Arnie Fletcher
Forest Lawn

- Required Surveillance
- Knowing the biker would be alone
- Knowing he stayed after his chores and played pool
- The side door was forced, yet the biker didn't react like he was threatened
- There were no defensive wounds and/or signs of a scuffle?
- He let the killer get close
- Again, personal.
- Use of broken pool cue is creative,
- and a different weapon.

Brad had history with the bikers and this bar. Two years ago, he'd confronted a Satan's Soldiers biker in the T&C, Lou LeBeau. LeBeau and his creepy biker friends had threatened to rape his then-girlfriend, Sarah Park.

In the ensuing fight, Brad dropped LeBeau and two of his biker friends. Unfortunately, the fourth biker took Brad down. Thanks to the timely intervention of the bouncers, and a discreet phone call by an undercover cop, Brad was hauled out of the bar by cops and he had to suffer the wrath of Briscoe. It had been worth it.

Wife-Beater, Thursday December 4
Vinnie Bevan
Sunalta

- Connection with Brad
- Beaten
- Not dead - yet

He and Griffin had caught Vinnie Bevan beating his girlfriend. Bevan decided he'd take it out on Brad. That didn't work out for Bevan. Brad had lost control and had to be pulled off Bevan, twice. He was lucky Briscoe and Griffin defended him, but it worried both of them about Brad's mental health. It came back to haunt Brad in court.

Brad sat back and twirled a pen between his fingers. It was a better idea than chewing another pen. No evidence tied him to the first two murders. It wasn't until the pimp and driver that evidence against him appeared. What happened after the second murder? Why him? Was framing him a bonus thrill of the kills?

Was it personal with him as well? He went back to his original notes about the evidence.

He thought about that. Who fits that statement?

- Crime Scene Investigators
- Cops

- Lawyers
- Judges
- Military—Military Police?
- Military—Special Forces—Airborne, SEALS, Rangers, Delta

The challenge was that when you matched the list of people who knew about crime scene evidence with the list of occupations that could kill multiple ways, there wasn't much of a crossover. That the killer was military was number one on the list. But a vigilante cop was a close second.

What cop would want to frame him? There were cops who didn't particularly like Brad. But he couldn't think of any who would frame him. Then again, despite all their bluster over a few beers at the Cuff and Billy Club, he couldn't think of a cop who would commit these murders. He had heard no rumors about a cop's sister, mother, girlfriend or wife as the victim of a sex crime. Well, except him. Brad had a few reasons to go after perpetrators of sex crimes. Annie had been held and raped. But Brad had sent Wolfe to hell. That case was closed. LeBeau had tried to rape Sarah, but LeBeau had died tragically in a car bomb. And Maggie—well, he resolved that issue at the same time he avenged Annie's assaults with Wolfe's death.

An argument could be made that Brad had already taken revenge. Why would he need to commit these killings? Not an argument he'd want to use in court.

When LeBeau died, there had been speculation that with Brad's tactical training, he had the knowledge and skills to make the bomb. True, but he was cleared. The two Internal

Affairs detectives, Genereau and Harker, who had grudgingly cleared him, were on his case. *Well, shit.*

What was with Griffin? They'd gotten along fine. Worked together well. Was it as simple as Griffin was pissed because Brad escaped? Brad shrugged. *Okay, I'd be pissed if someone disappeared on me.* But to turn against him? Hunt him for murder?

He grabbed his coffee, but it was empty. His stomach growled. He checked his watch: 12:45. He stood to leave, then had another idea. He headed to the rack of newspapers for the past five days. He hauled them back to his table.

A story buried on page twelve mentioned a traffic fatality in downtown Calgary. The traffic division was still investigating and asking for anyone who may have witnessed the fatal hit and run to contact police. Brad remembered Sturgeon working on this. Brad headed to the archives and found the newspapers for the day after the hit and run. On the surface, it appeared like a drunk driver hit a drunk crossing the road. But what if that wasn't all it was?

He grabbed his pen and made notes.

Hit and Run, Wednesday, November 26
Jimmy Duggan

- Fourth Avenue and Macleod Trail SE.
- Did this fit in?
- Drunk driver hit while crossing the road. By a drunk driver?
- Coincidence?

- Was the car stolen for the purpose of killing the drunk?

Then it fit with each killing being different.

The paper mentioned multiple drunk driving charges, yet he still had his license. How many charges exactly?

The cops easily found the car—it had been stolen, and the owner was cleared. He needed additional information on the victim—his entire court records. Steele and Zerr would definitely know a few ladies in the court records section they could charm into supplying them with this information.

Brad replaced the newspapers, gathered his notes, and headed to the elevator. He was content with his research and notes. But was he any closer to identifying the killer?

CHAPTER FIFTY-FOUR

Detectives Genereau and Harker were parked on the opposite side of the road down the block from the coffee shop. Genereau—a squat man, bald, with a wispy mustache and a nasal voice—was in the driver's seat. His partner, Harker, was riding shotgun. Harker was thin and gangly with wild red hair that clashed with his rust-colored suit. He sported a narrow mustache and a face of freckles.

"There's the reporter chick heading into the coffee shop," Genereau said. "On TV, you only see her upper body and face, but dang, I like what I see. Too bad she's wearing that huge parka." He vigorously chewed his gum, making smacking sounds.

"Do you mind?" Harker keyed his portable radio and updated command. "Units in place."

Genereau's eyes didn't leave the door to the coffee shop. "It's what I do on stakeouts."

"I don't give a shit, you're annoying me."

"Keeps me alert." Genereau snapped the gum louder.

"Go for a walk around the block. If you snap that gum one more time, I'm gonna grab you by your tie and drag you out of the car."

"Man, you're cranky. Maybe you need coffee. Head across the street. The chicks don't know you."

Harker snorted. "And the white shirt, tie, cheap suit and comfortable shoes don't shout out *cop*."

Genereau rolled down the window, then spit the gum onto the road. "There. Happy?"

Harker increased the heat. "Shut the frickin' window. I'm cold enough. I'll be ecstatic when you step out of the car, put your size twelves into the gum, and carry it to the next crime scene."

Genereau rolled up the window and swung to his partner. "What is wrong with you today?"

Harker shrugged. "This doesn't feel right."

"Staking out the chicks?"

"Stop saying chicks." Harker clapped his gloved hands together. "It's not the stakeout. It's the total mess with Coulter."

Genereau grinned. "I'm gonna take great pleasure slapping the cuffs on that asshole. Maybe he'll resist and we can rough him up. Fuckin' dirty cop."

"I'm not so sure."

"Oh, great." Genereau rolled his eyes. "Another Coulter hero worshiper."

"You know I'm not a Coulter fan. And I'd love to catch his hand in the cookie jar. But he's too smart. There's no way he'd leave all the evidence leading back to him. If he were doing the killing, we'd never know."

Genereau shrugged. "Since his fiancée got wasted, he's not the same guy. Who knows what demons he's fighting? Don't get me wrong, I'm glad he sent some shitheads to purgatory. It still ain't right about him being a cop."

Harker keyed the radio again. "You guys got anything out back?"

"All quiet here."

Harker keyed the mic. "Any unit see the suspect on the street?"

No reply.

"The meeting has started," Harker said. "Be alert. Let's see if Coulter shows."

"Do you think Coulter will show up?" Genereau asked.

"You're the one who thinks he's stupid, so why not," Harker said.

Genereau shrugged. "Sure. Maybe not *that* stupid."

They watched the front of the coffee shop. It did excellent business, people coming and going all the time. Genereau wondered if they'd give the cops free coffee like 7-Eleven. Probably not. Too many upscale hippy freaks.

The radio squawked. "We've got something in the alley. A tall guy dressed in black entered the back door. He appears shady."

"What the hell does shady look like?" Harker asked.

"Head down, shoulders hunched. For sure he didn't want anyone to see his face."

"You think it's Coulter?"

"Right size, right build."

"Roger that," Harker said. "Detectives and TSU, move in."

Genereau and Harker jumped out of the car and sprinted across the street. "I guess we won't be getting free coffee here anytime soon."

Annie figured two could play the game, so she arrived at the coffee shop twenty minutes early, ordered her coffee and took the seat in the back booth facing the door. Just before two, Sadie entered the coffee shop, stopped inside the store, and removed her sunglasses. She surveyed the tables. A thin grin appeared as she spotted Annie.

Sadie tossed her parka and hat onto the bench and slid into the booth across from Annie. "I see Brad has taught us the same thing." She set her gloves on the table.

Annie smirked. "Last time I arrived too late. I wasn't making that mistake again." Annie slid a cup across the table. "Got you an espresso."

"Thank you." Sadie sipped. "How's Brad?"

Annie surveyed the room. "His friends met him last night and dropped off supplies, cash, food, and clothes. Didn't he stay with you last night?"

Sadie shook her head and stared at her cup. "Not with me."

Annie sipped her coffee.

Sadie set her cup down and glared. "You don't trust me."

"Just being cautious."

"What is it I have to do?" Sadie slumped in her seat. "I've

never betrayed his trust. I could have turned him in a dozen other times. One call to 911 and I would have the scoop of the decade. I didn't."

Annie shrugged. "It's nothing personal."

"The hell it isn't." Sadie glared at Annie. "You know where he met Steele and Zerr last night?"

"I have an idea."

"But you won't tell me."

"It's better that way."

Sadie sat back and crossed her arms. "Fine. Tell me about your interrogation yesterday."

"They made a show of it. Two police cruisers and four cops came to my apartment and escorted me downtown."

Sadie's eyes were wide. "That's intimidating."

"That's what they think." Annie grinned. "I've handled worse."

Sadie sipped her espresso and nodded. "How'd you deal with them?"

Annie laughed. "I may seem like a teen, but I'm a hardened bitch. Detective Harker got nothing from me but grief. When he got angry, I asked for a lawyer. He said I wasn't being charged with anything. I said I still wanted my lawyer. He said fine. Who? I said Brad."

Sadie laughed.

"He said he'd be glad to call Brad and have him come in. I said, terrific point. I'll call Jenni Blighe."

"The crown prosecutor?" Sadie laughed. "Hilarious."

"That ended the interview."

"I'm not sure I'd be this calm about it." Sadie sipped her espresso. "Hey, why didn't they interview me?"

"You want to be interrogated?" Annie asked.

"No, it's just—"

"That's wonderful." Annie leaned across the table. "It means they aren't making any connection between you and Brad. We might be able to meet to get messages to Brad." Annie winced. "Today might screw that up, though."

"I thought Steele and Zerr were meeting him?"

"It worked last night because they ditched their tail. They got called in today by IA and asked questions about where they were for the hour last night when the surveillance team lost sight of them. Our homes are under surveillance and we're followed everywhere. They even follow Sergeant Briscoe when he's at work."

Sadie stared out the window. "Did they follow you here?"

Annie grinned. "I hope so."

"Why?"

A man dressed in black clothes, a black ball cap and hoodie slid in beside Sadie and pushed her over.

Sadie pushed back. "What the—"

"Sadie, quiet," Annie said.

The figure grinned at Sadie.

Her eyes went wide. "What are you doing here?"

"I just have a minute and then they'll be here," Steele said. "There was another murder last night. A drunk fell down the stairs."

"How is that a murder?" Sadie asked.

"They found a police Billy club under the couch. It's Brad's. They're keeping it quiet. Archer doesn't want Brad to know."

Sadie's hand flew to her mouth. "Oh, god."

"What do you want us to do?" Annie asked.

"Find Brad."

"You don't know where he is?" Sadie asked.

"No."

"Brad needs to know this," Annie said. "When are you supposed to meet him?"

Steele chewed on his lip. "Tonight, after nine." He leaned across the table. "Think, Sadie. Did he say anything when he was with you about his plans?"

Sadie shook her head. "No, he ... the note—"

"What?" Steele asked.

"He left me a note yesterday. It talked about visiting the Central Library today."

"What time?"

Sadie shook her head. "The note didn't say."

"Shit." Steele's eyes widened. "That's where he can do research where no one would recognize him." Steele pulled out a portable radio. "Central Library."

The front and back doors opened, there was a clanking sound, then an explosion and bright white light.

Annie was disoriented and blinded. She knew voices shouted at her, but she had no clue what they were saying. Then she was dragged off the bench and thrown to the floor. Her arms were wrenched behind. Her hearing returned. She heard the handcuffs clip into place. She was lifted from the floor and shoved back onto the seat. Her eyes cleared. The coffee shop was overrun with tactical cops and guys in suits. She recognized two of the suits—it was the Internal Affairs Detectives Genereau and Harker.

Assholes.

While a few cops kept their eyes on her, most were focused on the dark-clothed, facedown figure on the floor. One tactical cop had his knees on Steele's back while another cinched up handcuffs. They shoved Steele into a booth.

"Thought you could hide from us, huh, Coulter," Genereau said. "It's with the greatest pleasure I read you your rights."

Detective Harker reached over, flipped the hood back, and removed the ball cap.

"Bradley Coulter—" Genereau paused. "Steele?"

"Did we forget to pay our bill?"

Zerr was driving south on Fourteenth Street. He glanced in the rearview mirror. Four cars back, the dark sedan followed. Zerr had led them on an extensive tour of southwest Calgary. If something didn't happen in the next couple of minutes, he'd pull into the A&W and get a burger.

As he crossed Seventeenth Avenue, his cruiser radio came to life. "We've got something in the alley. A tall guy dressed in black just entered the back door. He appears shady."

A voice replied, "What the hell does shady look like?"

"Head down, shoulders hunched. For sure he didn't want anyone to see his face."

"You think it's Coulter?"

"Right size, right build."

"Roger that. Detectives and TSU, move in."

Zerr glanced in his rearview mirror again and watched

the dark sedan slide sideways in the intersection and head east toward the coffee shop.

Zerr passed the A&W. A burger would have to wait. Steele's voice came over the secure tactical portable radio. "Central Library."

Zerr skidded his truck to the curb outside the library. He tossed a sign that read "Police Business" on the dash and jumped out. That sign might buy him five minutes before they towed the truck. Rush-hour traffic did not like obstructions.

He raced into the library and up to the reception desk. He flashed his badge, then slid a photo of Brad onto the counter. "Have you seen this man?"

The librarian set her pencil down, closed the book she'd been writing in and glanced at Zerr. "Can I see the badge again?"

Zerr slid his badge out of his back pocket. As he pulled the badge away, the librarian grabbed his hand, and with her other hand slid on her glasses. Satisfied with the badge, she glanced at the photo, then back at Zerr. She released his hand.

"This is a police emergency." He pointed at the photo. "Have you seen this man?"

She picked up the picture and held it close to her eyes. "We get a lot of cops in here. We have a problem with the homeless."

"Right, uh, he wouldn't have been in uniform."

"Then this picture isn't much help."

"Check his face, not the uniform." Zerr was still surprised that people he dealt with daily when he was in uniform didn't recognize him out of uniform. He remembered every face, not the clothing.

"Maybe," she said. "A homeless guy was on the fourth floor. I was going to kick him out, but he was quietly reading newspapers."

"When was this?"

"About ten this morning."

"Have you seen him since?"

"No."

"You didn't see him leave?"

She slid off her glasses. "I believe I answered that when I said I hadn't seen him again."

"Right. Fourth floor?"

She nodded.

Zerr raced to the elevator. The librarian saw Brad over six hours ago. Zerr had a sinking feeling in his gut. He was too late.

CHAPTER FIFTY-FIVE

GRIFFIN, GENEREAU, AND HARKER SAT SILENTLY AT THE conference table in Deputy Chief Archer's office. Griffin's jaw was clenched so hard his teeth ached. Every muscle in his body was tense. He'd need a four-hour massage to loosen the tension. Working with Genereau and Harker was all he expected, and a lot less. Their assignment had been to follow Annie Sutton. Griffin was sure she was the key to finding Coulter. Everything had been going well, but they'd been set up. Fuckin' Steele.

Not that it was Genereau and Harker's fault, Griffin just didn't like the IA detectives. But now he was sitting waiting for an ass-chewing from Archer.

Archer had barely acknowledged them as his secretary escorted them into Archer's office to the conference table. Head down, Archer had continued to read a report on something. Finally, Archer shoved the paper to the side of his desk and pushed his chair back. He stood by the table, staring at them. Like Griffin, his jaw was clenched, but there was a pulse in his jaw as he clenched and unclenched.

Archer leaned forward and placed his hands flat on the table. His eyes, dark-black holes, bored into each man. "Forty-eight hours and nothing to show. Oh, except for another murder and our prime suspect is still at large." His hands slammed on the table.

Griffin winced. Harker might have pissed his pants. Genereau stared at a pen on the table.

Harker dared to glance up. "No one knows it was a murder."

Archer's eyes rolled as his head swung back. "That doesn't matter. I've lost count of how many are dead. Add one, subtract one, who gives a shit. The point is, we have arrested no one for any of them."

"Well, we know it's Coulter—"

Archer's finger was up and pointing at Harker, daring him to say another word. "You believe it's Coulter. Fine. Then arrest the fucker. End of the day at the latest. I want someone charged. I want someone in our cells. I want to tell the mayor and the press and the citizens we did our job. You know, the one where we arrest dangerous guys. Where the killing stops."

Genereau found his voice. "Some people, including the press, think drug dealers and pimps dying is okay."

Archer's eyes widened. "Is that what you think? Vigilante justice is okay? A seventeen-year-old murdered and put on display for raping a girl is okay? He deserves jail for a couple of decades, but not this type of justice. Not a death sentence. Find Coulter or clean out your desks, polish your boots and iron your uniforms. The three of you will be assigned to search prisoners in the arrest processing unit. Dismissed."

Griffin bolted from the room. He was pushing open the door to the stairs when Genereau called to him. Griffin took the stairs three at a time and shouldered his way out the back door into the alley. He didn't need those two slowing him down.

CHAPTER FIFTY-SIX

BRAD PARKED ON FOURTEENTH AVENUE AND HEADED TO THE 7-Eleven. He bought a large coffee, then headed around the corner, facing the tattoo parlor. The windows were boarded, and no vehicles were parked nearby. If the Russians had taken over the business from the Hells Angels, it was unlikely anyone would come there for several weeks, if ever. The Russians would know the cops have eyes on the place. Brad scanned the surrounding buildings and cars. Across Sixteenth Avenue, he spotted an older sedan parked in the parking lot of a strip mall. Same make and model as the two sedans parked near the entrance to Bowness Park, forcing the cancelation of his meeting with Steele and Zerr.

In the darkness, he spotted two people in the front seats. He twisted slightly and faced south. Down the block, he spotted another black sedan. They were too close to the streetlight and Brad could see their faces, not enough to identify them, but enough to know they were Narcotics undercover—beards, long hair and shabby clothes, not unlike what Brad was wearing.

Brad sipped his coffee and watched for half an hour. In that time, no one went near the house. One cop from the car down the street exited the car and headed Brad's way. Time to move on.

It was too early for the inhabitants of the night to come out of the darkness and seek food or drink at the store, so Brad continued west. If they weren't on the street, then they'd likely be at the Beacon Hotel Bar. Years ago, it was the meeting place for the Gypsy Jokers outlaw motorcycle club. Brad and his TSU team had been locked in their battle for control of the city with another gang, the Satan's Soldiers. When the war was over, most of the leadership of both clubs were dead or in jail. That left a void the Hells Angels were ready to fill. Nowadays most crime in the city was controlled by the Angels, including the hotels and prostitution. If the girls were back working, it was likely they were at the Beacon.

The Beacon was a popular bar with the working class. Known as "Peekin' at the Beacon," it featured the city's largest strip show, bringing talent from across Canada and the United States.

As Brad crossed Centre Street, he pulled his beanie low, hunched his shoulders, and tucked his hands in his pockets. The bouncer didn't give him a second glance as he entered the bar. He stood for a minute, allowing his eyes to adjust. Even coming in from the darkness, the bar was still dimmer. The odors of beer, popcorn, and sweat greeted him. The walls were cheap laminate paneling, peeling in spots. Wooden chairs without armrests encircled tables meant to hold four patrons, but the closest ones to the stage held six or seven guys with their eyes glued to the stage and their jaws dropped onto their chests. Their jaws closed momentarily to wolf whistle.

The bar was about three quarters full, with most of the clients close to the stage. Brad took a seat near the back with an excellent view of the two main doors, the stage and the bar.

The waitresses were rushing from the tables to the bar where two male bartenders poured beer and mixed hard liquor, mostly rye and ginger or rum and Coke. Then the waitresses headed back to the table with trays loaded with at least twenty glasses of beer and the occasional rum or rye.

After distributing her load, a waitress stopped by Brad, empty tray in her left hand, and right hand on her extended hip. She didn't make eye contact, and her eyes roved the bar as she smacked her gum. "What'll ya have?"

"Four draft beer."

"Ya got it." She drifted away, never once having glanced at Brad.

He leaned back and scanned the bar from one side to another. To either side of the long bar were doors. The door to the right apparently led to the kitchen, as trays of burgers, hot dogs and fries came out at regular intervals.

His gaze held on the left-hand door. To the handle side stood a beast of a man—six-foot four, at least, well over two hundred and forty pounds with a shaved head and piercing black eyes.

The waitress dropped off his beers, then hustled to more promising tables.

No one went near the left door while the show was on. Brad was on his second beer when someone announced the show would take a break. The waitresses pounced on the patrons, taking orders before they could think of leaving. After about ten minutes, a few men headed to the left door. They said something to the bouncer, slipped something into his hands, then the bouncer opened the door and they slipped past. For the next fifteen minutes, about a dozen men approached the door and gained entrance.

The intermission lasted approximately twenty minutes, then the lights dimmed, and unfamiliar girls took the stage.

While the third act was on, the left door opened, and a teenaged girl talked to the bouncer. She was a girl from the first show. He nodded and headed over to a table. He spoke briefly with the man, who then followed the bouncer back to the door where the girls stood. The man followed her down the hall, then the door closed.

He'd glanced at the first acts with slight interest. When the third act started, Brad almost dropped his beer. It was the girl from the video at the tattoo parlor. This girl had his undivided attention. If he was right, the girls performed on stage, then turned tricks in the back hall. He needed to figure out how this was arranged.

The waitress came back and stood with the same hip-out stance.

"Another round?"

"Sure," Brad said. "About the girls, can a guy get some time with them?"

"Maybe. Anyone in mind?"

"Yeah, the girl on stage."

She frowned. "You like them young, huh? I'll see what I can do."

She took a few additional orders, then approached the bouncer at the door. He briefly glanced in Brad's direction, then said something to the waitress who headed to the bar. He stared at the girl again. He was sure they'd say she was eighteen, but he felt she wasn't over sixteen. What he noticed was most were the same dead eyes he'd seen on the video. She was going through the motions, her body moving, but her mind was blank.

The teen left the stage and was replaced. The waitress brought him four draft beers but didn't say a word. Brad tossed a dollar on the table for the beer, then added a quarter as a tip.

Brad started working on a plan to get into that back hall. Maybe when the bouncer approached another table, Brad could slide through the door. The problem was that the bouncer never strayed far from the door or for long. That meant he wasn't the only one making arrangements for the girl. Brad scrutinized the bar and came up with at least three other possibilities, all bikers. Brad had noticed them when he came in but hadn't given them a second thought. Now he realized they were working a portion of the bar. He watched closer, then saw a waitress approach the biker on the far side of the room. She pointed to a table, and he nodded.

Brad sipped his draft beer and watched the bikers rather than the girls. The lights came up, and they announced another intermission. Again, the waitresses pounced on the customers before they could leave. Brad's waitress came by. "Another round?"

"I'm good," he said.

"Vic will come and get you when the girl is ready. Have a twenty ready and give it to him." Then she headed to another table and dropped off the drinks.

Brad tried not to stare at Vic, but he wanted to remember every feature, so when the time came, they would have a discussion about which hospital Vic wanted to go to.

Intermission passed, and the music started. Another girl took the stage. As he stared at her, a hand tapped his shoulder. He jumped, and his left hand headed to his hip.

"Follow me, bud," the bouncer said.

The bouncer opened the door and Brad extended his hand. The bouncer took his hand, and they made the exchange. He'd just given away most of the cash he got from Steele.

The teen met him in the hallway and took him to an eight-by-eight room. A bed was jammed against a wall and a coat stand sat next to the bed. She closed the door.

Brad smiled at her. Up close, he not only saw the dead eyes, but her posture was of one who had given up. Her shoulders sagged. Her movements were slow and spastic. When he peered at her eyes, he realized the pupils were pinpoint. They were feeding her narcotics.

"Ten minutes." She sighed and pursed her lips. "Blowjob or bed?"

Brad held up his hands and shook his head. "No sex. I want to talk."

"I no talk. Not English. Blowjob?"

"No. Listen. You were at the tattoo parlor."

She shrugged and shook her head. "No blowjob, you go."

He dug for some way to communicate with her. He held his hand up like it was a movie camera and with the other hand cranked it.

She stared at him. "Movie?"

"Yes." Then he noticed the tattoo on her chest, just below her clavicle and to the left. A crown with the initials *RFS*. He pointed. "Tattoo?"

She stepped back until she bumped into the wall. "No talk." She glanced at the door. "*Nyet*. Not happen. Go."

"Did you see …?" He made a gun motion with his hand.

"*Nyet*." she screamed.

Brad held out his hands, but she kept screaming. The door burst open and the bouncer and two of the bikers stormed into the cramped room. The girl kept screaming and pointed to Brad. One biker grabbed him and as he tried to shove him off, the bouncer swung his fist into Brad's gut. He nearly puked, then doubled over. The first biker held him up while the bouncer fired a half-dozen shots at Brad's face. Pain surged in his nose and he tasted blood. He had no play against the three of them in this compact room, so he slumped in the arms of the biker.

The bouncer punched the side of Brad's head again. The two bikers dragged Brad out of the room and through a back door. They tossed him on the ground. Each gave him a kick to the ribs, just for fun.

Brad lay on the cool gravel that dug into his cheek. The pain came in waves, then the storm lessened. He pulled himself into a sitting position. His head sparked with electric shots of pain firing around his face. He carefully reached up to his nose. It was swollen but didn't seem to be crunched or facing the wrong direction. It was filled with drying blood and he breathed through his mouth, which hurt his split lips.

He took a deep breath and was thankful there weren't any sharp pains in his side. At least his ribs were intact. His face, not so much.

He grabbed the wall and pulled himself up. The world spun, and his eyes wouldn't focus. This time, no one was coming to save him. No one would nurse his wounds. He was alone and couldn't reach out. He used the wall of the bar for support and staggered down the alley. By the time he reached the end of the wall, his vision had cleared, but he still stumbled as he headed toward his car.

Two cruisers, lights flashing, stopped in front of the Beacon and the cops raced inside. They didn't glance at Brad as he headed down Sixteenth Avenue toward his truck. As he passed a sedan, one of the undercover guys glanced in his direction. "You gonna be okay, buddy?"

Brad waved his hand and headed into the 7-Eleven. While he waited for the clerk to pour a coffee, Brad glanced at the security mirror above the cash register. *Ouch.* His nose was swollen, his lips split in at least three places. The flesh around his eyes was red, which he knew would be black and blue by morning. It had been a while since he'd had the shit kicked out of him. In a weird way, it felt good. He hurt, but he was invigorated. He hadn't learned a lot—well, except that he still did stupid shit—but he was sure all the girls from the tattoo parlor were working at the Beacon.

CHAPTER FIFTY-SEVEN

It was 8:45 when Zerr drove past Brad's former house on Thirty-Fourth Avenue. A dark sedan was parked farther down the block. Zerr continued to the entrance to Bowness Park and spotted another sedan parked on a side street facing the park entrance. "So much for the meeting tonight."

"The IA bastards have the park staked out," Steele said.

Zerr kept driving and eyed his rearview mirror. The second sedan pulled in behind them.

Steele glanced over his shoulder. "You going to lose them?"

Zerr shrugged. "No point. Let them follow us and feel useful. I'll head to the northeast to search for the hookers. We have to find them tonight. But the cold will keep most people inside. We need some of luck."

Steele peered out his side window. "It's going to take more than luck to save Coulter."

Zerr nodded, glanced out the window and chewed a

fingernail. "One thing at a time. This is the one we can work on. Every piece of evidence that's disproved is one step closer to clearing his name. Sturgeon has to figure out the crime scene evidence. We locate the girls and find out why they said they saw Brad's car."

"You probably meant to say we double check their information and see if there are any inconsistencies in their statements."

Zerr grinned. "Like I said, get them to say they didn't see the car." He steered onto Edmonton Trail and headed north. The sedan followed.

For the next two hours, they drove back and forth between Edmonton Trail and Sixth Street northeast from Sixteenth Avenue to Thirtieth Avenue. They traveled these roads so many times and talked to so many people that when they passed a second, or third, or fourth time, the people on the street just waved at them.

Dispatch asked for units to respond to the Beacon Hotel Bar for an unruly patron.

"What about the Beacon?" Zerr said.

"What about it?" Steele replied. "You want to break up a fight?"

Zerr grinned. "I wouldn't object to that. I was thinking—"

"That's a first."

"—maybe the girls had a few jobs. You know, make movies, strip, and turn tricks."

"That's a splendid idea," Steele said. "You think of that all on your own?"

"Screw you."

Zerr drove to Centre Street and parked the truck behind

two cruisers. They pushed past a biker at the door and entered the bar. The lights were on and some soft background music played. They split up, and each wandered around the bar. As they passed the tables, some patrons quieted. Others, feeling the false courage of booze, heckled. Steele just grinned and kept walking. But he made a mental note that one night they needed to come back with the entire team and settle a few scores.

When they reached the far wall, they backtracked and met at the door.

"Did you see anything?" Steele asked.

"I'm not sure what we're searching for."

"You'll know when you see it."

"Oh, okay. I didn't see it."

The lights dimmed, and the music roared. The patrons cheered as a tall girl wearing a nurse's uniform danced onto the stage and paraded in front of the men in the front row.

"We should head out," Steele said.

"Why?" Zerr asked.

"First, it's hard to see anything with the lights low, and second, this is not a pleasant image."

"First, the lights over the stage are just fine and I can see everything I want to. Second, no one gives a shit about us being here."

"What are we going to accomplish here?"

Zerr smirked. "Surveillance never hurt. Besides, we're showing the colors. Keeps everyone in line."

A waitress stopped next to them. "Can I get you a drink, boys?"

"No thanks," Steele said.

"On the house," she said.

Zerr grinned at her, but Steele put his hand on Zerr's arm. "We were just about to go."

"All right. You should have been here earlier."

"Why's that?"

"Some customer got out of hand and the boys had to tune him."

"He grab the girls, or what?" Zerr asked.

"Not sure. He was a quiet guy, not like the ones who commonly get out of hand. He'd had little to drink—well, at least from here. I doubt he'll be back. The boys are excellent at getting their message across. If you know what I mean."

Steele nodded. "Have a good night."

"The offer is always here if you get thirsty later." She winked and headed to a table.

They stopped outside the bar. "We've got a choice to make." Steele peered up and down the street. "Either we call it a night, or I need a coffee and to pee, and not in that order."

"Fine," Zerr said. "Take your break, then let's do another hour."

Steele sighed. "Okay. Fine with me." He drove south on Edmonton Trail and pulled into the 7-Eleven. They climbed out of the SUV and headed to the door.

Just as they stepped inside, three ladies headed away from the cash register.

"Hello, ladies," Zerr said.

"We've been searching for you," Steele added.

Steele had arranged for three cruisers to take the girls to HQ to be interviewed. At two in the morning, it wasn't difficult finding three free crews. He didn't want the girls to talk to each other and come up with a story.

They stepped into the first interview room. The teenaged girl was shaking. She appeared tiny in the small room. Her hair was blond, but not naturally. Her face was heavily made up with thick black eyelashes and bright blue around her gray eyes. Her arrest records had no date of birth but said she was twenty. Steele guessed no more than seventeen or eighteen.

They sat opposite her. Zerr reached over and uncuffed her.

Steele opened the file folder he carried, then glanced at the girl. "It seems we have various names for you. What do I call you?"

She stared at the table, rubbed her wrists. "Martina."

She pronounced her name with a heavy European accent, possibly Russian. "Okay, Martina, I'm Sam and this is Charlie."

"I don't know nothing."

Steele smiled. "I haven't asked a question yet. Where are you from?"

"I don't have to say anything."

Steele leaned back. "That's true. We'd like to help you."

Martina crossed her arms over her chest. "Police lie. They don't help."

"We don't want to keep you here," Steele said. "Answer a few questions and we'll let you go with your friends."

She sneered. "I give blowjob, you let go?"

Steele held up his hands. "Whoa. Nothing like that. Just a question. Well, the truth. Last week you were at the tattoo parlor."

"Parlor?"

Zerr rolled up his shirt sleeve and pointed to the tattoo on his shoulder—the US Army Ranger logo with a lightning bolt and the words *Ranger, Airborne.*

She nodded. "*Soldat?* You soldier?"

"I was."

"Worse than police." She spat on the floor.

Steele glared at Zerr. "Thanks for the help."

Martina grinned and pulled her top down, revealing a tattoo just below her left clavicle, **RFS**. Then she pulled the shirt down farther.

Steele held up a hand. "No. Stop."

Martina glanced from one to the other, then released the fabric.

"We need to know about the night the men were killed."

"Pigs."

"The man who killed them, what did he say?"

"Say go. Give money. We go."

"Nothing else?"

"Take money, go."

"Okay." Steele picked up the file folder.

"Wait," Martina said. "You said you help?"

Steele nodded.

"You keep us safe?"

"Absolutely."

She pursed her lips and sighed. "I talk to prosecutor. Make deal."

"What do you know?" Zerr asked.

She leaned back in her chair. "Prosecutor."

Steele opened the door to the second room. Zerr removed the handcuffs and again they sat. The lady, early twenties but appeared thirty or more, had unnaturally bright-red hair. Her face was overly made up with bright-red cheeks and thick red lipstick. She sat back in the chair, arms folded, almost black eyes glaring at them with an 'I'm going to kill you' glare.

Steele glanced quickly at the file folder. "What do we call you?"

She glanced at her red nails then chewed a cuticle.

"This says your name is Belova Komarova. You go by Belle."

"Why you ask, if you know?" Her accent sounded Russian.

Steele shrugged. "Okay, I'll call you Belle."

"Call me whatever." She leaned back and crossed her arms. "I don't talk to you."

"You speak English well."

"Dah." She grinned and leaned forward. "You understand, fuck you." She shifted in her seat then cupped her breasts in both hands and shoved them up. She grinned at Zerr. "Quiet one, you like?"

"I've seen better," Zerr grinned.

Belle laughed and sat back. "But you pay more."

"We have a few questions," Steele said.

"Am I under arrest?" Belle's eyes stayed on Zerr.

"No."

She pushed her chair back. "I go then."

Steele shook his head. "No."

"I buy coffee in store. That a crime in Canada?"

"A couple of questions and you can go."

She folded her arms. "Lawyer."

"Your choice," Steele stood and gathered the file folder.

"Leave quiet one here." She blew a kiss to Zerr and jiggled her breasts. "He likes."

"I can do the next interview alone," Steele said.

"Screw you." Zerr grabbed another Coke and they entered the third interview room.

This girl was hunched over and crying. When she glanced up, her brown eyes were red and puffy. She gasped with each breath, her chest rising and falling, on the verge of collapse.

Her brown hair was curled and hung a few inches below her shoulders. Like the other two, she wore a lot of makeup, but Steele was sure she hadn't seen her sixteenth birthday yet. She couldn't weigh more than ninety-five pounds.

"We want to help you." Steele slid a box of tissue toward her.

She grabbed a couple of tissues and blew her nose.

Zerr set the Coke in front of her. They waited as she blew her nose a second and third time. The gasping stopped.

They leaned back and waited. Zerr slid a file folder over. Steele opened it. Just a note—*No Record Found*.

Finally, she grabbed the Coke and took a long drink. Over

the next few minutes, she finished the Coke, but remained silent and never made eye contact.

Steele asked, "What is your name?"

Head down, she whispered, "Tatiana."

Steele understood he was talking to someone young and terrified.

"Tatiana. That's a lovely name." He tapped his chest. "I'm Sam."

She glanced up and sniffled. "Sam?"

"Sam."

Tatiana nodded toward Zerr.

"My friend," Sam said. "Charlie."

"*Militsiya?*"

Steele glanced at Zerr.

"Eastern bloc name for police." Zerr nodded to Tatiana. "*Militsiya.*"

Steele's head swung toward Zerr, his eyes wide.

Tatiana's eyes widened and her lips quivered. She wrapped her arms around her body and began rocking.

"Friend," Steele said.

Zerr leaned over and whispered in Steele's ear, "*Droog.*"

Steele tapped his chest again. "*Droog.*"

Tatiana shook her head. "*Zloy.*"

Zerr suppressed a smile and leaned toward Steele. "Wicked, sinister." Then he faced Tatiana. "English?"

"*Dah. Podsobit,* um, help."

Zerr nodded. "Yes." He pointed to Steele, then himself. "Help."

"Bring Martina," Tatiana said.

Steele and Zerr stood outside the first interview room, occasionally glancing through the window in the door. Martina held Tatiana close, her arm around Tatiana's shoulders.

"What the hell was with the Russian?" Steele asked.

"I learned a few words. I'm better at Vietnamese." Zerr grinned.

"Maybe we should ask for a Russian interpreter," Steele said.

Zerr rolled his eyes. "Sure, we've got hundreds of Russians on the job."

"You'll have to do, then," Steele said. "Bella is a hardened woman. I got the feeling she'd kill me if given a chance. Although she liked you, quiet one."

"Did you see her eyes?" Zerr asked. "Dark and dead. What the hell did they do to these girls?"

"You already know," Steele said.

"Ah shit." Zerr closed his eyes and groaned.

Steele peered into the room. "Martina knows more English than she lets on."

Zerr snorted. "More law, too. How many people would ask for the prosecutor, not a lawyer?"

"That was an interesting request," Steele said. "Martina has been in Canada for at least a few years. Tatiana is a recent arrival."

"What does Martina have to deal?"

Steele shrugged. "We'll find out when Blighe gets here."

The door at the end of the hall opened and the desk sergeant escorted a lady toward them. Steele almost didn't recognize Crown Prosecutor Jenni Blighe. He was used to seeing her in court, dressed professionally with her hair immaculately styled. Tonight, she wore a university T-shirt, jeans and sneakers. Her hair was pulled back into a loose ponytail. As she approached, she gave Steele and Zerr the 'this better be worthwhile' scowl.

"Why am I here at four in the morning?"

Steele started with the pimp killing to the tattoo parlor murders, and then that the evidence suggested Coulter was the killer.

"Are you kidding me? I saw the news, but even you guys think Coulter is behind the murders?"

"We don't think he committed them," Steele said. "But the evidence is more than circumstantial, it's damning."

"To be clear," Zerr said, "we know Coulter didn't do it. That's why we tracked down these ladies. We don't believe their statements."

Blighe shook her head. "That's a … I don't know what the word is … a fantastic story. Major motion picture quality."

"Except a career is on the line," Steele said.

"Let's see what she has to say," Blighe said. "Let's get in there."

CHAPTER FIFTY-EIGHT

STEELE KNOCKED, THEN OPENED THE DOOR AND STEPPED BACK. Jenni Blighe stepped into the cramped interview room. She sat across from Martina and Tatiana, crossing her arms. Steele noticed the tight definition of her biceps. He'd heard she'd been obsessed with working out since her ordeal with Jeter Wolfe. He retreated to the corner of the room.

"I'm Jenni Blighe. I am a crown prosecutor. I understand you want to speak with me."

Martina stared at Blighe. "Do I know you?"

"I don't think so." Blighe glanced at a file. "Martina, we've arrested you several times for prostitution and drugs. Perhaps you saw me in court?"

"*Nyet*. Not there."

Blighe glanced at the other girl. Tatiana slunk back in the chair, trying to slip behind Martina. Blighe sat back, relaxed her posture and smiled.

"Tatiana?"

The girl nodded.

"I need to know you are talking to me voluntarily, and the officers"—Blighe glanced at Steele—"have not in any way influenced your decision."

Martina stared at Steele. "We go to jail, no?"

Blighe shook her head. "No, you will not go to jail."

"They not make us talk. I decide is okay."

"This is your and Tatiana's choice," Blighe said.

Martina placed a hand on Tatiana's arm. "*Dah*, we choose. I talk for both. We talk, no jail."

Blighe nodded. "Correct. No jail."

"You help us be safe?" She glanced at Steele. "No men?"

"I guarantee that," Blighe said.

"Ask questions."

Blighe grabbed a pen and a yellow legal pad. "Were you two in the tattoo parlor when the murders happened?"

"*Dah*," Martina said.

Blighe's blue eyes darted between the teens. "Did either of you see the face of the murderer?"

"*Nyet*."

Blighe cocked her head "Did the murderer talk to you?"

"*Dah*."

Blighe straightened. "What did he say?"

"Gave money. Tell us to go. Said if cops get us, say what we saw, but tell cop's black car outside."

Blighe scribbled notes. "That's all he said?"

Tatiana whispered in Martina's ear. "Ya, bird on front of car."

"A bird." Blighe glanced at Steele. "Then what did you do?"

"We go out to street."

"Did you see the black car with the bird?"

"*Nyet.*"

"No car?"

Tatiana vigorously shook her head.

"Did the man say or do anything else?"

Tatiana whispered to Martina. "Why you think is a man?"

Blighe's head swung up from her legal pad. "I'm sorry? You said—"

Martina shook head. "*Nyet.* You said man."

"It was a woman?" Blighe sat back in her chair. Steele's eyes widened.

Martina shrugged. "Maybe, maybe not. Voice sounded, uh, different."

Blighe glanced from one girl to the other. "How so?"

"Like trying to be deep," Martina said. "Some words not deep."

"How big was the killer?"

"Big?"

"Large." Blighe gestured to Steele. "Like this man?"

Martina shook her head and pointed at Blighe. "*Nyet.* Like you."

Zerr waited in the hall outside the interview room. No sense jamming the room with people and scaring the ladies further. He watched through the window in the door for two minutes, then decided that was a waste of time. He headed down the hall and talked to the desk sergeant. At this time of morning, even the criminals were tired, so there were few arrests and the booking area was quiet.

The back door opened. Sergeant Toscana stepped in. "Hey, Zerr. What brings the TSU out in the wee hours of the morning? I heard nothing on the radio."

"Morning, Sarge. Steele and I were doing a follow-up. It took longer than we thought."

Toscana glanced around. "Where's Steele?"

Zerr jerked his head toward the interview rooms. "He's interviewing two hookers with Blighe."

"You've got the crown prosecutor involved?" Toscana's eyes widened. "At four in the morning with hookers?"

Zerr shrugged. "We think they have information about the murders at the tattoo parlor."

Toscana sucked on her lower lip. "This is huge."

"We hope so. I should check on the third girl." Zerr headed down the hall.

Toscana followed. "A third girl?" She peered in the window where Blighe and Steele were conducting the interview. Her jaw tightened. The second room was empty. In the third room a lady sat in a chair, eyes closed, head on the table.

"She won't talk," Zerr said. "I need to get her something to drink. I forgot about her when she said she wouldn't talk. Can you keep an eye on her? I'll be right back."

"No problem." Toscana stared at the woman through the window as Zerr headed down the hall.

The interview door swung open. Blighe stepped out and headed down the hall past Zerr.

"Wait," Zerr shouted. "What did they say?"

Blighe stopped and peered over her shoulder. "I'm in a rush, it's god knows what time. I need to write my notes, prepare a presentation for a judge, and, oh yeah, I'm in court at nine-thirty."

"I'm not asking for a detailed synopsis." Zerr stepped in front of Blighe. "What did they say? Can they clear Brad?"

"There's enough to their story to suggest his car was not at the crime scene until after the murders."

"It's all circumstantial," Steele added, joining them in the hallway.

Blighe shrugged. "Doesn't change the ballistic evidence, though."

"There's a lot of reasonable doubt," Zerr said.

"It's up to a judge or jury to decide reasonable doubt." Blighe put her hand on Zerr's chest and pushed him away. "How about we talk this afternoon? I need to go."

Zerr stepped aside. "Sure, no problem." His voice grew icy. "Forget that you owe your life to Brad."

Blighe kept walking and raised a finger.

CHAPTER FIFTY-NINE

DESPITE CAREFUL PLANNING AND AGONIZING OVER THE TINIEST details, the timetable would no longer work. The final act had to start immediately. It was an inconvenience. Not everything was in place. This was not a perfect time, but there was no option. With luck, it might work better. It would be Dice's crowning achievement and Coulter's farewell performance. With Coulter out of the picture, Dice would have to take a break, give things time to cool down.

Dice drove to the southwest community of Lakeview and cruised the streets. The early hour and the biting cold kept most people inside. Other than tow trucks and taxis, few vehicles were on the road. From surveillance, the odds were better than fifty percent that the target would arrive soon. He'd come by taxi, so picking out the vehicle wouldn't be as difficult as it would be if he caught a ride with a friend, although that was still possible—slim, but possible.

When a taxi drew close, Dice's heart beat faster, breath

deepened and eyes focused. Several times it was a false alarm. It was interesting how many people were out and using taxis.

Then brake lights shone as the yellow taxi pulled to the curb a block ahead.

The occupant stepped out and stopped at the driver's window. He waved as the taxi drove off. Dice pulled ahead and honked. The man faced the lights heading toward him. Dice rolled down the driver's window and waved the man over.

He stumbled through the snow and leaned into the window.

Dice swung a lightning-fast punch out the window. The man staggered backward, grabbing his nose, then fell on his butt. Dice jumped out of the vehicle.

They struggled in the snow, but not for long. Dice rolled the man on his face, secured his wrists and legs, shoved a cloth in his mouth, and placed tape over the gag. Dice dragged the man to the back of the vehicle, opened the door and, after several attempts, finally pulled him onto the back seat. A quick search produced a baggie of heroin and all the paraphernalia.

CHAPTER SIXTY

KEARSE'S SECRETARY OPENED THE DOOR AND WAVED ARCHER and Jackson into the mayor's office. Mayor Roger Kearse was pacing behind his antique oak desk. He was short and overweight with red veins weaving throughout his nose. Generally, his blue eyes sparkled, and his chubby face had a mischievous expression. His shaggy brown hair looked like he'd forgotten to brush it this morning. Kearse was pale, his eyes gray and dull, and his face sagged. He appeared twenty years older than his age of thirty-eight. Archer had never seen Kearse appear this ghastly.

Archer waited for Kearse to acknowledge their presence. Archer had been in this office a few times, but there were new photos on the walls. Kearse with the Prime Minister Pierre Trudeau, the Calgary Stampeders football players, some Calgary Stampede officials, in the Stampede parade, and even a photo of Kearse in the St. Louis Hotel Bar.

Kearse spun away from the window and glanced at the

men. "Take a seat." He pointed to two stuffed chairs, remained standing, then stared out his office window again.

Archer had no clue what this was about. All he knew was that the mayor's office called. The mayor needed to see Jackson and him immediately.

Archer sat back in the chair, crossed his legs, placed his hands in his lap and waited. Jackson was less patient. He sat back, then forward. He picked lint off his suit jacket, stared at his boots, then rubbed the toes on the back of his pants, satisfied that he'd gotten the slush and salt off and attained a shine.

Finally, the mayor spoke. "I have a nephew. Michael Trant. He's twenty-three. My sister's kid. He had it easy growing up, didn't want for much. He never learned to work because his parents gave him whatever he asked for. Somehow, that wasn't enough. In his teens, what he wanted was drugs. Usual story. Smoked some grass in early high school." Kearse shrugged. "Not a big deal then."

Kearse stepped back to the window.

"Then it was heroin," he said. "Before long, Michael was using in excess of the money he had, so he stole from his parents. Money at first, then he took stuff from the house and sold it or traded it for drugs. Small stuff to start. A pair of earrings—ones my sister didn't wear. Then valuable possessions went missing. A gold watch, a pearl necklace and a vintage guitar. They both covered for him—my sister the most. I don't know how many times I heard, 'He's a good boy.'"

Archer waited as silence extended between them.

Kearse let out a deep breath and his shoulders sagged.

"Early this year, Michael was stopped at the Calgary airport and his luggage was searched. They found four kilos of heroin and charged him with importing illegal drugs. He was facing ten, maybe fifteen years in prison. My sister begged me to help. I tried to convince her he wasn't a small boy, he was a man and needed to face the consequences of his actions. She was inconsolable. I contacted the crown prosecutor, the premier, and the RCMP. They kept it quiet. I brokered a deal. He provided the details of the drugs he received in Mexico and the operation here. In return, no jail time and mandatory rehab. The RCMP passed that information on to the Mexican Federales. The RCMP made dozens of arrests here, taking down an international smuggling ring. I'm not sure what happened in Mexico."

Jackson snorted. "Michael wasn't charged?"

"To make it appear legitimate, he was arrested and charged," Kearse said. "His trial isn't for another nine months to a year. By then, the other trials will be done and the smuggling gang in jail. Then Michael's charges will be dropped."

"How does he explain that he's not in jail?" Archer asked. "Surely, the dealers would come after him."

"Since it was his first serious crime, the court granted bail, ordered mandatory rehab, and he has a curfew."

Archer's patience hit a wall. "I'm not sure how this has anything to do with us. It seems the court has this under control."

"Michael is missing."

Jackson's head lifted. "How long has he been gone?"

"He didn't come home last night."

"With all respect, Mr. Mayor," Archer said. "We have a

major investigation going. I can get detectives over here to help find Michael."

"I'm not explaining this well." Kearse sagged like an enormous weight had fallen on his shoulders. "He was kidnapped."

"That would have been a perfect place to start," Jackson said, scowling. "When was he taken?"

"Sometime late last night or early this morning."

"From his house?" Jackson asked.

Kearse stared at his hands. "No. Probably not. He, uh, misses curfew a lot."

"So, anyone watching him would know that?" Jackson said.

Kearse nodded.

"How do you know he was kidnapped?" Jackson asked.

"I received a phone call at seven telling me that Michael had been taken."

"For Christ's sake, Roger," Jackson said. "What other important stuff are you holding back?"

"I thought it was important you knew the complete story."

"Did you record the call?" Archer asked.

"I didn't have the chance. The call was brief. The person said Michael would be killed unless—"

"Unless what?" Archer asked.

"He said there are a few demands. Michael is publicly charged and returned to jail. I admit what I did to get the deal and resign."

"That's it?" Archer asked.

"There's one additional thing," Kearse said. "We have to give them the four kilos of heroin, as well."

"Are you shitting me?" Jackson shouted.

"They want their product back, and revenge for snitching," Archer said.

"Michael is a screwup, but he doesn't deserve to die," Kearse said.

"We're not putting four kilos of heroin on the street," Jackson snarled.

Kearse put his hands together like he was praying, his eyes pleading.

"But my nephew is dead if we don't."

CHAPTER SIXTY-ONE

Jackson was the last one to arrive at the truck stop restaurant. He tossed his parka on a chair and slid in next to Steele, who was sitting across from Zerr.

"What's so important we had to meet early this morning?" Steele asked.

"It's eight-thirty." Jackson rolled his eyes. "Shit is hitting the fan."

"You think?" Steele said. "We haven't been to bed yet."

Zerr hunched over his coffee. "Coulter is about to end up in jail."

"Coulter isn't the pressing problem anymore," Jackson said.

"What the hell do you mean?" Zerr asked.

The waitress poured coffee and dropped three menus on the table.

"The mayor called Deputy Chief Archer and me to a meeting." Jackson glanced around the restaurant, then leaned over the table and whispered, "Mayor Kearse's nephew, Michael Trant, was kidnapped."

"What?" Steele said.

"Keep your voice down."

"Why kidnap him?" Steele asked.

Jackson related the story of the drug smuggling, the deal made, and the disappearance of the heroin.

"Well, I'll be damned," Zerr said.

"When did they take him?" Steele asked.

The waitress came by and refilled coffees. "Decided yet, boys?"

Jackson waved her off. "Kearse got the call this morning. Trant disappeared late last night or early morning."

"We haven't heard about this," Steele said. "We should be working on a hostage rescue plan."

"Kearse wants this kept quiet," Jackson said.

"No way Archer agrees with this," Steele said.

"He doesn't, but he hasn't figured out a game plan yet." Jackson sipped his coffee. "Keep in mind we learned about this thirty minutes ago."

Steele stirred some cream into his coffee. "What does the kidnapper want?"

Jackson sipped his coffee again.

"Well?" Steele said.

Jackson didn't meet his eyes. "The four kilos of heroin."

"No shit," Steele said. "They know there's no way we'll turn the drugs over to them."

Jackson nodded. "True."

"Who is the kidnapper?" Zerr asked.

Jackson shrugged. "Best guess is the kidnappers are the drug dealers that Michael was carrying the drugs for."

"Are we talking about the bikers?" Zerr asked. "Pickens and the Hells Angels? Pickens controls a lot of the crime in this city."

Jackson shook his head. "No, not local dealers or the Hells Angels. Those drugs were part of an international drug smuggling ring. He smuggled the drugs from Mexico, but no telling for sure where the heart of the operation was."

"What if it's a new gang?" Zerr asked.

"Possibly," Steele said. "The guys at the tattoo parlor were Russian. The hookers are Russian. It's possible the pimp and his chauffer were working for the Russians."

"No one will take on the Hells Angels," Zerr said.

"They might if they had backing, say a Russian mafia," Steele said.

"Oh shit. Another street war."

"I like your idea that it's the Russians," Jackson said.

"We can start checking into this," Steele said.

Jackson held up a hand. "Archer will get the drug squad and Tommy Devlin working on that side of it. You two need to find Brad."

Steele took a quick peek at Zerr.

Jackson peered at Steele, then Zerr. "You two assholes know something, don't you?" Jackson's face went from red to purple. Veins pulsated at his temples. He chewed a bottom lip and shook his head. "I'm stupid. I should have known. Tell me, now."

Steele swallowed hard. He told Jackson how they'd met Brad at Bowness Park and gave him supplies.

Steele swallowed hard and avoided eye contact with Jackson.

"Sometimes Brad contacts us through Annie and Sadie."

"Sadie Andrus, the reporter? Are you two insane? A reporter?"

"Look, Sarge, she hasn't used any of this information to her advantage. She could have."

Jackson shook his head. His lips moved, but no words came out.

"It was the only way," Zerr said.

Jackson nodded slowly. "If I needed to get a message to Coulter, Ms. Andrus could do it."

Steele shrugged. "It has worked in the past."

Jackson downed the last of his coffee, grabbed his parka and stood.

"Where do I find her?"

"She'd be at the CFCN station on Broadcast Hill," Steele said.

There was a knock at her door. Sadie glanced up. The receptionist stood in the doorway, eyes wide and flustered.

"There's a sergeant here to see you. He's quite insistent."

A tall, lean man with salt-and-pepper hair and a bushy mustache pushed past the receptionist. "I apologize, Ms. Andrus, but this is important."

Sadie nodded to the receptionist, who hustled away. "Please have a seat, Sergeant—?"

"Jackson." He slid off his blue parka, set it on one chair,

and took the other across from Sadie. "Staff Sergeant Kent Jackson, Homicide."

Sadie clasped her hands on top of her desk. "How can I help you?"

"I need to talk to Coulter."

Sadie leaned back, eyes wide. "Why are you coming to me?"

Jackson leaned forward, large hands on the desk, and glared. "Ms. Andrus, I don't have time for bullshit. Steele told me about you and Coulter. I don't care about what is or isn't happening between the two of you. But I need to talk to him, urgently. Not to arrest him. I need his help."

Sadie frowned. "I don't contact him. It doesn't work that way. Steele and Zerr see him every night. That's how the information is passed."

"Tonight will be too late." Jackson sat back in the chair. His shoulders sagged and confidence practically dissipated out of him.

Sadie sighed. "There might be a way. But a lot of things need to line up for it to work."

Jackson glanced up and cocked his head. "Anything is worth a try."

CHAPTER SIXTY-TWO

AFTER THEY LEFT THE TRUCK STOP, STEELE AND ZERR DROVE IN silence, each lost in their own thoughts. Steele parked on Crescent Avenue overlooking the city.

"Jackson has me wondering if Brad has lost it," Steele said.

"I might understand Brad losing it if Wolfe were still free, or even in jail." Zerr sipped his takeout coffee. "But now? What reason would Brad have to randomly kill criminals?"

"It's not that random." Steele watched a group of joggers dash past. "He has a connection to a few of them."

"Maybe they're individual murders, not linked at all," Zerr said. "Maybe Brad sees conspiracy in everything."

Steele glared at Zerr. "He was right about the snipers."

"That's my point. He's trying to link things that don't go together."

Steele took a deep breath, then exhaled slowly. "Brad's theory makes sense. Everything fits. Different murder styles, some needing a specific skill set. All criminals, all released from custody to do as they please on the street."

They sat in silence, working on their own theories.

Steele stared at his coffee cup. "You realize all we've eaten for the last couple of days is takeout?"

"I like burgers and fries," Zerr said.

"We work, we eat. It seems like weeks since I've seen Emma."

Zerr winced. "She's due anytime, right?"

"Yup, and I'm not around."

"I hate to say it, buddy, but this isn't the last time you won't be around for a special event—birthdays, Christmases—it's the job."

Steele peered out the window. "Yeah, I know, and she knows, but I should be there."

"Take the rest of the day off. I've got this."

Steele snorted. "Right. A couple of things wrong with that. First, if I leave you alone, you'll get in trouble. Second, do you think I can go home when Brad is in this mess?"

Zerr laughed. "I'd love to be there when you explain that to Emma."

Steele rubbed his chin and sighed. "What do we do now?"

"If it's not Brad, and with the skills needed, it's you." Zerr grinned as he sipped his coffee.

"You're a better candidate," Steele said. "I'll bet you did some nasty shit in Vietnam."

Zerr shrugged. "I could tell you, but then I'd have to kill you."

"See, it must be you."

"Other than Brad and us, who fits the bill?" Zerr asked. "What about Jackson?"

"Are you insane?"

"Hear me out. He had better training than us when he went to Los Angeles. He was injured in the explosion and he nearly died. But the important thing is, he's been involved in this since the beginning. He knows everything about the murders, and he has access to court files. You don't think of him because no one would."

"What's in your coffee?" Steele asked. "It's not Jackson and it's not tactical guys."

Zerr rolled down his window. "If it's a cop, then it is someone who has skills we don't know about."

"A cop with military experience?"

Zerr stared into his coffee cup. "Someone who is batshit crazy."

"That's most cops."

"Most prosecutors, also," Zerr said.

"Prosecutors? Are you crazy?"

"Jenni Blighe's life was twisted upside down by Wolfe."

"Now you're the one who is batshit crazy," Steele said. "What does she weigh? One hundred and ten?"

"Did you check her out when she arrived?"

"What?" Steele glanced at Zerr. "No. Did you? Does Annie know?"

"Listen, jerk, it was hard to miss. Her biceps and triceps aren't just toned, she's ripped. She might be small, but she is in great shape. I heard she was working out and taking self-defense classes, but it's beyond that."

"Being in great shape is one thing," Steele said. "Where

would she get the experience? It's difficult to kill. You know that. We both remember our first kill."

Zerr stared out his window toward the mountains. "Yup. And it will haunt me until the day I die."

"Did it make your second kill easier?"

"I guess so."

"Let's say Brad is right, and the murders started with the drug dealer two months ago. There were hesitation marks on the first dealer. Then months later, another murder with the same MO, but no hesitation marks. A clean kill."

"I still don't see it as Blighe," Zerr said. "There are other prosecutors who are frustrated."

"Or judges."

"I see where you're going with this."

Maggie was Judge Ethan Gray's only daughter. He and his wife, Olivia, withdrew from society for months after Maggie's murder. It was just recently that Judge Gray was back on the bench. Steele hadn't been to his court yet, but other cops talked about the judge having no sympathy for the criminals and frequently giving the maximum sentence. As a result, many of his cases were being appealed. Rumor around the courthouse was that he'd be asked to take a leave of absence.

Zerr chewed on the brim of his cup. "That's one angry man. If you think Brad took Maggie's death hard, Judge Gray took it worse. You can see it in his eyes. They are dark coals of hatred. He has a perpetual scowl and snaps at everyone."

Steele shifted in his seat and stretched his back. "He's angry and he may want revenge, but that's a lot different from being able to carry it out. I don't think it's Gray."

"We have a list of people it isn't," Zerr said. "That doesn't help us a lot."

Steele drummed his fingers against the steering wheel. "We're looking at the wrong people."

"How do you figure that?" Zerr asked.

"Right away we got stuck on the idea it had to be a guy like us, strong with extraordinary experience."

"Some of the murders were pretty precise."

"I agree." Steele swung toward Zerr. "But the Russian girls talked of a small person and were surprised when Blighe mentioned a man. I heard them say that, but I didn't pay attention. Martina thought she knew Blighe."

Zerr's eyes widened. "Blighe?"

"Why not. She is in great shape, she's angry at the court system."

"I don't buy that." Zerr leaned back and folded his arms.

Steele glanced at Zerr, "Annie."

"Now I know you're crazy," Zerr shouted.

Steele grinned and held out his hands. "My point is we need to think differently."

They sat in silence for a couple of minutes, then Zerr said, "We agree Brad didn't do any of the murders. I'm coming around to your idea the killer might be female."

"Why all the evidence against Brad?" Steele asked.

"There's that." Zerr squished his coffee cup. "No evidence pointed to Brad until after the two drug dealers were stabbed and the pimp and driver were shot. Brad was nosing around on those two low-priority killings. Then, by luck, he gets the pimp and chauffer killings. They still seem random, but the killer gets worried because Brad is investigating all four murders."

Steele leaned forward. "But how does the killer know Brad is poking around on the two dealer murders? No one knew he was doing it, except Sturgeon."

"And you and me and Sturgeon's staff and Griffin, Briscoe, Jackson, and …"

"Shit, lots of people," Steele said.

"That's my point."

"If not Brad, then who?" Steele asked.

"That's our mistake. We're checking people close to Maggie or Brad. What if it's not any of them? What if the killer has a hit list? The first killings didn't point to Brad. Then the killer got worried and decided the best way to get Brad off the case was to frame him."

Steele sat back, then nodded. "That's not bad, Sherlock. So now what?"

"We need to figure out who had access to Brad, Lobo, and his gun so they could plant the evidence."

"Makes sense. Who do you have in mind?"

Zerr huffed out an exhale. "Not a fucking clue."

CHAPTER SIXTY-THREE

Bright lights shone on Sadie as she presented the noon news broadcast. She stared at the camera as she read the prompts. "Calgary Police have extended their manhunt for Detective Bradley Coulter outside the province and issued a Canada-wide warrant for his arrest. Officials at the Canadian and US border have also been notified. As previously reported, Coulter is the primary suspect in several murders of known criminals in Calgary. Sources say the case against Detective Coulter is overwhelming and includes ballistic evidence." A photo of Coulter dressed casually from press conferences during the sniper crisis a month ago replaced Sadie's face. "If you know the whereabouts of Coulter or see him, police ask that you call 911."

The image switched back to Sadie.

"On a lighter note, the City of Calgary will host a Christmas light display at Heritage Park this evening. It promises to put everyone in a holiday mood. I know I'll be attending myself with my friend Sissy. I hope to hear from her soon. I'm Sadie Andrus, have a wonderful day."

The lights clicked off. Sadie headed out of the studio, giving her earpiece to a technician on her way out. She stepped into her office, closed the door and slumped in her chair. She rested her head against the back of the chair and closed her eyes.

A knock on her door startled her out of her nap. She leaned forward and rubbed her eyes. "Yes."

Her receptionist opened the door. "Sadie, there's a phone call for you from Sissy. I guess your friend is excited to get together."

"What time is it?"

"Almost two."

Sadie grabbed the receiver and punched the blinking light.

"Sadie Andrus."

There was a moment of silence, then a squeaky voice said, "It's Sissy."

Sadie could barely contain her laughter. It was the furthest thing from a female voice. "Hey, great to hear from you."

"How soon can you get away?"

"Five minutes."

"Pick you up outside the station." The line died.

Sadie grabbed her red parka, scarf and mitts and sprinted down the hall. As she passed the receptionist, she said, "I'll be back for my six o'clock broadcast."

"Where do I say you—"

Sadie was already out the front doors.

Brad hunched in his truck, the camouflage gear not providing much help. He spotted Sadie standing outside the station, her red jacket like a beacon. He swung the truck to the curb. Sadie was still sliding in when he pulled away.

"Jeez. You trying to kill me?" The momentum of the truck closed the door. "You in a hurry to get somewhere?"

"Might not be the best idea for me to hang around a TV station."

Sadie struggled with the seatbelt. "You picked the location. I could have met you somewhere else." She finally glanced at him and gasped. "What happened to you?"

Brad rubbed at his bruised face, not meeting her eyes. "It's nothing. Don't worry about it."

"Black eyes, scrapes, lips split and your stupid scraggly beard." Her eyes were wide. "My God. Do you ever win a fight?"

He turned onto Banff Coach Road and headed west.

"The city is the other way."

Brad glared. "I'm not in the mood for your snark. I've got a few things weighing heavily on me. You know, jail being one of them."

"Jeez, relax." Sadie leaned forward to increase the heat. "You know it's winter, right?"

Brad's jaw was clenched, eyes straight ahead.

"Okay, I'll dial it down," she said. "Where are we going? Banff Springs Hotel for brunch? Romantic getaway?"

"You call that dialing it down?"

"Wait, it's an abduction. That would be ironic."

Brad glanced at her, eyes squinting. "Why?"

"Because, asshat, that's the news I have for you."

"That you're being abducted?"

"Oh my god. Sometimes you are so dense." She sighed. "Mayor Kearse's nephew, Michael Trant, has been kidnapped."

Brad's foot slid off the accelerator, and the truck abruptly slowed.

"What?"

"Yup. Sometime last night, early hours this morning. Kearse got a ransom call."

"How the hell do you know this?" He pulled to the side of the road.

"Jackson told me."

He squirmed in his seat until he was facing Sadie. "Staff Sergeant Kent Jackson?"

Sadie rolled her eyes. "No, Michael Jackson."

"Spill it."

Sadie recited what Jackson had told her, including the kidnapper's demands. She added the part about another murder—a man falling down the stairs drunk, with Brad's police baton showing up under the dead guy's couch with Brad's fingerprints on it. The bad news seemed unending until Sadie told him Steele and Zerr located the hookers from the tattoo parlor and they admitted to lying about his car.

Brad stared out the window, then closed his eyes.

"I'm turning myself in," Brad said. "Might not hurt to make a show of my arrest at headquarters in case someone is watching."

"You think it's a cop?"

"I'm not positive, but I'm sure someone in the department is the killer or is helping the killer."

Sadie's eyebrows furrowed. "You're saying the killer and kidnapper are the same person?"

Brad nodded. "For sure."

"What evidence of that do you have?"

"It's the single theory that fits. Various methods of killing, all successful, using specific skills that required expertise. A knowledge of crime scene investigation. A knowledge of the victims—each one a criminal who went back into the public."

"Someone like you," Sadie said.

Brad cocked his head. "True. Or any TSU."

"The evidence points to you," Sadie said.

"Most of it's bullshit."

Sadie leaned tight against the truck door, arms across her chest. "Most of it?"

"Someone must have stolen my police baton and planted it. Anyone could find out I had a history with some victims and target them specifically to point back to me. The girls at the tattoo parlor were coached what to say by the killer."

"You realize how ridiculous that sounds."

Brad glared at Sadie, then stared out the front window. "The one I can't figure out is my gun matching the bullets with the pimp downtown and at the tattoo parlor."

"Ballistics doesn't lie."

"We already talked about this. I'd never use my gun if I were the murderer and then carry it at work? Over the years, I've had access to hundreds of guns I could have slipped in my pocket. If I didn't do that, then I could get one off the street in about five minutes with the asshat's fingerprints and they'd be arresting some street punk for the murders, not me."

Sadie shifted in her seat. "Tell me about your gun."

"What's to say? It's always with me."

Sadie cocked her head. "Always?"

Brad sighed. "Jeez, Sadie. It's on my hip ten to sixteen hours a day. Or it's locked up at home in my bedroom."

"Those are the only two options?"

"Yes."

"At home you always lock it up?"

"Yes."

Sadie leaned toward Brad. "So, on your hip or in a safe."

"Yes."

"At work, it is only on your hip?"

Brad rolled his eyes. "Yes."

Sadie pressed, "Never in your desk?"

Brad slammed his palms on the steering wheel. "No. Sadie, let this go."

"A little late to turn yourself in. Griffin is still pissed he let you walk away."

"He'll get over that," Brad said.

"You hope."

Brad leaned into the steering wheel. "I take the heroin and make the trade. Heroin and me, for Michael."

"Are you serious?" Sadie gasped. "He'll kill you *and* Michael and have four kilos of heroin. That's your plan."

"If I deliver the drugs, then I'll always know where they are. I can rescue Michael and arrest the sick bastard."

"The killer or killers will take the drugs, kill you, and then kill Michael. That's a stupid plan."

"It's the one I'm working on. I have no intention of getting killed."

"It won't be as simple as setting the heroin on a park bench, and when they grab it, you make the arrest. Whoever has Michael will make you run around the city until they know you're alone, then they'll still have Michael, but also have you and the drugs."

"I won't be alone. I'll have TSU close by."

"Oh, brilliant plan. Bet the kidnapper never figured you'd get your buddies to back you up."

"I'm counting on it."

Sadie snorted. "You have no idea what you'll be walking into. Maybe one guy, maybe five or ten. Archer confiscated your guns."

"They took the ones they knew about. The present from Annie for Sissy was two guns and ammunition. I'm using my older TSU Hi-Power and a CZ75, I uh, had as a spare."

Sadie rolled her eyes. "The kidnappers search you and take your guns. Then a strip search, beat the shit out of you, then kill you. They'll have the heroin and Michael is no longer needed. He dies. They never find your bodies. But we know they got the heroin because we see more overdoses and additional heroin deaths." She rubbed her eye and rested her head against the window. "Did I miss anything?"

Brad cocked his head to the side. "That covers it. Except in my version I come out with Michael and the heroin, and the killer is dead."

"You live in a dream world. Or have a death wish."

Brad dropped Sadie back at the TV station and swung out onto Banff Coach Road, heading east. He'd been frustrated with Sadie's questions about his gun. It was a part of him. He'd be lost without it. In fact, when he went out without the gun, he felt a part of him was missing. He couldn't think of a time he'd ever forgotten his gun for work, or any moment when he realized he'd set it down. It wasn't like a wallet or car keys. He always knew where his gun was.

Sadie was right, though. Ballistics on his gun was enough to convict him. Twenty-five to life for the pimp and his bodyguard, the three asshats at the tattoo parlor, and who knew how many more murders they'd attribute to him.

He followed Bow Trail past Shaganappi Golf Course toward downtown. The kidnapping didn't fit into the other crimes—all murders, though Vinnie Bevan was barely hanging on. Was he wrong? Was this simply a crime wave? Unrelated crimes, murders and an abduction. Was he creating conspiracy theories where there weren't any? Nope. Most of the crimes were linked to him. No one else.

The evidence pointed to him. Sure, some of it was circumstantial—except for his gun. Last year he had the new Hi-Power fine-tuned to his specifications by a gunsmith. He'd also had the barrel replaced since he'd fired thousands of rounds through the original barrel. That was the one time it had been out of his control.

He still spent a lot of time at the range and fired thousands of rounds each year. An hour at the range would be soothing. At the range—

His head jerked to his rearview mirror as a siren sounded. An unmarked police vehicle had pulled in behind him. *Shit.* Traffic cop. Brad's initial reaction was to hit the gas and flee. That might work in his Trans Am. Not a chance in the truck. He pounded his palms on the steering wheel and pulled to the curb. He rolled down his window and waited. Eyes ahead, he hoped it was merely a traffic violation for the expired plates. However, once he gave his driver's license, backup would be called. He'd be surrounded and arrested. He was sitting in his truck in his last few moments of freedom.

The crunch of boots in the snow approached his door. Brad glanced over his shoulder. His eyes widened. He knew who the killer was.

Sadie shook the snow off her red parka and stomped her feet. Her toes were frozen. Was it too much to ask that the truck had heat? The world appeared upside down. A decent cop was being hunted for murders she didn't believe he committed. She had the inside scoop on the story of the decade, and she didn't report it. She glanced out the door at the retreating truck. One man against the world. Then a dark van passed in front of the entrance doors and followed Brad out of the TV station's exit. *Oh, shit.*

It wasn't a marked police van, but something about it shouted *cops*. Had the cops figured out about her and Brad? Was it the Internal Affairs detectives?

Brad always said there was no such thing as coincidences.

She had no way to contact him. Even if she could, it would be too late. There was one chance. She raced down the hall to her office.

CHAPTER SIXTY-FOUR

FINALLY, DICE'S PATIENCE PAID OFF. SADIE ANDRUS SPRINTED out of the TV station and into an old truck. The vehicle pulled away from the curb.

Dice let the truck get several blocks ahead and then followed. Instead of heading into downtown, the truck veered right, out of the city. *Ms. Andrus, where are you going?*

During surveillance the past two days, Dice hadn't seen Andrus with the truck. Surveillance had been brief, but Dice discovered nothing about Andrus having a boyfriend. She was separated from her husband and according to court documents Dice acquired, it would be a long and nasty process. That's what happens when physical abuse is an issue.

Outside the city it was a challenge to keep distance while also keeping the truck in sight. Dice grinned, thinking about the mayor's nephew and his suffering. For hours, his own heroin had been administered, then reversed. The highs and lows had him screaming, begging for the drugs to stop. Now he knew the pain his smuggling activities had subjected hundreds of addicts to. Eventually an overdose would be given. But not before he lived through hell, over and over.

The brake lights of the truck interrupted Dice's thoughts. *Damn.* Daydreaming had gotten Dice too close. The only hope was to pull off the road. *Damn. Damn.*

Dice quickly pulled onto a farm lane, swung around in the farmyard, and slowly headed back to the road. There was no sign of the truck. Decision time. Head west on the highway or head back to the TV studio.

Out of town made no sense. Andrus might be meeting with someone with a news tip, or boyfriend for some afternoon delight. No matter, she'd have to be back at the studio for her broadcasts. *Shit.* Dice swung onto the highway and headed back to the TV station.

Twenty minutes later, the truck drove up to the main doors of the TV station. Andrus jumped out, then leaned back into the truck.

Goodbye smooch? Last words? Then she shut the door and jogged to the main doors.

The truck pulled away, sliding on the ice. The driver expertly steered through the fishtail and drove past.

"Coulter."

Sometimes all the planning in the world wasn't enough. Other times, luck was all you needed.

Toscana spotted the old truck driving along the Shaganappi Golf Course. Deep snow covered the fairways and greens. As she got close, she noticed the license plate tag was expired by two years.

She swung in behind the truck and hit the lights.

The truck's brake lights flashed once. The truck sped up, then slowed and pulled to the curb.

Toscana stopped behind the truck and exited her vehicle. With one hand on her gun, the other holding the long black tube at her left side, she approached the truck. The driver's window was down, and the driver sat motionless with his hands on the steering wheel.

Toscana stood at the driver's shoulder and leaned forward. "Good afternoon, Detective."

Coulter's head swung toward the window, eyes wide. "Toscana?"

"You look like shit. Talking again when you should have been listening?"

"Something like that."

"The entire city is searching for you."

"How did you find me?"

Toscana grinned. "Wild guess and a lot of luck. I knew your friends were being watched closely, yet you still evaded capture. Someone had to be helping you. Then I remembered a while ago some of my cops talked about you and the TV reporter, Sadie Andrus, and something about you two having breakfast. I took a chance and staked out the TV station."

"What happens now?"

Toscana watched Brads eyes as they flicked from side to side. He was evaluating options just like she knew he would.

"We're having a friendly chat while you wait for backup to arrive?""

Toscana saw Brad's left-hand slide toward his gun.

"Nope. No backup." Toscana jabbed the cattle prod into Brad's chest.

There was pleasure on the verge of euphoria as she heard sparking and watched incredible pain rip through Coulter's body as his muscles contracted and threatened to snap. His breath came in gasps, but he was unable to scream. His eyes widened as the pain increased, then he collapsed onto the steering wheel.

CHAPTER SIXTY-FIVE

STEELE AND ZERR WERE PARKED OFF ELEVENTH STREET, southwest by the Planetarium. Snow fell gently, and the wipers cleared the window every ten seconds. The clouds were low and gray. The weather matched their moods—dismal. No new leads. Archer still hadn't included TSU in his rescue plans for Kearse's nephew. They were in the dark.

"I hate sitting here doing sweet F-all." Steele stared out the window and chewed a nail.

Zerr spit sunflower seeds out his window.

"It's minus ten Fahrenheit and you have the window open."

Zerr shrugged. "I can spit the shells on the floor if you'd like."

"I'd prefer you not chew sunflower seeds."

"They're healthy for you."

Steele glared. "You use more energy eating than any nutrition you get."

Zerr spit out a wad of shells. "You're whiny."

Steele rolled his eyes. "Give me a handful."

They cracked seeds and stared at the falling snow. Their pagers buzzed one after the other. They read the message, then their heads swung toward each other. *"Call Sadie Andrus. ASAP or sooner."*

They jumped out of the Suburban and sprinted into the Planetarium. As they approached the reception desk, Steele said, "We need to use your phone. Police emergency."

The receptionist placed the phone on the counter. Steele grabbed it and dialed. He heard ringing.

"Sadie Andrus."

"It's Steele."

Zerr pushed his head next to Steele's "It may be nothing, but Brad picked me up at the station."

"What? Why?"

"No time for that now. When he dropped me off, a van followed him."

"Where was he going?" Steele asked.

"I don't know. But he headed toward downtown."

"What's he driving?"

"His old farm truck. Has he been arrested?"

"We've heard nothing on the radio," Steele said. "No one has said they pulled Brad over or called for backup. They'd be crazy to arrest Brad alone."

"Maybe it's nothing," Sadie said.

"No, go with your gut," Steele replied. "We're not far away. We'll head in your direction, then double back. I'll call you if we find anything."

They raced back to the Suburban and swung onto Sixth Avenue, then onto Bow Trail. Zerr sped up the hill.

"You in a hurry?" Steele asked.

"Time is important," Zerr replied.

"But we don't know where we're going."

Zerr grinned. "But we're making great time."

Steele glared at Zerr. "Glad you feel you're being useful." Then Steele's eyes widened as he stared past Zerr. "There. There."

Zerr followed Steele's gaze. "Holy shit." He swerved into the left lane, spun a U-turn at the next intersection, and raced back toward downtown. He slid the Suburban to a stop behind a truck. They jumped out, guns drawn, and headed up the sides of the vehicle.

Steele peered into the passenger's seat, then across to Zerr. "Shit." The truck was empty.

"You sure this is Brad's truck?" Zerr asked.

"Oh, yeah." Steele tried the door. It opened. The passenger's side floor mat was littered with empty coffee cups and fast-food wrappers. "At least his diet hasn't changed." He sifted through the garbage.

Zerr held up a thin folder. "Registration and insurance. Both expired."

"Where was that?" Steele asked.

"Driver's floorboard."

Steele frowned. "That makes little sense."

Zerr shrugged. "It's not like Brad's had this truck detailed —ever."

"True."

Zerr unfolded a small piece of paper that was loose in the insurance folder. "This is interesting."

Steele raised his head from the pile of garbage. "What?"

Zerr passed it over. Steele glanced at it. One word was scrawled on the paper.

"Toscana."

Briscoe parked his van behind the Suburban and headed to Steele and Zerr. As he hiked, he zipped his issue parka, slipped on gloves, and placed his fake fur hat on his head.

"Well?" Steele asked.

"Toscana is supposed to be off duty," Briscoe said. "But she signed out a van this morning."

"Does she have court?" Steele asked.

Briscoe shook his head. "Nope. She said nothing to anyone about why she needed the van."

"So, what's she up to?" Zerr asked.

There was silence as the three men shivered in the cold. Snow stuck to their clothing.

Briscoe stared at the darkening downtown skyline shrouded in low clouds. Fingers of exhaust reached to the sky from every building. "Did you two know Brad was using the truck?"

They shook their heads. "I didn't even think of it," Steele said. "He just uses it around the farm. Maybe an occasional trip to the dump."

"In an unregistered, uninsured vehicle?" Briscoe asked.

"He's a rebel, for sure," Steele said. "Probably get life for that."

"Smartass," Briscoe said.

"Maybe it was a traffic stop," Zerr said. "Some cop spotted the expired plate."

"I checked as soon as you called me," Briscoe said. "Communications says the plate wasn't checked through the computer. Coulter's name wasn't checked either."

"What about an alias?" Zerr asked.

"Are you serious?" Steele asked.

Zerr shrugged. "Why not? Maybe he made up one."

"Why would he do that?" Steele glared at Zerr.

"He might, if he were guilty," Briscoe said.

"That's bullshit," Steele spat. "I won't listen to that kind of talk. It's not helping us at all."

Briscoe held up his hands. "Don't snap at me. You need to accept that there may be things we don't know about Brad. If he wasn't a friend, we'd all believe he was guilty and hunt him to the ends of the earth. He's a friend, but he still might have committed the murders."

Steele threw his hands in the air. "Fuckin' great. Now Griffin has you thinking Brad is guilty. I'm sorry I called you." Steele stalked away to the shoulder of the roadway.

"I hit a touchy spot," Briscoe said.

"You just said out loud what we're all trying hard not to think," Zerr said. "You don't think Brad is guilty, do you?"

Briscoe dusted the snow off his parka.

CHAPTER SIXTY-SIX

STURGEON SWUNG THE DOOR OPEN AND STEPPED INTO THE GUN lab. The familiar odor of gunpowder and lead hung heavy in the air all the time. But he detected the odor of fresh gunshots. Gayle and Angie stood beside a long wooden table with stripped guns on top. A long fluorescent table light shone onto the guns. Analysis reports were taped to the wall.

Gayle grabbed Sturgeon's arm and pulled him to the table. "We've got it figured out."

"Great. Show me what you have."

"We took the pistol apart and examined each piece," Gayle said. "Hard to say when the gun was last fired, but it had been cleaned. Most of the gun was spotless."

"Most of the gun?" Sturgeon asked.

"Yes." Gayle picked up a black tube. "Except for the barrel."

"What?" Sturgeon took the barrel and peered down its length. "The barrel wasn't clean?"

"Sure, it was clean." Gayle pointed to a row of plastic containers. "We analyzed what cleaning solution had been used on each component."

"The department doesn't issue cleaning solutions," Sturgeon said. "Every cop buys their own."

Angie picked up two plastic bottles. "True, but would a cop clean all parts of the gun with one solution, and the barrel with another?"

"That would be unusual, to say the least." Sturgeon's eyes grew wide. "Two cleaning solutions for the same gun?"

"Exactly." Gayle nodded enthusiastically. "And there's one interesting thing."

Angie slid an analysis over to Sturgeon. "The barrel was not as clean as the rest of the gun."

"My guess is the barrel would be the cleanest," Sturgeon said. "It's the easiest part of a pistol to clean."

"Exactly." Gayle picked up a different gun. "So, we checked Coulter's backup gun."

Sturgeon's eyebrows rose. "And you found?"

Gayle grinned. "The CZ was cleaned with the same cleaning solution as Coulter's pistol."

"Except his barrel," Sturgeon finished.

"Exactly," Gayle said.

"But the serial numbers matched," Sturgeon said.

"On the frame. There aren't always serial numbers on a replacement barrel for a Browning Hi-Power."

"No shit," Sturgeon said.

"Our theory," Gayle said, "is that at some point, Coulter's barrel was changed for the killer's barrel."

"Excellent work, ladies," Sturgeon said. "I have to find Staff Sergeant Jackson."

CHAPTER SIXTY-SEVEN

AN UNMARKED POLICE SEDAN PULLED OFF THE ROAD IN FRONT OF the truck and plowed through snow as it stopped. The door opened and Sergeant Jackson hauled his lanky frame out. He zipped his parka and slid on gloves as he strode to Briscoe and Zerr. Steele ambled over. Jackson glanced at Briscoe. "Charming hat."

"Yeah, well, my ears ain't gonna freeze off and my brain stays warm," Briscoe said.

"You need a better hat then." Jackson glanced at Steele and Zerr. "How did you find the truck?"

Steele told Jackson about the call from Sadie and how they spotted the abandoned truck.

"Ms. Andrus got my message to Coulter," Jackson said.

Zerr glanced at Steele, then said, "I guess. You know?"

"What did you find in the truck?" Jackson asked.

Zerr told Jackson about the registration and insurance and the scrawled note with the word, *"Toscana."*

Jackson rubbed his chin. "He was leaving us a message. He didn't have much time. There are only two reasons you pull out your registration and insurance. If you're in a traffic accident and you are exchanging details with the guy. Or—"

"The cops stop you," Zerr said.

Jackson nodded. "Not any cop."

"Toscana," Briscoe said.

"She's all hot about tactical stuff," Zerr said. "She's built solid. In the TSU testing a few months ago, she bench pressed more than some guys on the team." Zerr glanced at Steele, who gave him the finger.

"I know she's at the range at least three times a week," Briscoe said.

"And she'd know all about crime scene investigations," Jackson said. "And how to plant evidence. Well, that fits with what Sturgeon and his team found."

"What's that?" Briscoe asked.

"You know, most of the evidence against Brad was circumstantial and easily disproved," Jackson said. "The most damning evidence was ballistics. Sturgeon's techs believe the killer swapped the barrel on Brad's gun for the killer's gun."

"How?" Steele asked. "None of us ever let our guns out of our sight unless we lock them up. You taught us that, Sarge. Brad told us that at every meeting. Every frickin' meeting."

"The only way we answer that question is by finding Brad," Jackson said.

"And Toscana," Briscoe added.

CHAPTER SIXTY-EIGHT

BRAD'S CAMOUFLAGE PARKA WAS ZIPPED, HIS COLLAR UP, AND his hands were behind his back. He hunched into the wind as he headed south from the crack houses of Victoria Park. The gray day from the low clouds was fast approaching darkness.

A freezing December wind whipped through him like he didn't have the parka at all. Ice needles peppered his body, mostly his face, which had no protection.

Minutes into the walk and Brad was chilled to the bone. He shivered, shoulders hunched, and chin tucked into the top of his parka. The crunch of snow was steady behind him. The cold steel at his neck reminded him he'd let his guard down for a second, maybe even less, and screwed up. The pain in his chest and the headache were a further reminder.

Toscana told him to stare ahead and keep walking. As he wiggled his gloveless fingers to get circulation flowing, the gun pressed harder against his neck. The voice said, "Don't."

His brain ripped through ideas for his escape. But a

confounding variable was Kearse's nephew. If Brad put up a fight now, chances are they'd never find Michael and not in time to save his life.

Brad continued south.

"So, where are we heading?" Brad asked.

"Shut up."

"Trying to make conversation," Brad said.

There was no response.

To pass the time, Brad thought about his mistakes. First, meeting Sadie had been dumb. He should have known the killer would figure that out. Second, he'd been slow to figure out who the killer was. By the time he knew, it was too late. And third, he was an idiot.

Capture was an interesting twist. He was with the killer and likely heading to wherever Michael was being held. All good. Not so good was his pistol and Maggie's gun, his backup, were gone. No doubt taken while he was unconscious. He was weaponless. He just needed to wait for the right moment.

"I would have bet money that you were taking me to Victoria Park," Brad said. "You know, end this where you started."

"I told you to shut up." The gun moved away. Before he could react, the butt of the gun slammed into the side of his head. The world spun, and he staggered a few steps. A hand grabbed the collar of his parka and pulled him upright. The gun was pressing into the back of his neck again.

"Keep walking."

Brad's vision cleared, and he tried to figure out where they were going. He'd been sure where the murders started would also be the end. Not for the first time today, he'd been wrong. That it would stop now, he was sure. He had no intention of it being Kearse's nephew or him. In his mind, just one person was going to die.

"Not a great way to continue a relationship."

The gun pressed harder into his neck. "You've had plenty of opportunities to have a conversation."

"Let's cut the bullshit, Toscana."

"You can call me Dice." She pronounced the name *dee kay*.

"Are you seriously calling yourself by a nickname? Wow. What the hell? Why *dee kay*?" He said it in a mocking voice.

"Dice in Greek mythology means Goddess of Justice."

That wasn't the answer Brad expected. "Is this about revenge?" He glanced over his shoulder.

The sidewalk was slick. Brad contemplated a slip, going down on one knee. Then he could either swing his arm around and take his assailant's legs out, or a whip kick would do the same. Then he was back to the same problem of finding out where Kearse's nephew was being held. No, it wasn't the time.

If he wasn't being taken to a drug house in Victoria Park, then where? No one was on the streets, and no one paid any attention from the few houses that still had glass windows.

He stamped his feet as he hiked, willing circulation to return and warm blood to flow to his toes. The icy wind was at their backs, with Toscana absorbing most of the blast.

"I need to know Michael Trant is okay."

Toscana smacked the back of Brad's head. "What part of shut up are you having trouble with?"

Brad caught the hint of hesitation in the voice. "I'm

having trouble with all of it. Maybe we weren't best friends, but you came to me for advice. I was straight with you about your chances for TSU. We had pizza and beer and some laughs. I helped you with Briscoe. I don't understand why you are doing this."

There was a snort. "Ah, are your feelings hurt? You know all you need to know. The last couple of weeks I didn't hesitate to kill. If you don't follow everything I ask, you will die. I'll leave your gutted and bleeding corpse splayed out. Then I will take pleasure in killing Trant."

Brad tried to figure out how he'd missed the warning signs with Toscana. She'd been on the periphery of events with the snipers, but there'd been nothing to make him suspicious. She was aggressive and career oriented. Driven to get ahead. Even at the range and having pizza, he had felt no danger. "If you keep killing, they'll know it wasn't me."

Toscana laughed. "Maybe. But forever you'll be remembered as a disgraced cop. I can live with that."

"There are people who won't accept that I did the killings. They'll keep hunting for you."

"Ah, isn't that cute." Toscana sneered and her voice mocked. "Your precious group of friends will fight to clear your name. They might try, but there is overwhelming evidence against you."

"The next time you murder, they'll pour over the crime scene, the evidence, the method. They'll find you."

Toscana sighed and shook her head. "Oh, Coulter. The dream world you live in. I tried to vary my modus operandi, but obviously I slipped up since you figured out the cases were connected. In the future, I'll plan better and make sure there are no breadcrumbs for your friends to follow. Even if they connect a few murders, it will be too late for you. You'll be in heaven or hell with your beloved Maggie."

Brad's gut clenched. He had an idea where they were headed. "Are we there yet?"

Pain ripped through the back of his head; the full force of the blow knocked him to his knee. He rolled onto his shoulder rather than having his face pounded into the ice. That happens when you have your hands tied behind your back. The icy cold was soothing. He blinked his eyes, his vision cloudy. He could nearly make out a face framed by the hood of a parka. As his vision cleared, he was yanked to his feet, the gun jamming into his neck.

"Stop being a smartass. Shut the fuck up and move."

They continued south. The city was in complete darkness. Clouds formed around the streetlights, giving an eerie, eighteenth-century-London feel. If Jack the Ripper had popped out from between houses, he wouldn't have been surprised. He'd rather take his chances with the Ripper. Pain pounded in the back of his head in time with the beat of his heart. If he could get his heart rate down, maybe the pounding would subside. Then Toscana jabbed the gun deeper into his neck. Yeah, his heart rate wasn't coming down anytime soon.

Toscana shoved him toward the abandoned building. Sandstone and brick walls had defied seventy years of harsh weather. The windows had not survived vandalism and were boarded.

"Open the door," Toscana ordered.

Coulter stepped through the doorway first, the gun still firmly against his neck. The room was in darkness, their footsteps echoed, and he sensed they were in an open area, maybe half the size of a school gym. Coulter stepped farther into the room. Toscana followed, one hand on his shoulder, the other holding the gun at his neck. They headed through the room. Coulter stopped and Toscana bumped into him. He listened. It was faint, but someone was moaning ahead. A sniffle, then moaning.

Toscana shoved Coulter toward the increasing sound. They came to a heavy door. "Inside."

Coulter opened the door.

The moaning ceased. A voice pleaded, "Please, stop."

The dark room flooded with light. When Coulter's eyes adjusted, he saw a young man secured by ropes to a chair. *Michael Trant*. He was slim, emaciated, and mid-twenties. His brown hair was long, to his shoulders, with a greasy shine. He looked nothing like Roger Kearse.

Blood oozed from dozens of cuts. His face was bloated like he'd been in a heavyweight championship fight. One eye was swollen shut. He had the vacant stare of someone high on opioids.

"Hey, are you Michael Trant?" Coulter stepped toward the man.

Toscana jammed the cold steel of the gun into Coulter's neck.

"Move and you die," Toscana said. "Slowly kneel."

Coulter knelt. "Hang in there, Michael."

Toscana pulled Coulter's head back by his hair. "Shut up. Stay on your knees."

"What the hell are you doing, Toscana?"

"Isn't it obvious? I'm executing the sentence they should

have received. The courts are gutless. These predators are allowed back into society to continue their depravity, to prey on the weakest. If the courts don't stand up for the victims, who will?"

"You?"

"Yes, me." Dice slid the cattle prod out of her pocket and jammed it into Coulter's side.

CHAPTER SIXTY-NINE

THE APB ON THE UNMARKED POLICE VAN FINALLY PAID OFF. A patrol cruiser had spotted the van parked in Victoria Park. Jackson coordinated TSU raids on several houses. They arrested a dozen with outstanding warrants, seized drugs from every house, but didn't find Brad, Michael, or the killer.

Steele tossed his helmet into the back of the Suburban in frustration.

"What a fucking waste of time."

"We kicked a hornet's nest of lowlifes and drug dealers in the area," Zerr said. "They'll be crapping bricks for weeks."

"You realize that they'll all be back onto the street before dark, right?" Steele asked.

"Sure, but it was fun," Zerr said.

"But it didn't get us any closer to finding Brad or Michael or the killer."

"You're being whiny again."

Jackson headed over to them.

"Get anything worthwhile, Sarge?" Steele asked.

"Not initially. There was a weird person hanging around here a few weeks ago. Dressed all in black and kept to the shadows."

"Probably doing surveillance for the second murder."

Jackson nodded and blew onto his fingers. "Yup. Another guy said at least an hour ago, two were people heading east toward the rundown Symons Mattress factory." Zerr and Steele exchanged glances. Every cop knew about the Symons factory. In the summer, on warm nights after shift, occasionally cops gathered for a brew or two after work.

"Homeless heading out of the cold to shelter in the factory," Zerr said.

"Maybe," Jackson replied. "He said one guy was dressed in jeans and a blue parka and the other person, shorter, was behind and dressed in black."

"Okay, you convinced me," Steele said.

CHAPTER SEVENTY

Brad was floating in cold darkness, then toward a light. He was over—well, he wasn't sure what he was over. People moved below him, hustling from one place to another. He floated across the street and over some steps. A door opened, and he continued. Another door opened, and he was in a courtroom. "It is clear, Your Honor, that Coulter is guilty," Jenni Blighe said. "His carelessness, his ego and his failure to protect the innocent all contributed to the death. You must sentence him accordingly."

The judge, Ethan Gray, glared at Brad. His words were obvious.

"Coulter? Coulter? You had one job. Protect my daughter. I release you into the custody of Dice. May the Goddess of Justice have mercy on your soul. Or not." His eyes blazed and an evil grin crossed his face. He laughed, a loud, maniacal laugh. The judge disappeared. Brad's body wouldn't move. The room went dark and he was freezing.

"Coulter."

He lifted his head a few inches and opened his eyes. It took a moment to focus. Then it started coming back. Toscana sat before him, grinning. Her hands rested on her thighs, one hand holding her gun. He glanced down. His camouflage parka, gloves, and beanie lay in a pile on the floor. His upper body, with only a T-shirt, shivered.

He was in a chair, his arms still tied behind his back, calves tied to the legs of the chair. Several loops of rope tightly encircled his chest, making it difficult to take a deep breath.

"What the hell?" Brad struggled against the ropes.

"For a while, I admired you." Toscana casually sat back in the chair. "With the shit you'd been through, I was sure you'd understand what needed to be done." She smiled sadly. "But you were weak." Her voice rose. "Unfortunate, really. We could have cleaned up the city. Partners." She let out an exasperated sigh. "Crime would decrease. Criminals we didn't execute would flee the city. Almost as good."

"You're out of your mind." Brad jerked his body in the chair.

"You're too smart for your own well-being. You slipped through my carefully planned frame-up. This isn't personal. But I can't let you stop me." Her nostrils flared.

Brad flexed and relaxed his hands and wrists. He slid his arms up and down and side to side against the ropes. Soon his arms were on fire from the rope burn, but he continued. He needed to create some slack in the ropes. He slid as low as he could in the chair. His fingers spread and he reached as far around his back as he could. His fingers searched for the cold metal he'd clipped to his pants under his belt. Nothing there.

"Searching for this?" Toscana held his tactical knife in her hand and waved it in front of his eyes. "Quite sneaky, clipping it under your belt." Toscana held her finger to her lips. "Now who was it that told me to always carry a knife?" She swung the hand holding the knife wide, then pointed it at Brad. "Why, it was *you*." She grinned. "The gun on your hip and your right ankle were easy. She flicked her wrist, and the blade flew open. She gently touched the edge across his face. "Oh, nice and sharp. I bet it would cut the ropes with no problem and you could escape. You won't find out." She closed the knife and slid it into her pants pocket. She glanced over at Michael. "There are too many who need justice."

"Your justice." Brad practically spit the words.

"My justice." Toscana sneered with an ugly twist of her mouth. "Does it matter? Like I said, if the courts won't do it, I will."

Brad laughed. "You aren't the Goddess of Justice. You're a punk, a thug with an overgrown sense of yourself. You're a cold-hearted killer with an over-confident sense of superiority, nothing more."

Toscana loomed over Brad, her face reddening.

Brad jutted out his chin. "True justice doesn't mete out punishment for a chosen few. The laws are the same for all."

Toscana leaned inches from Brad's face. "Those who died were guilty. They were also the scum of society. That's a win both ways."

Keep her talking.

Brad rolled his eyes, his chin high. "You haven't given the

justice system a chance. Heck, you haven't even given being a cop a chance. We see some evil stuff, and the courts don't always see it the way we do, but they take a lot of evil pricks off the street."

"Correction, pretty boy." Toscana straightened, legs wide, eyes blazing. "We arrest many people, but few of them end up in jail. Hell, most are out on bail before we've even completed the paperwork. Out to re-offend. Right back to the shit they were doing."

Brad's eyes peered around the room. His options for escaping weren't promising. His muscles were stiffening from the cold. She's slipped a cog. She was crazy. *Keep her talking.*

"It's not a perfect system, but it's better than every other freaking one."

She raised an eyebrow and laughed. "How did the perfect system work for you? Fiancée and baby dead." Toscana's tone was mocking. "All because the jail system couldn't keep Wolfe secured. He escapes jail not once, but twice. Each time he continues killing. Where's the justice in that, smartass? A perfect example of the failure of the system. I can't believe you would even try to defend that."

Brad clenched his jaw until he felt the pain up to his temples. He couldn't let Toscana distract him. *Keep talking and figure a way out of here.* There was no doubt she was going to kill him and Michael.

"Wolfe was a despicable piece of shit, I'll give you that," Brad said. "He's the exception, though, not the rule. What's the burr up your ass, anyway?"

"Fuck you, Coulter. You think your perfect family—oops,

sorry, the perfect family you let get killed—is the only one affected by shitbags?"

Brad sneered. "Let me guess, you've got some sad story you want to tell me. Something you want to get off your chest. Some vast *boo-hoo*. Tell you what, Toscana, I'm not fuckin' interested."

In three strides, Toscana was in front of Brad. She jabbed the cattle prod into his chest. He screamed and struggled against his restraints. Brad's entire body was on fire. He thought his head would explode.

Toscana stepped back, grinning.

Brad slumped in the chair and gasped for air. An involuntary shiver rolled through his body. He needed to come up with a better plan than pissing off Toscana. Maybe listening was the best idea.

"Tell me," he gasped. "What happened in your life that was so horrible that you needed to take revenge? What did any of these guys do to you? You didn't just kill them, you executed them, and then put some on display."

Toscana ignored Coulter and headed to Michael. She pulled a syringe out of her pocket, injected the needle into Michael's arm, and pushed the plunger.

Michael's head wobbled back and forth; his eyes grew wide. Coulter watched Michael's pupils constrict. His head bobbled a couple of times, then dropped to his chest.

"You're killing him," Brad said.

"That's the point." Toscana's lips curled. "Michael first, then you."

Brad strained against the restraints, wobbling the chair.

He was no closer to escaping. *Bargain.* "Let Michael go. Keep me here."

"Aw, isn't that amusing. Coulter being the bigger man." She touched her hand to her heart. '"*Take me, but leave Michael alone.*'" Her voice was mocking again. "Why would I want to do that? I have both of you. Neither of you are leaving alive. Your deaths, however, will be totally different. When you two are finally found, Michael will be dead from an overdose and you will have apparently committed suicide, not able to live with all the killings."

"Why not put the energy into making the system better? You're smart. You're on the fast track as a cop." Brad felt some give in one chair leg.

"I've done better in the last few weeks than you've done your entire career."

"Mutilating and killing? You call that better?"

"Dealing out justice, the courts couldn't. If there had been someone like me around twenty-two years ago, my skills wouldn't be needed. My sister would still be alive."

Brad rolled his eyes. Finally, Toscana was going to reveal her secret. He couldn't hold back the sarcasm. "All right, I'll bite. What happened to your sister?"

"Took you long enough to ask, asshat." Toscana straightened and paced the room. She'd become a performer in her own play. "See, that's your problem, you are so egotistical, you can't comprehend that others have something to say, might have an opinion."

"Just tell your story." Brad glared. "Cut the drama."

Toscana grabbed a chair, set it in front of Brad, and leaned close. "My sixteen-year-old sister was babysitting a couple blocks away. Never made it home. Mom and Dad didn't know until the next morning, when she wasn't at home and the bed hadn't been slept in. The police were called, but it was the usual crap. She was a teenaged girl, maybe she was out with her boyfriend. It hasn't been twenty-four hours yet. Didn't investigate it at all. Two days later, her body was found behind a dumpster in a park. She'd been raped and then murdered."

Toscana stood and twirled Brad's tactical knife between her fingers. "I was eight, so I didn't understand what was happening. All I knew was that my mom wouldn't stop crying. And my dad was angry. I was scared, I didn't understand what was happening, why my parents didn't have time for me." Toscana's chin trembled.

She stared across the room for a moment, then bounded back in front of Brad, her voice rising with venom.

"Police didn't have any suspects and stopped coming by." Brad was losing feeling in his body. He wiggled his fingers and toes and flexed his muscles in a vain hope he'd beat the cold.

She dug the knife into the arm of the wooden chair, twisting it.

"It wasn't until the third girl was kidnapped and raped a month later that they finally apprehended the murderer. He was the twenty-year-old son of a judge. A high-priced lawyer got him out on bail. It only took him two weeks to find his next victim. But as the girl was walking home from babysitting, the mother of the kids saw her being dragged into a car. She got the license number and reported it to the police. The police were close and surrounded the car. They negotiated with the guy inside. He threatened to kill the girl and himself. When the police felt negotiations weren't going anywhere, an officer with a hunting rifle killed him. The girl survived."

"That sounds like a perfect outcome," Brad said. "He was stopped and couldn't hurt anyone anymore. Saved the system a lot of money."

She stabbed the knife blade into the chair arm. "It has nothing to do with saving the system money. He didn't pay for his crimes."

"What do you mean?" Brad asked. "He died for his crimes."

Toscana shook her head. "No. He got off easy. He needed to suffer, like his victims suffered. The system had failed my sister and my family."

"I hear ya. But nothing was going to bring your sister back. That's the hard truth."

"We suffered." Toscana's hands were clenched. "I suffered. My family was never the same." She stomped a foot. "My mother cried herself to sleep for months. My father was an angry man till the day he died." Toscana gripped the arms of Brad's chair and glared into his eyes. "I was the forgotten child. My sister was beautiful and bubbly. Everything I wasn't. I was shy, quiet, and a tomboy. I wasn't the daughter they wanted, period." She pushed away from the chair, strode over to a shelf of cans and swept them all onto the floor. "How do I get closure? I didn't get to kill him. I didn't get revenge. My parents died within three months of each other of broken hearts when I was twenty."

"How does Michael fit into this? He's a drug addict. He

tried smuggling drugs, he got caught. He's not a sex offender. He's got nothing to do with your story."

Toscana rushed back to Brad's chair. "Weren't you listening? Why don't you understand? Michael was going to screw up people's lives with the drugs he was smuggling. He was no different from the others. His uncle used his connections as the mayor to get his nephew released. That's bullshit. It's another flaw in the system. A flaw I exposed. No sense restricting myself to just sexual predators. Any predators. Like the first drug dealers."

Brad shook his head and sneered. "I have to give you credit."

Toscana's head jerked back in surprise. "For what?"

"There are few female killers. You'll be famous. They'll write books about you." A grin played at the corners of his mouth. "Maybe a movie. They could get Kathy Bates to play your role. She does pure evil well."

"She's hardly a goddess."

Brad laughed. "Yeah, well, I was kidding. You're hardly a goddess. Just a pathetic murderer."

She strode over and swung her foot. It connected with his jaw.

Brad spit blood and a tooth. He swirled his tongue around his mouth. "I was going to get that tooth pulled, anyway." He spit at Toscana's feet. "It was hard for you the first time, wasn't it?"

"He needed to die."

"But you had trouble doing it. Hesitation stabs—just like in suicides." He raised his eyebrows and snorted. "Lack of guts. It's harder than you think, jamming in the knife. Lots of resistance. The muscles are tough, trying to shove the knife up and back." He glared directly into her eyes. "Maybe too hard for you to do?"

"Go to hell, Coulter." Toscana's shoulders shook with rage.

"Did you have nightmares after that? Do the others you've killed haunt you?" His eyes widened. "At night, do they visit? They should."

"Shut up," Toscana screamed. "You think you're the golden boy? How many have you killed? They make you a hero for doing the same thing."

Brad snorted. "I hardly think it's the same, princess."

Toscana's voice rose, as redness crept up her neck. "Killing is killing. We're the same."

"Not even close." Brad laughed. "You're thoroughly fucked up."

"Shut up!" She stepped forward. Her fist connected with Brad's jaw and his neck jerked to the right.

He shook his head, spit blood, and grinned. "Not bad for a girl."

She swung again. This time the force jerked his head to the side, and the chair toppled to the floor.

Brad struggled on his side. The punches got his blood circulating. He was less chilled. Or he was well into hypothermia.

With the last punch, he'd thrown his bodyweight onto the frame of the wooden chair. He'd heard the frame crack but didn't think he'd done significant damage. The ropes were still secure. He had little wiggle room. *Shit.* He'd need another punch. "That one was better. Maybe you need to get back to the gym. Try putting your hips into the swing."

Toscana grabbed the chair, jerked it upright and grinned. "I can do this all day. Do you think you can handle it?"

"Give it your best, Barbie."

This time Toscana used the butt of the gun. He felt a crack in his jaw. Brad pushed off with his legs as Toscana made contact, launching the chair into the air and landing hard five feet away. He screamed out as his back slammed into the floor. If he didn't have some wiggle room now, he wasn't sure he could handle another blow. This time, Toscana left him groaning on the floor.

CHAPTER SEVENTY-ONE

BRISCOE OVERSAW THE STREET COPS SURROUNDING THE BUILDING. His men would snag anyone trying to escape.

Steele led one TSU team while Zerr led the other into the mattress factory.

Knowing Briscoe had their backs, Steele and Zerr split, taking their teams right and left.

Steele's team stayed close to the left wall. Their flashlights illuminated a tiny portion of the warehouse. Mice scattered in the beams, scrambling from one pile of garbage to another. The stench grew stronger the farther into the warehouse they got. Rotting food, human feces, sweat and body odor. Steele rubbed his runny nose with the back of his glove. Even the cold didn't lessen the odor. He swung his flashlight to the right, and several pairs of red eyes peered back. "Police. Show me your hands."

Several other flashlights swung toward Steele's beam. A half-dozen men peered out from behind cardboard boxes.

"We ain't done nothin', Officer. We're just trying to survive the cold."

"How many of you are here?" Steele asked.

A man with long silver hair and a beard crawled out of a box. "Eight."

Steele swung his flashlight over the boxes. "Anyone else here?"

"Sure, there're guys all over. Every floor." Men slid out of the boxes all over the room. "Small groups, you know. We watch over each other."

Most of the men wandered over to Steele.

"Have you seen anyone who doesn't belong here?" Steele shouted.

There were murmurs all around, but no one came forward.

The old guy shrugged. "People come and go."

"I mean, not homeless. Dressed well?"

"Nope, ain't seen that."

Steele panned the room with his flashlight. Men shook their heads.

"Okay. Thanks for your cooperation."

Steele waved his team forward. They headed deeper into the warehouse. They came across five additional groups of men. None had seen any strangers. Zerr radioed that they'd had the same experience.

Steele's gut said this was a waste of time. They were in the wrong place. Every second they wasted here was a second Brad was closer to death.

Steele's team met up with Zerr near the back of the main floor of the warehouse. Voices were coming from a room in the corner. Low at first, then they grew louder. The voices were muffled, and it was impossible to understand what they were saying, but it was getting heated.

Steele and Zerr communicated through hand signals. One of Zerr's guys stepped to the door with a heavy ram. Steele nodded, and he swung the ram into the door. Steele tossed a flashbang into the dim room. After the explosion and flash of light, they entered. Steele entered first, followed by Zerr. The rest of the team followed and fanned out on either side of the room.

"Police. On the floor."

At least a dozen people were crammed into the room, some wandering, dazed. Others hit the floor in compliance. Steele shone his flashlight around the room. Three Coleman lanterns were spaced around the room, providing limited light and heat. Sleeping bags littered the floor with cardboard as dividers between.

"Coulter, you here?" Steele shouted.

No answer.

"Brad. Are you in here?"

Still no answer.

"I'll take a team and check the rest of the building," Zerr said.

A voice from the floor asked, "Who y'all here for?"

"Brad Coulter or Michael Trant."

"Can't say as I know anyone by those names. Course, some of us don't use actual names."

"How long have you been here?" Steele asked.

"Can't say for sure. Late September. Shelters won't take most of us. At least we're out of the cold here."

"You sure Coulter or Trant weren't here today?"

"We'd all help you if we could." He was pleading with his eyes. "We got a safe thing here. We'd help in a second, so you'd leave us alone. We don't want no trouble."

"Don't want no trouble about what?" A tall black man wearing a heavy overcoat and fake fur hat headed over to them. His gloved hand brushed snow off his shoulders.

"Hey, Gilly. These cops are searching for a couple of people."

Gilly nodded. "Few people out in this weather. I saw a man and a woman heading south."

"Wait," Zerr said. "A man and a woman?"

"Yeah, heading south toward the old CN Railway station. He was wearing a winter army jacket and pants. He was drunk or something. He kept falling. She was holding him up."

"How long ago?" Steele asked.

Gilly shrugged. "About fifteen minutes ago. Long enough for me to walk here."

CHAPTER SEVENTY-TWO

BRAD TRIED TO TALK BUT COULDN'T. HIS JAW WOULDN'T MOVE. Dislocated or fractured, for sure. He tried to breathe through his nose, but it was likely broken and was clogged with blood now. The best he could do was breathe through gritted teeth. Each breath was a whistle. His lungs screamed for oxygen.

Toscana was squatting beside Michael, injecting something into a vein. Michael's eyes rolled back in his head, a faint grin on his face. Then his lips curled, and he screamed out. His body convulsed and rocked the chair across the concrete floor.

Brad curled into the fetal position, shook with the cold, and stretched his arms. He could just reach his boot. He rubbed his leg on the floor, causing his pant leg to ride up above his boot top. He stretched his fingers inside the boot and got a finger through the rope glued to his shoddily repaired tactical knife where it was tucked into a leather sheath. Initially, the knife failed to budge. The rope cut into his finger. Brad scrunched as tight as he could, then stretched his legs and withdrew his fingers. The knife slid out of the sheath.

The struggle to retrieve the knife left him breathless. His eyes blurred, and the world spun. Despite the pain, he forced his jaw open to get extra air. Bones shifted in his jaw and searing pain shot to his temple. The world went white. But he could breathe and rapidly gasped for air. The pain subsided, his vision cleared, and his breathing slowed. He worked the blade over the ropes on his knees. Then he reversed the blade and sawed at the ropes around his wrists. The sharp blade easily cut through the rope … and his wrists. Compared to his other pains, the cuts were a minor inconvenience. With his wrists free, he could slide his arms around in front.

He cut through the rope across his chest and rolled onto his knees. When he glanced up, Toscana was standing next to Michael, her eyes wide. "How the hell—"

In three steps she crossed the room, swung her foot back, and kicked at Brad's jaw. He swiveled as the boot swung toward him. The heel grazed his head—pain shot up his jaw and he dropped the knife blade. He grabbed the swinging leg and yanked, pulling Toscana's other foot out from under her. She crashed to the floor, hitting the concrete with her ass first, then her head.

Brad pushed to his knees. His gut churned. Waves of nausea crashed into his body and the room spun. He reached out for something to support him. He sucked air through his clenched jaw. It was enough—barely. He rose to a crouch.

Toscana had rolled onto her stomach and was pulling the cattle prod out of her pocket. She stood, took a couple of unsteady steps, then reached out with the tube. As Toscana thrust the tube toward him, Brad spun to the side and stepped forward, his left hand chopping down on Toscana's wrist. She cried out and dropped the prod.

Brad snatched it off the floor and faced Toscana. He was staring at a gun.

She shrugged. "Like the saying about bringing a knife to a gunfight."

Brad glared.

"Cat got your tongue? Is your jaw broken? Just as well. I'm tired of your self-righteous rambling."

The problem was that Brad hadn't planned beyond cutting the ropes. Maybe a thought about weapons would have been useful. By his count, Toscana had at least three guns. Hers and Brad's two pistols. She had Brad's knife, and now he'd dropped the repaired blade. You'd think carrying a primary gun and a backup and a couple of knives would be enough. Did he need to carry three guns? Might as well carry a couple of grenades.

He had few options, so he went with his first one. "F … uck you."

Toscana laughed. "My god, that is funny. As far as comebacks go, that's weak. I would have expected better of you."

Brad's breath came in tiny gasps with a whistling sound with each breath. His pulse pounded in his temples and black spots appeared before his eyes. His chest spasmed, trying to pull air into his lungs. He slouched and then rested his arms on his thighs. His fingers tingled.

"Oh, poor baby. Having trouble breathing. Please. You're breaking my heart." Toscana bent to meet Brad's eyes. "I might not have to do anything. You're suffocating. You'll die, soon. Weird thing about not being able to breathe. Just not consistent with life."

Like in football, Brad's powerful legs propelled him forward and within two steps, he slammed into Toscana's stomach as hard as he'd ever done in football. They hit the floor, the wind knocked out of them.

Brad rolled off Toscana and tried to roll to his knees. He couldn't. Every time he moved, the room spun. He wasn't getting enough air. He glanced at Toscana, who was doing worse than Brad. Her lips puckered like a guppy as she struggled to breathe.

Brad scanned the floor. The gun was eight feet to the left, the cattle prod the same distance to the right. He wasn't sure he could get either. He didn't see the knife blade. It had to be the gun. Fighting her for the guns would be suicidal, but he was out of options. He sucked air between his teeth and then rolled left. On the third roll, he used his momentum to raise into a crouch. In two steps, he was reaching for the gun.

"Coulter, you fucker. Die."

Brad dove to the floor, grabbed the gun, and swung toward Toscana. Her first shot whizzed over his head, exactly where he'd been crouched. He swung the gun up and without aiming fired three shots. Two to the chest and one to the forehead.

CHAPTER SEVENTY-THREE

STEELE SPRINTED OUT OF THE FACTORY WITH OTHER TSU members close behind. Zerr limped to their truck. The cold was messing up his leg. Zerr hadn't closed the truck door when Steele swung the Suburban out of the parking lot. The truck fishtailed on the slippery road. Steele gained control and swung the truck south.

Zerr picked up the microphone. "Dispatch. TSU heading to the old CN Railway station. We have information Coulter may be there. Send backup."

"Roger," dispatch said.

Steele glanced over. "Maybe EMS."

Zerr's jaw clenched. "Dispatch, roll two EMS units please."

"Roger."

Steele swung onto Eighteenth Avenue. Four Suburbans followed bumper to bumper. As they approached the CN Railway station, the Suburbans fanned out on either side of the building. Every window and door was covered with a sheet of plywood.

Steele and Zerr jumped out of the truck and jogged toward a side door that was covered with plywood. Steele reached into a gap between the door and plywood and pulled. Nails screeched as they gradually released their grip on the ancient wood. Steele tossed the plywood to the ground and unslung his rifle. He placed his hand on Zerr's shoulder and they entered the dark building. Before they'd taken a dozen steps, three gunshots rang out. They sprinted through the darkness toward the sound.

Steele was the first one to the room. He swung the door open, stepped in so the door would bounce back on his foot, and surveyed the room over the sights of his rifle. Zerr did the same to Steele's left.

The air was thick with the odors of body sweat, blood, and body fluids. A body lay before them, face down and unmoving. Across the room, a man was bound to a chair by rope. Occasional moans escaped his lips. To the far right, a man lay face down on the floor. High-pitched whistles were heard.

Steele knelt and rolled the first person onto their back. Despite the bullet hole in her forehead and the blood, he recognized Toscana. He checked for a pulse and found none. Blood oozed from two bullet holes mid-chest.

Zerr was assessing the man in the chair, so Steele headed to the man on the floor, and rolled him onto his back.

"Oh, shit."

Zerr's head swung to Steele. "What?"

"It's Brad. He's badly injured."

"I've got Michael Trant here. I think he's overdosed."

Four TSU members, guns pointed, strode into the room.

"We need EMS here, now," Steele yelled. "Officer down."

Two TSU members sprinted out of the room.

Zerr left Trant with two of his team and slid across the floor.

Steele glanced at Zerr. "Where do we start?"

Puffy, dark bruises surrounded Brad's eyes. His nose hooked right, and his jaw was out of place. Whistling sounds came as air passed through Brad's clenched jaw.

"Ah shit," Zerr said. "His nose is broken and caked with blood. His jaw is broken or dislocated. He can hardly breathe through his mouth. I don't know."

CHAPTER SEVENTY-FOUR

JILL COOK SPRINTED ACROSS THE OPEN ROOM, FOLLOWING THE beam of two TSU flashlights. They separated as they reached a room and Jill stepped in. Her eyes scanned the scene. "What do you have?"

Zerr glanced up. "Three patients. One DOA. One overdose. And Brad, he's in awful shape."

Jill pushed Steele to the side and assessed Brad's face. "Oh, shit," she muttered. "He's ice cold."

"Broken nose and jaw," Zerr said.

"Yup. And he's not moving much air." She pulled an oxygen mask out of her kit and hooked it up to the oxygen tank. She handed it to Steele. "Hold this over his nose and mouth, but don't apply any pressure." She glanced at her partner. "Sharma, take two cops, get the spine board, stretcher, blankets, and hot packs. We need to get going."

As Amir left, Dixon and Thompson barged into the room. Jill pointed to Michael Trant. "Overdose."

She checked the rest of Brad's head and face. "He's got some large goose eggs on his head, and several lacerations. If I had to guess, I'd say he was hit with something a bunch of times, maybe a gun."

"Was he given heroin?" Zerr asked.

Jill shone a penlight into Brad's eyes. "They're equal and dilated. It's unlikely he was injected with an opioid."

Jill pulled out her paramedic shears and cut off Brad's T-shirt. Her jaw clenched when she saw a half-dozen pairs of red circles smaller than a dime on Brad's chest and stomach, along with an assortment of bruises. She listened to his lungs with her stethoscope. There was barely any air movement. She slid her hands over his ribs—they were intact. She checked his arms for any signs of injections—none.

Sharma set the spine board down next to Brad. They wrapped him in blankets and placed hot packs on his armpits, groin, and neck. They slid him onto the spine board and attached straps. With the cops, they lifted Brad onto the stretcher and raced to the ambulance.

Sirens blared as the ambulance raced through downtown toward the Foothills Hospital. Jill hung on to the roof rail as the ambulance swayed with each bump and turn. Briscoe hadn't given them a choice. They had a police escort and had a cop driving. She glanced up at Sharma. "I can't get a secure airway. His jaw won't move. Either it's dislocated or broken. His nose is full of dried blood. I tried to clean it out but it's like concrete."

"Can you get an airway past his teeth?" Sharma started a second IV line.

"Nope."

"All righty. Get ready for a surgical cricothyroidotomy."

Jill reached into a cupboard and pulled out a sealed bag. She ripped it open and carefully opened the wrap. Everything she needed to cut into Brad's trachea and open his airway was in the kit. She licked her dry lips as she mentally went through the process. She'd never done a cric on a person. Her training had been on pig tracheas in a lab.

She slid the stethoscope earpieces into her ears and listened to Brad's breathing. With all the surrounding noise, it was difficult to hear. She filtered out all other sounds and concentrated on Brad's lung sounds. They were faint. She glanced at the cardiac monitor as the heart rate increased to over one hundred and fifty.

"I can barely hear his respirations. His heart rate is too high. He's hypoxic."

Sharma nodded and leaned toward the driver. "I need you to slow down and keep it smooth." He slid into the seat at Brad's head and held an oxygen mask in place. He glanced at Jill and nodded.

Jill cleaned Brad's neck with an alcohol swab and then Betadine solution. She slid on surgical gloves and selected a scalpel. She slid a gloved finger down the middle of Brad's airway, over the Adam's apple to the notch just below.

With two fingers, she tightened the skin and secured the trachea. She made a horizontal incision about an inch across. Blood oozed from the cut. She held the trachea in place with one hand and wiped the blood with gauze in the other hand.

Then she inserted hemostats into the incision and opened them, creating a hole in the trachea.

Sharma handed her an endotracheal tube, which she inserted through the hole in Brad's neck. Sharma inflated the bulb on the end of the tube, then secured it in place with tape. Jill attached the bag-mask to the endotracheal and squeezed. Brad's chest rose, then fell. She ventilated a dozen times, then glanced at Steele, who was sitting at Brad's head in the airway seat. Color had drained from his face and beads of sweat ran across his forehead.

Jill shook his shoulder. "I need you to take over. You can do this."

CHAPTER SEVENTY-FIVE

Annie paced the hall by the triage desk in the emergency department. No one likes hospitals, but she was tiring of waiting to find out if someone she loved was dead or alive. And if alive, how badly hurt. It was less than two months ago that Charlie was severely injured in a helicopter crash. Brad had comforted her while they waited for the ambulance to arrive. This time, it was Brad she waited for.

She heard the swoosh of the electric doors and the rush of icy air. She spun toward the door. Sadie raced to her. "Any word?"

Annie shook her head. They stared at each other for a moment, then Annie pulled Sadie into her arms. "I'm so scared. I can't take this."

Sadie held her close. "It won't be long. The ambulance is on its way."

"How do you know?"

Sadie stepped back from Annie. "We scanned the police and EMS channels."

"Did they say how he is?"

Sadie shook her head.

Annie stared. "You know something."

"They … they're giving the ambulance a police escort."

"Oh my God." Annie's hands flew to her mouth. "That's bad. That's terrible."

Sadie grabbed Annie. "Maybe. You know how cops are. Get a laceration and they to go lights and siren to the hospital. I'm sure it's more courtesy than anything serious."

"Really?"

Sadie's jaw was clenched. Annie knew Sadie was barely holding on. Each were trying to be stronger for the other. This time Annie put her arms around Sadie and guided her to the waiting room. "We can watch for the ambulance from here."

The steady thrum of activity in the emergency department was interrupted by the sounds of sirens in the distance. Quiet at first, then louder and seemingly more urgent. Sadie and Annie stood at the entrance, staring out the window. Only sirens. Several cruisers blocked the intersection at Twenty-Ninth Street at the entrance to the hospital grounds. Then the first police cruiser swung off Twenty-Ninth Street toward the emergency entrance. The cruiser caught air as it flew over a speed bump. The ambulance, close behind, crossed the speed bump at a reasonable speed.

The speaker in the emergency department announced, "EMS arrival with critical patient. Trauma team to bed one."

Annie's knees weakened. Sadie grabbed her arm and held her upright, then they stumbled toward the ambulance entrance. They couldn't get close for the police officers, paramedics, and hospital staff crowding around the door.

The doors opened and Briscoe strode through. "Get the hell out of the way. Let EMS through." Anyone he felt was too close, he shoved. He was a snowplow clearing the road and nothing was stopping him.

Annie stood on her toes to get a peek. Steele jogged beside the stretcher. A paramedic, standing on the bottom rail of the stretcher, leaned over Brad's face as they rushed the stretcher to the trauma room.

Annie and Sadie tried to follow the paramedics, but a blue line formed in front of them. The cops weren't letting anyone past.

"Damn," Sadie said.

Annie took her by the hand. "Come with me." Annie led Sadie past the triage desk and down a hall. She made a right turn toward X-ray and then stopped at a door on the right.

"Now what?" Sadie asked.

"We wait."

"For what?"

Annie raised her eyebrows. "You'll see."

Thirty seconds later, the door burst open and an orderly rushed out. Annie stuck her foot in the doorway before the door closed and pulled it open.

"Let's go."

They entered the back of the emergency department

where three trauma beds were located. All the activity was in the bed farthest from them. They inched their way over and slipped behind the paramedics. Nurses, doctors, and techs surrounded the hospital bed. A nurse stepped away from the foot of the bed, giving Annie and Sadie their first view of Brad. They reached for each other at the same time and staggered back to the wall.

Aside from a tiny sheet across his groin, Brad was naked. IV lines ran from bags on hooks to both arms. Cardiac monitor leads crossed his chest. A nurse was taking his blood pressure. But the most terrifying sight was the tube that went into the middle of his throat. A lady in red scrubs was using a bag device to breathe for Brad.

Annie's vision blurred, and she slid down the wall. "Oh, God."

Annie heard the whispered voices first, then her eyes focused. She was in a chair in a small room, had a cold towel on her forehead, and a blanket across her body. "Where ... what happened?"

"You fainted."

Annie squinted and searched for the voice. "Oh God, Sadie. Really?"

Sadie patted her hand. "Don't worry about it. You just beat me to it."

"You're getting your color back." Annie glanced toward a paramedic she didn't recognize.

"Jill Cook."

Annie nodded. "Brad talked about you."

Sadie's head swung quickly to Annie, then Jill.

"My partner and I treated Brad ... Detective Coulter."

Footsteps thudded down the hall toward them. "Are you okay?" Zerr knelt next to her, a hand on her arm.

"I'm fine. Just embarrassed."

Zerr glanced from Sadie to Jill.

"Just syncopal episode," Jill said.

"What?" Sadie and Zerr said.

"I fainted." Annie straightened in the chair and swiped the cloth off her forehead. "How is he?"

Cook frowned. "Until they—"

Annie held up her hand. "No mumble-jumble bullshit. I don't give a shit about tests hours from now. I want to know how he is. You're a fuckin' paramedic, so tell me what you know."

Cook nodded. "He's had the shit beaten out of him. His nose is broken. His jaw is broken. He has contusions to his head. So, likely concussion. Tests"—she held up her hand—"will tell us the extent of the brain injury. He has electrical burns to his chest, back and stomach. His wrists have friction burns, likely from ropes and a lot of cuts. That's just the stuff we can see."

"You forgot to mention the tube in his neck," Sadie said.

"Right." Cook chewed her bottom lip. She took a deep breath and exhaled. "With his broken nose and jaw, he wasn't able to breathe well. I couldn't clear the blood from his nose and with the broken jaw, I couldn't put a tube into his lungs through either his nose or mouth. His heart rate was tachycardic, likely because he wasn't getting enough oxygen. I had to cut into his trachea—his windpipe—and slide a tube in."

"Was he without oxygen for a long time?" Annie asked.

"We don't know. That's what—"

"The tests will show," Sadie said.

Cook held out a hand. "Do you want to go see him?"

CHAPTER SEVENTY-SIX

Three Days Later

AFTER TWO DAYS IN INTENSIVE CARE, BRAD HAD BEEN MOVED TO a regular hospital room. Dull green walls, single window, TV mounted on the wall, hospital bed and nightstand. Flowers lined the shelf under the window with a view of downtown. In the space under the flowers, dozens of cards were lined up.

A portable tray table on wheels was next to the bed with a Styrofoam cup of iced water and a box of tissue. Zerr acquired two chairs from the waiting area and carried them to Brad's hospital room, past the scrutinizing charge nurse's eyes. He sat with Steele in two of the chairs in a semi-circle around the bed.

For two days, they met outside intensive care and watched Brad until Annie or Briscoe or someone else came.

Physically, the last hours of pursuing Toscana hadn't been that difficult. Heck, they trained harder most days. But emotionally, it was draining. It was always that way at the end of a challenging incident. Just that this one had gone on for days. Overall, it had been successful—if killing Toscana meant success. The entire department was reeling from her betrayal. Processing the shock, Toscana was a murderer. Someone they'd worked with, trusted as a partner, respected colleague, who was dead.

This was the second time he'd been in the hospital waiting for Brad to recover. For Steele, it was the third. He wondered what they needed to do differently. Maybe latch on to Brad with short ropes. Once he was out of their sight, they could reel him back.

On his own, Brad got into trouble, significant trouble, and it typically ended with Brad in the hospital, then taking time to rehabilitate. Sleep had been difficult to get the past two nights.

Steele was just as exhausted. He could barely keep his eyes open, and his head bobbed. They passed a box of chocolates meant for Brad back and forth between them.

"I like the fancy locally made ones," Steele said.

"La-de-da," Zerr said. "Aren't you the chocolate snob."

Jackson wandered in with a booming, "Morning, boys."

Steele rubbed his eyes and straightened. "Why are you so cheery?"

Jackson took the third chair, sat back and worked a toothpick from one side of his mouth to the other. "Blighe and I interviewed Michael Trant last night."

"Do tell." Zerr rolled his head and his neck cracked.

"It took the nurses two days to get him down off all the heroin Toscana injected. He'll be in hospital for another month while they deal with the addiction." Jackson spun the toothpick end-over-end in his mouth. "Trant may have overdosed from the heroin, but amazingly he remembered at lot of what Toscana said to Brad."

"Did he hear why Toscana was killing?" Zerr asked.

"Yup. Her sister was abducted, raped and killed twenty-some years ago. The killer wasn't caught until a third kidnapping but was released on bail. Then abducted another girl and was killed by cops."

"Was she telling the truth?" Steele asked.

Jackson stared at the remains of his toothpick, tossed it in the garbage and pulled out a fresh one. "I checked, and her story is accurate."

"On one hand, I get that," Zerr said. "But on the other hand, it's a tad extreme."

Jackson stared at Brad for a moment. "Toscana felt she was denied revenge and that the court system sucked. I'm sure we'll find she wasn't the person she presented."

"What did she want with the heroin?" Steele asked.

"Trant thought she only wanted to ensure it never hit the street and would have used some of it on him, and possibly Brad. But I think it was a red herring. She tried to point us in the direction of the drug gangs. She might have hoped we'd start a war against the Hells Angels and the Russian mob. They'd kill each other, we'd shoot a few, arrest others. We'd be doing her dirty work for her."

"Dang," Steele said. "That might have worked." He glanced at Zerr. "We were planning to pay a visit to the Hells Angels President Jeremy Pickens. It's something he'd mastermind."

"What does Blighe think?" Zerr asked. "Is she taking the word of a junkie? Michael Trant isn't a reliable witness."

"Blighe is waiting to hear Brad's side of things," Jackson said. "But that's not going to be an issue. Sturgeon has his team sifting through everything in Toscana's apartment. She has a wall covered in pictures and information on all the victims, including Brad. Vinnie Bevan died. So even in death Toscana adds to her total."

"Un-fucking believable." Steele sat back in his chair, yawned, and stretched his legs. "I'll feel better when the evidence against Toscana is added up."

"Legally, Brad will be cleared," Jackson said.

Zerr's head swung to Jackson. "What does that mean?"

Jackson gnawed on his toothpick before he answered. "He's innocent and won't be charged with a darn thing. He still must deal with Deputy Chief Archer. I'm not sure how he will handle Brad disappearing. Then there're our guys."

"What do you mean by that?" Steele asked.

"There are going to be cops who will believe Brad is capable of being a vigilante."

"That's bullshit," Steele shouted.

Jackson held up a hand. "Keep it down. I'm not saying this is right, but there's already been chatter. This last year, he's been through a lot. He's seen as a renegade. He plays by his own rules. Old-school cops don't like that."

"He gets results the gray-haired cops don't," Zerr said.

Jackson sighed. "You don't have to convince me. When he comes back to work, he's going to be on his own. I don't think Archer could even order anyone to work with him."

"Screw it," Steele said. "Promote me. I'd work with him in a heartbeat."

"Ditto," Zerr said.

Jackson laughed and choked on a piece of a toothpick. "Be careful what you ask for, boys."

Zerr admired how Jackson stuck by Brad despite the overwhelming evidence. His last comment had Zerr thinking about life after TSU. Maybe it was time to think of another career path. TSU was great, but not suitable for family life.

He grinned. He and Annie hadn't even discussed this, yet he knew that was where they were heading. They should do it now, while Brad was incapacitated. The thought brought a smile. He knew Brad would give him a hard time, but he also knew Brad was all for them.

Getting something past Brad was difficult, but this would be fun.

Brad made some rasping sounds. He'd been doing that regularly since they took the tube out of his throat last night. The nurses had been keeping him sedated though, and the closest to words was the rasping. Then words formed. "Wa ... ta. Wa ... ta."

Jackson bounced out of his seat and over to Brad's side. He grabbed the remote and raised the head of the bed. Brad leaned toward Jackson. "Wa ... ta."

"Yup. Got it." Jackson took the Styrofoam cup off the night table and slid the straw into the side of Brad's mouth. Despite the severe beating, an orthodontist had been able to repair Brad's jaw without needing to wire it shut. However, movement was minimal.

Water dribbled out of the corner of his mouth and onto his gown. Brad didn't care. He drank thirstily.

Jackson pulled the cup away. "That's enough for now. Let's see if the water bubbles come out of the new holes in your body."

Brad growled. "A … ss … hat."

Brad woke with a start. His eyes darted around the strange room. The ugly paint wasn't from his house. His face throbbed, and each breath brought the odor of plastic. He tried to sit up but was too weak. At the end of the bed, Zerr and Steele slept in chairs. The third chair was vacant.

A tray sat on the portable table. Chicken noodle soup mixed with the plastic odor from the oxygen mask. The combination churned his stomach.

Bits and pieces of conversation came back. Jackson talking about Michael giving a statement. He was alive. Thank God. Toscana had been injecting heroin into Michael with abandon. Either Michael had a high tolerance, or the stuff wasn't that pure. Either way, he'd made it. He didn't know what was real and what he'd dreamed. He knew there had been nightmares. Real or from his subconscious, he wasn't sure. He tried to move his jaw but couldn't. His face felt frozen. The hits and kicks from Toscana exploded into his consciousness. He winced and tried to cry out. A squeak escaped his lips. Not enough to bring Zerr and Steele out of their snooze.

The quiet was okay and he closed his eyes. Emotionally,

his tank was empty—from the soaring high of the investigation to the low of another near-death experience.

It pissed him off that people he worked with and trusted had been so quick to believe he was the killer. You'd think they'd understand he got results, if, maybe, unorthodox. He knew his closest friends had stuck by him. Still, he felt alone, and a heaviness settled over him.

CHAPTER SEVENTY-SEVEN

BRAD WAS IN A SITTING POSITION, STILL UNABLE TO TALK, BUT the fog of two days was lifting. His eyes followed Archer and Griffin into the room. Jackson stood and offered his chair to Archer.

Steele and Zerr jumped up. "They can have ours," Steele said. "We were just leaving. Enjoy your hospital dinner." Steele glared at Griffin as he passed. Zerr dropped his shoulder and bumped into Griffin on his way out.

"They're pissed," Jackson said. "Can't say as I blame them." Jackson glanced at Brad. "He doesn't talk much. Enjoy it while it lasts." Jackson squeezed Brad's shoulder and left.

Archer stepped to the bed and shook his head. "I don't know anyone tougher than you. I don't always agree with your methods, but I can't argue with the results." Archer stared at the vital-sign monitors. "As deputy, I have to play by the book. But I stuck too close to protocol."

Brad and Archer locked eyes. Brad read sincerity in the gray eyes, and maybe concern. Brad nodded. "Tha … nks."

Archer nodded. "No need to talk. We'll have plenty of time for that."

Brad wasn't so sure about Archer and wasn't looking forward to another trip to the principal's office.

Griffin pushed away from the door and stepped to the bed. "I don't think there's anything I can say to repair our relationship—partnership. To me, your actions were those of a guilty person. I let IA get in my head. For what it's worth, you're a damn fine cop. Speedy recovery." Griffin nodded and left.

That's it, Griffin? "I know you hate taking time off," Archer said. "But you don't have a choice. Enjoy Christmas with family. Go somewhere warm in January. I hear Hawaii is beautiful. Come back when the doctors say you can. Know that I will double, and triple check documents saying you are ready for work."

Archer read some of the cards scattered around the room, then held up one. From the mayor. "Kearse invited you for drinks at the St. Louis."

"Make … me … buy."

Archer laughed. "No doubt. Don't be surprised if he stops by. Heck, he might even bring the beer."

The nurse brought in dinner, all liquid. Archer glanced at the tray and grimaced. "Perhaps that food is punishment enough." He started for the door, then turned. "Excellent work."

Brad stared at the door for a moment, not sure how he felt about Archer and Griffin. Archer had been in a tough position, and Brad hoped he'd never have to make that type of decision. Brad knew he wasn't making it easy for Archer either. From forging back-to-work documents, then two months later accused of multiple murders. No doubt there was a huge lack of trust between them.

Archer was the sort of guy you admired and wanted to have a beer with but scared the heck out of you at the same time. There would be consequences, but the quick talk gave Brad hope he still had a job—although it might be writing parking tickets.

Griffin's actions hurt, though. They hadn't been partners long, but you get to know each other well. Brad had enjoyed working with Griffin and they were a sound team. Their personalities were different, but that's what made them successful. Apparently, he didn't know Griffin as well as he thought. Even Griffin's apology felt hollow. Not an apology, rationalizing his actions. Perhaps it was guilt on Griffin's part, but Brad's gut said Griffin still thought Brad was guilty. Is this what Jackson had been talking about to Zerr and Steele?

It's important for a cop to know that his partner, and other cops, have his back. If Jackson was correct, suspicion would be all around. How could Brad count on any partner to back him up?

Potential partners he trusted with his life were down to three—Steele, Zerr and Briscoe. Well, four. Lobo was a loyal partner.

It wasn't like Brad could go to Archer and say, "Hey,

Chief. I need a favor. I'll only work with Steele, Zerr or Briscoe. Is that okay with you?"

Then a thought hit him. He tried to grin, but pain shot up his jaw. Any of those three guys writing parking tickets with him was funny.

CHAPTER SEVENTY-EIGHT

THE NURSE WAS TAKING AWAY THE DINNER TRAY WHEN BRAD heard a loud commotion down the hall and Briscoe's voice in an argument. The nurse hurried out the door. Brad saw other nurses go by his door, jogging toward the noise. Then Annie scurried into the room, Lobo on a leash beside her. Once Lobo saw Brad, there was no way Annie could control him. He leaped for the bed, jerking the leash out of Annie's hand. He scrambled up the bed until he was over Brad. Lobo's wet tongue slashed over Brad's face and neck. Brad reached up in vain to stop the slobbery assault.

Finally, Lobo was content lying beside Brad on the narrow bed, wiggling until he was comfortable, and Brad was teetering on the edge of the bed.

"Hel ... lo," Brad rasped.

"Hello yourself. You don't need to talk. Just enjoy Lobo. He's been driving me crazy. He whines all day and carries your boots around. Oh, and you may need to buy some new socks. He chewed a few. Having a break from him even for a few minutes is worth it."

Brad scratched behind Lobo's ears. He made a low rumbling sound, then rewarded Brad with another slobbery kiss.

"How was dinner?"

Brad made a face.

Annie laughed. "I had salmon and rice."

Brad gave her the finger. "Milk ... sha ... ke."

Annie grinned. "Tomorrow. Smuggling Lobo in was enough for one day."

There was a knock at the door. Briscoe strode in and glanced at Brad.

"You look like shit."

"Briscoe," Annie said.

Briscoe shrugged. "He does." He grabbed a chair and picked up the TV remote.

"Really?" Annie asked.

"Not like we will have a conversation with him." He clicked through the channels, found the one he wanted and sat back. He reached into his coat pocket and pulled out a beer. "You can't have one. Doctor's orders."

Brad's eyes were wide, and he flipped the bird.

Briscoe took a gulp of the beer. "Ah, that hits the spot."

The theme music for the evening news came on. Briscoe increased the volume.

"CFCN Evening News with Sadie Andrus."

The screen switched from the station logo to Sadie.

"Good evening, and welcome to the evening news. I'm Sadie Andrus. Today, Calgary Police held a news conference and provided further details on the kidnapping of the mayor's nephew, Michael Trant, and his rescue by Detective Brad Coulter. We'll take you to a portion of the news conference with Deputy Chief Archer."

The screen changed to Archer at a podium with the Calgary Police flag in the background.

"Two days ago, Detective Bradley Coulter was taken hostage by a killer. While being held, Coulter was severely assaulted, including the repeated use of a cattle prod. Despite injuries from the shocks, a broken nose and jaw, Coulter freed himself from the rope that held him to a chair. In the ensuing fight, Coulter recovered a gun the suspect had dropped. As the suspect fired on Coulter, he shot back, striking the suspect three times. The suspect died at the scene. The heroic efforts of Coulter saved the life of Michael Trant. The suspect was also responsible for the string of murders over the past few weeks. Coulter is recovering in the hospital."

Archer paused and shuffled his notes.

"The suspect died on scene," Archer continued. "We regret to say that the suspect was Calgary Police Sergeant, Caterina Toscana. Detectives are still working to piece together the events that led Sergeant Toscana to commit the murders."

The screen changed to a video of the Foothills Hospital and a stretcher being rushed down the hall through a sea of blue. A framed picture in the corner showed Sadie.

"The video shows a severely injured Detective Coulter as he was rushed to the trauma room," Sadie said. "Deputy Chief Archer may be understating the lengths Detective Coulter went to rescue Michael Trant. He nearly gave his life in the rescue. If it hadn't been for the timely intervention of paramedics, Coulter would have died."

The screen switched back to a full image of Andrus. "Police are unwilling to discuss their previous manhunt for Coulter, although it is clear he had nothing to do with the string of murders. Considering Coulter's role in concluding these murders, perhaps he is owed an apology by the Deputy Chief. We certainly need a detailed account of the events."

The screen returned to Andrus.

"With the biting cold and snow, streets were a mess with the city seemingly unaware there'd be snow again this winter. Efforts to clear the roads started too late and were insufficient. City police reported over one hundred and fifty accidents during rush hour this morning. So far tonight, there have been over one hundred during the afternoon rush hour."

Briscoe decreased the volume.

"Brad deserves an apology," Briscoe mimicked with a high, squeaky voice. "For doing his fucking job. I need another beer."

Just after seven, Sturgeon stepped into the room and glared at Briscoe. "What the heck. I got frisked before I came in and played twenty questions on why I was here, and you're drinking beer. Even when I showed my gold badge, the constable wasn't impressed."

Briscoe grinned and waved his beer. "That's because your

gold badge doesn't carry as much weight as mine. Besides, he works for me."

"Why the security? Hero boy isn't in any danger."

"Just from the nurses."

Lobo popped up his head.

Sturgeon nodded. "I get it now." He set a large container on the night table.

Brad cocked his head.

"Extra-large chocolate milkshake from Peters' Drive-In."

Brad's eyes widened.

"Yup. Who's your real best friend? Not only did my team disprove the ballistics, I'm the first one to bring you authentic food. You need to let it thaw so you don't pop out your jaw sucking on the thick milkshake."

Brad reached for the container. Annie pulled it away. "Weren't you listening? Jeez."

Briscoe stood. "I gotta get home to Elaine and the kids. Too many days since I've seen them, and I'm out of beer. Not that the boys care if their pops is there or not." Briscoe winked. "Take care, rookie."

"Wait for me," Annie said.

"Wha ... 'bout ... 'obo?" Brad asked.

"He gets to do a sleepover," Briscoe said.

"The nurses will have a fit," Sturgeon said.

Briscoe nodded toward the door. "I've got guys posted outside all night. When Lobo needs a walk, they'll take him out. You owe me."

Briscoe and Annie left.

Brad stared at Sturgeon. "Ball ... ist ... ics."

"Ah, yes." Sturgeon grinned. "You want to know about

my team's brilliance. You already knew the other evidence was circumstantial and weak. Nothing you'd ever be convicted with. But the ballistics was another matter. With the ballistics match, all the other evidence supported you as a killer."

"Not ... my ... gun."

Sturgeon cocked his head to the side and narrowed his eyes. "Yes, and no. It was your gun frame, just not your barrel."

"Re ..." Brad swallowed with difficulty. "Replaced."

"Yup. I remember that." Sturgeon set a photo of two gun barrels on the table in front of Brad. He pointed at the top barrel. "Some replacement barrels don't have a serial number. Yours didn't."

"Barrel ... switched."

Sturgeon sat back with a smug grin. "You've got it."

"Toscana."

Sturgeon's eyes widened. "How did you figure that out?"

"Only ti ... me didn't have."

"Ah. The one time your gun was out of your possession. But how did Toscana get at it?"

"Range."

Sturgeon nodded. "Anyway, the way Gayle and Angie figured it out was that the gun cleaning solution on the barrel differed from your other gun, and the frame. Yesterday when we tested Toscana's gun, the cleaning solutions matched."

Brad nodded, gave a thumbs-up, and eyed the milkshake.

Sturgeon figured that was as close to a thank-you as he'd get.

Brad awoke with a start in darkness. He felt something around his arms but realized he could still move them. A faint light glowed from his right. He tried to call out, but his mouth wouldn't move. A wave of panic flashed over him. He could barely breathe. Where was he? He remembered fighting with Toscana—Dice. She shot, he shot. He was sure she missed. Did he miss? Did she still have him captive? What about Michael?

"Brad. Are you okay?"

Brad's vision was blurred. A priest hovered over him. *I'm dying. But why a priest? I'm not Catholic. But, hey, if it's my time, might as well do all I can to get to the right place.*

"Brad. It's John Branton."

Branton? Not a priest. Preacher or reverend or something.

"Bran … ton."

Branton smiled. "Ah, you're awake. I was worried for a while. You were having flashbacks or nightmares. I was about to call my friend, a priest, so he could do an exorcism."

Brad's chest heaved as he contained a laugh. "Saw … the …movie. Scared … me."

"I hope they didn't serve you pea soup."

Brad held up a hand.

"Right," Branton said. "I won't tell any further jokes. I won't stay long. It's well past visiting hours, but my dark suit and collar get me free access in the hospital. I wanted you to know I enjoyed our talk, and you know where to find me."

Brad blinked. The one part of his face that didn't hurt, despite the swelling.

Branton clasped one of Brad's hands in both of his. "Is it okay if I say a prayer?"

Brad nodded and closed his eyes. As Branton prayed, Brad felt the burdens that had been weighing him down lift away. Then he slipped into the deepest sleep he'd had in over six months.

Brad's eyes popped open. He struggled to sit up. A hand pressed gently on his chest. "It's okay. Lie back. You're in the hospital."

Brad blinked a couple of times and his eyes adjusted to the dim room. The light from the corner backlit the face peering down at him. A soft hand stroked his cheek, then came to rest on his hand.

"Sadie?"

"I'm going to put the oxygen back on your nose. I know it's hard to breathe, and I know it's hard for you to understand, but the oxygen canula you keep knocking off is helping you. Leave it alone."

"Nose."

"Yes, your nose was broken. They've straightened is as best they could. You'll have a cute hook to it now. But the blood is cleaned out, so don't breathe through your mouth, only your nose."

Paws pounced onto the other side of the bed and Lobo's head popped up.

"He's barely left your side since last night. The cops had to drag him out to pee."

"Las … night?"

"This is your third day in the hospital. Annie and Briscoe smuggled him in yesterday."

Brad remembered that, now. Lobo lay on the bed for hours, edging Brad toward the floor. The nurses were not impressed with Lobo barking every time they came into the room. He got particularly angry when around needles.

"Time?"

Sadie yawned. "About four in the morning."

"How … long … you … here?"

"I came after my last show at ten."

"All night?"

"Yup. You've been out cold since I got here. I slept for an hour. Then listened to you snore, wheeze and whistle. I read a novel. Briscoe told me about it. He said I'd get an insight into cops." She held up the book. "The Choirboys by Joseph Wambaugh."

Brad tried to grin. It hurt. "Favorite."

"So I'm told. It's, um, interesting reading. Especially the choir practices. Briscoe said where they found you has been used for choir practice."

Brad glanced away.

"I figured so," Sadie said.

Brad chewed his lip for a moment. "Desk. Saw … papers."

Sadie nodded then stared out the window at the shadows of the downtown skyline. "I wondered if you had. My whole desk was messed up. And all without a search warrant." She tried to laugh, but instead sniffled.

"Sorry."

"That part of my life is over." She shrugged. "Now's not the time to talk about it. I don't want to, and you can't talk."

"You ... okay?"

She grabbed a tissue and wiped her eyes. "I'm better than you." She forced a smile. "You should sleep."

"Not ... tired." Lobo's head lifted. He stared at the door and growled.

Then a nurse strode into the room. "You don't scare me, Lobo." She scratched behind his ears and he rolled his head toward her. "You're a baby." She gave him a digestive biscuit.

She checked Brad's blood pressure, replaced an IV bag, and withdrew medication into a syringe. "We'd like you to sleep a few hours longer." She injected the medication and patted his hand. "Nighty night."

Brad's eyes grew heavy, fluttered, then closed. Brad rolled onto his side up against the bed rail. Sadie grabbed her red coat, black gloves, and white wool hat. She stood over him. "Sleep tight."

Then Sadie set the coat back on the chair and removed her knee-high boots. She climbed onto the bed and curled next to Brad. Lobo shifted and positioned his head across Sadie's ankles as he kept watch on the door, daring any nurse to interrupt.

TO THE READER

I hope you enjoyed *Goddess of Justice*, Brad Coulter Thriller #5. I can't believe that this is novel number five. It's only three years ago, in April 2018, that I published *Crisis Point*. It is a lot of fun writing the Coulter Thrillers. I'm so appreciative of my fans who have stuck with me while I learn to write and while I just beat the heck out of Brad Coulter.

Goddess of Justice is a little different from the first novels because it is not based on an incident that happened in Calgary. I had the idea for a vigilante, which has been done many times in novels, TV and movies. The key was to find something slightly different. If you haven't read the novel yet, stop reading now, because there might be a couple of spoilers coming in the next few paragraphs.

Having a female antagonist isn't new either, but I thought the idea of combining a serial killer and female killer was intriguing. Of course, I had to make life miserable for Brad,

TO THE READER

which I did when he became a suspect. When times get really rough, that's when you find out who your friends are.

I'm a mystery/crime/thriller writer and there's a joke I like:

> A good friend will help you move,
> a great friend will help you move a body.

I'm not sure whether I should put this in print, or mention it at all, but I have a few friends that I'm pretty sure I could call on to help move a body.

Luckily for Brad, he has those friends, too. But there were some relationships that soured. You know by now that everything can't be bright and rosy for Brad—I don't think you'd be satisfied, and I wouldn't enjoy writing that.

There are times I have cried while writing a novel. Where my heart is pounding and racing, because frankly I don't know how Brad is going to get out of the dilemma. I didn't want Brad's friends rescuing him. I didn't want him to simply shoot his way out, either. I reached the point where Brad was captured—and then stared at the screen. Every author will understand that. You're on a roll writing, and then you hit the wall. You stare at the screen and you come up with possibilities and you quickly eliminate them. It's not until you're on your tenth, twelfth or twentieth idea that you finally hit on one that you know will work. Then you're back in business.

Brad Coulter #6 is in the planning stages. The working title is **Bonded Labor**. It carries on from the end of **Goddess of Justice**. So, the teaser is, some characters you have already met will carry over into *Bonded Labor*. That novel will be released in spring 2022.

My Team

I am lucky to have a great team supporting me. None of this would be possible without the love and support of **Valerie West**. She is always supportive, gives me the time to write, and is always my first beta reader. I can't do this without her.

Taija Morgan is my editor. She is absolutely brilliant. I've said it before, but I truly believe she understands the stories better than I do. Her edits are detailed, her comments are funny, and she doesn't let me get away with any lazy writing.

Over the last year and a half, she has been teaching me as well. So hopefully you have benefited from that. The characters are described better, the scene settings are stronger, and the conversations and banter are funnier. You can feel yourself in that cruiser with Brad and whoever he is working with. Thank you, Taija.

I've told the story of meeting **Jonas Saul** three years ago at the Creative Ink Festival in Burnaby, British Columbia, where we were both presenting. We hit it off and, fortunately for me, he became a mentor. I guess that's good for you, the reader, too. He's been a great support in my writing and a great mentor. He does the last proof on the novel and always has great suggestions or areas where he is confused, or areas where I could write just a little better.

I love writing the novels, but I'm not as keen on publicity, marketing or social media. Thankfully, I met **Jennifer Cockton**, Online for Authors, who assists me. When I say assist, I mean she guides me in all aspects of social media. The exception is Facebook. Facebook is fun for me. I love searching to find the funniest and most bizarre memes and then post them. So, I hope most days you get a laugh from them.

Mickey Mikkelson of CREATIVE EDGE CLIENT GROUP handles my publicity. He hung in there with me when I wasn't the best client. There are times I'm disorganized and overwhelmed with everything. He's done a great job keeping me on track, arranging interviews, guest blogs, and reviews for the novels. He has a reach into the area of publicity that I could never attain.

Maybe you can judge a book by its cover. I receive fantastic comments about the covers. That's due to **Travis Miles**. He has created all my covers and is working on covers for the next two novels—*Speargrass -Vengeance* and *Bonded Labor*. I know they will be awesome. That's just the way he works. I'm so excited by the color scheme he has for the Brad Coulter Thrillers and a completely different color scheme for the Speargrass series. Thank you, Travis!

When I have a police procedure question, my go-to guy is retired **Calgary Police Service Sergeant Bill Sturgeon**. You'll recognize him from the series as he has a starring role as the Sergeant in charge of the crime scenes unit. I hope I have been able to portray Bill in a way he is happy with. In the novels, Brad and Sturgeon have many verbal sparring confrontations. That's exactly the way it is with Bill and me. I love hanging out with him. I love his sarcasm and he is a clever character in the novels. He thinks Sergeant Sturgeon should have his own series, and maybe that's in future plans. He and his wife

TO THE READER

Susan (retired RCMP) are early beta readers of the novels and always offer brilliant suggestions.

Sheila Clayden—Mom. She is my biggest fan and the reason I read and write.

A Final Note To My Readers

After a break writing *Speargrass—Opioid*, it was great to get back into the Brad Coulter Thriller series. *13 Days of Terror* and *Goddess of Justice* were fun to write. I hope you enjoy them as much as I enjoyed writing them.

As I write this at the end of February 2021, I am working on the second novel in the Speargrass series, *Speargrass—Vengeance*. This novel picks up a couple months after *Speargrass—Opioid*. Franklyn Eagle-child has a new challenge when a series of ritualistic deaths occur in Speargrass.

Riley Briggs knows drug dealers are laundering money, and he's leading a task force to figure out how. Both Franklyn and Riley have new members on their teams, which create new challenges and provides a few laughs to the novel.

The past year has been a challenge for everyone. COVID-19 has affected us all in ways we never expected. For me, being isolated at home has given me the opportunity to do a lot of writing. For you, I hope you have been doing a lot of reading.

On the negative side, I miss seeing my friends and family, as I'm sure you do. I miss talking with my readers. It was a nice break this past summer, to be able to attend some markets and talk to readers. Let's hope that we are on the rebound, and we can return to normal activities, spend time with friends and family, go outside and maybe even travel!

TO THE READER

Thank you so much for your support. I was reading a book the other day on marketing and there was a comment about the problem of "writer's ego." The problem was that writers lacked an ego, were self-depreciating, and lacked confidence in their work. Fortunately for me, on those days when I'm wondering why I'm writing, when I hide out for hours in my writing cave staring at the computer monitor, I'll receive a text or an email or see a review from a reader and then I remember why. If my novels give you a few hours of entertainment, a few laughs, a few hours away from the stress of everyday life, then I have accomplished what I set out to do. Although I'm not sure my novels are stress free!

I'd love to hear from you. Email me anytime.
   dwayneclayden@gmail.com

If you enjoyed *Goddess of Justice,* please consider leaving a review on Amazon, Kobo or Goodreads. Reviews are what keep authors like me writing!

If you are not already receiving my newsletter, please email me or sign up at www.dwayneclayden.com for updates, a glimpse into the writing process, and access to exclusive Advanced Reader Copy review team opportunities.

Take care, stay healthy and be safe.

Dwayne

ABOUT THE AUTHOR

Dwayne Clayden combines his knowledge and experience as a police officer and paramedic to write realistic crime thrillers.

His first novel, *Crisis Point*, was a finalist for the 2015 Crime Writers of Canada Arthur Ellis awards.

The Brad Coulter Thriller Series includes *Crisis Point*, *Outlaw^{MC}* , *Wolfman is Back, 13 Days of Terror and Goddess of Justic*e .

In 2022,The Brad Coulter Thriller Series continues with **Bonded Labor.**

Dwayne released the first novel in a new Modern Western Thriller Series, S*peargrass-Opioid*. If you like Longmire, you'll love *Speargrass-Opioid*. The second novel in the series, *Speargrass-Vengeance* will be released in Fall 2021.

Dwayne's short story, **Hell Hath No Fury**, was published in **AB Negative**, an anthology of short stories from Alberta Crime Writers.

His vast experience working with emergency services spans over 40 years and includes work as a police officer, paramedic, tactical paramedic, firefighter, emergency medical services (EMS) chief, educator, and academic chair.

Dwayne is a popular speaker at writing conferences and

for writing groups, providing police and medical procedures advice and editing to authors and screenwriters. The co-author of four paramedic textbooks, he has spoken internationally at EMS conferences for the past three decades.

DwayneClayden.com

dwayneclayden@gmail.com